# INTO THE CAGE

# CAGE

## R.D. BRADY

BOOKS

# BY R.D. BRADY

Vinci Books

vinci-books.com

Published by Vinci Books Ltd in 2024

1

Printed and bound in Great Britain by Clays Ltd, Elcograf S.p.A.

"Everything has changed, and nothing has altered. Oh, what a fate."

A.H. Septimus

# CHAPTER 1

## DETROIT, MICHIGAN

"So that's when I told her that, you know, we should just kind of, take it easy." Dr. Gregory Schorn, lead scientist for the U.S. Department of Extraterrestrial and Alien Defense (D.E.A.D.), moved to push his glasses up his nose before he remembered he no longer had glasses. He'd gotten Lasik a month earlier, but the nervous habit remained.

He quickly shifted to pushing his dark-brown hair out of his eyes. He needed to get it cut. As soon as he had time, he'd see to it.

*And by then, my hair will reach my waist*, he thought with a sigh.

Mitch Haldron, the tall African American leader of the D.E.A.D. response team, flicked a glance at him and then immediately returned his gaze back to the street. "That's interesting, Greg, but we really need to be keeping an eye out for the Seti. So maybe a little less talking?"

Greg winced. "Right, right, sorry."

Seti, Search for Extraterrestrial Intelligence was what they had taken to calling the escapees from Area 51. The list of genetic hybrids created from alien and animal DNA and pure-bred aliens recreated from alien DNA taken from crash sites by the U.S. government was simply too long. Generally, when they went on one of these capture missions, they didn't know exactly what type of Seti they were going after. They just knew the U.S. government never intended for them to be running free within society.

Greg was part of the response team created to track them down. He was the only scientist. The rest of the team was composed exclusively of former military. Since Greg had spent most of his life as a poster child for Geeks "R" Us, they weren't exactly his usual social group.

But unlike a lot of the former military types that Greg had run into during his years working with the government, Greg really liked Mitch. He was a good guy, focused on the mission, but his muscles were not accompanied by a head full of rocks. Being Mitch had also been a Special Operations capabilities specialist with the Marine Corps, Greg was doubly happy that he wasn't either a muscle head or completely squared away.

A sympathetic look from Mitch was aimed Greg's way. If it had come from any other member of the team, Greg might have thought it was sarcastic or mocking in intent. But not coming from Mitch. He was married with two kids. Dating hadn't been an issue for him in over a decade. "Any idea what kind of creature this one is?"

Greg shrugged. "Nope. It's not in the database."

"Well, that's a shocker," Mitch deadpanned.

Greg grunted in agreement. The D.E.A.D. files were a mess.

A year ago, after everything had happened with Martin Drummond and the world practically ending, Greg had had a few golden moments when he'd thought that the alien threat was over.

Of course, it only took a few days before everyone remembered that a ton of aliens had escaped Area 51, and that the D.E.A.D., which Martin had been in charge of, was the agency directed to round them up. But with Martin dead, the D.E.A.D. was in shambles, and no one was hunting them down.

Add in the computer virus Martin Drummond had left in the system, which had wiped most of the project files, and it was a complete disaster. The virus had run riot after he'd died, one last present for humanity. A computer specialist managed to stop the virus before it destroyed everything, but it had done a lot of damage. And surprise, surprise, the virus had focused on the Seti files.

After about a week of the D.E.A.D. stumbling along without a head, the media began to catch on that something weird was happening across the country. There were more and more reports of unusual sightings of mutated animals. The government had to quickly swoop in and reorganize the D.E.A.D. Greg had volunteered to be one of their top scientists because ... well, actually, he wasn't sure why he'd volunteered.

The plan after everything happened was that he'd sleep for a week, and then maybe take a vacation. And he'd done that. He'd gone to Orlando and gone to each of the Disney parks and the Universal ones as well, then he hung out on a beach in the Keys for a while. But once two months passed, he was back in Norway with everyone, and he was kind of bored. Maeve Leander and Chris Garrigan had the triplets. Matilda and Adam were settled down with Sebastian. Sammy had gotten a job down at the docks. Even Alvie had settled in, running R.I.S.E. research project analysis out of the Norway base.

Then Norah said she was going to take Iggy back to the States to run the D.E.A.D. She asked if he wanted to come along as a scientific advisor to help with the reorganization. He'd said yes before she even finished explaining what the job would entail.

Ariana Mitchell, Martin Drummond's biological daughter, had agreed to work with them as well. He knew that was a big reason why he'd jumped at the chance. He thought it would give the two of them more time to get to know one another, in a more normal setting. At least, as normal as his life got.

Like he'd just been telling Mitch, things with Ariana were now strange. At first it had been great. They worked on almost all cases together. They lived next door to each other. There was something there. He knew that. She knew that. But apparently after learning that you're a half alien and having your full alien mother be part of your life, you wondered what other kinds of changes you were up for in this world.

So they weren't exactly broken up because they hadn't really been together, but things had definitely cooled down. And Greg wasn't really sure what to do about that.

Ariana had taken off two months ago to spend time with her mom. They were somewhere on the planet. Ethera was teaching Ariana about her nonhuman family. Greg hadn't heard from her in about two weeks. Before that, for a month, it had been only texts, which had grown shorter and shorter.

But that was fine, really. After all, he had this glamorous job to keep him busy.

He cast a glance at the street with a sigh. They were in Detroit now, in a neighborhood that had definitely seen better days. Most of the homes were boarded up and tagged with graffiti. Weeds had replaced the lawns and broken through the sidewalks and lined the edge of the road.

All in all, it looked like a post-apocalyptic movie set. All that was missing were the brain-seeking zombies ambling down the street.

Of course, seeing as how they didn't know exactly what type of creature they were following, it was entirely possible it was something of the brain-seeking-zombie variety.

*And apparently my love life is so bad that walking down an*

4

*abandoned street looking for what is probably an alien hybrid with some sort of cloaking ability is a step up. I'm living the dream,* he thought sourly.

"Heads up," Mitch said softly.

Greg's head jolted up. His eyes narrowed. He strained to hear anything or see anything in the dim light. The overcast sky definitely wasn't helping. Then he heard it. The sound of something or someone moving in the building to the left.

He slid the M4 that he'd left hanging along his back around to the front of his chest. The last couple of months, he'd gotten pretty good with it. And he knew how quickly these situations could go downhill.

"Should we call it in?"

Mitch shook his head. "Not yet. Not until we know there's something to call in about. It could just be some squatter or a cat. Heck, it could be a door swinging in the wind."

That was entirely possible. Greg's cheeks still burned thinking about the last time he'd called the entire team in. It turned out to be two cats getting it on in an alley, not the class-five Seti they'd been chasing.

Besides, Hannibal was on the team tonight. He was every stereotype of a muscle-bound jock rolled into one trigger-happy package. He was every bully Greg had come across in school. And like those bullies, Hannibal liked to take shots at Greg every chance he got. Greg would never hear the end of it if they called the team in for a stray cat or a loose kitchen door.

"Right. We'll check it out and then call if we need them." Greg hefted the M4. "You first."

Although, Mitch rolled his eyes, he didn't say anything as he made his way forward, stepping through the downed remnants of the chain link fence without making a sound.

Following behind him, Greg stepped over the metal framing of the fence, his head on a swivel as he watched the house but also checked the area around them. It was quiet.

Mitch paused at the base of the wooden porch steps and then moved to the right-hand side of the stairs. He stepped onto the sagging wooden porch. A loud creak shattered the silence.

His heart rate ticking up, Greg winced as his body went still. Ahead, Mitch had halted as well.

Greg braced but nothing came charging out the door at them, and there was no sign of anything scampering out the back door either.

Ignoring the front door, Mitch walked over to the window. Wood had been placed over it, making it difficult to see inside. Greg stepped onto the porch, and Mitch nudged his chin toward the door.

Greg swallowed.

You'd think after all the situations he'd been in that he would have gotten used to this kind of stuff.

But … no.

He moved to the side of the front door. The holes in the frame on the side indicated that there'd been a screen door at one time, but who knew where that was now.

Grabbing the handle of the wooden door, Greg looked back at Mitch. Mitch moved to the side of the doorway before he gave Greg a nod. Taking a breath, Greg flung the door open and flattened himself against the side as Mitch stepped inside.

Taking a breath, Greg followed him.

The wood covering the windows made it difficult to see, draping the house in shadows. Mitch flicked on the flashlight attached to his scope. The floor in the front hall sagged. Some of the wood had completely rotted through. To the left was a living room with an old brown threadbare couch.

Garbage was strewn throughout. The distinct aroma of urine filled the air.

His eyes beginning to water, Greg wrinkled his nose. "Man, it stinks."

"Dog." Mitch pointed to a turd on the ground as he slowly made his way down the hall.

Careful to step around the poop, Greg grimaced, making sure he didn't step anywhere else that would require him to scrub his boots later.

Another hand signal from Mitch stopped Greg in his tracks. The soldier pointed to the kitchen. Greg could just make out the soft noises coming from within.

Perched at the edge of the kitchen doorway, Mitch raised two fingers and bent them forward, the universal sign for *come on, let's go*. Greg was sure there was some sort of official military term for it, but he had no clue as to what it might be.

Mitch held up three fingers. Greg tensed as Mitch counted down. God, he hated this part. His stomach always rose like he was at the top of a roller coaster about to plunge to the ground.

At one, Mitch darted into the kitchen. Greg was right behind him. A squeal sounded as their lights scanned the area.

"There!" Mitch yelled.

The tail end of something moved at the edge of Mitch's flashlight beam. Whatever it was, it was small and fast. It darted across the room and out the doggie door.

"Damn it." Mitch grabbed his radio, calling the sighting in as he moved to the back door.

But Greg stepped forward to the spot where the creature had been. Something else was moving.

"Mitch," Greg hissed as he pulled his M4 tighter into his shoulder.

Lowering his radio, Mitch nudged his chin toward Greg as he stepped forward. "I got you."

Greg swallowed, moving toward the corner of the room.

A broken wooden kitchen table lay on its side. Greg moved carefully around the metal frame of a chair missing its seat. Finger on the trigger, he glanced over the table and then jerked his head back. His mouth fell open. "What the—"

7

He peeked again as a low growl sounded. He quickly backed away, not sure what to make of what he'd seen.

"What is it?" Mitch asked.

"Puppies. A mama pit bull and her puppies." Greg inched forward again and glanced down at the dogs. The mama looked up. Her blue eyes focused on Greg as she let out another growl.

But it was weak. She was weak. Her back legs were splayed at an odd angle. A takeout bag with some chicken still lay next to her.

Greg frowned, looking at the bag. It was relatively fresh. But there was no way the mom went out to get it, not with those damaged legs. He shone the beam of his flashlight around and caught a trail of something wet.

The trail led to the back door. Glancing back at the pups he frowned. "I think—"

Hannibal's voice burst out over Mitch's radio. "Subject sighted. All teams converge. Lethal force authorized."

Greg scrambled for his radio as he sprinted for the door. "No lethal force! I repeat, no lethal force!"

Static was his only reply.

He burst through the kitchen door, Mitch on his heels. "What's going on?"

"The subject's not dangerous. He's—" Greg cut off as he saw another team two houses down. He burst forward, his legs pounding on the ground.

The creature darted out from the bushes with a squeal. It was only about a foot tall and looked like it was covered in an almost translucent skin.

Hannibal's team raced around the side of the building, Hannibal in the lead. His six-foot-two frame battered the ground, his muscles accentuated by the black sleeveless shirt he wore under his tactical vest. A smile of triumph alighted across his face as he caught sight of his target. Hannibal let loose with a spray of gunfire.

"Wait!" Greg darted forward as the creature let out another squeal. Greg sprinted toward it, jumping in front of Hannibal, blocking his shot just as the creature began to glow.

With a curse, Hannibal pulled his finger from the trigger. "Move, Schorn!"

Heart pounding, Greg held up his hands as he stared at Hannibal. "No, wait."

With a grunt, Hannibal dashed to the side and opened fire.

"Stop!" Greg covered his head with his hands as he whirled around.

A giant bubble of translucent material erupted in front of him. Greg tried to move, but the bubble captured him in less than a second.

Greg stared at the little creature and realized that the bubble he was in was actually *part* of the creature. It looked like it had expanded its size to include Greg in its protective sphere. The creature stood suspended as well, only about two feet away from Greg's face encased in the bubble, about three feet from the ground.

The bullets from Hannibal's gun bounced off and slid harmlessly to the ground. The creature looked at Greg with big violet eyes and blinked. The bubble burst around them. Greg winced, feeling the cold gelatinous muck slide down his head and over his skin.

The creature sprinted forward, having dropped to the ground, and grabbed onto Greg's boots. Small stubby arms appeared from the gelatinous stomach and wrapped around his calf.

Mitch walked forward slowly, his weapon pulled into his shoulder. He wore a look of confusion on his face. "Greg? You okay?"

A large piece of goo dripped down Greg's forehead between his eyes and off the edge of his nose. "It slimed me."

# CHAPTER 2

The good news was the slime didn't appear to be toxic. The bad news was Greg didn't find that out until after he'd had a radiation shower in the middle of the street.

Now it was still a few hours before dawn, and Greg stood outside the hangar at the McCarran Airport, leaning against the Hummer they had rented, toweling off his hair while wearing a bright-orange *Albuquerque Rocks* T-shirt and Bermuda shorts.

He'd used up his extra supply of clothes on the last mission and had forgotten to replace them, so this was all that was available.

The jet was being refueled, which meant he had some time to kill before they could load up.

Which was a good thing because Greg was still trying to clean up. Even after the street-view shower, he'd used the small bathroom in the back of the hangar to change his clothes and to wash his hair as well as he could in the sink. But he still felt like he was covered in slime.

Now he leaned against the hood of the Humvee, running a

towel through his hair to get the excess slime that he'd missed. And apparently he'd missed a good chunk.

*Great.*

He wiped at his ears, and the towel came away with more of the substance. He'd already put a bunch into a test tube for testing later. He just prayed the stuff didn't have any long-lasting effects. Kaylee, the team medic, had only been able to run a few immediate tests. Back at the lab, they would do a full deep dive.

The stuff was strange. Greg had been completely paralyzed while encapsulated. It wasn't a bad feeling, necessarily, more like getting stuck in a waterbed or really thick syrup.

*"Chirp."*

Greg eyed the cat carrier on the hood of the Hummer with distaste. The creature seemed to be able to ooze its way out of almost every enclosure. And each time, it ended up standing next to Greg. They'd finally put it in a cat carrier, and as long as it could see Greg, it stayed put.

Greg hoped this was not a sign of things to come. The group back at the base would be able to figure out a containment unit that would keep it restrained.

Hopefully.

Mitch walked up, carrying one of the puppies from the abandoned house. The boyfriend of one of the response team members ran a rescue, and they were going to bring the puppies and the mama back with them. This puppy was predominantly gray with a couple of white spots and had bright-blue eyes. Mitch rubbed its head, carrying it in one hand.

Eying the small little guy, Greg smiled. He was awfully cute. A lot cuter than the translucent blob that seemed to be his souvenir from the trip.

He reached out a hand to scratch the puppy, and Mitch

pulled the puppy away with a frown. "Are you sure you're not contagious? Radioactive or something?"

Greg rolled his eyes. "No, I'm fine. The slime is just, well, gross, but not lethal."

Mitch studied him for a long moment before putting the pup within scratching range. Greg reached out, feeling the soft fur. "He's really cute. You getting attached?"

His white teeth flashing even in the dim light, Mitch grinned. "I know we have the new baby and all, but Marissa has really been wanting a puppy. And I like the idea of kids growing up with a dog."

"Are you going to be able to convince Maya of that?"

Shrugging, Mitch moved the puppy a little closer to Greg's face. "Could you resist this little face?"

Greg reached out and rubbed the puppy behind its ears. Its tail started to wag frantically. "Nope, most definitely not."

"Are you thinking of taking one?" Mitch asked.

Sighing Greg pulled his hand back from the puppy. "Nah. It's just me. And you know the hours I work. That's not good for a dog."

But the idea of coming home to someone, even a four-legged someone, was awfully appealing. What he'd said to Mitch was right, though—his hours were too crazy to put a dog through that. Take tonight, for example. He'd left upstate New York with less than thirty minutes' notice. He wouldn't be able to find a place for a dog with that short a lead time, not without having a roommate or a significant other. And for various reasons, both of those were impossible right now.

There was a different situation waiting for Mitch back home. He was married with two kids. He and Maya had been together for at least ten years. And she was currently home on maternity leave. But not everybody had such a stable home life.

Hannibal walked by and glanced over with a smirk. "Missed a spot."

With his annoyance growing Greg watched him go. "Does that guy own any shirts that have sleeves?"

Mitch chuckled. "Probably not. But he is good at what he does."

"Yeah, killing things. But not everything needs to be killed."

The puppy squirmed in Mitch's hand. Trying to regain control, Mitch tipped it closer to the cat carrier. A purring erupted from inside.

Mitch stepped back quickly.

But Greg smiled as he tilted his head studying the carrier. "I think it likes the puppy. It was taking care of them. I think it likes that the puppy's in good hands now."

"That bubble was pretty amazing," Mitch said.

"It's a defense mechanism. It's pretty powerful." Greg frowned. "I'm a little worried about what will happen once the Department of Defense finds out about it. We need to make sure that they don't."

It was a conversation he and Mitch had had a few times. And Greg had been glad to find an ally who agreed with him.

"Norah will keep it locked down. Although I wouldn't be surprised if they end up with a sample," Mitch said.

Greg ground his teeth. He'd joined the D.E.A.D. to protect the people of the United States, yes, but also to protect these creatures. Not all of them were killing machines. And the ones that weren't, well, they had no say in the fact that they existed. And they certainly shouldn't be treated like lab rats.

Whenever he thought about that, and that maybe it would be okay to lock them all up, he imagined Iggy or Alvie being one of the lab rats, and he automatically knew it wasn't.

He flicked a glance at the cat carrier. And it looked like he now had someone else to protect.

Stepping away from the Hummer, Greg stretched his back.

Mitch frowned. "You hurt?"

Shaking his head, Greg grimaced. "Nah, it doesn't really hurt, more of a dull ache. But I think it was from the mission before this, not this one."

"That one was a little dicey. But hey, maybe we'll luck out and get a little time off. We're due for a break," Mitch said.

Greg groaned. "You just assured that we're not getting one."

Mitch shrugged. "You never know. Things could start to calm down."

Greg slapped his hand to his forehead. "Oh, I can't believe you just said that."

"What are you talk about?" Mitch asked with a frown.

"You're totally jinxing us," Greg explained. "You know that means things are going to start getting fast and furious."

Mitch chuckled. "Now you're just being ridiculous. We've been at this for months. We've taken in, what, three dozen creatures? We have to be reaching the end soon. Maybe there won't be a next one."

Greg groaned even louder. "Please stop talking."

A deep belly laugh escaped Mitch. "You're too easy, man. You can't believe in those kinds of superstitions."

Greg flicked a glance at the alien specimen sitting on the hood of the car. "Yeah, well, it turns out I believe in a lot of things these days."

# CHAPTER 3

## BROOKLYN, NEW YORK

The metal door slid open. Trevor Austin looked up from his large antique wooden desk. It was clean and shone brightly, even in the dim light, a marked departure from the rundown appearance of the scarred wooden floor, cracking plaster walls, and rusted metal door. When he was younger, he'd seen a desk like this in a movie, and to him it had always been the ultimate in taste.

Even though the walls that surrounded him were peeling and the door that had just slid open was rusted in spots, he still insisted on the Queen Anne desk in his office. The dilapidated location was necessary for his current lucrative endeavor. That couldn't be helped. But his comfort was not a matter that was up for debate.

Neil Tedeschi stepped into the room, his whole body seeming to vibrate. He was about five ten but rail thin, making him appear taller. He had dark-brown hair that often fell across his face, forcing him to shove it back impatiently. He wore a pale-gray suit with a dark-blue shirt and matching tie.

It was a good suit, an expensive suit. Trevor would know, seeing as how he picked it out and paid for it.

But even though he knew Neil had only put it on less than an hour ago, it was already a disaster: wrinkled, shirt untucked, tie askew. Something about Neil made it impossible for him to look polished, or even just neat.

Neil's gaze darted around the room before focusing on Trevor. He bounded over to him, every limb seeming to shake. He had the appearance of a junkie. He never seemed to be able to stand still. But he wasn't a tweaker. Trevor had made sure to have him drug tested often the first year he'd come to work for him. All the tests came back clean. It had to be something like ADHD or even a neurological disorder.

It was hard to keep Neil focused on one topic. But he was dependable, and that meant a lot to Trevor.

Neil bounced up to the desk. "Hi, boss. That big shot you were talking about, Mr. Fischer? Yeah, well, he's here. His car just rolled up. It's a … what do you call it? A Rolls-Royce?"

Trevor raised an eyebrow. "He brought a Rolls-Royce down here?"

Neil shrugged, or maybe it was just him bouncing up and down. "Yeah. I thought that was kind of crazy too. But I guess he'll be on the floor any minute now."

Pushing back from the desk, Trevor stood up and pulled his black suit jacket from the back of his tall leather office chair. He flattened the lavender tie against his white silk shirt and then pulled the jacket over it, securing the one button. The suit had cost him $3,000, and it was on the cheaper end for his collection. But he tried not to wear the good stuff when he was working on site.

Moving ahead of him, Neil stepped out of the office, nearly tripping over his own feet. Neil's suit also cost a few thousand, but no matter how much money Trevor spent on a suit for him, he always looked like he just got it off a J.C. Penney clearance rack, or from underneath the rack. He sighed. "Fix your tie, Neil."

Neil looked down at his tie and quickly shoved it toward his neck. It didn't help. He still looked rumpled. Like he'd slept in the suit and maybe rolled around on the floor in it for a couple of minutes. How did he manage that in such a short time?

Trevor had stopped mentioning such things to him. There was no point. Neil tried, but much like the shaking, it just seemed to be out of his control. "Will you make sure the VIP box is ready? Make sure there's champagne chilled."

"Sure thing, boss. Sure thing." Neil hurried down the hall, disappearing through the door that led to the stairwell.

Trevor continued along the concrete hallway. Lights had been strung up, as the property's electrical systems hadn't been used in decades, and Trevor certainly wasn't going to rewire the place.

Back at its creation in 1922, it had been called the Red Hook Grain Terminal. In 1944, it had been taken over by the Port Authority before finally being decommissioned in 1965. The place was completely falling apart, but some areas were in good enough shape for Trevor's short-term needs.

He had the lease for a full year, but he would only be using it for three weeks. Most of the properties he picked up for his latest financial endeavors were similar short-term prospects. Abandoned for years, he could get them for a steal. And as they tended to be in the back and beyond, no one paid too much attention to what went on there. And he had security that kept any nosy parkers out.

It took a lot of money to make this kind of enterprise fly, but the money put in was nothing compared to what Trevor made. Yet on paper, he looked like an average guy. As far as the U.S. government was concerned, he made $32,000 a year through his pawn shop.

In fact, the pawn shop had been one of Trevor's first acquisition decades ago. He'd grown up in the Bronx. Trevor's mom struggled to make ends meet after his dad had left when Trevor was just five. All he remembered of the man was that he had big hands, which he liked to use on him and his mama. She was a good woman, his mama. Cancer took her when he was only fifteen years old. Trevor had been on his own since then.

But he was okay with that. In fact, he liked it like that.

He never went to college. He never even finished high school. He liked to think, cliché as it sounded, that the streets had been his education. Over forty years ago, he'd started as a runner for Handsome, one of the drug dealers in his neighborhood, when he was only ten.

Eventually he'd become the drug dealer in the neighborhood. But even then, he'd known that was not how he was going to make his living. It was good for the moment, but he was thinking bigger.

And drugs were just the tip of the iceberg. Because Trevor understood what drugs stood for: a demand. And as a drug dealer, he was simply a supplier.

But as he expanded his drug empire, he realized that drugs were not all that people wanted. And the more wants people had, the more money he could make. He'd left the drug game years ago and now considered himself one of the preeminent leaders in the field of acquisitions. He was a libertarian at heart. He believed government had no role in what people did with their money or their free time.

And as far as Trevor was concerned, he was an enabler of freedom of choice. He helped people get what they wanted. If they could afford it, then Trevor was their man. It didn't matter what it was. If they wanted to go hunt down some exotic animal in some foreign land but the government said no, Trevor could make that happen. If their lustful intentions ran to individuals of a younger age, Trevor could make that happen too. Whatever people wanted, Trevor could provide.

Two years ago, he'd heard about another want that people were itching for. And he realized that this could be his most creative and lucrative endeavor yet.

Trevor's footfalls echoed off the floor as he made his way to the elevator at the end of the hall. The floor was cement with dark spots crusted in over the years. The whole place would be a great setting for a horror movie shoot.

Which made it the perfect setting for his new project.

His bodyguard stood at the elevator doors, arms crossed, and gave him a nod. Camden was seven feet of pure muscle. He was former Delta Force, with tours in Afghanistan and Iraq, before he came to work for Trevor. The man looked like a mountain. Just his appearance was enough to make anyone who had a problem with Trevor think twice.

Dylan, who worked the other twelve hours of the day, was almost Camden's twin. One of them was with him at all times, sometimes both.

In Trevor's line of work, security was perhaps his most important expenditure. He had a security force for the operation, of course, but Camden and Dylan's job was to keep Trevor protected at all costs.

The elevator opened, and Camden moved to stand in front of it. He glanced inside, stepped into the elevator, and held his arm out to keep the door open. Finally, he nodded. "You're good."

Trevor stepped in. Hans Fischer stood in the corner of the elevator. From the file Trevor had read on him, he'd expected Hans to be a big-boned German, strong and imposing. Instead he stood five foot four and looked like a strong wind could blow him over.

Whenever Trevor got a new client, he always liked to put the picture at the back of the file. He'd read through everything he could on the person and then guess what they looked like. It was amazing how many times he was wrong. People's files were never really indicative of what they looked like. It was a good lesson to never let appearances deceive you.

Hans, who looked like he got beat up a lot in high school, was actually the number one gunrunner out of Southern Africa. He walked into hotspots that most people didn't even like thinking about. He sat across the table from men who'd gutted entire families and still wore the bloody knife to the meeting. Hans had brought his own security. Two guards who were slightly smaller than Camden stood on either side of him.

"Mr. Fischer. It's a pleasure to meet you." Trevor smiled but didn't extend his hand. Hans didn't shake hands. He went into some of the largest cesspools of the world and was notoriously careful not to get any germs from those locations. So he just made it a habit not to shake anybody's hand.

Hans inclined his head. "Mr. Austin. It's good to finally meet you. I wasn't sure at first that I had the address correct. The location is unusual."

Trevor grinned more broadly. "Thank you. That *is* the idea. The cops tend not to come down this way. But even if they did, we want to make sure that no one would be interested in stepping inside."

What Trevor didn't mention was that the reason the cops didn't come inside was because most of them had been paid off. It was a small business expense and well worth the hassle it avoided. Plus, Trevor cleaned up his own messes, so he never left anything for the cops to handle.

"Of course," Hans said smoothly. "I, too, find it is best to remain inconspicuous."

"Well, I think that you will be very impressed by the entertainment tonight. We've got some incredible matches lined up."

Hans's eyes showed the first glimmer of interest. "Yes. I've seen the matches online. I am hoping that, in person, it will be even more thrilling."

"Oh, it will be. I can promise you that," Trevor assured him.

The elevator doors opened. Trevor stepped through first. The rumble of the crowd washed over him. In front of them was a metal catwalk that led to stadium seating surrounding a large octagon. Unlike in mixed martial arts, though, this cage was made of metal, was twenty feet tall, and had a metal mesh roof as well. Plus, barbed wire ran through the metal bars. What couldn't be seen, however, was the electric current that could be released through the cage in the event of any escape attempts. That particular safety option had to be used at least once a night.

Which Trevor completely understood. Blood lust was not easy to control.

"This way, Mr. Fischer," he said as he gestured to the path to the left.

Hans fell in step behind him as Trevor headed toward the VIP box. The box was located ten feet above and only four feet from the edge of the cage, providing the perfect view of the octagon.

Trevor led the way in. There were four tall leather chairs that looked like thrones. A table of food had been set on the left-hand side of the box, and a silver ice bucket of champagne sat chilling next to it as well.

Clare, dressed in a black cocktail dress, her makeup heavy but tastefully applied, stood waiting. Her dark hair was pulled back, and she gave him a small nod with a smile. "Good evening, Mr. Austin."

"Good evening, Clare." Trevor turned back to Hans. "Would you like anything to drink or eat?"

Hans shook his head as he stepped in. "No, no. We ate before we came."

His two bodyguards peered around the room and into the cage before stepping back against the back wall.

Trevor nodded. "Well, I will leave you to the show. Clare here will see to any of your needs. Enjoy your night. And if you have any requests, please refer them to Clare."

Taking a seat, a smile began to spread across Hans's face as he peered into the cage. "Yes, thank you."

The tone made it clear that he needed nothing more from Trevor. Not bothered by the dismissal, Trevor turned on his heel and headed out of the VIP room. The door locked shut behind him. The VIP room was a steel cage. The safest spot in the auditorium.

Well, the second safest.

The safest was Trevor's own box. Heading toward it, he nodded at a few of the well-dressed guests sipping champagne and harder drinks. Making his way down the metal gang-plank, he glanced up at his lighting director and nodded.

The lights along the ceiling began to circle and flash. An excited murmur rumbled through the crowd as they all turned their attention to the octagon.

Over the loudspeaker, a voice called out. "Welcome, ladies and gentlemen! Tonight will be a night you will never forget. First on the scorecard is a former UFC champ. You've seen him battle before, but you've never seen him battle like this. Let's hear it for Chad Kaz!"

The crowd clapped politely. Chad stomped out of the hall-way, looking up and raising his hands with a glare, expecting more applause. But the people weren't here for him.

At the end of the plank, Trevor stepped into his own VIP box. Camden slipped in behind him and locked the door. Trevor stepped over to the reinforced glass windows that looked into the cage. He'd stay for the duration of the fight. After all, that was where the greatest threat would come from.

The buffet table called to him. He wandered over and

grabbed a handful of fries. There was another door across from him that led to a hallway that could get Trevor out of the building in less than ten seconds. Unbuttoning his suit coat, he slipped his jacket off and hung it on a tall chair set in the center of the room. He took a seat, grabbing the glass of scotch from the table next to the chair, took a sip, and then grabbed a cigar.

He lit it as the announcer introduced Chad's opponent. "And now, ladies and gentlemen, feast your eyes on the challenger. He's had four fights and zero losses. He is from God knows where. The one, the only, the Guerrilla!"

Trevor took a puff of his cigar and then blew it out. Through the smoke, he saw the creature emerge from the hallway. Blue skin covered its muscular body as it loped down the caged alleyway and into the cage on all fours, just like an ape would.

But this was no ape. Trevor didn't know what it was. As far as he knew, no one else did either.

Its face was flattened and featured two rows of sharp teeth that became visible a second later when it roared. The crowd gasped in response and then cheered. The creature pounded the ground, the metal floor of the cage shook in response.

The creature's opponent looked dumbstruck. Trevor loved these moments. Chad's mouth hung open in shock.

Apparently Chad hadn't seen one of these fights before. Not that that was a surprise. After all, who would agree to this kind of a fight if they knew what they were fighting against?

Pounding on the ground again, the blue gorilla let out an even louder roar. Chad rolled his shoulders and raised his machete.

Trevor took another puff on his cigar. This was going to be good.

# CHAPTER 4

## CLAY, NEW YORK

66 I just don't understand why we haven't seen you in a year, Gregory." The tone in Evelyn Schorn's voice was painfully familiar. It was a mix of guilt-tripping, annoyance, and disappointment all rolled into one.

Sighing, Greg slumped down lower in his office chair. He was in his office at the D.E.A.D. Headquarters in Clay New York, just twenty minutes north of Syracuse. The Headquarters consisted of four three story buildings that had been created to serve as a business park. However, when the money for the project fell through, the buildings and the acres around them went on the market. The US government snatched it up for a song and immediately made adjustments to the buildings and the surrounding areas to turn it into a Top Secret base.

Greg's large office was on the second floor and had a great view of the rest of the base, that consisted of mainly trees, the four buildings, and one apartment complex.

Generally, he liked his job, especially the office part. And the day had been going pretty well. He'd finished up his report from the Detroit mission. He'd had a chance to run some data that he'd wanted to take a second look at, and he'd even sent a text to Ariana. Not that she had texted back, but that was okay.

Then his mother called. And he'd spent the entire conversation trying to *not* explain where he'd been for the last year.

"Mom, I can't tell you. It's a government thing."

"Government shmoverment. I'm your mother! I should know where you are. You've missed so many important things. Giselle graduated, and you weren't there for her. She was very disappointed."

Closing his eyes, he ran a hand over his face. Part of him wished he could just hang up. For a moment, he contemplated faking an emergency. But then he'd just give his mother more ammunition for the next phone call. "It was a kindergarten graduation, Mom. I'm pretty sure she didn't even notice I wasn't there."

"And whose fault is that? Maybe if you showed up more, she'd know who you are instead of wondering who Uncle Greg is."

Lowering his head to the desk, he contemplated slamming his skull into it. He settled for laying his head down, his ear pressed to its top. "Mom, it couldn't be helped. But all that is behind me now, and my life is a little more normal. So I will make every effort to be there for my family obligations."

"Obligations? *Obligations*? These are *celebrations* of our family. You should be happy to be at them. Do you know how many people don't have a family to celebrate with?"

*And how lucky they are,* he thought.

A knock sounded on Greg's door before Norah Tidwell, director of the D.E.A.D., former Marine, and Greg's friend, popped her head in. He raised his head from the desk as she raised her eyebrows, looking like she was about to disappear.

But Greg waved her in, happy for the distraction. "Mom, my boss just stepped in, I need to go."

"Well, you'll be free for your father's birthday, right? Everyone will be there."

*That is not a selling point, Mom.* Out loud, he said, "I'll see. Probably. It depends if something comes up with work or not."

"Dinner's at three o'clock on Saturday. I expect you to be there. Your family misses you. *I* miss you. I love you, Greg."

Guilt rolled over him again. He knew his mom loved him. His sisters and father, he wasn't so sure about. But he did feel guilty about not seeing his mom. "I'll try to be there. I'll probably be there."

"I won't be here forever, you know," she warned.

Rolling his eyes, he rubbed his face hard. "Mom, you just ran a half marathon last month. I'm not exactly worried about you kicking off anytime soon."

"I could get hit by a car. It could happen."

He tried not to laugh. "Okay, Mom. As long as nothing comes up, I will be there on Saturday."

"That's all I ask," she said. "Love you."

"Love you too, Mom. And I'll send you a reflective vest to make sure the cars can see you." He disconnected the call, then blew out a breath as he slumped even further down in his chair.

Taking a seat in front of his desk, Norah straightened her black suit. It was strange seeing her in a suit every day. "So how's Mom?"

"She's improved her guilt game. Apparently I'm supposed to feel guilty because my niece, who doesn't even know who I am or care beyond what present I bring, had a kindergarten graduation, and I wasn't there for it."

Norah laughed. "Well, you don't get to choose your family."

"No, you definitely don't." He shook his head, brushing away his thoughts. "So what's going on?"

Once again she raised her eyebrows. "You tell me. You're the one who said you wanted to talk."

Greg sat up in his chair, grabbing for his mouse. "Right, right. Sorry, my mom just kind of ..." He waved his hands. "Anyway, I wanted to talk about the numbers. They're just not adding up."

She frowned. "I looked at the data you sent me, but I don't see the problem. I mean, there seems to be a pretty close link between the subjects we've tracked down and the ones that escaped Area 51."

"Yeah, and that's the problem." Greg stared at the spreadsheet on his monitor, the feeling of dread flowing over him again.

After everything that happened, and being part of the team that had essentially saved the world, Norah had been put in charge of the D.E.A.D. And through that, they'd learned *all* the subjects had been released from Area 51 and that there were more than they realized. While Greg had been busy running them down, he'd also been running some models to predict different outcomes. But no matter how he tweaked the algorithms, the numbers all came back the same: they were missing a lot of the creatures.

"The numbers are similar," Greg agreed. "But the problem with that is some of these guys should've reproduced by now. So the numbers should actually be higher."

"Reproduced? Are you kidding?" Norah asked.

"Sadly, no. As *Jurassic Park* taught us all, nature always finds a way."

Norah stared at him and then shook her head, apparently deciding against debating the wisdom of Dr. Ian Malcolm. "But do you have any proof of that?"

"Proof? No, but there's no way that *all* of these creatures escaped and not a single one reproduced. Statistically, it's practically impossible."

"But some of them will have died, right? Hostile environments, unable to find food, etcetera, etcetera?" Norah asked.

"Yes, that's true, but I accounted for that in the models. Even with that, we should be seeing more creatures. Something is wrong. There should be more of them," he said.

Norah frowned. "So what do you think is going on? Where do you think they are?"

Greg shook his head. "I have no idea."

A chirp erupted from Greg's desk and he winced.

Norah raised an eyebrow. "That's not what I think it is, is it?"

With a resigned sigh, Greg opened the bottom drawer of his desk. The small gelatinous creature that he'd found in Detroit lay inside in what could only be described as a blob formation. Small olive-green warts had broken out across the creature's body.

Norah stood up and glanced over the desk. She shook her head. "Greg ..."

Frustration rolled through him as he held up his hands. "It's *not* my choice. Every time they lock him up, he figures out a way to get out of it and comes to find me. The cleaning staff is getting sick of cleaning up the slime trails all over the building. So for now, he's just staying with me until the engineering department can create something that will hold him."

Shaking her head, Norah settled back down. "Well, you did say you wanted a little buddy like Iggy or Alvie."

Greg groaned. "Yeah, but I wasn't exactly thinking of a slimy, wart-covered blob. I thought, you know, someone cute. But Pugsley is definitely not cute."

"Pugsley? You named him Pugsley?" She asked.

He shrugged. "Well, Ugly seem like a horrible name to give him, so I thought Pugsley was close enough."

Shaking her head in mock sympathy Norah said, "Poor little guy. All alone, looks to you like a dad, and you give him a horrible name."

"Hey, I didn't sign on for this gig." He closed the desk drawer with his foot.

"Not sure any one of us truly volunteered for this gig. But here we are. Is he okay in there?"

"Yeah, that's one of things that we found. He really likes the dark. And saltines."

Norah stood up. "Okay, well, let me know if you figure out anything about the numbers." She turned to the door and stopped, pulling a sheet of paper from her suit jacket pocket and placing it on the desk in front of him. "And I'm guessing this was your recommendation to the committee for the new name for the agency."

"Um …" He glanced down at the sheet, although he was pretty sure he knew what was there. *H.A.L.T.* was written in bold red letters in the middle of the page. Underneath was the translation in parentheses: *Help! Alien Life is Terrifying.*

"Really, Greg?" Norah asked.

Greg tried and failed to hide his grin. "What? It's a perfect name."

"Yeah, well, the committee wasn't amused."

"Well, they have no sense of humor," he muttered,

Norah gave him an overly bright smile. "You know what? I think you really should go see your family this weekend. I'll make sure you're cleared to go."

Greg groaned. "What have I done to you that you would be so cruel to me?"

Grabbing the paper from the desk, Norah waved it at him. "But seriously, you should go. I come from a family of five brothers. They're always getting on my case. But family is family."

"Yeah, yeah," he grumbled.

She crossed her arms over her chest, staring at him.

"Fine, fine. I'll go. They're in Connecticut. If you need me for anything, anything at all, though, just call. If someone needs to remove staples from some old paperwork, I'm your guy. Just give me a call."

Norah grinned. "I think we'll be good. Have fun with your family. And I'll ask Alvie to take a look at your data. Maybe he'll see something that we haven't. I'm surprised you haven't asked him already."

Alvie was working over in Norway, but Greg had been consulting with him online about a couple of different things.

"I know. It's just, everybody's throwing stuff at him these days. So maybe we should hold off on that. I don't want to overwhelm the guy."

Norah shrugged. "Your call. You know, maybe for once we just got lucky, and the numbers are real, and these guys never actually managed to reproduce."

Greg laughed without mirth. "Norah, when it comes to aliens, when have we ever gotten lucky?"

# CHAPTER 5

## GREENWICH, CONNECTICUT

The Fowler home looked like most of the other multimillion-dollar homes in the Greenwich Proper neighborhood of Connecticut. The homes had been developed about ten years ago to look like testaments to the wealthy who lived inside. Most were owned by hedge-fund managers or well-to-do doctors who worked in Manhattan, making the commute when necessary.

Officer Denise Sandra pulled up in front of the two-story contemporary glass-and-concrete home and put the squad car in park.

Her partner, Michael Wu, glanced at the home. "Quiet."

Denise nodded as she stepped out of the car. "Doesn't change the fact that the alarm went off."

Michael stepped out on his side. "Probably some kids setting the alarm off. Come home from college, forget about how it works."

Denise knew normally that was right. They'd been called out

to more than a few false alarms in the area because of just that kind of scenario. But that didn't apply to the Fowlers. "They don't have any kids. They do have a maid-slash-dog trainer."

Michael raised an eyebrow. "A dog trainer?"

"Elaine Fowler shows champion miniature poodles. Her trainer, Shelby, came over from England to help train them. In exchange for free board, she also does some light house-keeping."

"You know her?" He asked.

Denise nodded. "Shelby and I met at the gym. She's nice. She says the Fowlers aren't too bad. Pretty decent, in fact."

Nodding to the house, Michael close this car door. "Well, let's go say hi."

Together, the two of them walked to the front door. Denise scanned the drought-tolerant front garden, but there was no sign of anything amiss. While Michael went to the front door, Denise moved to the windows to the left of the door and glanced inside but saw no signs of life.

Michael rang the doorbell. The peal of the bell could be heard clearly through the walls. Yet nothing inside stirred. There wasn't even a bark from one of the dogs. Denise narrowed her eyes and then shifted a little farther to the right. Through the other window, she could just make out the leg of one of the poodles. It wasn't moving. Uh-oh.

As she made her way back to the front door, she slipped her gun from its holster. With raised eyebrows, Michael did the same.

"I saw one of the dogs. It's not moving," she said.

"Is an unmoving dog probable cause?" Michael asked.

"It is for this family." She reached out and grabbed the doorknob, surprised when the door swung open. It hadn't been fully latched. She glanced at Michael, who gave her a nod. She pushed the door wide.

She was about to call out when Michael whispered, "Look."

On the front hallway rug, underneath a circular pedestal table, lay a part of the dog. One of its paws, tendons dangling, lay in a small pool of blood.

Denise swallowed what she had been about to say, along with the bile that was trying to make its way up her throat. She stepped inside, quickly checking the corners. The rest of the dog lay to the left. The leg she'd seen through the window was sprawled next to the couch. She'd thought the rest of the dog was simply out of view.

She supposed that was technically true. The poor thing's head laid on its own on the white couch.

"Who the hell could do something like that?" Mike whispered.

Denise just shook her head. A quick glance showed that it wasn't a nice, smooth cut from a knife. Dangling strands of blood and gore indicated the head the head had been wrenched off. She struggled to imagine how a human could manage it.

Michael gestured to the right. Denise nodded her head to the left. She walked past the remains of the dog, only giving it a quick glance. She needed to find what had caused that but she didn't need all the gory imagery in her head.

As she moved, she tried to remember how many dogs Shelby said the couple had. She thought it was three, one a puppy, but she couldn't be sure. She'd last spoken with Shelby two days ago. They'd met at the gym and then went out for a light dinner afterward. Shelby had seemed fine. No stress, no worries. She'd mentioned the Fowlers, but only in passing, when she told a story about trying to get the puppy to learn how to walk on a leash. Nothing bothered her about them.

But had Denise missed a sign?

The living room had long windows along one side with

pale-gray drapes framing them. A long white sectional ran along the room to the left. There were blonde hardwood floors and a white shag rug.

How on earth did they keep this place so spotless with dogs? It wasn't exactly the most crucial question at the moment, but it sprung into Denise's mind nonetheless.

A small sunroom just off the living room shared a two-sided fireplace with the living room. The second dog lay sprawled on the couch in the sunroom, in similar condition to the first.

Denise backed away, not seeing any sign of what had caused the damage. Was it possible that one of the Fowlers was on drugs? She'd heard stories of PCP causing incredible rushes of adrenaline. She'd never seen it for herself, but she supposed it was possible, although it would be an unusual drug of choice for a couple in their mid-forties who were well-to-do suburbanites.

She walked back through the living room and caught up with Michael in the dining room. The room had a two-tiered ceiling and metallic paint along the walls. Shadow boxes outlined the lower half of the room, with a silver and white stripe on the top half. An enormous dark metal chandelier hung over the dining room table, surrounded by twelve high-backed upholstered chairs.

Denise noted all of that in just a glance. Her attention was pulled to the one part of the room that obviously had not been part of the decorating scheme: the body on the ground around the side of the table. She could make out a pair of dark loafers and dress pants.

"Mr. Fowler," Michael said softly from the other side of the table.

"Call it in," Denise said.

Looking a little pale, Michael nodded. Denise didn't look at the body as she made her way into the kitchen. She'd seen what the dogs looked like. That was going to be enough to fill her nightmares. She didn't need to see the human equivalent.

But Denise's plan to avoid further visions of blood and gore were foiled the second she stepped into the room.

Mrs. Fowler lay sprawled next to the kitchen table, her eyes open, blood splashed across her face. Her chest had a giant, gaping hole in it that went almost from her collarbone to her pubic bone. The ribs were spread wide. It almost looked as if something had wrenched the ribs open. It reminded her of an autopsy she'd seen once. What on earth had happened here?

A small noise came from behind her.

Pulse racing, Denise whirled around. Distracted by the body, she'd failed to check the corners. Light shone in through the row of glass doors along the back of the house that over-looked a large pool. Gray cabinets with a pristine white coun-tertop ran along the wall to the left. A matching island nearly the length of the wall separated the table and the cabinets.

There wasn't a dish out or a piece of food. Everything was spotless. Not a sign of violence except for Mrs. Fowler on the floor and the blood caused by her condition.

The only sign of anything else out of place was a small door to the left of the cabinets. It was slightly ajar.

Denise had been in enough of these types of home to know it was most likely a pantry. She walked forward and carefully nudged open the pantry door with her foot and swung her gun muzzle inside. Rows of canned and boxed goods lined the shelves, all carefully organized. It was a meticulous pantry, and Denise had no doubt that if she checked the labels, she would find it organized according in some sort of specific order. It looked like something from a magazine shoot.

In fact, just like the kitchen, everything looked perfect except for one glaring and obvious factor, yet again not part of the design scheme. Shelby sat on the ground at the back of the pantry, her knees crushed to her chest, a small white poodle in her arms. Blood was splashed across the two of them as she rocked back and forth.

Denise walked up slowly, her training kicking in. Was Shelby a victim? The perpetrator?

Even as her mind rebelled against the second possibility, she could not discount it. She kept her finger on the trigger as she approached. "Shelby? Shelby, are you okay?"

Rocking back and forth, Shelby just stared straight ahead, holding on to the small dog.

Denise crouched down and reached out a hand. She touched Shelby's shoulder. "Shelby?"

The woman flinched, her eyes blinking before she turned her head slowly to Denise. Recognition flashed through them. "Denise?"

"Yeah, it's me. What happened?"

Tears filled Shelby's eyes as her words came out in a rush.

"Oh my God, Denise. You can't be here. It will get you too. It got the Fowlers."

"What got them?"

Sirens sounded in the distance, growing closer. A scream rang through the house, long and filled with pain.

Denise vaulted to her feet. Michael.

Shelby clamped onto her hand. "No. You can't."

Denise tried to shake her off. "Let me go. I have to help him."

Terror filled eyes met Denise's gaze. "You can't. Your gun won't do anything."

Chills crawled over Denise at the conviction in Shelby's voice.

"Who's out there?"

"It's not a who. It's a what. And it's not human."

# CHAPTER 6

## PORT CHESTER, CONNECTICUT

Birchwood Lane hadn't changed much in the last year and a half. In fact, it didn't seem to have changed at all. The homeowner's association made sure of it.

Greg stepped out of the Uber and stared at his family's home. It was a white-and-brown split-level that dated to 1965. The long lawn was manicured but not ostentatious. Two Acura sedans, both dark gray, sat in the driveway. Two Acura SUVs, these ones silver, were parked along the curb.

There was a small flowerpot with pansies by the front door. Greg knew the pansies were replaced every month with the appropriate flowers. Except during winter, when they were replaced with a small Christmas tree. That little pot was the only outdoor decoration that his mother allowed.

The Honda Civic that dropped him off pulled away from the curb, yet Greg continued to stand there. He'd been around the globe. And he'd quite literally been to the end of the world, and even off the planet. He'd had his life on the line he didn't know how many times. He'd saved more than a few people's lives over the last few years.

And yet somehow, standing on the sidewalk facing his family home, he felt like an awkward fourteen-year-old kid who never seemed to measure up. Even as he acknowledged the ridiculousness of feeling insecure, he felt his shoulders hunch and his chin drop, the posture of teenage Greg Schorn. He consciously made an effort to straighten, but it was almost as if gravity at this particular part of Connecticut was stronger than anywhere else, on or off the planet.

He'd read somewhere once that family dynamics made it very difficult for people within a family to accept when one member had changed. In families, everyone got assigned a role: the good one, the smart one, the athletic one, the funny one, the loser, and so on.

Greg knew which role he'd been given early on.

It didn't matter how many degrees he got or how well he did in school, in his family's eyes, he was always the loser. Long ago, his parents had decided that his sisters were smart and Greg merely mediocre. No matter what grades Greg got in school, he could never change that opinion.

He'd been the surprise child. And apparently not a very welcome one. There were ten years between him and the younger of his sisters. Twelve between him and his older one. Maybe that was why he felt so out of touch with them.

But he knew what the real reason for the division between him and the rest of the Schorn family was: instead of going into the family business—taxes—he'd gone off into the world of science, confirming his black sheep status. Other kids were classified as black sheep because they got into trouble. Greg was a black sheep because he studied biology and engineering at MIT instead of accounting at Lehigh University.

Gripping the handle of his suitcase a little harder, Greg wondered why exactly he had come home. Okay, Norah had ordered him. But he could have just gone somewhere else for the weekend. Heck, he could have contacted Sammy and asked him to take him up to Norway. Seeing Maeve and the gang would have been a nice pick-me-up.

For a moment, he contemplated heading down the street and calling another Uber to come pick him up. But just as he thought it, the curtain in the kitchen shifted, and someone glanced out.

Crap. Too late to retreat now.

He straightened his shoulders, which had somehow hunched even more while he stood there, and headed for the front door. A few moments later, he opened the door and stepped inside. He was greeted by a staircase split into two. He'd always thought split levels were uncomfortable. Whenever someone walked in, they automatically had to make a choice of up or down. Too much pressure.

He glanced toward the downstairs. His bedroom had been down there, along with the family room and a single bathroom. Everyone else's bedrooms had been upstairs, which he realized now was pretty much a perfect example of his relationship with his family. They were all on one level, and he was most definitely on another.

"Greg."

His gaze shifted to the top of the stairs. His mother, Evelyn, smiled as she headed down the stairs toward him. His mom was sixty-one, but it was hard to tell from where he stood. Her hair was dark, with only a light sprinkling of gray that somehow made her look more intelligent. Dark eyes were set in a face that was just starting to get a few wrinkles. She was absolutely rigid with her food and exercise schedule.

Her nails were bright red, which was not a surprise. He didn't think he'd ever seen her actual nail color in his entire life. She always had them painted. She reached out her hands for him. He automatically placed his two hands in hers.

Leaning up, she kissed him on the cheek, squeezed his hands, then stepped back, releasing him. "Greg. It's so good to see you."

Greg straightened his shoulders again. "You too, Mom. Is everybody here?"

"Of course. You're the last, as usual."

Little boy Greg winced. Two seconds in the door, and already his failings were being pointed out. But he tried to ignore the slight. "Where's the birthday boy?"

His mother nodded toward the downstairs. "He's out on the back deck. Why don't you drop your bag in your room and go see him?"

Without waiting for a reply, his mother headed back up the stairs. Greg watched her go with a sigh as he grabbed his suitcase from where he'd set it down. This was going to be a long weekend.

He headed down the stairs and turned into the first door right off the staircase. The room his mother called his looked nothing like the room he'd grown up in. Back in the day, Greg had a twin bed pushed up against the wall. A bookcase sat along the other one, with a long desk that held his computer and all his LEGO creations. A couple of posters had decorated the walls.

Even back then, his mother had hated it. She had wasted no time redoing it when he left for college. But apparently she had redone it again. Now it had white wicker furniture and a bright floral comforter.

He stared at the wicker furniture in dismay. His grandparents had that furniture. He'd always associated it with old people or summer spots. Connecticut was not a summer spot. His mother had hated it when he was growing up too. He wondered if she was just storing the outdoor furniture in here until the weather cleared.

He placed his case next to the bed, looking around. There

was a small narrow window above the bed. This part of the house ran into a hill, not allowing for a full window. When he was younger, he knew if there was a fire, he was a goner.

Apparently, if there was a fire this weekend, he was still a goner. He shook his head, chasing away the thought. Man, he'd been here less than five minutes, and already it had him contemplating his demise.

*It's just a weekend, Greg. You can make it through the weekend,* he reminded himself as he stepped out of the room.

He passed through the family room, which had a large leather sectional facing an enormous TV, and made his way out onto the back deck. His father sat in an Adirondack chair at the edge of the deck, just staring out into the nature preserve behind the house. The preserve was acres of untouched forest, although trails had been made by animals over the years. Greg had escaped there innumerable times during his childhood. He'd even set up a little camp. He'd felt more at home there than in his actual home.

Although the door made a loud click as Greg slid it shut, his dad didn't turn. Greg cleared his throat. "Um, hey, Dad."

Jeff Schorn turned around and then slowly placed his tumbler of scotch on the deck next to his chair as he stood. Jeff was an older version of Greg. He normally wore glasses, but like Greg, he'd gotten Lasik a few years back. He turned to Greg, extending a hand. "Greg, good to see you."

*Gee, Dad, don't get all mushy.* Greg shook his hand. "You too, Dad. Happy birthday."

With a nod, his dad accepted the sentiment and then sat back down.

*And that ends the emotional portion of the weekend,* Greg thought.

His father gestured to the chair next to him. "Take a seat."

Greg glanced at the other Adirondack chair and then back at the house, looking for someone to save him. He and his

42

father rarely talked. In fact, he couldn't remember the last time he'd spoken with his father alone. He almost always communicated with his family through his mom.

No movement came from inside, so he took a seat. "Uh, so how you doing, Dad?"

"Good, good. We got a couple of extra clients this year, which will really make things busy come April. We could use another accountant or two." He gave Greg a sidelong glance.

*And it begins,* Greg thought.

"If you'd been with our firm, it really would've helped out," his father finished.

"Well, I'm sure there are some perfectly capable accountants that you can find."

Jeff shook his head with a sigh. "But it's not the same as family."

Apparently his mother had been giving his father some guilt-tripping tips. "Right. Um, so how are my sisters doing?"

"Doing great. Each of them brought in quite a few clients of their own. We might even have to expand soon."

Greg nodded as his father began to tell him about those clients. He tried not to feel jealous at the pride he heard in his father's voice. After a twenty-minute recitation on the accomplishments of his sisters, his father finally asked, "So how's your military thing going?"

"It's good. I'm running a new division. We're based in upstate New York now."

"Well, that's good, I suppose. I think I'll go top off my drink." His father stood.

"You know, I think I'll just stay out here for a few minutes. It's nice and quiet."

"Suit yourself." His father headed inside, closing the door behind him.

Greg's whole body sagged with released tension. How was it possible that he'd only been here for a short time and already he felt like he been put through the ringer? He leaned his head back against the chair. *I should have just sent a gift.*

The door slid open behind him. He glanced over his shoulder as his older sister, Martha, stepped outside. He tried not to groan. *Oh, come on. I just wanted a few minutes.*

She walked over and kissed him on the cheek. Her dark hair hit Greg in the face, and he got a nose full of perfume. "Hey, Greg."

"Hey, Martha. How's it going?" He asked.

"Oh, you know me, can't complain," she said as she took a seat next to him.

Greg nearly laughed out loud. Complaining was Martha's specialty. She was a younger version of their mother, right down to the nails being done every week. He didn't think he'd ever seen her real nails either.

"So, I wanted to ask you a favor," Martha began.

Greg raised an eyebrow. "Really? I mean, what kind of favor?"

"I'd like you to speak with Kal."

Kal was Martha's oldest son. He was … Greg scrambled, trying to remember. Sixteen or seventeen. His full name was Kal El Hadid. Martha's husband Doug was a huge Superman fan, and for some reason, he'd thought it would be a good idea to name their child after the Kryptonian son.

Of course, being that Doug was a massive geek, and that Kal also had the Schorn genetics mixed in there, Greg had known that would be a disaster of a name. And sure enough, there had been more than a few incidents at school because of it. Which was really unfair, because Kal was a good kid.

Actually, out of everyone in his family, Kal was the one who Greg liked the most. It was probably because Kal reminded him of himself. He wasn't athletic. He wasn't cool. He was just a nice, smart kid.

Silence stretched between them, which, when it came to

Martha, was normally a sign of something bad on the horizon. Greg wanted to let the silence play out, but he knew his role. "Something wrong?" he asked.

She blew out a breath, drumming her fingers on the armrest of her chair. "Oh, something is most definitely wrong. So you know how Kal is in his senior year?"

He nodded, even though he'd been about a year off in his age estimate. Which meant Kal had just turned eighteen a few weeks ago. Greg had sent him this video game that Norah somehow got before it was publicly released. "Of course."

"Well, he got accepted to pretty much all of the schools he applied to, but he's dead set on one."

For the life of him, Greg couldn't figure out why that was a bad thing. "Which one?"

Martha spewed the name at him with a glare. "MIT."

Surprise flashed through Greg. "He applied to MIT?"

"*And* he didn't tell us beforehand. He just did it. He's got some stupid idea that he's going to major in biochemistry. I mean, we can't let that happen. We don't want him to be like ..." She gestured toward Greg.

Ouch.

She continued. "I mean, you know you've made choices for your life, and they're fine for you. But my son is not going to go into that kind of lifestyle."

"Martha, I have two PhDs. And I work for the U.S. government. I'm not exactly a drug dealer."

She waved away his words. "What kind of life has it given you, Greg? I mean, we never see you. And do you even have an important relationship in your life?"

A vision of Ariana floated through his head. "Well, actually—"

"He's *not* going into *biology*." She managed to put as much derision into that word as humanly possible. "He's a smart kid. He'll be an amazing accountant."

Greg had to keep himself from shaking his head, knowing it would just set off his sister. It was true: Kal *was* a smart kid. He was an incredibly smart kid. And if he didn't want to be an accountant, Greg couldn't think of a life that would be less appealing.

Greg himself had been pushed toward being accountant. And by push, he meant with a verbal cattle prod. But the idea of simply staring at rows of numbers and sheets of paper and trying to figure out whether or not someone was due this deduction or that deduction ... even the thought of it gave him a headache. And if Kal was anything like him ... God, that poor kid.

Martha, believing that for some reason he was on her side, and seemingly unaware of how much she'd insulted Greg, continued. "So anyway, I need you to speak with him and tell him that this is just a really horrible idea. I mean, tell him about your life. Once he sees that there is no future in it, I'm sure it'll change his mind. In fact, you can bring him to your work someday just to show him how boring it is."

He tried to imagine bringing Kal to the New York facility. Maybe he could arrange it so that he showed up on a day when Alvie and Iggy were there, and, of course, Pugsley, who would escape the lab and ooze his way down the hall toward Greg's office, right on time. "Yeah, we really aren't allowed to bring guests. It's all classified."

"Whatever. Just explain to him that it's not a good lifestyle, okay?"

She stood up without waiting for his answer and went back inside, closing the door with a thump. Greg rubbed the bridge of his nose, contemplating whether he should just jump the deck rail and start walking down the street. He could call an Uber once he was away from the house. He really didn't need his suitcase. There was nothing important in there anyway.

The door slid open again, and Greg wanted to drop his

head and start crying. *Seriously, can I please just get a single pig in a blanket before getting thrown into all this family drama?*

But instead of his mother or one of his sisters, it was Kal. Kal was tall for his age. About six foot three, he had dark hair that kept falling into his eyes. Like Greg did before, he had glasses, and like teenage Greg, he also still had some acne. Kal had a couple of inches on him, and Greg had put on some muscle these last few years, but otherwise they were pretty similar in appearance. He wore old ratty jeans and a T-shirt for a band that Greg had never heard of.

"Hey, Uncle Greg."

This time as he stood, the smile came easily to his face. He really did like Kal. He walked over and gave him a hug. Kal hesitated for a minute and then returned the hug.

When Greg released him, he stepped back, looking up at his nephew. "It's really good to see you. Man, you've gotten tall."

A smile spreading across his lips, Kal ducked his head. "I shot up like six inches last year. I'm taller than Dad now."

Greg chuckled. "I'm betting he doesn't like that."

Kal grinned back at him. "No, he doesn't."

Flicking a glance at the two Adirondack chairs perched on the edge of the deck, Greg frowned. They'd already been the scene for two uncomfortable conversations. He didn't want them tainting his conversation with Kal. "Hey, how about if we take a little walk through the woods?"

His nephew nodded. "Yeah. That sounds good."

The two of them headed toward the woods and fell into an easy silence. Greg had really missed Kal. He was probably the only member of his family he could say that about. When Kal was younger, they'd play board games together whenever they saw one another, and Greg had been the one who'd introduced him to video games. Even now, they still occasionally played online together.

But, of course, last year, when he'd been in hiding, he hadn't been able to reach out to him. He watched his nephew from the corner of his eyes. His chin was down, his eyes clouded with worry. His shoulders were hunched, just like Greg's had been at his age.

"Hey, Kal, I'm really sorry I haven't been able to link up with you over the last year. Things got really crazy at work, and it just kind of became impossible."

Kal shrugged. "It's okay. I understand."

After studying him for a moment, Greg stopped walking. Kal stopped too.

"I mean it, Kal, if I could have reached out to you, I would have. But I was in a situation where, well, I couldn't contact anyone. I really wish I could have."

Kal looked at him and gave him a nod, some of the tension seeming to leave him. "It's okay. Seriously."

Feeling a little better, Greg nodded, and they continued their walk. "So you got into MIT. That's awesome."

A grin split across Kal's face. "I couldn't believe when I got the letter. I mean, I applied, but I never thought I'd get in."

"Why not? I mean, your grades are awesome, and that project you did freshman year with the AI program? People at MIT love that stuff."

"Yeah, but I mean, I'm not going to be able to go."

The happiness that he'd seen on his nephew's face disappeared with the utterance of those words. Greg sighed, not sure what to say. He wanted to tell Kal to just do what he wanted with his life.

But he also knew how tough that road was. At the same time, the last couple of years had been the most rewarding of Greg's life. He couldn't imagine that being an accountant in the family firm would have come anywhere close.

"My mom wanted you to talk me out of going MIT, didn't she?" Kal asked.

Greg nodded. "Yep."

"Are you going to?"

"Nope."

Kal's mouth fell open before he shut it. "Why not?"

Thinking about how to respond, Greg paused for a moment before answering, He didn't need to think much beyond today's interactions. His parents hadn't seen him in a year, and he received the welcome of a returning repairman. Greg sighed. "Look, our family is not exactly warm and fuzzy."

Kal scoffed. "Yeah, that's an understatement."

"True. But they mean well. Your mom's just worried that you will have an unfulfilled life. She's worried that you won't be around much. I mean, I don't see the family very often. But your mom and Aunt Sally, they both see your grandparents every day. And I think she just kind of wants that for you."

Kal sighed. "Yeah, I know. But the idea of just staring at numbers every day, I mean, God, that just sounds so boring."

"Yeah, I know what you mean." Greg smiled as he said it, but he also knew how tenacious his sister could be when she had an idea in her head, especially when it came to her oldest son. "Does MIT have an accounting program?"

Kal nodded. "Yeah, actually, they do."

"Okay, well, maybe just take a few accounting classes to make sure that it's not what you want, and then hopefully, by the time you declare a major, she will have come around."

"Do you think that's possible?"

Greg wanted to lie to him, but he made a point of always telling Kal the truth, and he really didn't want to change that now. "No. But by then you'll be older and be better able to handle it."

The path wound its way back toward the house. "Kal, whatever you decide to do, there will be consequences. As long as you're aware of them, then you should be able to make your own decision."

"Do you ever regret not going into the family business?" Kal asked.

Once again, Greg thought about lying, but Kal didn't deserve that. "No. I can honestly say that at no point in my life have I ever wished I was an accountant."

Relief flashed across Kal's face. Obviously, he just wanted to talk to someone who understood. And Greg most definitely did.

"Yeah, that's what I thought." Kal smiled.

Greg's phone beeped just as they stepped onto the back lawn. With regret, he pulled it out and glanced at the screen. He'd missed a call from Norah. Cell reception was spotty in the preserve. He frowned at the notice indicating that she'd left him a voicemail.

"Everything okay?" Kal asked.

"I'm not sure. My boss left me a message. I need to check this."

Nodding, Kal headed toward the house. "Okay, I'll wait for you inside."

Greg quickly pulled up his voicemail and listened as Norah's voice spilled across his speaker. "Hey, Greg. Sorry to call you during your family weekend, but we have a situation, and it's not that far from you. I have a tactical team on the way. But I think I need a science guy, and you're the closest one."

Greg closed his eyes in relief. *Thank God.*

# CHAPTER 7

The tactical team would pick Greg up down the street from his parents' house. He couldn't have them pick him up right at the door because there'd be too many questions. As it was, his mom was already annoyed when he kissed her on the cheek, said he had a work emergency, and that he'd be back as soon as he could.

She narrowed her eyes, her hands on her hips for only a second before she threw them up in the air. "What kind of emergency could you possibly have?"

His sisters both glared at him over the bowls of pasta they were setting on the buffet table. His father and brothers-in-law were too involved in their ball game to notice, so he didn't even bother trying to explain. "Sorry. I'll be back as soon as I can."

Kal stood playing with his phone at the front door as Greg walked down the steps. He gave him a hopeful look that disappeared when Greg opened his mouth. "Sorry, I have to go do a work thing."

"Are you coming back?"

Visions of the different creatures these types of calls

involved floated through his mind as his stomach dropped. Still, he tried to keep his voice upbeat. "I hope so."

With a resigned sigh, Kal gave him a nod and headed up the stairs as his mother called.

Greg felt like ten different kinds of a heel as he watched Kal go. That poor kid. He felt about as much a part of the family as Greg did.

*I need to make more time for him*, he thought as he walked down the sidewalk of Birchwood Lane. He could play a few more video games with him at night. He didn't need to sleep a full eight hours, right?

Or maybe he could just shoot him a few more texts during the week, just to check in. That was the least he could do.

Lost in his thoughts, he didn't notice the black SUV until it pulled to a stop with a squeal of brakes. He jumped, whirling around, his heart racing.

Mitch sat behind the wheel with a grin. "What's up, Doc?" he asked as Greg stepped into the passenger seat.

Greg groaned. "You really need to come up with some new material."

Mitch shook his head as he pulled away from the curb. "Nah, the classics are always good."

"What are you doing here, anyway? I thought you were back at base."

"There were some reports of unusual activity over in New Hampshire. Turned out to be a bust. But it meant my team was closest when this call came in." Mitch nudged his chin toward the tablet in between the seats. "The file's in there."

Pulling over the tablet, Greg started flipping through the little information they had as Mitch pulled away from the curb. It looked like the case had been initiated by two cops who'd been called to a home. Homeowners were deceased, along with a couple of the family dogs. There was one survivor. Local cops were already on scene but were told to stand down until the D.E.A.D. arrived.

"How did you guys even find out about this?"

"Monster watch," Mitch said.

Greg grunted. Monster Watch was the shorthand for the intelligence program that analyzed all cellphone communication in the United States for certain key words. A team was put on alert if further analysis indicated any emotional responses that indicated fear and/or alarm. The program was designed to differentiate between fear caused by say a scary monster movie and an actual Seti event.

The whole thing seemed like a civil rights violation but Greg couldn't help but admit that it did give them a jump on some situations.

Mitch nodded toward the tablet. "I thought it was a long shot given the location but when we touched down, we got a report of a 911 call in the area. So here we are."

"What's the chance the cops will wait until we get there?" Greg asked.

"Probably zero."

With a nod, Greg said, "Yeah, that's what I figured too. How far from here?"

"Only about ten minutes. Lucky you were so close."

Ten minutes? His mind raced, trying to figure out where they would be going. There weren't a lot of options. Their sightings tended to happen in less populated areas. Most of their subjects didn't show up in shopping malls. "Yeah. I'm feeling awfully lucky," Greg murmured.

Mitch nudged his chin toward the backseat. "Your gear's in the duffel behind you."

Reaching back, Greg pulled the black duffel into his lap. Grabbing the body armor, he slipped it over his shirt. He pulled out the P90 and checked the drum. It was good. He locked it back in place and then put it on his lap. It all took three minutes. He was really getting used to this.

Mitch grinned. "I have to say, you're looking a lot more comfortable with that weapon. The first time you picked it up, I was afraid you were going to shoot yourself in the foot with it."

Greg grunted. "I almost did a few times. But like they say, practice makes perfect."

Mitch's security clearance wasn't quite as high as Greg's, but it was high enough that he knew about some of Greg's previous involvement with the creatures from Area 51.

Greg turned back to the tablet and flipped through the file again, surprised to see their destination. "Greenwich? Are they serious?"

"Yeah, I was surprised too."

Greenwich, Connecticut is one of the richest areas of the United States. It's known for being a haven for the wealthy. Located an hour outside Manhattan, it's an enclave comprised of hedge-fund managers and the super-rich of Wall Street.

The house was located in Belle Haven, an exclusive gated community within the Greenwich community that once had homes owned by Diana Ross and hedge-fund mogul Paul Tudor Jones. The home in question belonged to a couple named Elaine and Michael Fowler. Both were forty-four and had been together for twenty years, no kids. He owned a small computer security firm, but the bulk of their money came from her work as a hedge-fund manager.

Their only hobby seemed to be their dogs. Apparently they had won a ton of awards in dog competitions in the last few years. They'd even placed at the Westminster Dog Show.

Closing the file, Greg glanced over at Mitch. "This is not normal."

"Agreed. What the hell is one of these things doing in a neighborhood? Especially a hoity-toity neighborhood?"

Greg had no answer for that. So far, the only Seti they'd encountered in a neighborhood was Iggy. Most had been found in more out-of-the-way locations. These things might not be from around here, but their survival instincts were good, and they knew to stay away from highly populated areas. And none had been found this far east.

So how did one of them end up in a house in one of the richest neighborhoods in Connecticut? Something definitely didn't make sense.

Two more SUVs fell in line with them, one in front and one behind as they pulled onto the highway. They were only on the highway about five minutes before they pulled off again. It seemed that every car they passed was a high-end luxury brand: Lexus, Lucid, Mercedes, even a few Rolls-Royces and one Bentley.

Five minutes later, they were pulling through the gates of Belle Haven. It was not what Greg expected. The first couple of houses looked almost normal, even though he was sure the price tags would make his eyes pop.

The houses here weren't the gaudy pop-up McMansions of the new wealthy. This was understated wealth. Everything was tasteful, as if waiting for the photographer from *Traditional Home* to arrive.

As they drove, each home and yard became progressively larger. Each house had a perfectly manicured lawn, impressively maintained landscaping, and not a sign of life. No cars were parked out front. No kids toys were in the yard. That would be frowned upon in this kind of neighborhood. They seemed to think it was best if the houses looked perfect and unlived in. God forbid they looked as if someone actually spent time there.

But up ahead, police cruisers marred the perfection of the street. One was parked along the road, its lights flashing, their doors thrown wide. One more was in the driveway, but there was no movement.

For a moment, Greg thought that maybe, just maybe, they'd actually waited. Maybe they'd just set up a perimeter while waiting for Mitch and Greg to—

Gunshots rang out through the air.

Mitch punched down on the accelerator. The two SUVs with them did the same.

"They never wait," Greg grumbled.

# CHAPTER 8

"Going in hot!" Mitch yelled as he stepped on the accelerator, weaving around the cop cars in the driveway and pulling up in front of the house.

It was a nice-looking house. It had to have cost at least two million. But that was all Greg had time to notice. The SUV in front of them slammed to a stop seconds before Mitch did, and already all four members of the tactical team were out and moving toward the house. A cop stumbled out the door, his arm hanging by a thread, his face ashen.

Kaylee, the team medic and a former Marine with three tours in Afghanistan, grabbed him and pulled him behind the SUV. She quickly got to work on his wound.

Greg knew that the guy wasn't going be able to keep his arm. He'd seen enough of those wounds to know the score. Immediately, his mind categorized the wound and what could have caused it.

The arm hadn't been cut off. It looked more like it had been pulled. Like something had grabbed a hold and yanked. Something with heightened strength.

Greg processed all that in seconds. Mitch was out the door

as soon as the car stopped. Taking a breath, Greg bolted from his own seat. He wasn't built like these other guys. The rush of adrenaline did not make him want to run forward. If anything, it made him want to run away screaming. But this was the job.

With only a slight hesitation at the door, Greg followed Mitch into the house. The other four members of the tactical team had already spread out. The SUV behind him had unloaded its members, and they were making their way to the back of the house.

Two members of the first team headed up the stairs as Mitch nodded his head to the left. Greg fell in step behind him, the P90 pulled into his shoulder. A quick glance at the couch indicated that parts of one of the dogs was missing. Their subject was definitely a carnivore. The other pieces hadn't been flung about, which meant they had most likely been eaten.

The file hadn't indicated what kind of creature they were tracking down, but it definitely wasn't a Maldek like Iggy. Greg tightened his grip on his gun. *Just please don't be a Hank.*

Hanks were officially classified as Kecksburgs and then designated by what generation they were: AG1, AG2, etc. They'd been created from the remains found at the Kecksburg UFO site back in 1965.

Greg had worked with a Hank, a very nasty one, back at Wright-Patterson. Unbeknownst to him, that Hank hadn't been the only one. The former director of the D.E.A.D., Martin Drummond seemed to take a liking to the creatures and had created his own special pack, which he controlled.

It was not surprising that Drummond had an affinity for them. They were brutal killing machines. They killed not to protect, not for food, just because they could. Greg swallowed, picturing those things back in Drummond's underground bunker in Arizona where they'd chased him down a hall. He had hoped that all of them were destroyed, but like he'd told Norah the other day, when were they ever that lucky?

He and Mitch did a sweep of the first floor. Besides the two bodies, they didn't see any movement. In the kitchen, they stopped at the pantry. The door was dented and scratched but not fully closed.

Mitch waved Greg to the side. He called softly through the door. "Federal agents. We're opening the door." Staying to the side, Mitch pulled on the door slowly, saying again, "Federal agents."

The cop at the back of the pantry held her gun on the doorway anyway. Sitting next to her was a woman with dark-brown hair, holding a small white puppy. The officer only lowered her weapon when she caught sight of Mitch and Greg.

Greg stepped inside. "Are either of you hurt?"

The cop shook her head and cleared her throat. "No, we're good, but my partner ..."

A voice came through his earpiece. *"One body upstairs. Police officer."*

Greg cringed.

"We found him," Mitch said.

"Is he ..." The cop let the rest of her question drift off.

Greg shook his head. "I'm sorry. But can you tell me what you saw?"

The officer took a deep breath, pulling her emotions back. She let it out slowly before speaking. "There was this scratching, this really loud scratching, something really big was heading toward us, and there was the scream that came from upstairs. It was a screech. It wasn't human."

She swallowed. "I went to go check on my partner after I heard him scream. I was about to step out of the kitchen when the door flew back at me. Something heavy pushed against it, pinning me to the wall. I fired through the door. My backup arrived then. The pressure on the door disappeared. I opened the door as the front door was flung open.

Her eyes troubled, a tremor rolled through her before she continued. "Sharon and Nate stepped in, guns drawn. I sent them upstairs while I stepped back into the hall and cleared the front of the house."

"Did you get a look at it?" Mitch asked.

"No, not at all."

"What about her? Can she tell us anything?" Greg asked.

The officer looked back down at the other woman. She sat rocking the puppy curled up in her arms. The cop frowned. "This is Shelby. She works for the Fowlers. I haven't really been able to get her to make much sense. She said it's ... I don't know, she's just rambling."

"What did she say?"

The officer looked up at Greg, meeting his eyes. "Tentacles. She keeps saying it had tentacles and so many teeth."

# CHAPTER 9

There was no sign of the creature. The cop who'd had his arm ripped off had seen it upstairs, and he'd been the one to fire off the shots. But then he'd been grabbed. The others had rushed up the stairs but hadn't seen it at all. All they found was one of their fellow officers lying in a pool of blood and the other with his arm nearly pulled off.

Greg stepped outside, watching as the officer from the pantry helped Shelby into one of the waiting squad cars.

Mitch stepped up next to him. "What do you think?"

"I have no idea." Greg kept looking around, trying to see if there was any sign of the creature, but nothing stood out. There were no clues, no trail on the ground that anyone had found. Not that that was surprising, being it had been able to get all the way to the middle of Connecticut without raising alarms. The teams were going through the house again, and then they'd start on the neighbors. This thing had to be here somewhere.

Greg turned to Mitch. "A house like this has to have some sort of security setup. Were there any cameras?"

Mitch shook his head. "No, but the alarm had been tripped, which was why the cops showed up."

"Great," Greg said still confused how any of this was possible.

"I'm going to help them canvas. You want to come with?"

Greg shook his head. "No. Not yet. I'm going to run through the house again and see if I see anything."

"Okay, Max and Kaylee are still here. The rest of us are going to head to the neighbors and see if we can figure anything out."

Watching Mitch walk off, Greg's mind rolled through the possible explanations for the creature's disappearance.

None of them were good.

He turned to stare at the house. How the hell had this Seti even arrived in Connecticut? And why couldn't they find it?

The possibilities were terrifying. Did this thing have some sort of camouflage? Or God forbid, could it actually go invisible? Or maybe it could fly. But so far Sammy was the only creature they knew of who could fly.

He ruled absolutely nothing out at this point, though. He'd seen too much to say that anything was off the table. He headed for the house. One more sweep and hopefully he'd see something to help figure out what they were looking for.

He didn't even know what he would put into the D.E.A.D. computer to search for this. Tentacles and teeth? There were more than a few creatures that had tentacles. There were definitely a lot that had terrifying teeth. He wasn't sure those two descriptions were going to narrow anything down.

From the cop's description, it sounded like it was on the larger side, but again, that didn't help a whole lot.

Stopping on the stoop, he turned around, scanning the neighborhood. What really bothered Greg was the fact that this thing was on the East Coast. The creatures had all escaped from Area 51, thousands of miles southwest of here. Other creatures had made it as far east as Ohio, but there was always a trail of sightings. How had this one gotten all the way out here without a single person seeing it? Had they just missed the reports?

He discarded the thought almost as soon as he had it. This thing was brutal, and its attacks were pretty unique. Some creatures' attacks could be mistaken for an animal attack, but not this one. If it had traveled from Las Vegas, there should have been a string of bodies missing hearts in its wake.

Iggy went undetected in a neighborhood because he didn't cause any destruction. The thing they were tracking right now did not have the same pacifist tendencies.

He stepped into the foyer and this time headed to the right. Michael Fowler was still splayed out on the floor. There was a slash across his face, another across his neck, and then there was the gaping hole in his chest identical to the wound in his wife's chest.

It looked as if the creature had taken their hearts. That was just gross. Why couldn't it have been a cute little alien? Or at least not a serial-killer type?

A flash of movement outside the window pulled his attention.

A muffled yell of fear came from the left-hand side of the yard. Greg sprinted to the front door just in time to see someone disappear into the woods to the left. And only about twenty feet behind the figure was an undulating mass of brown and green that looked like an octopus on steroids.

"I found it!" Greg yelled as he burst out the door.

# CHAPTER 10

Fumbling to pull the P90 up as he ran, Greg sprinted toward the trees. He got a grip on the trigger and automatically felt better.

His feet pounded the ground, tearing off after the creature. Its coloring was almost identical to the ground below it. If it stayed still, it would be really hard to see. He wondered if that was its actual color or if it shifted to replicate its surroundings.

All those thoughts, though, were just background musing. Right now, he needed to get to the creature before it reached the poor person it was chasing.

Greg didn't know who it was after: one of his team or maybe some neighbor that just happened upon the situation. Whoever it was, they were definitely going to be in a world of trouble if Greg didn't get to them soon.

Screams traveled through the trees. "No! No!"

And Greg, the man who in high school was voted most likely to jump at his own shadow, sprinted forward, knowing that he was the closest to the creature and therefore the only one that had a chance of helping whoever this thing was currently tracking.

At the same time, his mind sorted through what he had seen. The creature used its tentacles almost like legs. It didn't stand up on them. They remained nearly flat on the ground. It moved them in more of a seesaw fashion. The process should have been slow and awkward, yet it moved incredibly fast.

The creature was almost entirely brown now, suggesting it did in fact have a chameleon-like ability. It was entirely possible it had just been lying flat in the backyard and they hadn't even realized it. They could have walked right by it and not noticed a thing. The idea made Greg's stomach bottom out. His life was officially a horror film.

Perhaps it had been sitting there digesting its meal. Then when it was done, maybe the neighbor had strolled by, trying to see what was going on, and the creature had taken off after them, looking for dessert. If the neighbor hadn't come by, they might not have even found it. They could've left, and this thing would've gone back to work. Or worse, at night, when they were closing up the scene, it could have grabbed one of their people.

His stride lengthened as he raced to the edge of the lawn and burst through the trees. Then he pulled up short. The creature was only thirty feet away. It was bunching itself together, growing taller at the base of a pear tree, almost as if it were going to try to climb it.

Greg didn't wait. He raised the P90 into his shoulder and pulled the trigger, setting off shots in short bursts.

The creature squealed as Greg's aim proved true. The creature flattened back to the ground. But a small head emerged from the center of its body. It let out a roar, showing off rows of sharp teeth.

All the hair on Greg's body stood at attention. But he held his ground, knowing that he was the only thing that was going to keep the person up in the tree alive.

Gunfire sounded from behind him. From the corner of his

eye, he saw Kaylee and Max approach as they added their fire-power to his own.

The creature roared again. It started to move to its right, away from them, trying to escape. But now it was moving much slower. Yet it was still fast enough that they had to jog to keep up with it.

"You get the civilian, we'll track it down," Kaylee said as she and Max strode forward.

His weapon pulled tightly to his shoulder, Greg followed them, making his way toward the tree, waiting until he couldn't see his team members or the creature. Then he lowered his weapon and looked up.

The individual who'd run across the lawn was only about seven feet up. Almost level with Greg's head, his sneakers were a familiar pair of blue Converse.

He grinned down nervously at Greg as he pushed his glasses up his nose. "Uh, hi, Uncle Greg."

# CHAPTER 11

**W**ords completely failed Greg as he stared up at Kal. He was pretty sure that upon pain of death, he would not be able to utter a single coherent sentence at this moment in time.

And once he had to face his family, he knew his heart or brain would quite literally explode from the stress.

"Uh, is it safe to come down?" Kal asked.

his mind misfiring, Greg continued to look up at Kal. "Ubba, um, whose …"

Shoving the glasses up his nose once again, which nearly caused him to fall off the branch he was precariously perched upon, Kal frowned. "Uncle Greg?"

"Uh." Greg gave himself a mental shake and lowered his weapon, quickly hiding it behind his back. "Uh, yeah, come on down."

Crouching down, Kal dangled his feet over the edge before jumping the last of the short distance. He wiped his hands on his jeans before looking pointedly at Greg's right arm. "I know you have a gun, Uncle Greg."

His words shook Greg from his paralysis. Yes, Greg had a gun. And he had a gun because there was a scary, scary Seti still out here.

And his nephew was standing right here too. Bolting forward, he gripped Kal's arm. Then he pulled him back toward the house as he scanned the area. "Come on. It's not safe here."

Releasing Kal, he pushed him forward while he stayed behind him to cover their retreat. Every sound and rustle in the area seemed to be magnified. The hair along his arms stood upright, and his heart seemed to be working overtime, just like his thoughts. *I cannot let Kal get killed. Getting Kal killed would definitely be worse than letting Kal be almost killed.*

They stepped out of the woods. Kal stopped, but Greg pushed on his shoulder. "We need to get back to the house."

"But I thought that thing, I mean, your friends have it, right?" Kal asked.

It was sweet how much faith he had that the good guys would easily catch and kill the big scary monster. But Greg didn't want to have the chat about how that wasn't how these situations always played out. "Hopefully. But they don't always cooperate."

Kal frowned. "Your friends?"

"No, the thing my friends are chasing. Just go." Greg's mind rolled as he tried to figure out a way for this not to be a complete and utter disaster.

Kaylee's voice came through on his earpiece. *"We got it. I need a body bag. A big one."*

*"Good. Get it bagged and out of there. I'll be on site within twenty minutes,"* Norah's voice replied.

Greg tapped the mic at his throat. "Norah? What are you doing around here?"

"I flew out so you could leave and get back to your family

dinner. I know you don't want them getting any ideas about what we really do. And running out this weekend is a tough one to explain," she said.

Staring at his nephew, who walked silently next to him, Greg nodded. "Yeah, you have no idea."

# CHAPTER 12

Visions of everything that could have gone wrong flashed through Greg's head as he paced in front of the SUV. "What were you *thinking*? You could have been killed."

Kal sat in the backseat with the door open, drinking a bottle of water, his hands shaking. "I just saw that you were going to be nearby, and, well, I saw those guys pick you up. I'd already cloned your phone. So I thought maybe I could see—"

"Wait, you cloned my phone?" Greg asked as he stopped his pacing.

"Well, yeah. I mean you're so secretive about your job. I thought maybe if I kind of figured out what you did, maybe you know it would give me an idea about why you're always gone."

Running a hand over his face, Greg groaned. The feeling that his head was about to explode, not in anger but in a combination of fear and stress, returned. Not only had Kal nearly been killed, but he'd cloned the phone of a federal agent. That couldn't be legal. "I have no idea how to explain this to your mother."

His nephew winced. "I was kind of hoping we weren't going to tell her."

"I think that's kind of a good idea, although I'm not quite sure how to manage it."

A large van pulled up in front of the fountain. Together, they watched as two stretchers were rolled out from the back and taken toward the front door.

Kal's eyes widened. "Are those for bodies?"

As Greg winced, his left eyelid started to twitch. God, this just kept getting worse and worse.

"Uncle Greg, what was that thing? I mean, it looked like some sort of mutated octopus."

A mutated octopus. Perfect. Greg latched on to the explanation. "That's exactly what that was. Yes, that's exactly what it was. It was a mutated octopus. There was a chemical spill and, yeah, it was just horrible."

Kal stared at him. "An octopus? That can live on land and breathe air?"

"Yeah. Nature's weird," Greg muttered.

Kal gave him a dubious look. "Uncle Greg ..."

A Prius pulled up at the side of the road. Norah stepped out.

Thank God. Norah would have a plan. Some sort of "save Greg from the hell his life is about to become" plan. He nearly sagged in relief before turning to his nephew. "Okay. Stay here. Just stay here. Don't move. Like, at all."

He started to head toward Norah and then turned back. "Don't say anything. Don't touch anything. Don't look at anything. Just stay here with your eyes closed. Yeah, that would be great."

Then he turned and jogged over to Norah.

Norah grinned when she saw him. "Hey there. So I hear you found the thing and even saved a civilian in the process. Nice job."

"Yeah, about that civilian. He's kind of, well, my nephew."

Norah stopped for a moment, her whole body going still. "You brought your *nephew* on a case?"

This time Greg did try to tear his hair from his head. "No, of course not. He followed me. I mean, he saw Mitch pick me up, and I don't even know how he ended up here. I heard a yell, saw the thing tearing across the lawn, and I went after it. It stopped at a tree. Then I shot it, not knowing it was my nephew up there, and then Kaylee and Max took off after the thing. I looked up in the tree. There's my nephew, and oh my God, my sister's going to kill me."

Spots appeared before Greg's eyes as he imagined his sister's face. He bent over. "I think I'm having a stroke."

Norah rubbed his back. "Okay, okay. Calm down. This might not be as bad as you think."

Greg glared up at her. "Really? Really Norah? How exactly is this not as bad as I think?"

Norah grimaced. "Okay, it probably *is* as bad as you think. Didn't you say that your nephew is the only member of your family that you actually like?"

Straightening Greg swayed for a moment as the world seemed to blur. "Yeah, I mean, he is kind of the only one that's not a jerk. And he does actually want to go into biochemistry. He got into MIT."

"Okay, so we'll figure out a way to get him to keep quiet."

Hearing Norah being on board made him feel a little better. "Well, technically he did just turn eighteen, so I mean, I guess legally I don't have to tell his mom if we can get him to agree to not say anything."

"Look, the situation is wrapped up. We'll explain the policy to your nephew about witnesses."

Greg's stomach rolled. He'd forgotten about that. The "policy" was basically something straight out of the Men in Black urban legends. Backed by the power of the Department of

Defense, anyone who saw aspects of a D.E.A.D. operation was informed that any revelation of any aspect of the operation would result in fines, jail time, and potentially exile. Basically, you talked, you disappeared.

Spots danced at the edge of his vision as his eyelid started to twitch again. Yeah, he was, he was definitely about to have a stroke. And right now, that would be a good thing.

Norah smiled, unaware of the physical manifestation of stress currently trying to choke Greg. "So now we can just get your nephew back home. No harm, no foul."

Mitch's voice cut into Norah statement. "Director? Dr. Schorn? There's something you need to see."

# CHAPTER 13

The location Mitch wanted them to see was only two houses down from the Fowler house, but due to the size of the lawns, it was a good half-mile walk. Greg left Kal in the car under Max's supervision while he and Norah walked to the other scene.

While they walked, Greg had visions of what would have happened if he hadn't reached his nephew in time. That was enough to make his blood run cold.

But then he also envisioned Kal telling his sister, who of course would tell his mother and his other sister. And then they would all gang up on Greg even though Kal was the one who had snuck out to follow him.

Honestly, he was tempted to never see a single member his family ever again. That would be less painful than having to deal with the reaction to Kal being here. So that was what he would do. He would drop Kal off at the curb and then hightail it out of there.

"It's going to be okay," Norah said.

The laugh that burst from his mouth was not a happy sound. Even to his own ears, it sounded like he was on the edge of hysteria. Which he had to admit was pretty good because he was full-on hysterical in his mind. "Okay? Are you crazy? It's not going to be okay. My sisters had a full-on melt-down at Christmas one year when I brought the wrong kind of rolls. Rolls, Norah. They wanted potato rolls, and I brought Hawaiian rolls. You'd have thought that I stabbed them. And now I brought my nephew—granted, unintentionally—to the scene of a murder. No, wait, a triple homicide, and not just any triple homicide but a triple homicide by an alien! Oh, yeah, it's going to be great."

Norah was trying to hold back a smile. "Well, Kal seems like a pretty decent kid. And he's handling it surprisingly well. Look, we've both seen cases where after seeing something like that, people are incapable of even talking. Your nephew's holding it together."

Greg had to admit that was true. But the fact that his nephew was handling the existence of aliens on this planet well wasn't exactly his focus at the moment. Because while he might be handling it well, the rest of his family was definitely not going to. "Yeah, my sisters going to kill me, so Kal's ability to adjust is not really the problem."

"No, but it could be the solution."

"What do you mean?"

"Well, I was thinking about starting an internship program."

His jaw dropped as he stopped and stared at her. "What?"

"An internship program. A lot of agencies have them. And we really need some new blood to start the next generation."

"To start— Are you crazy? We're going to let teenagers wander the halls of HQ?"

"Well, I was actually thinking more like college or graduate students, but we can make an exception for Kal since there's a family connection."

Greg's mind was a complete blank. He didn't know what

to say. The idea of an internship program, especially in the science wing, was probably a good idea. But the idea of Kal being part of it, that was where he just wasn't so sure. Although he had to admit, it would be nice having at least one family member who he could talk to about work stuff.

"Look, just think about it. You said he got into MIT and he's interested in biochem. It could be a good fit. And he seems like a good kid."

"He is," Greg admitted grudgingly.

"Plus, this way he would really understand that he can't say anything. He'd have the full weight of the U.S. government on him if he did."

Greg rubbed his forehead with a groan. "Yeah, that's not helping."

Norah let out a laugh. "This doesn't have to be life-ending."

Greg shot a look at her.

She raised her hands. "Sorry, sorry, bad choice of words. I just mean that maybe this could be a good thing. Biochemistry is an area that we're interested in recruiting from. So instead of having to hide everything from your family, you could actually have a member of your family working with you."

Panic, fear, and horror were battling each other inside Greg to see which one was going to dominate. Logic and thinking things through when it came to Kal just wasn't going to be an option at the moment. "I get it, but I just can't think about this all right now."

Norah nodded. "I understand. Just mull it over when the shock has worn off some."

"Yeah, yeah, as soon as I turn fifty, I'll give it some thought."

They turned down the cobblestone driveway. Greg frowned as he walked along the ground. "I've never really understood cobblestones. I mean, it looks cool and everything, but it's hard to walk on. And cars shake like mad when you're driving on it."

"Cobblestone drives actually started with the Romans to make it easier to travel from town to town. The rocks are rounded because originally, they were taken from rivers and streams. The force of the water wore off their sharp edges, and back then they were everywhere, so they were an easy resource for streets."

Greg stared at her. "How do you know that?"

"Grandpa was into random trivia. He shared all kinds of facts and stories when we went on long walks when I was a kid."

He tried to picture a Norah walking along with her grandfather. He couldn't do it. Every time he tried, he pictured Norah as a little girl in pigtails taking down some bully in a schoolyard. Which, knowing Norah, was probably accurate.

Mitch stepped out of the house and nodded to them. "This is where your guy came from."

The house itself look like a re-creation of a castle, complete with two turrets on either side, albeit, it was a small castle, which meant it probably topped out at only about ten or eleven thousand square feet. But still, it had a heavy stone façade with a wide, thick front door. There were even small red flags waving from each turret.

"Who the hell owns this place?" Norah asked as they stepped inside. The castle's appearance continued inside, with floors and walls that had been created to look like light-gray stone.

"This is the home of Kevin Johansen," Mitch said.

"Why is that name familiar?" Norah asked.

"Because he's the CEO of about half a dozen companies, all of which are ridiculously well-known and successful," Mitch said.

Greg knew some of the guy's work. He had the normal

apps: directional services, voice recognition, voice translation, even a few critical banking apps, but it was his online dating app, Synchronicity, that put his name in the news. You put your answers into a form, and then it provided you with prompts to create a better profile. It was aimed at those who weren't quite as adept in the social arena as others. A kind of romance aid for geeks.

"He created Synchronicity," Greg said.

Norah looked at Greg with raised eyebrows. "Do *you* use it?"

"What? No, of course not. Why would you say that? You know that Ariana and I are, well, we're … You know what? Forget it. We're here to do a job, and we should just focus on that."

Norah turned away with a smile. "You're right. Where are we going?"

"Basement." Mitch said, trying unsuccessfully to hide his own smile.

Greg groaned. In all his cases, that word never resulted in something good.

# CHAPTER 14

Johansen's basement was like no basement Greg had ever seen. Being the man had designed his home like a castle, Greg half expected the basement to continue the motif with a nice dungeonesque decorating scheme.

But instead of chains and a torture rack, it was a state-of-the-art entertainment room. There were virtual reality games. More arcade games than should be legal outside of a business. There was even a large octagon like the type used in the UFC. Greg stopped when he caught sight of it. "Does Johansen fight?"

For some reason, Greg figured that Johansen was a small, kind of a geeky guy.

Mitch shook his head. "No. He's five foot nine and weighs in at about two hundred. No way he's bouncing around an octagon. Plus, he's sixty-two. Even if he was a fighter back in the day, there's no way he would risk that kind of fighting at his age."

"So what's the octagon for?" Norah asked.

"I don't know," Mitch said. "But that's not what I wanted to show you. Back this way."

Mitch led them through the entertainment section and down a large white hall. Greg turned back to look at the entertainment center and the hall and realized that the footprint for the basement was actually larger the first floor of the house. Johansen had created a larger subterranean area than there was aboveground. Strange.

And it just got stranger.

Mitch stopped in front of a gray wall without so much as a picture on it. The only décor were two sconces that matched all the other sconces in the basement. To the left was a large bathroom, and to the right was a small office. But Mitch made no move toward either of them.

"Mitch?" Norah asked.

Mitch grinned at both of them. "Okay, this part is kind of cool."

He reached up to the sconce on the right and twisted it. The sconce moved. A slight whirring sounded from behind the wall, and then the wall slipped away from them.

Greg's mouth fell open. "A secret room. That *is* cool."

"I knew you'd like it." Mitch's smile dimmed. "But what's inside is not quite as impressive."

But Greg barely heard him. His gaze shot to the large structure in the center of the two-hundred-square-foot room. It was a large glass cage that went up about twenty feet to just below the ceiling itself. The sides were fifteen feet by fifteen feet. A small vent was attached on the left-hand side. Another vent was attached to the top of the system.

Greg stared at it in horror. "Oh my God."

Norah stared at the container and then back at Greg. "What is it?"

"It's a containment unit." Horrific visions flashed through his mind. "The same type they had at Area 51."

# CHAPTER 15

As Greg stared at the containment unit, memories of escaping from Area 51 washed over him. He pictured the Hank slamming up against the glass. He pictured the desperate escape through the hallways with Leslie. His heart began to beat rapidly, and he took a step back. He'd been dealing with these flashbacks for a while. He'd thought he had them under control. But seeing the containment unit here, just out of the blue … he hadn't been prepared for it.

"You okay, Greg?" Norah asked.

"Yeah, uh, yeah, I just … I wasn't expecting this. Not here." He took a deep breath, noting that there were four other guards around the room. Okay. It was okay. Everyone here was safe. None of the tactical team looked nervous. It was safe. All safe.

The words sounded good, but there was still some residual fear in the corner of his mind that wouldn't quite let go yet. He took another deep breath.

Mitch nodded to the side of the container. "We found

Johansen over there. We think he's the origin of the Monster Watch hit."

He and Norah followed Mitch to where Johansen lay sprawled on the ground next to the small vent on the side of the container. A surprised look, his eyes wide, his mouth hanging open, was splashed across his face, along with his blood. Just like in the Fowler home, Johansen's heart was missing, his chest caved in.

His phone lay ten feet from the body.

Greg shook his head. "You idiot."

"Greg?" Norah asked.

Greg nodded to the vent in the door. "That's the feeding vent. I'd bet anything that he was feeding this thing, then got distracted by a phone call. He probably left the vent open while he talked."

Norah frowned. "And then that thing got out? But wasn't that thing huge?"

As soon as Greg saw the containment unit, the vent, and Johansen lying on the ground, he knew what had happened. The creature that had chased Kal did bear an uncanny resemblance to an octopus. One of the facts a lot of people didn't know about octopuses, or maybe just didn't think about, was the fact that they had no bones. Their beak was the only hard part of their body.

At Area 51, they had done all sorts of experiments with alien DNA, usually involving crossing alien DNA with animal DNA. It was entirely possible somebody thought it was a good idea to cross alien DNA with octopus DNA to see what came out. The resulting creature would be able to squeeze through a small opening just like this one if given the chance.

Gesturing to the unit, Greg shook his head. "When Johansen was distracted, the creature squeezed through that hatch. Without bones, it wouldn't be difficult. And to be honest, I've seen stranger things. I'm willing to bet anything that's how he got out. Johansen didn't have a chance."

"Why would he even have this thing?" Mitch asked. "I mean, it's just asking for trouble."

Looking around Norah frowned. "And how did he get it? This is a professional setup. He didn't just find this thing and throw it in a fish tank."

Mitch stared at the setup and then at Johansen on the floor. "No, but Johansen was rich. The rich can get what they want. You just have to find the person who can get it for you. And with Johansen, price is no object."

Norah's phone beeped, and she glanced down at it. "They've got the security tapes from Johansen's system. I need a tablet."

One of the tactical team members walked over and pulled the tablet from his satchel, handing it to Norah. She nodded her thanks before queuing up the security feed. Greg and Mitch crowded around her as it began to play. Sure enough, the creature had been in the container. Johansen walked in with a container full of rats.

Imagining what was to come, Greg grimaced. Johansen attached the container to the hatch and then slid open the door. The creature slid one of its tentacles inside and yanked the rats out, pulling them toward its small mouth. Once all the rats had been eaten, Johansen patted down his pockets and then pulled out his phone. He started to talk while disengaging the feeding box he'd attached.

But he failed to close the hatch before he did so. He pulled the box off and placed it on the floor, turning his back to the container as he continued to speak.

The creature wasted no time. Tentacles shot through the opening and pulled its body through. Johansen noticed the thing when the creature was halfway through.

He turned around, still on the phone. The phone dropped,

Johansen's mouth fully open. Even though there was no sound, it was clear he let out a scream as he started to run. The tentacles shot out and grabbed him by the leg, yanking him back.

Greg winced again as Johansen was slammed face first into the ground. The creature yanked him back, keeping him there as it oozed its way out of the small hatch. The creature oozed over to Johansen and covered him with its body.

From the camera's angle, they couldn't see exactly what it did to him, but Greg didn't need to see that. He had enough nightmares as it was. Once the creature was done with Johansen, it slid past him and headed for the door.

"Well, that was horrible," Mitch said. "But at least we know where the guy came from."

Norah shook her head. "No. We know where it was held. We need to find out where he *really* came from. Someone set this up for him. Someone was able to get ahold of this creature. That shouldn't be possible."

Fear crawled over Greg's skin as he stared at the setup. "But that's not the biggest question."

Mitch turned to Greg. "It's not?"

"No. The biggest question is: Does whoever sold this thing to Johansen have any more creatures? I mean, there could be other ones locked away in basements all across the country." Greg looked at Norah. "This could explain what's wrong with the numbers."

"You really think there's a whole black market for alien creatures?" Norah shook her head as soon as she was done speaking. "Never mind. Forget I even said that. Of course there's a black market for alien creatures."

Imagining what happened at Area 51 occurring at a shopping mall, Greg shivered. "Yeah, and we need to track them all down before this happens all across the United States."

# CHAPTER 16

The walk back to the Fowler home was somber. Greg kept replaying the images from the security feed through his mind. What other creatures were out there? And what the hell was wrong with people who thought it was a good idea to keep them in a basement?

He knew that rich people liked to collect strange things. They spent hundreds of thousands of dollars on ridiculous items just because they could. A pink diamond Barbie was sold at auction for over $300,000. A seventy-three-year-old bottle of French wine sold for over half a million dollars. A website called Toilet Paper Man sold a 24K roll of toilet paper for over a million dollars.

Keeping one of those creatures in a tank in your basement, though, that was a whole other level of crazy.

When Greg first started working on the A.L.I.V.E. project, he'd gone through rigorous security protocols. Even then, he'd been terrified for the first couple of weeks that he'd worked with the Hank. That terror had never really gone away, even though he'd grown more accustomed to its presence. The fact that he had an armed guard at all times helped drive home the point that he had every reason to be terrified.

Johansen hadn't had any security at his home. He'd treated the creature in his basement like a pet. He'd forgotten for a moment that the creature would kill him if given even the slightest chance.

And it did.

The entire time Greg worked with his A.L.I.V.E. project, he'd never once forgotten that. That had been the running fear in the back of his mind. Because he knew how dangerous these creatures could be. When he'd worked at Wright-Patterson, his assigned guard, First Lieutenant Leslie Cole, had saved his life. He'd slipped up once, and if Leslie hadn't been there, well, he didn't want to think of what could have happened.

But whoever was selling them was not going to be stressing over the danger of them. Not the way the government had when Greg had been put in charge of one of the projects. These people were going to look at it as just another sale. Just another rich-person extravagance.

Which meant they weren't going to take it as seriously.

Which meant people were going to die.

They needed to find the source of these things and shut them down and then track down every last creature. Greg shook his head. What was wrong with people?

It had only been a few months ago that he and his friends had literally saved all of humanity. The Council thought that the human experiment had run its course and that humanity had demonstrated that they were not capable of being trusted. It was only through finding Ariana's mother and her pleading the case for humans to the Council that humanity actually survived.

Yet very few people knew about that. Maybe the government should have told more of them. Maybe then humans would start behaving better. At the same time, he knew that wasn't true. There were always going to be humans who behaved as if the world owed them rather than the other way around. They felt entitled to take what they wanted because they were born to a certain family or had a certain number of zeros in the bank account or because they didn't have any of those things. It was hard some days not to think that maybe the Council had made the wrong decision.

Humans really did suck sometimes.

"Uncle Greg?"

His head jolted up as he spied Kal sitting in the backseat of the SUV. Holy crap. He'd totally forgotten about Kal. Guilt washed over him. But then he let himself off the hook. Finding out there was now a black market for alien species was a totally reasonable thing to chase every other concern from your mind.

"Kal, hey."

Norah nodded at Kal. "Mr. Hadid, I'm Director Norah Tidwell. Do you understand the legal jeopardy you will be in if you divulge anything that happened here today?"

Greg's nephew squirmed in his seat. "Um, yeah, a really scary agent explained it all."

"Good. Remember, we will be watching." She turned her back on Kal and winked at Greg. "Why don't you get him home? I'll wrap up the scenes and send you the report once we get all the information."

He knew that she'd be able to write that without him, but he was really looking for any excuse to postpone the scene with his family. "I could stay if you want me to. I mean, I'm sure there's something I could—"

Norah grabbed him by the shoulders and looked into his eyes. "Greg, you have to go see your family."

He groaned. "I'd really rather do the paperwork."

# CHAPTER 17

itch drove Kal and Greg back to Greg's parents' house. Greg was tempted to have Mitch drive them around the city to stretch out the car ride. He still didn't know how the heck he was going to do this. If Kal said anything to their family, not only would he be in legal jeopardy, but his family would kill Greg.

Literally.

"I won't say anything, you know," Kal said.

Since he'd been contemplating flinging himself from the moving car, it took Kal's words a moment to register. "What?"

"I get it. Your job is important. I don't know what that thing was, but if you hadn't been there ..." A shiver ran through Kal. "And I have to think I'm not the only person you've helped like that."

"Your uncle's helped more people than you know," Mitch said from the driver seat without turning around. "In fact, I think it's safe to say that your uncle has saved thousands, if not millions, in the course of his work."

Greg's jaw fell open at Mitch's words. He didn't think Mitch knew about any of that. Or that he thought that way about Greg. Sappy though it was, a little warm glow appeared in his chest.

But now wasn't the time to focus on the fact that Mitch might actually respect him. He turned to Kal. "Look, I just need you not say anything, okay? What you saw, I really wish you hadn't seen. You're not supposed to see that kind of stuff. No one is. Our job is to try and keep all of that quiet while keeping the public safe."

His nephew stared at him, eyes wide. "So *this* is what you do for the U.S. government?"

Feeling a little out of his element, Greg squirmed. He never discussed his job with people outside of his work. Although, he supposed Kal was no longer on the outside. "For the last couple years, yeah."

"And they ... gave you a gun and everything?"

Ignoring the shaking of Mitch's shoulders that indicated he was silently laughing, he nodded. "When necessary. Most the time I'm the science arm of the team. Guns not required."

"It's still pretty cool." Kal grinned.

As Greg studied his nephew he weighed the pros and cons. But he realized Norah was right: Kal was handling this really well. "Well, my boss mentioned that she was starting an internship program. She suggested that you might be a good candidate, if you pass all the background checks."

"Really?" Kal's grin grew wider.

"Yeah, I don't really know the details or anything, but once I see what it's all about, I can send you the information, and if you're interested ..."

"Oh, I'm totally interested," Kal answered quickly.

Greg sighed. "Your mom's not going to be happy about this."

"I won't tell her," Kal promised. "About any of this. And I mean, maybe for the internship we could just tell her I'm doing accounting or something for your organization."

A laugh bordering on hysterical burst from him. His sister would never agree to Kal coming to work with him, even for an internship. "That's not going to work. But I like the enthusiasm."

Mitch pulled up to the curb in front of Greg's parents' home. Greg stared at it, his stomach tying up in knots.

"You want me to wait?" Mitch asked.

Greg shook his head. "No. I'm staying, I think. And if not, I'll just grab an Uber. Thanks, Mitch."

He and Kal stepped out of the car and started to walk up the front path. Greg's feeling of dread grew with each step they took. Oh God, this was going to be bad. How was he going to explain this? His mind was a complete blank. He couldn't think of a single explanation as to where he and Kal had been.

The minute he walked in, they were going to know that something was up.

He slowly and quietly opened the front door, slipping inside, Kal right behind him. Their stealth proved useless, as Martha appeared at the top of the stairs, her hands on her hips before he'd even shut the door. "Finally. We've been looking for you guys. It's dinnertime."

Kal started to climb the steps toward his mom. "Oh yeah. Uncle Greg and I went for a walk after he got back from his work thing. He wanted to talk to me about college and stuff."

Martha raised an eyebrow, looking down at Greg and then back at her son. "And how did it go?"

His nephew didn't hesitate. "He explained that while biochem is like a really cool field, it's hard to get jobs in. And that maybe it's a good idea if I have a backup, you know, just in case. So I was thinking that maybe I can do a double major in biochemistry and accounting. I mean, I still love biochemistry, but I need to be smart, right?"

Smiling, Martha kissed her son on the cheek. "And that

you are." Then she hugged him and mouthed *thank you* to Greg over his shoulder.

Greg nodded, leaning against the banister in relief. Okay. Maybe this wouldn't be so bad after all.

Martha pulled away from her son. "Did Uncle Greg tell you how little he makes? You know, it really doesn't lead to a great lifestyle."

*On second thought, maybe I should just call Mitch and escape.*

"Greg? Greg, honey? Are you coming?" his mother called from farther in the kitchen.

Sighing, Greg gripped the banister and starting up. "Yes, Mom."

# CHAPTER 18

## DETROIT, MICHIGAN

The footsteps of Trevor's dark Italian loafers echoed off the walls of the Michigan Central Station. He had to admit that this place was one of his favorites. It had opened in 1914 and was the tallest railroad station in the world at the time, thanks to its three stories and eighteen-story clock tower. It had been designed by the same architects who'd designed Grand Central Station, which was another of Trevor's favorite spots. By 1988, the station had sent out its last train, all its beauty locked away. It had sat dormant until Trevor had taken on a short-term lease.

This was the fourth location he'd utilized for his show. They moved every six weeks. In part to allow the clientele to access the show from all over the country, but also because it made it easier to get the stars of the show to the venue. After all, transporting these things wasn't exactly as easy as hiring a U-Haul.

Already his team was planning on how to dismantle their current set. As soon as the show was over and the last of the audience left, they would have the entire spot broken down in an hour. There were a well-oiled team, his crew. There were twenty-four of them. Half were just security. The twelve main guys ran the program and the sets and carted everything away.

But his two main guys were Jerry and Brad Schroeder, and Neil, who was more of a glorified gopher. He, Jerry and Brad had grown up together. Brad was a few years older, but Jerry and Trevor had always been tight. Brad had done a stint in the Army right after high school, not exactly voluntary. He'd been given a choice between jail or the military.

He'd been with Trevor since he'd gotten out. Brad oversaw Trevor's security operations.

Jerry was in charge of all technical aspects of the projects and deals. Jerry had no formal schooling, but he'd always been good at figuring things out. Together, the brothers made sure these setups went on without a hitch, which made them all more money.

Trevor smiled as he stepped into the main room. He liked being here before any of the crowds arrived. It was as if the whole world was just on the edge, waiting for its moment to shine.

He'd made a million dollars each of the last three nights, from those in attendance and those watching online via the dark web. Buy-in online was twenty thousand dollars. But that only got you ten minutes. Each additional minute was another five grand. The audience was intentionally small, but they had large bank accounts. In-person attendance cost a flat fifty-thousand for two people.

Tonight would bring in close to another million. His shows were designed for a select audience. Only people with deep pockets were invited and they paid handsomely to be entertained.

After all, for people with money who could buy anything,

they needed something out of the ordinary to keep their interest.

And Trevor was the only ticket in town for that.

Tonight would be the final match. He wanted to do something different. Maybe have a tag team against one of the creatures. After all, it wasn't like he was going to bring the creatures with him.

He shuddered. He certainly wasn't going to travel with those things. What if they escaped? He was all for these things killing in the name of money. But he wasn't for them killing just for the sake of it.

Neil rushed down the aisle toward him. "Boss, boss, you got a call from Jerry."

Jerry had left last night to start getting the next site ready. Once he had the teams working, he'd head back here to oversee the shutdown of this one. He was the front man. Jerry never called during that stage.

Trevor grabbed the phone. "Jerry? What's the matter?"

"We got a problem, boss."

"What? I thought the site was solid." Trevor walked over to the stands and took a seat.

"No, no, Marino's good. It's not that. It's Johansen."

Trevor cursed softly. He didn't like Johansen. The man was too rich. And for Trevor to admit that someone was too rich was saying something. But there was actually such a thing as too much money.

Johansen had more money than he could spend in a lifetime. The media only knew a part of his financial kingdom. He had dabbled in illegal activities across the globe while keeping a squeaky-clean, albeit nerdy, public profile.

"What's going on? What does he want now?" Trevor asked.

"Nothing. He's dead."

That was not what Trevor was expecting to hear. Some of his clientele lived dangerous lives, though. But the fact that

Brad was sharing the information was perhaps more surprising than the death itself. "What happened?"

"What I told you would happen," Jerry said with heat.

*Oh, crap.* Trevor winced, remembering what type of client Johansen had been. The man had come to him, saying he wanted one of the creatures for his collection. He wanted to put the damn thing in his basement. Trevor had offered to stuff one so he could hang it down there, but Johansen wanted a live one.

Johansen wasn't the first one to come and ask him for a trophy. But he was the first one to ask for a live one. Trevor had planned on saying no. But like the movie cliché said, he was given an offer he couldn't refuse.

A few others had made offers in the intervening months. Each time, Trevor had upped the price. And in each case, the clients had agreed willingly.

It had turned into an excellent secondary stream of revenue. The creatures he handed over would have been destroyed anyway, so it was no loss to him. Brad had been concerned, but the money had quickly swayed him. Jerry had taken longer to convince.

"What about the specimen?" Trevor asked.

"Escaped his house, went two doors down, killed the couple there, and a cop, before some special government agency showed up and grabbed the thing."

It had to be the D.E.A.D. Brad had a friend who'd worked at Area 51 when everything had gone down. He'd gotten drunk one night and told Brad everything. At first, Trevor hadn't believed him when Brad had told him the story, but then Trevor had done his research. He'd verified where the guy had been stationed with some of his contacts. And then he started looking for stories in the news.

And he found them.

It hadn't taken long for him to figure out how to track these things down. Capturing them was a little more difficult, but you just had to know where and when to spend money. And spending money on a team that could track these things was well worth it. He had stables in different parts of the country for them. He'd wanted to put on a show in New York, but he didn't think any of these things would get anywhere close enough to make it financially feasible. But then a few had shown up in Pennsylvania.

The power of these creatures was incredible, and Trevor respected it greatly. He didn't for one moment think that humans had anything on these things. They were like lions, tigers, and bears combined. You let your guard down with them for even a second, and they would eat your heart out.

That was probably exactly how Johansen had gone. The specimen Johansen had been given had a fondness for his captor's hearts. The creature had only been showcased in one of Trevor's shows. Because while the crowd might be all for the blood sport, once the creature dug into his opponent's chest, ripped out his heart, and ate it, well, suffice it to say, that had not gone over well.

The plan after that display of carnage had been to kill the thing straight away. In fact, Brad had told him he needed to. But then Johansen had shown up. Trevor didn't even know how he'd learned about their shows. Trevor certainly hadn't told him. But one of his audience members must have.

Johansen had watched one of his shows and then told Trevor if he didn't sell him one of the creatures, he was going to rat out the entire operation. Plus, he'd give him two million dollars for the thing.

Trevor wasn't sad the guy was dead. He hadn't liked him to begin with. But now the dead jerk was causing him problems. "Is there any way they can tie it back to us?"

"No. Johansen paid to the Archimedes front. And the

money was run through the Caymans. There's no way to link it back."

Nodding, Trevor considered the options. The jerk was dead. The creature was no doubt too and there was no way to pin it back to him. "Good, good. With Johansen dead, it's literally a dead end. Hopefully this whole thing will blow over."

# CHAPTER 19

The rest of the weekend with Greg's family went surprisingly well, in the sense that they completely ignored him during most of their conversations. Only occasionally was his career held up as an example of wasted potential. His mother, however, did add a new schtick to the whole guilt routine: lamenting the fact that she was never getting any more grandkids, specifically from him.

But all in all, it went pretty well. And by pretty well, Greg meant that there had been no alien attacks. The bar for pretty well was particularly low when it came to his family gatherings.

Yet he was surprised to find himself a little reluctant to leave that Sunday afternoon. And it had nothing to do with his sisters, brothers-in-law, or his parents. It actually had been really cool talking to Kal. They'd taken some time to talk through what had happened in Greenwich, and Kal asked a bunch of really good questions about the creature's anatomy. He'd observed a lot, despite his heightened state of terror. It was nice talking to someone who was as intrigued by alien biology as he was. Since Maeve, he hadn't really had anyone to discuss this stuff with.

He also couldn't believe how confident Kal was. He definitely had more confidence than Greg had at his age. He really was taking the "alien chasing him across the lawn" thing pretty well. Greg had practically been a basket case the first time he'd been chased down by an alien. And even then, he'd had Leslie with him.

Although he supposed he'd been Kal's Leslie in this situation, which was completely mind-blowing.

Maybe Norah was right. Maybe the internship would be a good thing for Kal. As difficult as his world was, Greg loved it. He wouldn't trade it for anything. Being in the middle of all of this, it gave him a sense of purpose. Maybe not the firefights, but the research, the helping people, that he definitely loved.

So he felt a lot better than he normally did when he left. Usually he felt like a ten-pound boulder had been dropped on his shoulders, with all the criticisms aimed at him. But talking to Kal meant he'd managed to avoid talking to the rest of his family as much as he normally would, and surprise surprise, that made for a better trip.

When he arrived back at the office on Monday morning, he was feeling pretty good about the future. And then he got one more welcome surprise. He stepped into the secure wing of the D.E.A.D. building to a familiar figure walking down the hall toward him.

"Alvie!"

A feeling of love and friendship wafted over Greg as the four-foot-tall gray being headed toward him wearing a pair of jeans, a long-sleeved navy T-shirt, and hiking boots.

Greg smiled, leaning down as Alvie hugged him. "Always good to see you too, buddy. How is everybody? How are the triplets?"

R.D. BRADY

Alvie was from the first generation of the A.L.I.V.E. projects, but unlike the others, Alvie wasn't the result of some genetic combination in a lab. Alvie was the clone of a being who had lived in Mexico nearly a hundred and fifty years ago. Its skull had been found in a cave and brought to the States about a century ago.

Apparently, Alvie's brother had been the Council's first attempt at seeing if humanity was ready to accept the existence of life beyond their world. His death had proven that they were not. More recent events suggested that the world at large was still not ready for that knowledge. But Alvie and the triplets' connection to Maeve, Chris, and the rest of them had convinced the Council that we at least had the potential to be more than a warlike race.

And despite his half-human genetic code, Alvie himself looked all alien. His head was wide at the forehead and came down to a point at his chin, almost as if his whole head was a soft rounded triangle. His eyes were massive, much larger than a human's, and almost completely black. His mouth was tiny and used strictly for food, as Alvie couldn't speak.

But he could communicate.

A vision of the triplets, who were clones of Alvie, wafted through his mind. He saw them playing with two redheaded children. Greg's mouth dropped open, and then he grinned. Maeve had said that the triplets had been on some play dates, but to see it was something else.

"That's awesome," Greg said. "How are you? Are you enjoying working at the headquarters?"

After the whole situation with the world nearly ending, R.I.S.E., the United States government's secret space program, had set up a base in Norway. Alvie's intelligence, which they still hadn't found a way to accurately measure beyond saying it was extremely high, had landed him a job there. Maeve had been a little worried, not sure if he was ready for it, but by all accounts, Alvie was thriving in the position. He ran analysis and calculations on a range of projects for the U.S. government.

Another image appeared in Greg's mind, of Alvie sitting in a room filled with computers. And sitting across from him was Penny Johnson. He could feel the acceptance and attachment between the two. Penny was a computer savant at only thirteen years old. She was also autistic and had a difficult time connecting with people. But apparently, she and Alvie had forged a bond.

Which meant Alvie had a friend, one *he* had made.

More images followed of Alvie spending time with the other Maldek, Claude. And then more images flowed through Greg's mind of Alvie spending time with Sammy, Maeve, Chris, even little Sebastian, Adam and Tilda's adopted son.

Greg felt a sense of contentment roll through him, and this time it wasn't the result of Alvie's emotions. It was his own. Alvie meant the world to Greg. He viewed Maeve and Chris as family, but family he actually liked. And Greg would lay his life on the line for Alvie or the triplets in a heartbeat. So to see him happy and thriving just made everything better. "That's great, man. I'm really happy for you."

He stood up and then frowned. "But what are you doing here? And why didn't Maeve let me know you were coming?"

As soon as the words were out of his mouth, he realized what had happened. He'd gotten home late last night and had seen that there was a message from Maeve. But he'd been so tired because he'd been sleeping on the couch for the previous two nights at his parents' place, since Kal decided to stay over. Greg had given him the bedroom.

He'd grabbed a shower after he got back to his apartment, so he hadn't checked the message. He'd planned on checking first thing this morning, but he'd slept through his alarm, and it had been a rush to get to the office.

"Never mind. What are you working on?" Greg asked.

An image of the creature found in Connecticut splayed out on an autopsy table appeared in Greg's mind, followed by rows of numbers.

"You're going to run the data? That's great. If anyone can find anything, it's you."

Before heading to his office, he walked with Alvie to the cafeteria. A few people did double takes at the sight of him, but then they went back to their own meals. Everyone had seen weirder things than a simple gray dressed like he was ready for an afternoon hike. The two of them took a table in the corner and caught up over breakfast before Greg dropped him off at Norah's office. Alvie was going to be running the data from there. She had a large office with a separate desk and terminal set up for him.

Making sure Alvie was comfortable, he left the two of them to it and made his way down the hall to his own office. As soon as he stepped in the door, he closed it behind him and dialed Maeve.

She answered quickly. "You didn't call me back."

He placed his coffee cup and messenger bag on the desk. "Sorry, sorry. I was at my family's house this weekend. I didn't get in until late last night."

"Oh, well, now *I'm* sorry. How'd it go?"

"Well, it was pretty normal until the alien attack one town over, which my nephew also became involved in."

"*What?*" Maeve exclaimed.

Holding the phone away from his ear with a wince, Greg waited until her volume came down a bit and then returned the phone to his ear. He gave Maeve the rundown of the whole situation.

She was silent for a moment when he finished speaking, then she asked. "So what are you going to do about him?"

Greg slumped into his chair. "Actually, I mainly spoke with Kal for the rest of the weekend. It was pretty nice. Norah wants to set up an internship program, and she thinks Kal would be a good candidate. So for right now, we're going to kind of see where it goes."

"That's kind of good."

"Yeah, I know," he said. "I'm surprised too. Anyway, I'm calling about Alvie. I just dropped him off in Norah's office."

Maeve's relief was palpable across the phone line. "Good, that's good. I mean, Norah said she'd look after him, but I wanted you to be around him too. So he's okay? I mean, he looks okay, right?"

"He's fine. He actually looks good. He seems happy."

There was a smile in Maeve's voice when she answered. "Yeah, he is. The job has been going really well, and he's been spending some time with people outside of the house. He needed it. It's good for him."

"Are you trying to convince me or yourself?"

Maeve sighed. "I don't know. Both? I know it's good, I do. It's just ... I've been taking care of him his whole life. I've been keeping him a secret his whole life. It's hard to just let all that go, you know?"

"Yeah, I know."

Maeve had been raised with Alvie. Her mother had been the one who'd developed the procedure that had created him. And Maeve had spent most of her upbringing at the lab on Wright-Patterson. She didn't know any different. To her, it seemed like a perfectly normal upbringing.

But once her mother passed away from cancer, Maeve had taken over as the lead on Alvie's project and became Alvie's surrogate mom. Because while Alvie was intelligent, and even though he was basically the same age as Maeve, there was something about him that was incredibly childlike. There was a kindness and naivety to him that someone his age generally didn't have.

So Maeve had always been very protective. They were all

protective, which begged the question: "Why is Alvie here anyway?" Greg asked. "Couldn't he have done this work from there?"

"Yes. But he wanted to start doing some things on his own. And I mean, we can't exactly let him go off to the mall with friends to catch a movie. Norah wanted him to look at some stuff, but she didn't want to send it over. She wanted to keep it in house. You know how she gets with security."

Before Norah had taken over as director of the D.E.A.D., Greg hadn't realized how security conscious she was. There were a lot of files that she kept locked away, refusing to allow them to be sent via email. "Everything can be hacked," she'd said more than once.

Maeve continued. "So I figured this might be a good chance for Alvie to be a little independent, with both you and Norah there to look out for him. Jasper brought him over."

Picking up a pen from his desk top, Greg twirled it in his hand. "So you have a tracker on him?"

"Why would you ask that?" she asked, sounding defensive.

Greg laughed. "Because I know you and Jasper. If you didn't put one on him, Jasper did."

Jasper was Jasper Jenkins, an agent who'd been with R.I.S.E. for decades.

"Yes, we put one on him," Maeve grumbled. "But he doesn't know. And I want to keep it that way. I just need to know he's safe."

Greg smiled. "It's okay, Maeve. I would feel the same way. I'll keep an eye on him while he's here. Do you think he'd want to stay with me? I have an extra room."

"That would be great. But it's secure, right?" She asked.

"It's secure. Norah lives right next door with Iggy. It's on the base and in the secure area, so no one can see him. And at least in the building, he can wander around."

"Great, that's great. Thanks, Greg. I really appreciate it."

"No problem. And it'll be good to have Alvie's eyes on the situation in Connecticut. I have a feeling there's a lot more there than we realize."

Concern and a little curiosity slipped into Maeve's voice. "More how?"

He opened his mouth and then shut it. Maeve had been living in Norway for the last couple of months trying to keep herself and her gang safe. Finally, she had stepped out of the life. Greg wasn't going to be the one to pull her back in. "You know what? It's just a normal case. But you know Alvie always has a different way of looking at things. So it'll just be good to have some fresh eyes."

"Okay." Maeve drew out the word to let him know that she did not believe him, but she wasn't going to push it. "Hey, how's Ariana doing?"

The pen he'd been twirled slipped out of his hand. Wincing, Greg wished for any other question. He squirmed in his chair, then tapped the pen along the desk. "I don't know. I mean, we're good, I think, but she's off visiting her mom for a little while, and I just don't know what the situation is."

"Hey, but you have a situation. That's definitely a step in the right direction."

He tossed the pen onto the desktop with a laugh. "Okay, Pollyanna. Some of us have work to do."

"I'll have you know, I had them create a home lab for me off the back of the house. So I also have work to do."

"I didn't mean it that way. If anyone deserves a little time off, it's you."

"Well, I tried that for little bit, but apparently just sitting at home twiddling my thumbs really isn't my thing. I need some hobbies."

"You and me both, sister," Maeve muttered.

Brightening, Greg said, "Hey, when Alvie heads back,

maybe I'll hop on the plane with him and come visit for a little bit? I haven't seen you guys in a while."

"That would be great, and I'm sure Sammy could take you back home whenever you need to get there."

"Yeah, Sammy," Greg said, even though his stomach rolled at the idea of traveling with Sammy. Still, it would mean he could get back a lot quicker. "Actually, that sounds good. Hopefully by the time Alvie's ready to go back, I'll have this case finished, and I'll put in a request for some free time."

"Well, I've got an in with the boss if you need it."

"Thanks, Maeve." From the corner of Greg's eye, he noted liquid seeping into the carpet under his door. He groaned. "Oh, crap."

"What's wrong?"

"Oh, nothing, just my new little buddy coming to say hi."

The rest of Pugsley slid underneath the door and then slowly formed into a round cylinder. Its big eyes blinked wide at Greg, and it let out a happy chirp before wobbling over to him, two arms extending from the gelatinous blob. It wrapped around his leg with another happy little chirp.

Greg sighed. "Morning, Pugsley."

Maeve laughed. "I really need to meet this guy."

"Well, I've got to go put on a clean pair of pants because the bottom half of my leg is completely slimed. I'll talk to you later."

She laughed again. "God, I miss you, Greg."

# CHAPTER 20

Alvie had been in town for two days and Greg had to admit he really liked having a roommate. They'd had a Star Wars marathon yesterday which had been awesome. But it was more than that. Greg just liked having someone around. It was going to be tough when Alvie left.

This morning the two of them had come in early and it had been a busy morning. Now, Greg pushed back from his desk, needing a little break. Maybe he'd wander down to the cafeteria and see if they had anything tempting. His gaze flicked to his phone that lay on his desk. The text from Kal was still on the face of it.

*Thank you so much!!*

Greg smiled every time he glanced at it. Norah had had the HR department draft an internship application. She'd sent it to Greg, who'd sent it out to Kal this morning.

He still had reservations about introducing Kal to this world. Although he supposed the cat was out of the bag on that at this point. But he still worried. At the same time, it was kind of nice, the idea of having Kal here, especially after spending time with Alvie. And he'd make it so that Kal worked only in the office and not near any of the secure zones.

Not that that should be a problem. Even if Kal got the internship, he didn't think Norah would be sending him on missions. Paperwork was in his nephews future, not action.

His phone beeped, and he glanced at it again. The text was from one of the research analysts. They'd been doing the deep dive on Johansen. He pulled up the file from his email.

From the corner of his eye, he saw Pugsley slip under his door yet again. Greg groaned. Apparently the latest escape-proof containment unit created by R & D had failed.

He eyed the trail of slime with resignation. *Now I have to clean the floor again.*

Pugsley was oblivious to Greg's dismay. He slid over to Greg and wrapped himself around his boots. His whole body hummed.

In a stroke of genius, Greg had started wearing galoshes to work. They were much easier to clean off. Grabbing the waterproof gloves on his desk, he pulled them on and then reached down and patted Pugsley's head. "Hey, buddy. How you doing this morning?"

Pugsley gave off a small little chirp and nestled his head in a little closer to Greg. The warts he'd previously had were gone and now Pugsley was a soft blue color. If not for the slime, he'd be pretty cute.

Reaching down, Greg opened his bottom-right desk drawer. Pugsley climbed in, curling up on the waterproof dog bed. Pugsley gave a contented sigh and closed his eyes. He'd be asleep in seconds.

Greg smiled. It was hard not to like someone that liked you this much, even if they left a slime trail wherever they went.

With some regret, he turned his attention away from Pugsley and back to the computer screen and the file on

Johansen. The man had a lot of money, like *a lot* a lot. Greg's eyes nearly popped out of his head looking at all those zeros.

There was something incredibly wrong with a world where one man could have the wealth equal to the GDP of a small, or maybe a not-so-small, country. He shook his head and continued to scan the background. There were pages and pages of property and business interests. The analyst went in depth, describing each acquisition, price, dates purchased or sold.

The background on Johansen's personal life was much more scant. It was only two pages long. He had no strong personal relationships. No significant other. He was an only child, and both his parents were deceased. He was definitely on his own. He had business acquaintances but no actual friends.

*Well, I guess I'm richer than you in that, Mr. Johansen.*

A knock sounded at the door.

"Come in," Greg yelled without even looking up.

Norah walked in, her hand still on the door handle. "Hey, Greg. Did you get a chance to-" She let out a shriek as she slipped on Pugsley's slime trail. Her grip on the door handle was all that kept her from completely wiping out.

Greg cringed. "Oh, sorry about that."

Norah straightened and glared at him. "You need to stop letting Pugsley in here," she said through gritted teeth.

"Let him in? I don't *let* him in. He finds me. The gang downstairs haven't found a single container that he will stay in."

Norah still looked annoyed as she took a seat at one of the chairs next to his desk. "Did you see the critical lines from the report? From the financial disclosure?"

"Which ones? The guy was rolling in it. The financial statement alone is like a hundred pages long."

"Sixteenth page, fourth line from the bottom."

Greg quickly flipped over to the spot Norah referenced. His eyes scanned the screen before they landed on the lines Norah was talking about. He let out a slow whistle. "Multiple payments over six months. That's a pretty hefty donation to Archimedes Art. Who are they?"

"Technically, they don't exist. They are supposed to be a nonprofit that provides art instruction to underprivileged kids. But there is no program. It's a front."

"So who exactly got two million bucks?"

Norah shrugged. "Don't know yet. But he finished making the payments just before Mr. Johansen's new pet showed up in his basement."

"You know when he got him?"

Norah nodded. "We have security footage from the neighbors. A white-panel truck showed up at Mr. Johansen's home the day after the last donation was made. It was at night, but we could tell that they set up the cage, and then they brought something in that was completely covered."

"So Johansen bought it from Archimedes Art."

Norah crossed her arms over her chest. "Yep. Now we just need to find out who exactly that is. I'm going to light a fire under the analysts. Do me a favor and rerun those calculations? And I want you to estimate how many creatures you think we should be looking for."

Greg nodded, turning back to the screen and flexing his fingers. "Your wish is my command, fearless leader."

With a roll of her eyes, she said, "You know, a simple 'sure' would be okay too."

He nodded, already calculating the new variables he wanted to develop and the time it would take to create them and then run them. "But not nearly as much fun. I'll have something to you in about three hours."

---

Two hours later, Greg's phone rang. He grabbed it without looking. "I said three hours. It's only been two,"

"Dr. Schorn, this is Rhonda from Dispatch."

Rhonda was Rhonda Graves, Norah's second-in-command. She was tough, no nonsense. She had yet to be won over by Greg's charm. But Greg knew it was only a matter of time. He straightened in his chair as if she could see him slouching through the phone. "Rhonda. How are you doing today?"

Ignoring his question, she got right to business. "Sir, we have a situation."

"I figured. What's happening?"

Rhonda hesitated. "Actually, I don't know. Director Tidwell said she would contact you with the details through the secure network."

Greg wasn't surprised by that either. Norah had decided to play everything very close to the vest after the Johansen case. She didn't know who she could trust entirely, even though they'd cleaned house of all of Martin's people. So Greg simply nodded as he strode toward the door. "Is the response team at the airfield?"

"They're on their way now."

"Tell them I'm on my way too." He disconnected the call and then winced, turning around. He opened up the bottom desk drawer. "Sorry, Pugsley, but I think you need to head back to the lab."

Ten minutes later, after escorting a very depressed Pugsley back to containment, Greg pulled into the airfield. The airfield had been constructed on the base after they'd determined it would be the new D.E.AD. base. It made for faster response times.

Stepping out of the SUV, he nodded thanks at the D.E.A.D. guard who'd given him a lift. "Thanks, Marvin."

"Anytime, Dr. Schorn. Happy hunting."

Ducking his head against the wind, Greg headed across the

tarmac. The Embraer Lineage 1000 was ready for takeoff, the engine running. Greg quickly climbed the stairs and stepped into the fuselage.

"Dr. Schorn," Max said as he reached past Greg to pull up the stairs and close and locked the door.

"Hey, Max. Good to see you." Greg peered into the fuselage, letting out a relieved sigh when he didn't spy Hannibal or any of his buddies. At least he could avoid that uncomfortableness.

He wound his way through to the back of the plane and took a seat across from Mitch.

"You made it. I was beginning to get worried," Mitch said.

"What, and miss all the fun? You know I live for danger."

Chuckling, Mitch nodded. "Oh yeah. That's what I always say about you: Greg Schorn, daredevil."

Greg grinned back at him. "How did the barbecue go?"

"It was great. I made my famous pulled pork. I saved you some. It's in the fridge back on base. I'll get it to you when we get back."

"Thanks. I appreciate that."

"You get any details yet?" Mitch asked.

Pulling his laptop out of his bag before storing it under his seat, Greg shook his head. "Got the call from Rhonda just a few minutes ago. I came right here and didn't have a chance to check."

He opened up his computer and went through the laborious process of logging in. It took a while. Finally, he was in and saw the file waiting from Norah. Greg scanned it quickly and flipped to the back where there was a cage almost identical to the one found in Johansen's basement.

"Oh no," Greg murmured.

"What is it?" Mitch asked.

Gaze locked on the file, Greg said, "It looks like another case like Johansen."

"How many dead?"

Scanning the form, he found the number of casualties and winced. "Six, but they haven't finished clearing the scene."

"What about the creature?" Mitch asked.

"The team out there is already tracking it. But they haven't nailed it down yet."

"Dammit, that's not good. They have any idea what it is?"

His heart starting to pound as he read the addendum from the field team, Greg nodded. "It looks like it's a Hank."

# CHAPTER 21

A Hank.

Greg's mind seized up at the thought. He pictured the Hank back at Wright-Pat, and then the ones that Martin had used in New Mexico, and then the other ones he had used in Arizona. Of all the creatures they faced, these were the ones Greg dreaded the most. Not that the others weren't terrifying. Just two months ago, they'd dealt with a creature who bled acid, actual acid.

But Hanks had an intelligence and a cunning the others were missing. They were cruelly efficient killing machines.

They had no conscience. It seemed as if their entire focus was killing, like the velociraptors from the *Jurassic Park* movies. But not Blue from *Jurassic World*, who seemed to sort of like humans.

After his last run-in with the Hanks in Arizona, he and Norah had scoured the D.E.A.D. computer files, the ones that were left, searching to see how many Hanks had been created. They hadn't actually found any information on them. Those were some of the first files that had been destroyed by Drummond.

Yet another reason to hate the bastard.

Why would anyone create such creatures? When he'd first started working with a Hank at Wright-Pat, he'd marveled on a scientific level at the strength and cunning of the creature. But that had been all about biology. He'd never even considered weaponizing it. It was like a zoologist considering weaponizing a lion or a silverback.

At the same time, his mind had reeled at the idea that the U.S. government had created this thing. Why on earth would they think that was a good idea? He'd been told that the Hanks had been created to help America understand the threat that they would one day face.

Greg had believed them, or maybe he just wanted to. He wanted to believe that the only reason such a nightmare would be created was to give the United States an idea of what threats might be coming at them from the stars.

But he'd known somewhere in the back of his mind that the Hanks would be weaponized. That some evil mastermind would figure out a way to take the Hanks, control them, and use them to their benefit.

And that mastermind had been Martin Drummond. He'd taken the Hanks and made them work for him. He'd created control devices so that they were basically trained killers.

Killers that were very hard to kill. Standing at around six feet tall, they had been mixed with alligator DNA, giving them incredibly tough skin that was hard for some bullets to penetrate. Their mouths and eyes were similar to the Draco in that sometimes a shot to either was the only way to kill them. In hindsight, Greg realized that the Draco were probably the models for the creation of the Hanks.

The Hanks were also incredibly fast. They had sharp talons on the ends of their feet and hands. God, he didn't want to go up against one of those things again.

Mitch leaned toward him. "Greg? You okay?"

Greg nodded slowly. "Yeah, just thinking."

Mitch glanced down the pathway between the seats and then back at Greg, lowering his voice. "You've run into these things before, haven't you?"

Greg nodded slowly, not sure if he was violating one of the million contracts that he had signed and not really caring. "Yeah. Yeah, I have."

"How bad are these guys?"

"They are the worst. Whatever firepower you think you need, double it. You think he's dead, just keep shooting until you're sure. Actually, to be safe, pack a couple of grenade launchers and just blow the thing to pieces. Even an injured one can kill you."

Mitch watched Greg, his eyes serious. "This thing has got you spooked."

"Yes, it does. And it should have you spooked too. Tell your team to take zero chances. No one goes anywhere alone. In fact, you need to contact the other team and make sure they don't spread out. Hanks like to pick off the weak links. The team needs to stay together."

Mitch nodded, pulling out his phone.

Greg leaned his head back. They'd be in the air for only an hour, maybe less. He was going to try and get some sleep. But as he closed his eyes, he pictured the first Hank he'd ever met. Its real name was Kecksburg-AG2. But Greg had started calling him Hank, and the name had stuck.

Greg shut his eyes tighter, hoping that he would sleep. He prayed that by the time they got there that the Hank had been killed. But he couldn't help but wonder just how many people the Hank would take with him before that happened.

# CHAPTER 22

## SOUTHAMPTON VILLAGE, NEW YORK

The flight was uneventful. They didn't even have a burst of turbulence to interrupt it. Greg had slept, although it had been more of a doze, with images of the Hank running through his mind. As the landing gear dropped, Greg's eyes opened. The rest of the cabin was quiet. Most of the team had slept. He'd learned that these guys took every chance they had to sleep, knowing the chase could go long.

Greg flipped open his laptop and looked for an update on the case. He let out a breath at the new designation at the top of the file: Killed.

The team had taken down the Hank. He closed his eyes. *Thank God.*

Mitch looked over at him, his dark eyes crinkling with concern. "Greg? Everything okay?"

Relief flowed through him. He opened his eyes, nodding with a small smile. "Yeah. They got the Hank. It's just an investigation now."

It was a twenty-minute trip from the private airfield on the eastern edge of Long Island to the home where the Hank had been stored.

The home belonged to Rachel Dracmore. Greg paused at the name. Dracmore. It sounded an awful lot like Draco.

Rachel Dracmore was a trust-fund baby. She had houses all over the globe and five in the U.S. alone. She was forty-two and had never married. She hadn't been at her home in the Hamptons during the attack. Which begged the question of who exactly had been taking care of the creature.

As soon as he stepped into the 15,000-square-foot home, Greg got his answer. The first body lay by the front door. Deep gouges had been scraped into the man's back, and his right arm had been torn clean off, although Greg didn't see it anywhere nearby.

Lucinda Collins, the team leader on site, nodded toward the body. "That's Chip Higgins. He is one of Rachel's newest friends. He'd been staying at the home for the last two weeks."

Greg tilted his head, staring at the man's face. "He looks awfully young."

"Twenty-one."

Greg raised his eyebrows. "And he was living with Rachel? Isn't she in her forties?"

Lucinda narrowed her eyes. "And if it were a girl who was twenty-one and the guy was forty-two, would you make a comment about that?"

Heat crawled up Greg's neck as he fumbled for some words. "I'm sure I would."

Lucinda grunted before heading down the hall. Mitch shook his head at Greg before following her. Greg hurried to catch up with the two of them.

"It appears that Chip had a few friends over," Lucinda explained. "We found some of them down in the basement, a few along the halls, a couple out by the pool."

"How many total?" Mitch asked.

"Eleven deceased. We haven't found any survivors. For some stupid reason, they thought it was a good idea to party with the Hank. We're not sure yet if they let the thing out or if somebody just got careless. It was kept in the basement."

Just like with Johansen's Seti. What the hell was wrong with these people? Was it a rich-people thing? These things were not meant to be pets.

"Where is the Hank now?" Mitch asked.

"The team found it ten miles away. It attacked a horse farm. Two horses were killed before the team reached it, but no other humans. They've bagged and tagged the body and are bringing it back here. Once we get this scene cleaned up, we'll take everything back to the plane."

Greg nodded, looking around. "I'd like to see the basement first."

Without a word, Lucinda headed toward the kitchen and then took a left. The stairs to the basement were open and about six feet across. The basement actually had a wall of floor-to-ceiling windows that looked out over the Long Island Sound. The first room they stepped into had to be about 200 square feet, with a giant, ivory sectional, a large movie screen along one wall, a bar along the back wall, three mangled bodies, and a few body parts strewn across the place.

His breakfast threatening to return, Greg swallowed it back down, but still re-tasted the egg sandwich. He'd never gotten used to the scenes. He hoped he never did.

"This way." Lucinda headed to the left to a wide hallway.

They passed two bathrooms, a bedroom, and a full kitchen before they stepped into a massive workout room. An entire weight system that wouldn't have looked out of place in a professional gym dominated the left-hand side of the space. The ceiling rose up twenty feet, and Greg realized they must have been going downhill when they were walking in to make that possible. He hadn't even noticed it. There were mats and martial arts equipment on the right-hand side by the door, and then in the back-right corner was a giant cage.

The system was similar to the Johansen setup. The food exchange was different, however. Food was placed on a conveyor belt. It would lock down on one side before it opened up on the other side.

That was smart. The Hank would take any small breach in security and exploit it.

There were two bodies in this room. One was over by the obvious area of escape—the cage door, which was wide open.

Greg stared at it, his mouth dropping open. "They *let* the thing out?"

Lucinda nodded. "We managed to pull up some cell phone footage. The guys were daring each other to open and shut the cage door. It locks as soon as it closes. So they would take turns flinging it open and shoving it closed just as quick. On the third time, the Hank struck, slamming into the door and crashing it open. After that, the guys never had a chance."

Greg stood rubbing his face anxiously, as if he could remove the stupid from the room. The Hanks looked like alligators, and most people thought of alligators as slow, dimwitted creatures. But alligators could be fast when they needed to be. They'd been clocked going at twenty miles per hour. They weren't cheetahs, but they definitely weren't sloths. That speed was the equivalent of jacking a treadmill up to twenty. Why on earth these idiots thought tempting the Hank was a good idea was beyond him.

After a moment's thought, though, he knew why. They were young, stupid, and bored. And they all thought that they were invincible.

The Hank had shown them just how wrong they were.

"Did you process the scene?"

Lucinda nodded. "Yeah, but I thought you might want to take a look around first and then sign off on it."

"Okay." He knew Lucinda would've done a thorough job. He liked when she was the one in charge. She always made sure that she crossed every T and dotted every I.

He took the tablet that Lucinda offered and had just started to scroll through when Lucinda's phone chirped. She pulled it out and glanced at the screen. "The Hank's body just arrived."

A chill crept over Greg, even though he knew the creature was dead. "I'll just review the scene, and then we'll head up."

Lucinda nodded and headed for the door. Greg glanced up at the cage and then at the body right in front of its door. The kid's face was half gone. But the half of his mouth that was left was open in a scream.

They really needed to find out who the hell was handing these creatures out like they were party favors. Because if they didn't, more people were definitely going to die.

# CHAPTER 23

Lucinda had definitely been thorough. Greg took his time in the basement, reviewing her work and checking to see if there were any additional avenues that needed to be investigated. He found the Hank's food closet and shook his head as he looked inside. They'd been trying to feed the Hank a vegetarian diet from the looks of it.

What a stupid idea. That would only make the Hank hungry and therefore more dangerous. Hanks were most definitely carnivores. And like most carnivores, it wouldn't be happy with a salad.

Someone had pulled up some of the earlier feeds from the boys' phones. They had taken turns feeding the Hank different foods and then laughing hysterically. Twinkies, cake, potato chips. The bottom of the Hank's cage was littered with wrappers screaming one thing: sugar. Which meant lots of carbs.

Greg wasn't sure what impact those kinds of foods would have on its system. The Hanks hadn't really been exposed to it before, at least not while in captivity. It had a very strict meat-only diet. But he had to think this wasn't the first time the creature had been fed stuff off the military diet list.

For about the twelfth time, Greg found himself trying the cage door. He knew he needed to head upstairs, but he was still dragging his feet.

He really hated Hanks, even dead ones. His response wasn't quite a full case of PTSD, but it was definitely in the area. But he supposed he didn't have a choice on this one. So he squared his shoulders, stepped away from the cage, and headed toward the door.

Mitch, who'd been leaning against the back wall during Greg's inspection, straightened as Greg approached. "All good?"

A bead of sweat rolled down Greg's spine. His gaze immediately shot to the holster at Mitch's waist. "Just make sure you're ready to use that, okay?"

"The subject's dead."

Greg just looked at him.

Mitch nodded slowly. "Don't worry. I got you, doc."

And Greg knew Mitch was telling the truth. Mitch wouldn't let anything happen to him. "Okay, then. Let's go."

They made their way back through the massive entertainment room and up the stairs. Lucinda had been busy while he'd been working. Most of the bodies had been cleared from the entertainment room and the halls. The cleaning crew had now started their work removing the bloodstains. Greg never asked how exactly they explained these kinds of incidents. He wondered how they were going to manage to explain eleven dead bodies.

But that wasn't his headache to figure out, so he stepped past the cleaning crew and headed out into the bright sunlight. The trailer had been pulled over by the garage and stood in the shade. Greg walked toward it.

Michaela, the medic for the other response team, gave him a nod as she opened up the back of the trailer. "Hey, doc."

The trailer looked like a regular U-Haul, but it was a refrigerated unit that they used for specimen retrieval. Greg hauled himself into the back of the truck, and there, sitting on a slab, strapped down, was the Hank. Greg stayed at the edge of the truck for a moment, just taking it in.

Mitch climbed in and stood at the other side of the trailer, his sidearm in his hand.

The creature's talons were caked with blood, and it looked like one had been ripped off. Or maybe it had been shot off. Greg knew how dangerous those talons were. Hanks liked to slash their victims' torsos, disemboweling them before finishing them off.

This Hank lay still on a stretcher. Greg stared at its chest, looking for any sign that the creature was even a little bit alive. But it lay perfectly still.

Done with his visual inspection, or at least what he could see from his spot at the very edge of the truck bed, he moved closer. There was a large gaping wound in the Hank's chest. It went straight through. That was the obvious cause of death. Whoever had taken the shot was smart. It looked like they'd used a 50 caliber to take the thing out.

Inspecting the wound, Greg noted the scars along the Hank's torso. Apparently this one had gotten banged up quite a bit. The Hank's mouth gaped, frozen in a snarl. One eye was open, staring at nothing, while the other was shut. Greg frowned, staring at the closed eye. He peered at it closely. It wasn't closed, at least not naturally. It had been fused shut.

Greg called out over his shoulder. "Michaela. Do you have your bag with you?"

The soldier climbed into the back of the truck and slipped her backpack off her shoulders. "Of course. What are you looking for?"

"A scalpel."

Michaela raised an eyebrow, but that was her only response

as she opened up the bag and took out a small black case. She pulled a sharp scalpel out and handed it to Greg, handle first.

Greg nodded his thanks and then nudged his chin toward the eye. "You guys took pictures and stuff, right?"

"Yes. It's been documented," Michaela said.

"And this is being filmed?" He asked.

"Yeah. Go ahead." Michaela nodded to the camera in the corner of the truck before tapping the camera on the lapel of her jacket. Then she crossed to the other side of the stretcher so she'd have a better view of what Greg was doing. He leaned over the creature's face and carefully cut along the Hank's eyelid. And he found himself cutting stitches.

Michaela frowned, leaning in. "It looks like someone's sewn his eyes shut. Who the hell would do that?"

Greg had the same question. "I have no clue."

He completed the cut and then carefully opened the eyelid. He nodded, expecting what he found, which was nothing. "His eye's gone."

"Gone?" Michaela asked.

He straightened, staring at the creature, cataloging all of the scratches and scars along its body. This body had been through some fights. Some of the scars were older than others. And then there was the eye. "Whatever happened to this guy, someone patched him up before they sent him to Dracmore."

Michaela stared at the creature. "Who would do something like that?"

Greg pulled off his glove, shaking his head. "I have no idea. But I don't think that's the biggest question."

"What is?" Michaela asked.

He imagined all that would have been involved to treat the Hank and then the care taken to make sure its wounds didn't become infected. "The biggest question is why."

# CHAPTER 24

They had flown in from the Hamptons late last night. Greg had given Norah a rundown on what they had found this morning, highlighting his concerns about the medical procedures done on the Hank.

Norah looked just as concerned as he was. They still had no information on who was providing these people with the aliens. And that really was information they needed.

While Greg was gone, Alvie had finished his analysis of Seti data. He agreed with Greg's projections. There were more Setis out there than the official numbers suggested. And now they knew someone was actually selling them, and maybe even treating them.

Something had come up back in Norway, and Alvie was needed, so Sammy had stopped by and picked him up. Greg felt bad that he'd missed him but thought it was probably for the best that Alvie had gone back. Greg was exhausted.

A yawn threatened to dislocate Greg's jaw as he walked down the hall toward his office. God, he was so tired. He'd slept a little on the plane, but it was a short trip. And then once he got back to his apartment, his sleep had been filled with nightmares about Hanks. He must have gotten up three times to check that all the locks were secure. Maybe tonight he'd take a sleeping pill to let him catch up.

Or better yet, maybe he'd see if Norah would mind if he bunked in her guest room. He'd sleep easier with Iggy and a well-armed Norah right down the hall.

As he turned the corner to toward his office, an extra shine on the dark tile floor caught his attention. He sighed at the slime trail leading straight to his door. Apparently Pugsley had escaped the engineers' latest attempts at a containment unit.

Careful to avoid the slick surface, he pushed open his door and headed to his desk. A slime trail covered the side of his lower desk drawer on the right-hand side. Greg had left it open in case Pugsley made his way here while he was gone. Plus he was getting sick of cleaning the front of that drawer and the one above as Pugsley slid through. Leaving it open cut down on at least some of the mess.

He sat down without making a sound as Pugsley was contentedly sleeping, a small wheeze coming from him.

The glow from Greg's monitor gave his office a nice soft light. Greg went through his emails, trashing those that were unimportant and answering a few. Then he turned to some lab results from recent acquisitions, but nothing really grabbed his attention.

Pugsley woke up, giving a little chirp to let Greg know. Greg took a handful of peanuts from the jar on his desk and dropped them down to him. With a happy chirp, two hands darted out of Pugsley's chest to catch them, Now he sat on the waterproof dog bed, happily eating the legumes, shell and all. In the dimmer light, it was clear that Pugsley had become less translucent than when Greg had first met him. Now his soft pale blue almost seemed to have a light glow to it.

Rubbing his eyes, Greg wondered if it was just lack of sleep making him see things. But no, there was definitely a light glow. None of the lab reports on Pugsley mentioned it though.

Greg couldn't help but smile as Pugsley looked up at him and chirped again followed by his contented hum. He was actually kind of cute, except for, of course, the slime trail he left wherever he went. But Greg was beginning to think even that had been reduced.

Or maybe Greg was just getting used to it.

He reached over his head and stretched, staring at the file on the screen. The analysts were still nowhere on figuring out who had sold Johansen that creature. The financial trail was a complete dead end. Archimedes Art had been used only for the Johnsen purchase. Greg had no doubt a second fake company had been created for the Dracmore purchase.

Not that Greg was surprised. He hadn't exactly expected them to put a name and address down with the accounts. Whoever had access to that creature would also make sure that they had completely scrubbed their trail.

If there was a way to connect them, Greg was not seeing it. His mind was a mess right now. He needed something else to focus on.

After locking his door, he returned to his seat and pulled up the file he had yet to share with anyone. As far as he was concerned, the ideas and hypotheses within it were well beyond top secret. And they weren't actually related to any of the work he did for D.E.A.D.

Because Greg was trying to find out more about the Council.

The Council was a group of seven beings. They controlled the universe, or at least this part of the universe. Greg wasn't sure if that control extended beyond this part of it. But they had set up a base on the moon centuries ago to watch their human creation flourish.

The human race had come close to being destroyed not that

long ago because the Council had decided that their creation was a failure. It was only by pure dumb luck that they'd managed to find Ariana's mother in time. She had been able to convince the Council to give humanity another shot.

But what everyone seemed to have forgotten was that the Council hadn't decided that humanity was out of the woods. Really, all they'd done was extend humanity's trial phase. They could still pull the plug at any time.

Greg had been through a bunch of myths and wondered if maybe Zeus, Hera, and all the rest had actually been members of the races that the Council represented. In his free time, he'd spent his evenings diving into the ancient tales. It had been interesting reading, but making those intuitive leaps was beyond his skill set. He didn't have a background in mythology.

He did, however, have a background in science.

So that was where he started his search. The first thing he was looking for was something old. The Council had created humanity hundreds of thousands of years ago. Sadly, he didn't have a firm number on when exactly that had occurred. Humans themselves kept pushing back the date when they'd first shown up on the planet. Lucy had made all of the media go crazy back in the 1970s, and she'd fascinated schoolchildren ever since. She was the first modern upright human skeleton, although she was a human ancestor and not a *Homo sapien sapien*. She was 3.18 million years old. But now Lucy was a youngster compared to some of the other branches of humans that had been discovered.

The oldest complete skeleton had been found in South Africa. It was 3.67 million years old. But the oldest hominid found, albeit incomplete, was uncovered in Ethiopia, at 4.4 million years old. That was a million years older than Lucy.

But in order to create an entire race millions of years ago, the creator race had to have been around for even longer.

Humanity was just now beginning to figure out genetics and how to combine species. The Area 51 projects were a nightmare example of what could go wrong with that process. But even on a smaller scale, society had been dabbling in genetics and had created everything from cows that produced human breast milk to animals bred to serve as organ donors, complete with human organs.

So after millions of years, humans had finally figured out how to at least put aspects of one race into the genetic code of another. The A.L.I.V.E. projects were proof of that. But in those cases, they had created one, maybe two creatures. The Council, or at least their forebears, had found another planet and essentially colonized it with their hybrids. That was a whole other level.

Which meant they had to have been around for much longer than humans.

And that was where Greg was running into a problem. Odds were that the races that made up the Council came from an organized galaxy, or at least a stable galaxy. Unstable galaxies would make it too difficult for them to exist. But stable galaxies hadn't really existed until long after the Big Bang.

Of course, it was entirely possible that his assumptions were wrong. It seemed the world was always finding out new things about the universe that made all the previous ideas look oh-so-cute when faced with the daunting reality that was the universe. From thinking Earth was flat to believing that the sun revolved around Earth. Even now, all the facts were constantly developing, like learning that the moon was actually younger than Earth by millions of years.

Today, though, his project involved reviewing the research on the different galaxies across the universe that could support life. It was actually daunting when he considered just how many there were. Scientists at the University of Nottingham recently declared that using a variation of the Drake equation, there could be as many as thirty-six intelligent communicating life-forms in the Milky Way alone. The critical factors were, of course, the Goldilocks Zone, an area not too far or too close to a sun to allow life to flourish, but also the stability of the galaxy. Not all galaxies were stable. A system must be stable, they hypothesized, for at least four billion years before it could produce life.

Four billion years ago just so happened to be when the Milky Way was formed, making it one of the younger galaxies. But one of the other limiting factors to the research was the lifespan of a civilization. A civilization would have to exist for thousands of years before it was technologically capable of sending out a signal that could reach another civilization on another planet. Earth was only about a hundred years into that technological ability, despite being around for thousands of years.

And then the question became one of longevity: What if the civilization developed and then died out before achieving that feat? There were undeniably civilizations that flourished and disappeared on our own planet, never mind on the countless others that hadn't even been found yet.

But even with those ideas, the universe was throwing out facts that countered what limited knowledge we had about how it functioned, such as the Wolfe Disk galaxy. It had formed a mere 1.5 billion years after the Big Bang, had been discovered to be stable and not chaotic. That flew in the face of what scientists believed the early years of the universe were like. The galaxy was a mind-blowing twelve billion years old, which meant it had an additional eight billion years to develop a species.

No one suggested that a civilization could have lasted all that time. But even if the civilization were only double the age of humans, Greg couldn't help but wonder at all they could do. When the space program was in its infancy, all the computers on board had the power of a coffee machine. Now Greg had twenty times the computing power of the first space missions in just his cell phone. The last fifty years had seen an exponential growth in technological advancement. What would the next fifty years bring? Or one hundred? Or one thousand?

Greg sat back, staring at the screen and the image that someone had created of the Wolfe Disk. Was that it? Was that where the Council, or at least some of the races of the Council, had begun? Even as he thought it, he knew it was entirely possible that he was way off base. The true vastness of the universe was hard to comprehend. The Milky Way was approximately 150,000 light-years across. The universe, however, was ninety-two billion light-years wide and over thirteen billion years old. Which meant there are easily thousands upon thousands of galaxies out there that humans were unaware of. The depth of what we didn't know was staggering.

Yet, humans always made statements with such hubris. Humans had declared that Earth was flat, then they declared that Earth was the center of the universe, followed by a declaration that the sun was the center of the universe. There were some fools who still argued that Earth was only 10,000 years old. Apparently, the Council hadn't exactly perfected their formula when creating humanity.

And while humanlike creatures had been around for close to four million years, civilization as a complex web of human settlements dated back to only the Mesopotamians, who flourished less than five thousand years ago. Yet, archaeological evidence kept popping up, pushing those dates farther and farther back into the past.

Every time humans made some sort of declaration, something somewhere came up and proved how wrong that claim was.

Greg had no doubt that when it came to the universe and humanity's thoughts on the Council and the plurality of worlds, humans would once again be proven to be arrogant in their assumptions. He rubbed his eyes and shut the monitor off. That was enough for one day. He was moving into the realm of the philosophical. And nothing good came from that realm, at least for him.

Pugsley let out a little chirp and looked up at him. Greg leaned down and patted him and then winced, realizing he forgot to put on the gloves. Oh well, there was no helping it. Pugsley leaned into Greg's hand with a happy little sigh.

"Hey there little buddy. I think it's time to call it a night."

Now it was a sad little chirp that Pugsley emitted. Greg thought Pugsley was beginning to understand Greg's words. He didn't think it was a high level of understanding, but more like a dog's understanding of what the word *out* or *sit* meant. Greg had been trying to use the same words over and over again to help Pugsley figure things out.

He had to admit, the guy was definitely growing on him. He hated the fact that he was here alone at night. There were always people in the building, of course, but Pugsley was a one-guy kind of hybrid.

At least Pugsley would be safe. But not for the first time, he wondered about maybe taking him home one night, just to kind of show him the place. Without Alvie, the apartment felt awfully lonely.

He knew, though, that Norah would have an absolute heart attack if he even mentioned it, and the risk was too great, so he wouldn't do it. As much as he liked Pugsley, he still didn't know enough about him. And he seemed to be experiencing some physical changes. Even Norah had noted that his appearance was different each time she saw him.

So Greg knew he couldn't take Pugsley home, at least not yet. He glanced at the couch at the back of his office. He could always bunk in here a few nights. There were showers down at the locker room. He looked down at Pugsley. "Tell you what, buddy. I'll bring in some clothes and stuff, and that way I can stay here a few nights a week, okay?"

Pugsley gave a little hum, his body vibrating. Greg had started thinking of that as his happy sound. Greg smiled as he stood up. "Okay, I need to call it a night. I'll see you—"

His cell phone beeped three times. Groaning, Greg pulled it out and read the text: *Seti sighted. Airfield, ten minutes.*

# CHAPTER 25

## LAS VEGAS, NEVADA

The casino was jumping tonight. Trevor walked through the ARIA's main room. Slot machines covered the majority of the floor. Tourists in their colorful shorts and shirts sat, trying their luck while pulling lever after lever.

Or more accurately, punching button after button.

He wasn't sure they even realized how much they were spending on the off chance of actually making a few bucks. It used to take longer. You'd have to put a nickel or a dime or a quarter in and pull the lever. But now, with everything going automated, you could just punch a button quickly, one right after the other, until, before you knew it, you'd blown two hundred bucks in five minutes to make five.

Yet no one looked unhappy. Everybody looked like they were enjoying themselves. Trevor liked wandering the floor of the regular casinos, even though he only played at the high-end areas at the back. He liked seeing the normal people. He liked it even better when they noticed him. More than a few could tell he was someone important. There was always something about the attitude that indicated someone had money and power. And somewhere along the way, Trevor had picked up the ability to exude both.

Hungry eyes followed him now, envious of the lifestyle they imagined he lived.

And the truth was, they should be jealous. He lived a life that most people couldn't imagine. He had more money than he would ever know what to do with.

It was a strange problem to have, too much money. And it was a far cry from his early days.

His mama would be proud.

His personal concierge, Kenneth Taylor caught sight of him from across the room and quickly crossed to him. Tall and wispy thin, he was what Trevor imagined an English butler in some manor house would look like. He even gave Trevor a slight bow as he reached him. "Mr. Thomas, I didn't realize you'd be joining us tonight. Anything I can get you?"

Trevor was well-known in all of the casinos. He liked to spread the wealth a little bit. He liked Caesars the best. He knew it was his New York roots, but something about it just called to him.

"Good to see you again, Kenneth. Actually, I think I'll try my hand at a baccarat table."

Kenneth smiled. "Of course, sir. I'll get that set up. Would you like your usual drink?"

Trevor nodded. "Yeah. And set me up for seventy to start, would you?"

"Of course, sir. I'll have it ready for you as soon as you sit down."

"Great."

Kenneth gave him a small inclined nod before he hurried off to get everything set for "Mr. Thomas." Thomas was Trevor's Vegas name. He very rarely used his actual surname anymore. Trevor, however, he always used. He knew it was smarter to choose a completely different name, but his mom had given him that name. He thought it would be disrespectful not to use it. And he would never disrespect his mother. His father gave him his last name, and he owed that jerk nothing. So he really didn't care about his last name.

He wended his way through the Twenty-One tables. Two tables in, a poor slob in a food-stained white linen shirt sat gripping his cards tightly, sweat on his brow as his foot tapped nervously on the edge of his chair.

That guy was in for a world of heartache soon. He'd obviously come to Vegas hoping to get himself out of some sort of hole. Desperation was written all over the man's face. The guy was losing his shirt if the paltry amount of chips in front of him was any indication. It was going to be a bad night for him.

Trevor shrugged as he walked on by. If you couldn't handle the loss, you shouldn't bet the farm.

He knew he was considered a risk taker by many. After all, he was a criminal, and had been for decades. But his risks were always carefully calculated. Betting on a game like Twenty-One, where the odds were in the house's favor: absolutely not, at least not seriously. Losing seventy grand at baccarat, well that was just an evening well spent. But for him, seventy grand was chump change. He'd never bet enough to get himself in a hole.

No, gambling was entertainment. It was not a way to solve financial problems. When it came to Trevor's real money, he took all sorts of precautions. In fact, he tried to reduce that risk to practically nothing. Besides, there was a separate set of rules for the wealthy.

In his pocket, his phone buzzed. He pulled it out. Brad's name was splashed across the screen.

Like his brother Jerry, Brad never contacted him on his off time unless there was a problem, and a big problem at that.

Trevor stepped out of the main casino area and into an alcove, waving at Kenneth. The concierge quickly had three staff members take up posts ten feet away from Trevor to make sure no one bothered him.

"What happened?" Trevor said by way of greeting.

"The Hampton install. It went bad."

Dammit, that made two. Trevor struggled to remember who that involved. "Rachel? Is she okay?"

He liked Rachel Dracmore more than most. She was smart, tough, and didn't suffer fools. She was too old for him to date, but he'd seen pictures of her in her younger days, and she been a looker.

"Rachel's fine. She wasn't at the house at the time. Her latest pool boy was killed, along with a large group of his friends."

"What about the creature?"

"Killed. And the bodies have all have been removed. It's being reported as a boating accident."

He grunted. He didn't know much about this secretive scientific group, but they were very good at coming up with excuses for what had happened to people. A boating accident was an interesting choice.

"Yeah, there's only a few bodies that have been found. The rest are being reported as lost at sea. The Coast Guard is even doing a search for them."

That took some balls. He'd like to meet whoever was in charge of this agency. Because they obviously had some big ones.

"Is this going to be a problem for us?"

Brad was quiet for a minute. "I don't like it. I mean, one case they could write off, but two cases so close together? They're not stupid. They're going to be looking for us."

Trevor had known it would come to this at some point. You couldn't run a scheme like the one he'd been running without expecting to attract some attention. It had been good while it lasted. "All right, where are we with the Chicago lineup?"

"It will take me about two days to get everything set up."

"Okay. Well, it's going to be our final show. We'll close up shop after Chicago and lay low for a little while. Have you made any headway in getting something on this organization?"

The frustration was clear in Brad's voice. "No. I mean, I've got photos of them from both the Connecticut scene and now the Hampton one. But I can't get a trace on them. All the guys that I've run down are ghosts. They no longer exist. I can try some facial recognition and age them to see if maybe they show up in pictures somewhere, but that'll take time."

Trevor paused for a minute. "Is there anyone that was at both scenes?"

"Yeah, one guy. I don't think he's military, though. Hold on a sec." Trevor's phone beeped a second later, indicating that Brad had sent him a quick video. Trevor pulled it up and realized it wasn't the LEOs from the Hamptons. He immediately knew which guy Brad was referring to. Almost all the people in the shot carried themselves with a military bearing: straight shoulders, focused gaze, eye-on-the-prize kind of people. There was one guy, though, whose hair was a little longer than the others, with his shoulders slouched. If this were one of those "which of these is not like the other" puzzles, that guy would be the answer.

"Okay, get on it. Find him. Get a full background. I need someone that I can work with if things go sideways."

"I'll find him. There's always one," Brad said.

Trevor knew Brad was right. No matter how big the agency or organization poised against you, there was always a weak link. There was always a way to get what you wanted.

There was always one.

"There's something else. But I don't know if it's a good time," Brad said slowly.

"What is it?" Trevor asked.

"We got a line on another one. It's actually in Vegas. But maybe we should hold off."

The fear at Brad's initial statement abated replaced with excitement. Another creature. That was good. If this was the last show, he wanted to go out with a bang. "No. Track it down. We continue with business as usual until I say otherwise."

"You're the boss," Brad said before disconnecting the call.

Slipping his own phone back in his pocket, he grinned. *Yes, I am. And I'm about to be a much richer one.*

# CHAPTER 26

The lights from the Las Vegas Strip blared out into the night sky. Greg stepped out of the SUV and stared over at the well-known sight. They'd just flown into McCarran Airport.

Being here was making Greg feel strange. This was where, in many ways, it had all begun. His research had, of course, first begun at Wright-Patterson Air Force Base. But it was Project Vault, which Martin Drummond had created at Area 51, that had set them all off on their current trajectory.

Most of the creatures in Project Vault were hybrids, a mix of alien DNA and animal DNA from Earth. Although in the last couple of years, the U.S. government had started to expand upon its replication of pure alien DNA. Iggy was an example of it.

Greg wasn't really sure what the other examples were. There were hundreds of creatures listed in the D.E.A.D. files. And he hadn't had time yet to actually go through all of them. Each one required traversing several layers of security in order to access the information. And that all took time. So far, he'd only had time to go through the creatures directly related to his cases.

But Pugsley had him thinking maybe he needed to carve out the time to go through the other cases. Maybe he could get Penny's and Alvie's help. They could create some sort of program that would identify likely environments for each of the species. It might help run them down faster.

Mitch walked over to him and handed him an M4, pulling Greg from his thoughts. Greg slung it over his shoulder after checking the magazine. The rest of the response team made their way over as well, standing in front of Greg. Greg nodded at all of them. "Okay. Our Seti is about one and a half to two feet tall, three feet long. It has twelve legs and is dark brown in color. It's got two antennae on the top of its head and pincers on its mouth."

Max shuddered. "What the hell?"

That had been Greg's response as well when he'd first read the description. "Yeah, it kind of looks like a giant centipede. It was seen early this morning about a block from here. We think that it's been in the sewers and just recently stepped outside."

Kaylee shook her head. "So we're basically looking for a centipede the size of a Labrador retriever?"

Greg paused for a minute and then nodded. "Actually, yeah, that's pretty much it. They probably prefer dark spaces, so keep that in mind."

Mitch stepped forward and broke everyone up into groups before sending them out. Mitch, Max, and Greg were grouped together and headed west from their current location. It took them to an old neighborhood in a suburb of Las Vegas.

Looking at the homes they passed, Greg wondered if the people inside had any idea what had been created just a few miles away. He doubted it. Greg was still amazed that the government had managed to keep the breakout so quiet. No one really knew except for occasional reports that most people dismissed as being sensational. The plans of the U.S. government to nuke Area 51 if the breakout wasn't contained definitely hadn't made the papers either.

Although for this area, that wouldn't exactly be unusual. About ninety miles to the west was the site where they had tested nuclear bombs without the public's knowledge. And, of course, there had been a spike in cancer rates in the areas nearby.

But did the government then step forward and take responsibility and help people out? Of course not. The people had to sue the United States government to get them to at least pay for their cancer treatments.

He knew that similar payments were going out to people who were harmed by the escapees at Area 51.

Of course, that was for the people who actually knew that some sort of strange creature had harmed or, even in some cases, killed their loved ones. Where it was possible, the U.S. government kept it under wraps and labeled things as industrial accidents or car accidents or, in one disgusting case, a hiking accident. Greg didn't agree with the lying, but he understood the fear of what would happen when the government actually admitted that they had been creating aliens for the last couple of decades and that those aliens had, in fact, escaped.

In recent years, however, there had been a slow picking up of revelations about UFOs. More astronauts, including astronaut Scott Kelly, had provided testimony, or even pictures, in Kelly's case, of UFOs they'd seen while they were in space.

In fact, in 2020, the U.S. government even admitted, or at least the Navy did, that there were some objects in the sky that they simply could not identify. In the spring of 2020, the Department of Defense released three videos of unidentified aerial phenomena. The Pentagon stated that the videos were real and that they could not explain or identify the craft that seemed to defy the laws of physics. They did not declare they were ships piloted by little green men, but they at least confirmed that they had no real answer for what they were.

A former Israeli space security chief even went as far as to reveal the Council, declaring that humans were in contact with a galactic federation. But those news items had received very little fanfare. In fact, in the last few years, it seemed that governments around the world were slowly allowing the concept of UFOs to gain credibility within society.

While Greg was a fan of full disclosure, he knew that governments generally were not. Which made him question what exactly the governments were up to. Greg had a feeling that within the next couple of years, there was going to be a big reveal that they hoped, with the slow leak of information, wouldn't destroy society the way the *War of the Worlds* radio broadcast could have when it freaked everyone out decades ago.

A garbage can rattled, and the three of them turned quickly to the side. His own gun, he happily noticed, was raised just as quickly as those of the other two. A cat strolled down a driveway and slipped underneath the car.

Greg let out a breath, darting a glance at the other two. His nerves were always on high alert on these types of missions. But these two always looked cool as a cucumber. He wondered if there would ever be a time when he was as easygoing about possibly facing death.

He doubted it.

Max stared at the car. Waiting for the cat, Greg supposed. He walked next to Greg. "Greg, what about shape-shifting? Is that a possibility?"

Greg paused, looking at him. "You mean could a Seti have the ability to shape shift?"

Max nodded. "Yeah."

Shape-shifting, the ability to shift from one shape into

another or from one organism into another, was not really something he'd thought about in relation to the Area 51 creatures. They were a stalwart of science fiction and fantasy novels, though. He gave it a moment of thought before answering, thinking about what would really be required for that to happen.

Greg shook his head. "I doubt it. So far, all of the creatures that we've come across have certain biological limits that they have to live by, just the way creatures on Earth have biological limits that they have to live by. I mean, you've got some creatures such as the octopus that had, um, no bones, and thus it could fit into certain containers or spaces a little more easily, but they couldn't actually change their structure."

"Like that thing back in Greenwich," Max said.

Greg nodded. "Exactly. But even the octopus is restrained because it's got a hard beak. That can't change shape, so being able to go from a fluid shape to a more hardened shape, which would be necessary to replicate other organisms, seems unlikely. I mean, the closest anyone could do is replicate the noises one makes or change its color. But a pure shape-shifting ability seems highly improbable."

"Huh, that's pretty disappointing. I have to think that would have been really cool to see," Max said.

A grunt was the only response Greg gave, because he was pretty sure a shape-shifting Seti would be terrifying, not cool.

They walked in silence as they made their way down the street. It was a nice, quiet neighborhood. Every once in a while, there were signs that kids live there, a swing set in the backyard, a bike leaning against a garage. One of those big plastic red-and-yellow cars that seemed to be issued whenever a kid became a toddler.

"But," Max said, breaking into Greg's thoughts, "who says they have to follow the rules? After all, they're nothing like us, right?"

"Actually, that's not true. They follow the same rules of development that we do," Greg said.

Max stared at him. "But we're looking for a Labrador-sized centipede. There are no Labrador-sized centipedes in this world."

Greg grinned. "True. But that's because of the way our world is. The amount of sunlight, the amount of water, the amount of grass, the type of game that's available, all of those affected how we developed. We started walking upright because we were trying to get fruit off of trees. If the trees were lower to the ground, we never would have walked on two legs. We would have been on all fours our whole lives."

Max look taken aback. "Seriously?"

"We're not the pinnacle of development. We didn't influence how we are ourselves. Our environment determined how we turned out. Take for example, skin tone. There are at least six different skin tones in the world, right?"

Max nodded.

"Well, let's look at the palest of them. Which tends to be the people in grayer or rainy locations like Ireland or Scotland. Their skin tends to be extremely pale. And that's actually a biological adaptation. Because we all need to get vitamin D from the sun. But for them, they don't get as much sun because of where they live, so their skin adapted over time so that they need to be in the sun for less time to get that hit of vitamin D. For most people you need to be outside for up to thirty minutes. Pale people can get that same hit in a much shorter time."

Frowning, Max nodded. "Yeah, but then they're in trouble when they go to a sunny area. I had a friend back in high school who, I swear to God, he got burned as soon as he stepped outside on a sunny day."

Inclining his head, Greg nodded. "That's true too. So, they are well-adapted to one environment. But when they leave that environment and go to another environment, they need to be able to take protections, like sunscreen and clothing that keeps the sun out, to protect their skin because it can't adapt that quickly to the new location. But their *skin tone* is a product of the environment. So all humans have been affected by where their ancestors grew up. It determines how they look."

Greg could tell that Max was still skeptical, so he pushed on. "There's actually been research that indicates that animals will develop in a smaller size on islands than they will on larger continents. And the reason is there's less food available. So those creatures adapt to the smaller food supply by requiring less food for their systems."

"So how does this relate to these things that we're chasing?" Max asked.

"Well, there are over two hundred billion suns in the Milky Way alone."

Max cut in. "Wait, what? Two hundred billion? Billion with a *B*?"

Greg nodded. "Yup. So far, what we seem to know is that at least half of those has at least one habitable planet. Which means theoretically, there're over a hundred billion potential life-providing planets in our galaxy alone.

"Each of those planets, though, is going to have a different environment and atmosphere. Some of them will be incredibly rocky. Others will have very little water. Others will essentially be a water world. Some of them will be far from the sun and thus be shrouded almost entirely in darkness. Others will be closer to the sun and therefore be perpetually in bright light. All of these different environments affect how creatures develop. The creatures that live on a darkened planet are more likely to develop huge eyes to compensate for the lack of light."

"The Grays," Max said.

This was probably the first long discussion he'd had with

Max, and Greg had to admit he was really impressed with his questions. "Exactly. It's theorized that the Grays come from a planet where light is at a premium. As a result, they had to evolve into creatures with better eyesight, which meant larger eyes. That would also account for why their color is gray versus something that sees the sun a little more often."

"And why they're so scrawny," Max added.

"Without a great deal of sun, food is probably tough to come by—at least, nutritious food. So yes, that's probably part of the reason as well," Greg said.

"And what about this giant centipede we're following? What's his home planet like?"

Pausing, Greg contemplated what they knew about this creature. "Well, I'm not sure if the centipede is something that was mixed with something else or he's a purebred. If he's a purebred, I'm guessing that they probably developed a hard exoskeleton to deal with a violent environment. Maybe one that doesn't have a strong atmosphere, and therefore the planet's constantly getting bombarded with radiation and meteors. The hard exoskeleton would keep them safe. Without it, they'd be stuck in caves and underground. Or maybe they do live in caves and underground, and their body structure was a way to get through smaller spaces. Standing upright and trying to get through a small, cramped cave would be difficult. You'd have to crawl uncomfortably on all fours."

"Wait, wait, wait. You're not saying that these things are intelligent, are you?"

"I'm not sure. Some of them are. They don't look like us, but they are intelligent. We're not the only intelligent species on the planet. We're just the only intelligent species that looks like *us* on the planet. We know that dolphins are incredibly intelligent. Some even argue they should be considered people in their own right. But we tend not to recognize the intelligence of other species, even when they demonstrate it to us.

"I mean, dolphins are not going to be Mensa candidates, but there're a lot of humans who aren't either. But we know that dolphins have empathy. We know that they can think things through. So it doesn't seem crazy to think that creatures coming from another planet would have similar ranges of intelligence. As for what range of intelligence the one we're chasing right now has, I don't know.

"But it's been months since it was freed. And yet this is the first time we are seeing any sign of it. The rest have been a few here or there, but they're ones that we've seen before. This is the first sighting of this guy. That indicates either some level of intelligence or an incredible survival capacity. So if you're asking whether or not this guy is intelligent, I'm saying err on the side of it being intelligent. Because if we err on the other side, well, that could cause us a lot of problems."

The soldier stared at him for a long moment. "I don't know, Doc. I think I preferred when I thought aliens were just little green men that occasionally stopped by, grabbed a person, and left."

Sighing, Greg nodded. "Yeah, I think I preferred that too."

# CHAPTER 27

They'd been searching for ninety minutes now and still hadn't seen any sign of the creature. Greg wasn't overly surprised by that. If it had managed to hide out this long, he doubted that they'd be able to find it quickly. He had a feeling they were going to have to call in another strike force to aid in the search.

He, Mitch, and Max had wandered away from the residential neighborhood and into an old business area. Everything was closed up tight for the night. They walked along a strip mall that contained a long-abandoned Radio Shack, a pawn shop, a coffee place, and a Dollar Store. Greg peered in the windows as they passed, but it was dark inside, and he couldn't see anything. Although Greg had a feeling that this creature probably liked the dark.

While centipedes could thrive in a variety of environments, they tended to be found in more desert-like areas. In addition, they spent most of their time under stones or in the dirt. They weren't a bask-in-the-sun kind of creature.

Mitch stopped at the end of the strip mall and looked around. "This is not going well." His frustration was palpable.

150

Greg felt it too. There'd been no sign of the creature at all from any of the groups. Normally they at least had a sign of something. Maybe some disturbed garbage cans or even some tracks. More often than not, they had an eyewitness, even though they always managed to talk the eyewitness out of what they believed they had seen.

But on this trip, no one had reported anything. The only sighting of the thing had been through a security camera.

Mitch nodded to the street up ahead. There was another strip mall. And then there was one across the street on the other side, and then there was another one back the way they came. "All right, Max and I are going to go check out the next strip mall. Greg, why don't you call in the other strike force and update Norah? I think we're going to need more help."

Greg nodded. "Yeah. Okay."

Mitch and Max took off across the street. The other strip mall was similarly bathed in darkness.

Leaning against the brick column of the old Radio Shack, Greg pulled out his phone. He quickly typed a message to Norah, explaining where they were and the need for more help.

Norah got back to him quickly. *Reinforcements will be there in about an hour.*

He typed his thanks and then slid his phone back into his pocket. A clang sounded at the back of the Radio Shack.

Head tilted, Greg stepped away from the wall, his M4 in his hands. He craned his neck and listened, but no other sound came. He glanced over at where Mitch and Max had disappeared, but he couldn't see them in the shadows.

Pausing for just a moment to collect himself and shove down the panic, he rounded the building. He wouldn't go in because he wasn't crazy, but he could at least check and see if there was any sign that something had made its way inside.

Nerves danced along Greg's skin. God, he hated these

moments. Once again, he wondered how the guy picked last for every team in gym had somehow managed to end up with a career that required him to do physical stuff on a regular basis.

Although Mitch told him often enough that he wasn't that scrawny kid from gym class anymore, Greg still thought of himself that way. He knew he'd put on some muscle. And Mitch had been training him in self-defense. He was getting not bad. He wasn't quite ready to say he was good, but he was definitely getting better. And his aim with the M4 was definitely improving as well.

Inside, though, he still felt like a skinny twelve-year-old kid. And he had a feeling he was always going to feel like that adolescent beanpole.

But he ignored the memory of his bespectacled, teeth-braced, and acne-clad tween self as he walked down the side of the strip mall toward the back of the building. The strip mall connected to an overgrown lot along the back. There was a sign on it indicating that it was for sale, although why someone would buy such a decrepit lot in this neighborhood was beyond him.

Greg noted that the fence surrounding the lot was falling down. It would be easy for something to escape into it or out of it. Not necessarily the creature they were looking for, but any stray animal no doubt could. There was a good forty feet between that lot and the back of the building.

As Greg walked along the back of the mall, he noted that the door to the Radio Shack looked to be locked tight. And there were no windows back here for something to go through. But there was a line of dumpsters along the back of the building, and it looked as if the neighborhood had been using this area as their dumping ground. There were old couches and lamps, an occasional shoe or dish.

There were way too many hiding spots. He needed to ask

for help. Something rattled up ahead as he reached for his radio. Greg immediately grabbed the M4 with both hands. Bringing it to his shoulder, he scanned his surroundings.

The sound had come from halfway down the mall. Around the other side of the strip mall, two figures appeared. Both held long guns. Greg let out a sigh of relief. He moved forward slowly, indicating that a noise had come from up ahead. Mitch and Max moved toward him, cloaked in shadow. Greg did the same as they converged on the spot.

Another rattle sounded, closer to where Mitch and Max were.

The two of them turned and stepped toward it, moving into a spot of light from above.

And that's when Greg's heart nearly leapt from his chest.

It wasn't Mitch and Max.

# CHAPTER 28

The two men at the end of the darkened alley were not part of the response team. Their uniforms were slightly different, more of a dark gray than a black. And he didn't recognize the weapons they held. The D.E.AD. response team all used M4s for their long guns.

The noise came again, and Greg reached for his radio, stepping back toward the shadows and hoping the men ignored him. He whispered into the radio, "Mitch. Behind the strip mall. We've got company."

"We're on our way. Do *not* do anything." Mitch's voice was on the edge of frantic.

His concern didn't exactly make Greg feel better.

A third man Greg hadn't noticed appeared from the shadows. Heart racing, Greg tried to slip deeper into the shadows, hoping to be unobserved.

Heading jerking up, the man aimed his weapon at Greg.

"Shit!" Greg dove toward the dumpster next to him as gunshots rang out.

He wasn't sure which building was next to him, but he didn't hesitate. He shot out the lock on the door and yanked the door open. He burst into an old stock room and realized he was in the Dollar Store.

He crashed through a set of double doors and careened into a display of toilet paper. Rolling along the ground, careful to keep his finger off the trigger of his M4, he came to a stop. Scrambling to his feet, he bolted down the first aisle as footsteps hastened toward him. He tapped the mic at his throat.

"I'm in the Dollar Tree. I'm being chased by a human," he whispered into the mic, not wanting to let whoever was following him know where he was.

But, of course, he was in the first aisle near the display of toilet paper that was all over the place. So obviously his pursuer was going to know where he was. Greg quickly darted to the end of the aisle. Shots rang out behind him. Greg ducked his head and then, dove for the ground, sliding around the end of the aisle.

Shaken, he stood up in front of a display of action figures. They were about four years out of date. He noted Rey and Kylo Ren and gave them a nod, then flicked a glance around the corner of the aisle. The gunman had disappeared. Greg stayed quiet and then inched toward the other side of the aisle to get a look.

At the last second, he crouched down low and peeked from only about three feet high. Gunfire blew off a couple of Reys and Kylos from the display where he'd just been standing. He flattened himself to the ground, quickly set up his M4 on the floor, and let off four shots. The guy standing in the middle of the aisle was caught out in the open. Greg's shot caught him in the shin, and he dropped with a scream.

Not wasting any time on finishing the guy off, Greg hustled to his feet. Making sure the guy was completely out of commission was definitely not his department.

Sprinting to the front of the store, he pulled the M4 in front of him and shot out the glass in the door before bolting through. He tripped over the frame but managed to get one hand down. He shoved himself to the side, rolling away from the front of the store. He scrambled to his feet as he reached the narrow brick wall that connected the stores.

Mitch and Max sprinted across the parking lot toward him.

Blood pounded in Greg's ears and his arms shook as he took position against the brick wall. He gulped in some air as they reached him. "I heard a noise around the back of the strip mall. I went to go check it out. I thought it was you two coming in from another side. But it wasn't. There are three other gunmen here."

His eyes hard, Mitch scanned the area. "Locals?"

Greg shook his head. "It looks like another team. They're tracking this thing too."

"All teams converge on my location. I repeat, all teams converge on my location." Mitch barked into his radio before he looked at Greg. "You okay?"

Greg knew he wasn't asking if he was hurt but rather if he was ready to go again. He rolled his shoulders. "Yeah. I'm good. I shot one. He's in one of the aisles of the Dollar Tree."

Mitch nodded. "All right, let's head around the back. They're probably going to come through the front."

"I'll go in through the Dollar Store," Max said. "I'll meet you two out back."

"Give us thirty seconds before you go in." Mitch didn't wait for an answer. He turned around and headed for the side of the mall. Greg jogged quickly behind him.

Gunfire burst from the back of the strip mall.

Max couldn't have gotten back there that quick. So who were they shooting at? Catching himself at the stupidity of the thought, he realized it had to be the Seti.

Ahead of him, Mitch had reached the corner and flattened himself against the side of the building. He peered down the alley. Greg stopped at his side. With only a quick glance at

Greg, Mitch rounded the corner, his weapon tight to his shoulder.

Taking a deep breath, Greg followed, copying Mitch's approach. Two men stood in the alley, firing toward the back of the Dollar Store.

Mitch let off two shots. They found their mark, right in the neck of each man. Greg winced as they dropped.

The two of them walked down the alley quietly. Mitch kept his eyes on the two gunmen, but Greg was scanning the area. Those men had been shooting at something, and he doubted it was the third partner, who was probably still in the store.

A scrabbling of feet was all the notice they had before the creature burst out from around the dumpster. It had a massive mouth and two tusks that acted as pincers on the end of it. Its head had to be at least a foot wide. Its body was closer to four feet long, and it stood two feet off the ground. Of course, right now it was in the air as it leapt toward Mitch.

"Mitch!" Greg opened fire, but his bullets just bounced off the thing.

Turning quickly, Mitch let out a yell as the creature landed on him, dropping him to the ground.

With a curse, Greg dropped the M4 and pulled his knife from its sheath. Mitch had the creature by the neck and was barely keeping it from goring his face. Greg sprinted over and hesitated next to them, looking for an opening.

Then he saw it. The plates of the creature's skeleton moved. Each one was individually connected to its body, which meant that there were gaps in between. The design allowed it to move more easily, but it also meant that Greg had a target.

Greg plunged his knife in between the creature's plates. It reared back, trying to lash at Greg. But Greg simply pulled his knife out and plunged it in again and again and again. The creature struggled to run away, but Mitch held it tight, and finally, the creature stopped moving entirely.

As Greg stepped away, Mitch rolled the creature off of him . He lay there for a minute, panting, and then sat up. "Thanks, Greg."

The door to the Dollar Store burst open. Greg whirled around, knife in hand, knowing that he wasn't going to be able to get to the gun in time.

It was Max. He looked between the two of them and then the creature on the ground. "You guys okay?"

Mitch slowly got to his feet. "Yeah. What about the guy inside?"

"He's toast," Max said.

Greg winced.

Max caught the movement and shook his head. "It wasn't you, Greg. He pulled his gun on me. I had to take the kill shot."

The description did not help settle Greg's stomach.

Mitch looked at the two gunmen lying on the ground, their blood seeping into the old concrete. "Who are these guys?"

Greg stared at them and their gray uniforms. "I think these are the guys that have been collecting the creatures."

He walked over to one of them and pulled the gun from the man's holster. He held it up. Mitch walked over and grabbed it. Pulling out the magazine, he nodded. "Tranquilizers."

Greg had noted the guns as well. "They were here to take the creature, not kill it."

# CHAPTER 29

## CLEARWATER, FLORIDA

The waves were definitely not calming Trevor down today. He'd flown in last night after speaking with Brad. He didn't want to be in Vegas if one of those things was around. It might seem cowardly to some, but to him it was common sense.

He'd had this place built two years ago. It was the crowning jewel of his properties, his dream house. He loved it down here, although he didn't get here very often. In fact, he would be leaving again later today for St. Bart's. But he needed the peace his hideaway provided him. But he found none of it here today.

He moved away from the window before he did something he regretted, like breaking it. Gripping his phone, his knuckles turned white as Trevor seethed. "What do you mean we lost the subject and three guys?"

Brad's voice was calm, but Trevor could hear the anger underlying it. "That government group was there. They ran into our guys. They took them out as well as the subject."

Trevor slammed his mouth shut, trying to hold back the yell. He'd been working on his temper. It was still a work in progress. "What the hell kind of clown car operation are you running out there?"

Brad sighed. "Look, it was Danny. Normally he's pretty good. I don't know what happened this time. They reported that they saw someone behind a strip mall. Danny went after the guy, and the guy took him down. And then two others showed up. It was a clusterfuck."

"And the creature?" Trevor demanded.

"Toast. The guy that took down Danny, he destroyed it."

"God damn it." Trevor threw his cell phone across the room. It slammed into the wall and then shattered into a dozen pieces.

He immediately regretted it. He grabbed the house phone on the desk and quickly dialed Brad. "I want to know who this other team is. I want a way in."

"I just sent you the pictures we got last night. Two of the guys we've seen before."

Trevor took a couple of deep breaths and then sat down at his desk, pulling up the file that Brad had just sent him on his laptop. He quickly made his way into his email and pulled them up. He recognized the tall African American man. He was obviously a soldier. Everything about the man screamed lethal.

But it was the image of the other guy that gave him pause. This was the weak link. The guy had been at the other site as well. "Have you found anything on him yet?"

"Not much. We know his name is Greg Schorn. He's got degrees in biological sciences. He graduated top of his class from John Hopkins. And then he went to work for the United States government."

"Doing what?"

"I can't access that data," Brad said. "There's no record of the projects that he worked on. Everything is top secret. In fact, I can't find an address or current picture."

Trevor sat back, staring at the picture on the frame. "What about social media? Where is he?"

"He doesn't have any. No emails, no websites, no social media accounts. This guy's a ghost online."

"There's got to be something. No one can disappear that completely. Dig deeper. Pull on our military contacts."

"You want me to call in some chips?"

Trevor paused for a moment, considering the implications. Over the years, he'd done more than a few favors for those in the higher echelons of the Pentagon. After all, they had needs too. He'd been holding onto the favors owed for something big. But unless he got a handle on this, there might not be a chance to cash those chips in down the road.

"Use them. Call me back when you have something," Trevor ordered.

He disconnected the call and stared at the image on the screen. There was another file attached to the images—a recording from the strip mall. Trevor brought it up and leaned forward. It was dark, so it was tough to make out. He saw his two guys go down, and then the creature leap for the big guy. The big guy held it up while the scientist watched. He'd fired at it at first but quickly realized that wasn't working so he went to plan B—his knife.

Trevor grunted as he paused for a second, realizing that the man was analyzing, trying to figure out the creature's weak spot, before he launched himself at the creature. Seconds later, the creature was dead.

Pausing the image, Trevor zoomed in on the man's face. He looked terrified. But he'd done what he needed to do nonetheless.

Grudgingly, Trevor had to admire that. He also admired the fact that the guy didn't just keep blasting away when it was of no use. That was smart. He wasn't used to seeing smart when it came to dealing with these creatures. Most of the time when they were in the ring, people just started wailing away at them. They didn't pause to figure out what the best approach was.

Of course, if you had one of these creatures racing at you, you might not take the time to figure that out either.

But there was something intriguing about that approach. This guy might be interesting in the ring. Plus, if they could get a hold of this guy, he had a feeling that would help slow things up for these government commandos, whoever they were. They'd be too busy looking for this guy.

Studying the guy's face, Trevor sat back. So this guy was one of the brains behind the operation. If he could figure out a way to target him, then maybe, just maybe, he could slow things down long enough for this last show to run. One last windfall, and then he could retire, or at least hide away for a few years before he came back out again. He smiled. Yeah, that was the approach. That was what he needed to do. Now they just needed to find the guy.

For the next hour, Trevor conducted research of his own. Now that he had a name, it was easier. He grunted reading through the guy's educational record. He really was a brainiac. He even skimmed through some of the guy's publications. He only read the abstracts, but that was enough to convince him that this guy was definitely not a soldier. Soldiers did not use phrases like the "genomic basis of homopolid hybrid speciation."

No, this guy was definitely an egghead. His phone rang, and he picked it up quickly. "What have you got?"

"I think I might have found him. Sending you files now."

Trevor immediately brought up the files on his laptop and scanned them. They were from a Facebook page of someone named Kalel Hadid. Trevor rolled his eyes. Talk about setting your kid up for failure with that name. "What am I looking at?"

"Go to the photos. Look at the most recent ones. They're from a birthday party. Just family. Look at the guy in the back."

He skimmed through the files and noted who Brad was talking about. It was Schorn. Trevor leaned forward. "Where is this? Who's he with?"

"According to public records, this is Greg Schorn's family. Mom, dad, two sisters, husbands, and a few nieces and nephews."

"He keeps in touch with them?" Trevor asked.

"I was able to get into the nephew's texts. It looks like he and his uncle keep in touch pretty regularly."

Trevor smiled. "So we have an address?"

"Almost. I'm still trying to track that down. But worst-case scenario, we follow the kid."

Trevor leaned back in his chair. "Keep an eye on the nephew."

"Electronically or in person?"

"Electronically for now. Let's see how this all plays out. Maybe we won't have to do anything." Trevor paused for a moment. "But otherwise, we go dark. Close things down. We'll let everything settle and see which way the wind is blowing."

# CHAPTER 30

## CLAY, NEW YORK

The office was quiet with four response teams out. Norah had called back the second response team after the notification from Mitch that they'd taken down the subject.

But she was disturbed by the fact that another group had been on site.

She sat at her desk, running through the different government agencies, seeing if any of them might have sent out a separate response team. Government agencies ideally all worked together. But the reality was that, more often than not, they competed with one another for resources.

She knew that more than a few of them liked the idea of these creatures as a way to fight against other countries. Different branches of the military were always looking for the secret serum that was going to magically turn their soldiers into Captain America. If they had a legion of Hanks under their control, they wouldn't have to risk any human lives.

Norah shuddered at the thought of the Pandora's box that would open.

Her job was to make sure that that didn't happen. Her job was to make sure that the powers of these creatures stayed as far away from traditional warfare as humanly possible.

Martin Drummond had created the whole project with the idea that the world was going to, at some point, need to protect itself from alien invaders. He had created the projects under the belief that they would one day be able to be controlled and fight on the behalf of humanity. So far, that hadn't happened. Although she could grudgingly admit that Martin had made some impressive "progress" with the Hanks. They had actually been under Martin's control through some sort of cranial implants.

But by and large, the idea was crazy.

Besides, Norah had seen what they were up against. A couple of super-strong aliens wasn't going to make a dent in the technology that would be arrayed against them. And she prayed that they never needed to rely upon that.

She also knew that she couldn't write off the possibility of an invasion one day. They had only learned about the Council within the last year. And they were still keeping an eye on Earth.

Yet Norah had gotten the distinct impression that it was more than that. She had a feeling that they were also in some ways the guardians of Earth, keeping someone or something from interfering. Which meant that perhaps the people of Earth still had something else that they needed to worry about.

Her computer beeped, drawing her attention back to the topic at hand. It was a file from the analysts. They'd been going through the phones of the men who had been killed at the Hampton home.

A short note was attached: *You need to watch this. We're trying to track the source.*

Frowning, she clicked on the icon. There were a dozen video files. She clicked on the first one. At first, she thought maybe it was a clip from some sci-fi movie.

But the more she watched, the more she realized this was live and horrifying. It was some kind of fight club with Setis. She watched as humans fought Setis, and always lost. And then she watched as Setis were set against other Setis. But the most disturbing part were the humans in attendance. All of their faces were blurred to hide their identities, but she could recognize the wealth in their clothes and jewels.

Her mouth nearly hit the ground, her mind rolling at the threat this posed for U.S. security.

She flipped through the remaining films, long enough to determine that they were the same type of recording and that they had all been made at different locations. Whatever group was responsible for this, they moved around, which was smart.

She flipped to her files from the Hampton case and brought up the autopsy results. She sucked in a breath. Damn it. Greg was right. The creature had serious scarring and evidence of medical interventions.

She flicked a glance back to a still screen of the fight. Humans versus Setis. She didn't need to be a psychic to know how this would end.

She grabbed her phone and dialed quickly. Maxine down in the tech division answered. "Yes, director?"

"You need to put together a team. Your best and brightest. Track down where these transmissions are coming from. We need to find them."

"We've already IDed two of the locations," Maxine said. "The invitations seem to get sent out through the dark web. The invites don't go out until right before the fight."

Stomach tightening as she pictured horrific scenario after

scenario of those creatures breaking free, Norah said, "Find what you can. And get us on that guest list."

# CHAPTER 31

ONE WEEK LATER

LAS VEGAS, NEVADA

T he hallway of the Wynn extended twenty-five feet above Trevor and was another twenty feet wide. He liked the Wynn. He'd stayed at all the big hotels: the Venetian, the Bellagio, Caesars.

But he felt a kinship with the Wynn's founder, Steve Wynn. He was a man who saw what he wanted and went for it. He'd been pushed out due to a bunch of sexual assault allegations, but in Trevor's mind that was more proof that the guy was a go-getter. He didn't let things get in his way. And he'd run the Wynn organization for years, only getting pushed out in his seventies, after decades of debauchery. The man knew how to wield his power.

Yeah, the Wynn was definitely Trevor's kind of place.

Trevor had been in Monte Carlo for three days before Vegas. And Saint Bart's for three days before that. Neither was his kind of place. But he wasn't going there for fun, or at least not only fun. He needed to find new contacts, make new connections. If this was going to be his last show coming up, he needed to make sure it was an incredible haul.

Besides, finding new clients was the part of the job he loved. He thought of himself as a lion roaming among the gazelles, looking for the perfect prey. He spent his time analyzing and researching each target's background—their wants and needs—and then, if suitable, he made his pitch. He had an eighty percent success rate with this approach.

And Monte Carlo was all about the excessively wealthy. People who had money and had had it for generations. They were the ones who were bored with their Ferraris and their palaces. The ones who were looking for something new to make their gilded cages a little bigger. Poor trust-fund babies. All that money and still bored with their lives.

In Monte Carlo, he'd seen one kid who couldn't have been older than nineteen blow a million dollars in just fifteen minutes at a blackjack table. The kid just shrugged and moved on to the baccarat table.

If he'd had a million dollars at nineteen, he would've taken the world by storm. And that little brat was throwing it all away. The kid had the look of someone who'd never done a hard day's work in his life. He was soft, entitled.

That didn't get in the way of business, though. Trevor cozied up to him, and he was now on the list to be invited to the next show.

But Trevor was still debating when to make that happen. The site in New York had been shut down and completely cleaned. And he held off on starting up the Chicago site. After Johansen, Dracmore and the disaster in Vegas, he needed to lay low for a little bit. But so far as his people could tell, no one was the wiser about his company's involvement in the affair.

If he were smart, he'd wait another year until things had really cooled down.

But Trevor missed it. He liked the thrill of putting everything together. The steps he had taken to make sure that he wasn't discovered. He missed the smell of the crowd in the arena when the fear took over and they realized what it was they were actually paying all that money to see. And then he liked the look on all those pampered faces as they realized that he was the one who was showing them something they had never seen before.

He had a site picked out already. He just had to give the go-ahead. He'd had his people quietly put out feelers and make sure that all the other pets they'd rehomed were firmly in their cages. There were only about six across the globe that he'd allowed to be purchased. And so far, all of them remained secure.

In fact, one had even called in to his people and demanded that they take the thing back. He'd charged them three million dollars for the removal.

He smiled. He'd made more money retrieving the thing then he'd gotten for selling the thing. And now he could use the creature in one of the shows. That was easily one of his most lucrative endeavors.

It made him think that maybe he should be selling more of them, if only to get people to sell them back. That was a possibility for down the road. Right now, he needed to make sure that he stayed under the radar. Money was good, but he couldn't spend it if he were locked up.

Or at least, he couldn't spend it the way he wanted to.

So he'd wait and see and then decide whether or not he wanted to expand his in-home services.

He strolled out onto his balcony and took a seat, closing his robe over himself as he did so. Heat fell over him like a blanket. *God, I love Vegas. I love the heat.*

In his mind, he viewed Vegas as an introduction to Hell. People came to indulge in their wildest fantasies. Even some over-the-hill couple from Iowa would find themselves doing things they never imagined they were capable of. He'd brought that out in more than a few people. He liked to be there and watch them as they gave up all their morality and their decency. He didn't partake himself. That wasn't what got him excited.

What got him excited was watching other people drop into their own pits of despair and debauchery. And then he'd follow them the next day to watch the shame as it rolled over their faces.

That was what really got him excited.

He inhaled deeply, imagining the smell of society's moral decay as he sat there. At times like this, he wondered if perhaps he himself was actually a demon sent from Hell to corrupt the lives of those he came across. He smiled at the idea. It didn't seem so far-fetched to him.

A silver dome-shaped cover sat over his breakfast, keeping it warm. When he was younger, that always seemed the epitome of class. He pulled the cover off his breakfast and placed it on the side of the table in front of him, then snapped out his napkin and placed it in his lap.

He'd come a long way from sleeping in alleys in Queens.

Mama would be proud.

He took a bite of the eggs Benedict, the yolks running across the plate. He appreciated every moment of the meal. Unlike others in his field, he knew that everything could disappear at any moment. You couldn't take the little things for granted. So he appreciated the moments like this, when everything was peaceful.

His practice of meditating had really helped with keeping him centered and in the present. At first, he'd balked at it, thinking it was something stupid, entitled jerks did. But he could truly see the benefit. It kept him where he needed to be. It kept him appreciative of what was right in front of him.

And it also made him understand what the possibilities could be.

This latest round of entertainment had been his most successful endeavor yet. At this rate, he would be able to retire comfortably in less than a year. His money right now was already multiplying in a couple of very lucrative investments.

He smiled at the thought. Investments. When had he become that sort of guy?

Nonetheless, the sentiment was accurate. He didn't need the business the way he had back when he first started. In fact, he made more now from investments then he did from his business.

But the business kept him sane. It kept him grounded. It reminded him of who he was. More important, it reminded him he wasn't like those other stuffed shirts. His business was his drug. He knew that. He had no illusions about it.

But he would need to shut down for a little while. Now he just needed to finish with one last, death tinged show that would knock off people's socks. He just needed to take precautions.

One of the biggest issues was the military group that was dogging his steps. He'd finally got a little background on them. They'd been created years ago, after the Area 51 outbreak. The former directors had disappeared. But people that disappeared like that weren't sunning themselves on a beach in Aruba. They were sitting six feet under or had taken a quick trip to the oven before they spent the rest of eternity as specks of dust.

Whoever the new director was, though, had really ramped up security. None of Trevor's contacts had been able to find him any information on the guy.

And Trevor did not like the unknown. When you could put a name on a group, you could predict how they would respond. Right now, he had nothing. It seemed whoever had taken over had cleaned house of all the people who had previously been part of the organization. Which he had to admit sounded like a good plan, if the previous director had been as much of a tool as he seemed to have been.

He respected the approach. But it definitely made his work a lot tougher. He finished up his breakfast and then moved to the edge of the balcony. He wasn't overly worried about some nameless government organization now. There was always a way in. The reason most people didn't succeed in these situations was because when faced with this kind of enemy, they often gave up too early. They thought it was a huge organization, and that they couldn't take on that large a problem.

But Trevor had learned it was never necessary to take on the entire organization. No, you just needed to find one or two individuals within the organization. Once he tapped into those, they would bring down the entire place.

His phone rang, and he smiled as he answered it. "Jerry, how you doing?"

"Hey, good, good. It's been good to get away."

"Where you at these days?" Trevor asked.

"Down in Atlantic City. Been here for a few days. Had a run on the tables last night. It was awesome."

Trevor smiled. He was genuinely happy for Jerry. The guy worked too hard. If anyone deserved a break it was him. "That's good. Real good."

"Yeah, I'm getting bored, though. I wouldn't mind getting back to work," Jerry said, a hopeful tone in his voice.

"Well, then, your lucky streak is continuing, as I do indeed need you to get back to work."

"That's great. I sent you a couple new sites," Jerry said.

"I saw them. I like the Chicago site. What do you think about the security? Will there be any problems?"

"Nah. They didn't know we started in there. No one should know we'd been there. So we should be good," Jerry said.

Excitement rolled through him. This feeling was why he still did this, even though he didn't need to financially. He was a junkie, and this was his drug. "Good. Then let's get back to work."

———

Three weeks later, at his Clearwater home, Trevor's optimism from Las Vegas seemed like it had been a lifetime ago. He didn't like what he was hearing.

Jerry stood in front of his desk with the latest report on the government agency. "So they've found two of the other sites. I mean, there's nothing there. We cleaned up really well. But some people posted some pictures on social media, and they've hauled them in for questioning."

Running his eyes, Trevor shook his head. "Who are they?"

Jerry rattled off some names.

Trevor leaned back in his chair. He didn't know any of them. That was good. Because if he didn't know their names, then they definitely didn't know his. They were probably guests who were brought in. He should have tamped down on that. But it was too late for that now. The plan had been to wait and see. But now they could see way too clearly that the net was closing in.

"How long before they find us?" Trevor asked.

"They're doing a pretty good job of ticking through our locations. It won't be long until they come up with the latest one. We're going to need to go into hiding. I suggest we shut everything down and cut our losses. I think we should scrap the Chicago show."

That was not something that Trevor had ever done before. He'd always figured out a way to make a buck, even when things were falling down around him.

And he wasn't about to change that now.

He turned around his chair and stood up, walking to the window to look out at the Gulf. But he supposed if Jerry was right, this would be one of the last times he saw this place for a while.

He'd planned on staying here until he moved to the Chicago site. He did have a place down in Mexico, though, that looked over the Gulf too.

But it wasn't quite the same. Trevor wasn't really a fan of Mexican food either. He supposed he could make it work for a while just to lay low.

But they had so much inventory. He could destroy all of it, true. What a waste of money, though.

Plus, his guys had spent so much time tracking the things down, it seemed like an insult to them. He debated while watching the waves gently wash up on the rocks. He spoke without turning around. "How long do you think until they find us?"

"I'd say a week, tops," Jerry replied.

Nodding, Trevor made the calculations in his head. That would place him right on the last day or two of the exhibit. And once that last exhibit was done, well, then there wouldn't really be anything left to lose. He had already been planning on that being the last show. All the exhibits would be killed, as was standard practice. If he could just make it until then, he could have one last payday before he had to pull up stakes.

And it would be quite a payday. He might even let the audience watch the destruction of the subjects.

He mulled it over, imagining the crowd and the response. Yeah, that could work. In fact, maybe he could even set up some sort of auction for the crowd to determine *how* he killed the subjects. That could definitely bring in some cash.

In fact, if he played it right, it could end up being his biggest payday ever.

But none of that was going to happen if the feds got to him

before the last night. Which meant he needed a way to slow them down. He needed to give them something else to focus on or something to distract them.

Or maybe even a couple of somethings.

"What about that scientist guy? Have you got anything on him?"

Jerry's eyes lit up. "Actually, yeah. They just caught something this morning. It looks like the nephew is going to visit him. He's somewhere in upstate New York."

Trevor turned back around to look at Jerry with a smile. "I've got an idea. If this is going to be our last show for a while, let's make sure we go out with a bang."

# CHAPTER 32

## CLAY, NEW YORK

T he smell of smoke drifted into Greg's consciousness. His head jerked up, his mouth falling open as he noticed the white smoke coming from the oven.

"Oh, crap."

He tumbled out of his chair at the kitchen table and hustled over to the oven. Grabbing the oven mitts, he yanked open the oven door. Smoke poured out.

"Crap, crap, crap." He reached in and pulled out the baking sheet, placing it on top of the stove before turning the oven off.

With a grunt, he threw the oven mitts on the counter and walked over and opened the window. Waving the smoke toward the window, he glanced up at the fire alarm which remained silent. *Guess I need to change the batteries.*

On the counter, the black lumps that were supposed to be chocolate chip cookies still smoked. He sighed. *Damn it. I really wanted some cookies.*

Kal was coming over for the weekend. He had some sort of

school event in town, and his mother had agreed that he could stay with Greg for the weekend.

At first, Greg had been resistant to the idea of Kal coming over. But things had been really quiet at work lately. It had been a month since they'd run into that other team. And in that time, Greg had gone on two other missions. So life had been pretty normal. He'd even been sleeping at the office a few nights a week with Pugsley, who he really could swear was getting less slimy. He'd even dropped a note to the lab to see if they noticed but hadn't heard back yet.

So when Kal mentioned being in Syracuse only twenty minutes south of Greg, Greg had agreed to let him stay with him. Now he was surprised at how excited he was to have his nephew over. It had gotten him thinking about when they were younger. Kal's favorite cookies were chocolate chip, and Greg thought it would be nice if they had some this weekend.

But he'd lain down on the couch for just a minute after putting the cookies in the oven and now his attempts at home baking were a charred mess.

Smoke still hung in the air. He went into the bedroom and got a fan, then tried blowing the smoke toward the open window. Ugh. This was not the impression he wanted to make. He headed out of the kitchen and started pulling open all the windows in the apartment. By the time he was done, there was still a scent of smoke in the air, but it was definitely not as noticeable. Of course, now the temperature in the apartment had dropped.

But worse, he was still hungry. Luckily, he'd also bought a backup of ready-made cookie dough. Hopefully, he and Kal would be able to bake some after dinner and not start a small fire.

It was still hard to believe that his nephew was actually coming over. He'd been shocked to get the text from him. But he'd been downright flabbergasted that his sister had allowed him to come. He supposed she was just happy that he'd finally agreed to major in accounting, and that Greg had helped.

Greg shuddered at the idea.

That wasn't the most shocking news that Kal conveyed to him: His sister had somehow miraculously agreed to allow Kal to take the internship this summer with Greg. He supposed this weekend was a trial run to see how it would go.

He still had his own misgivings about Kal and the internship. It had nothing to do with Kal's interest in the biological side of life and had everything to do with the subject matter of Greg's work.

Of course, that cat was already out of the bag after the incident in Greenwich. And it's not like he could go back in time and change things.

He sighed as he made his way back to the kitchen and grabbed the oven mitts, picking up the tray and scraping the remains of the cookies into the garbage can. He'd been thinking a lot about his life and where else he could have ended up. If Maeve hadn't mentioned that she was working for the government, maybe Greg would never have looked into it. But working with Maeve, having that friendship, it had meant the world to him. It still meant the world to him. She was more his family than his actual family was. And he wouldn't trade that for anything.

But he also knew how dangerous his work could be. He'd already lost count of the amount of times he'd been in a life-threatening situation. And honestly, he'd almost grown immune to them.

Almost.

Could he really invite Kal into that world? It was true that he and Kal were very similar. They were both the black sheep in their family. Although, he wasn't sure if when there were two, they could technically still be considered the black sheep. And he did have to admit that Kal had handled the situation in Greenwich much better than Greg could have ever imagined. He remembered how impressed Norah had been and smiled.

Dumping the baking sheet in the sink, he sighed and ran cold water over it. Turning off the water, he glanced at the clock. Kal would be here in another fifteen minutes or so.

There was a scratch of movement by the door. Greg frowned. Was Kal early? He could picture him standing on the front step, not wanting to ring the bell before he was expected. That would be just like him.

A smile spreading across his face, Greg walked down the hall to the front door. He was looking forward to this weekend. They were going to have a video game marathon tonight. Tomorrow, the latest Marvel movie release was on the agenda. And there would be lots and lots of junk food.

He hadn't actually had a weekend off like this in, well, probably about three months. And that time, all he'd done was laze about the apartment by himself. It would be nice to actually have someone to do stuff with. He just wanted this to be a nice, normal weekend.

Greg's steps slowed as he reached the front door as a small blue shape appeared oozing under the door. "No, no, no, no, no."

Pugsley slid his way under the front door and stood blinking at Greg before letting out a little chirp and bolting over to him, leaving a small trail of slime in his wake.

# CHAPTER 33

**T**wo arms emerged from Pugsley's chest as he scooted over to Greg. He wrapped his pudgy little arms around Greg's leg with a little hum.

Greg groaned. "What are you doing here?"

Pugsley let out a happy little chirp in response.

Greg ran a hand over his face. Oh, this wasn't good. He'd snuck Pugsley home with him three nights last week because he'd felt bad for the little guy being stuck at the base on his own. The other nights he'd spent on the base, and it had been nicer having him here. But he most definitely had not brought him home today.

And how was he going to hide him now? He certainly didn't have time to take him back to the lab before Kal showed up. He could tell Norah, but Pugsley getting out of the building was a pretty big deal. He'd have to tell her eventually, but what about Kal?

*Oh, God, this is not good.* He reached down and picked up Pugsley, noting that he was even less slimy than the last time. Progress.

"Okay, little buddy, here's the deal. My nephew is coming

to town, and he cannot see you. So you need to just hide, okay?"

Pugsley blinked at him in response. Greg groaned again, realizing this was going to be an absolute disaster. The sound of a car engine came from outside.

Greg hustled over to the window, pulling back the curtain. Kal sat behind the wheel and reached into the back seat.

*Oh crap. Oh crap. Oh crap.* Greg hustled down the hall to his room and placed Pugsley in the small plastic basket with the waterproof pad that he'd picked up for him. Then he crouched down in front of him. "Okay. You need to stay here. Don't make a sound. Don't come out."

Pugsley chirped, blinking his bright eyes.

*Oh, this is so not good.* He stood, and as he straightened, his shirt stuck to his chest. A glance down indicated the problem: it was completely covered in slime from where he'd touched Pugsley. Apparently less slime was still enough slime to ruin a shirt.

He yanked it off and quickly grabbed another one from the closet without looking. Throwing it on, he hurried back down the hall. The doorbell rang out just as he reached the front hallway. He stopped, took a breath, and then opened the door.

Kal grinned, a duffel bag held in his hand. "Hey, Uncle Greg."

Greg hugged him tight. "Kal. It's so good to see you. Come in, come in."

Kal stepped inside, looking around the apartment. As he did, he slipped a little in Pugsley's slime trail. "Uh, this is cool."

His tone suggested it was anything but. And for the first time, Greg looked at his apartment with new eyes and cringed inwardly.

Interior design wasn't really his thing. It never had been. Maeve had been the only reason he did anything with his college dorm room. But being she was in Norway, this apartment had not received any of her extra touches. It had come furnished. He figured that meant less work for him. It was perfectly serviceable furniture with blonde wood frames and tough pale-gray fabric. But the furniture looked like rejects from a 1980s dorm.

The living room was on the right, the kitchen straight ahead, two bedrooms down the hall to the left, as well as a workout room and another two bathrooms.

Greg shrugged. "Sorry, I don't spend a lot of time here, so I haven't really done much with the place."

"No biggie," Kal said. "Hey, I saw there's a Comic-Con in Syracuse this weekend. Maybe we can go and get a couple of prints for your wall."

His walls could use a little personality. "Actually, that sounds good. Maybe we can do it before the movie tomorrow."

"Sounds like a plan. Where should I put my stuff?"

Greg waved toward the hallway that led to the bedrooms. "Uh, second door on the left is yours for the weekend. I'm going to, uh, go, uh, see what's in the fridge."

He turned and started for the kitchen.

"Uncle Greg?"

A tremor ran through Kal's voice. Greg winced as he turned slowly, closing his eyes, not wanting to see what he knew had caused the change in Kal's tone.

But he could only keep his eyes closed for so long. He squinted through his lids, and sure enough, Pugsley stood in the middle of the hallway, blinking at the two of them.

# CHAPTER 34

**T**error, shock, maybe even Kal running screaming from the apartment, those were all responses Greg was prepared for.

Yet Kal expressed none of those. Instead, just as he had at the site in Greenwich, he took Pugsley's presence in stride. Tilting his head, he stared at the little blob of alien. "Uh, what is that?"

"Still working on that one. I call him Pugsley."

"Is he safe?"

"Um, yeah. He's not toxic or aggressive. He's just kind of slimy. And *he's not supposed to be here*," Greg said, directing his last words to Pugsley.

"Do you think he'd be upset if I took a closer look?"

"No, actually, he'd probably like it."

Moving slowly, Kal lowered himself to the ground to get a better look. He lay flat on his stomach.

Pugsley stood in front of him, not backing away, blinking his large eyes and turning his head this way and that.

"Has he always been this color?" Kal asked.

That was an interesting question. And it was something

Greg had just noticed in the last week when he was looking back at pictures from when Pugsley was first brought in. "No, actually, he was more translucent when I first found him. At the time, he was taking care of a nursing mom and her pups. The mom's leg was broken, so we think Pugsley here was bringing in food for her."

"Huh. So he's a compassionate guy."

He'd never really thought about it that way. "Huh, actually, he is. He has a habit of finding me whenever I'm on base. He can get out of absolutely any container he's put in."

Kal grinned. "That's pretty awesome. And you said you don't know what he is?"

"They've been running tests, but his DNA is unusual. They haven't been able to pin it down yet. Partly because it literally runs off the slide before they can test it."

"Do you think ... I mean, would he be okay if I touched him?"

"Yeah. Just be warned, your hand will come away pretty soggy."

Holding his breath, Kal reached out with one hand first, placing it in front of Pugsley like one would for a dog. Pugsley leaned forward, blinked at it, and then looked up at him. Kal leaned forward a little bit more before reaching out and touching Pugsley's stomach. Pugsley blinked twice and then let out a little chirp.

Kal snatched his hand back, backing up quickly.

Greg chuckled. "Actually, that's a good sound. It's the way he communicates."

Pugsley wobbled a few inches closer to Kal, and Kal reached his hand out again. Pugsley leaned his head into it and gave a little sigh.

"That is so cool." Kal's grin was ear to ear. He looked up at Greg. "You said he used to be, like, translucent?"

Greg pictured him from those first few days. He'd seen

Pugsley practically every day since, so it was hard to note the changes. But the images had made it clear. "Yeah, you could practically see right through him."

Tilting his head as he studied him, Kal said, "I wonder if he's developing into something else, aging, for lack of a better term."

Yet again, a great observation. Maybe Kal *was* cut out for this. "We were thinking the same thing. That he's going through some fast stage of development. We don't know what he's going to turn into. I just hope he doesn't change much by way of personality."

And that was something that did have Greg worried. Baby lion cubs were adorable. Grown-up lions, not so much. So Greg really hoped that whatever Pugsley was turning into, he was going to at least retain his sweetness.

If he didn't, Greg wasn't sure what they were going to do. They couldn't contain him, which meant there would be only one option left available to them: destroy him.

And Greg really hoped it didn't come to that. The little guy was really starting to grow on him. It was kind of nice that whenever he got to the office, Pugsley tracked him down. They were still trying to figure out how he knew Greg was there. Apparently, when Greg wasn't at the office, he didn't go roaming the halls looking for him. But Pugsley had no nose, so it definitely wasn't scent. They were leaning more toward some sort of telepathic intuition that was guiding him.

Greg wondered if maybe that intuition also worked with types of people. Kind of like how dogs seemed to be able to sense whether someone was good or evil. He wondered if Pugsley had the same ability. There'd obviously been no way to discern that, at least not yet.

He paused, wondering if maybe he should have had Alvie meet Pugsley. Maybe Alvie could have told them something about Pugsley's communication abilities. He pulled out his phone and dashed off a request to Norah to see what she thought about maybe getting Alvie back over here to talk to Pugsley. Sammy or Ariana should be able to bring him over and then return him the same day.

His gut tightened when he thought of Ariana. He hadn't heard from her. He wasn't sure if she had gone off on another mission or had gone back to see her mom. She had pretty much cut off all communication.

He tried not to let that hurt, but it did. He could understand if she didn't want to get romantically involved, and it wasn't like they had actually taken that step. But he did kind of think she needed some friends. She was going through a lot, and there wouldn't be a lot of people that she could talk to about it.

He shoved his phone back into his pocket along with his concerns about Ariana. That was not for today. Today was all about spending time with Kal.

And Greg was really looking forward to it. He clapped his hands together, rubbing them. "Well, I'm hungry. How about if we raid the fridge and then begin the *Halo* marathon?"

Kal grinned. Standing up. "Can Pugsley join us?"

Greg shrugged, flicking a glance at Pugsley, who looked up at him with those big blinking eyes. "Sure, why not? Besides, I don't think he's going to give us a choice."

# CHAPTER 35

The raiding of the fridge had been very short. Greg opened up the door to find only condiments, the extra tube of cookie dough, and one half-gallon container of expired milk. Kal leaned over the door and shook his head. "I'm guessing you don't eat here a lot?"

Greg closed the door. "I've been kind of busy at the office. I stay there sometimes now because I don't like Pugsley being on his own. How about if we go on a food run? Pizza, potato chips. We'll stock up and then just hunker down."

"Ice cream?" Kal asked.

The question reminded Greg of when Kal had been little and the two of them had gone to the ice cream store every single time Greg had come into town. Greg grinned. "Of course ice cream."

Twenty minutes later, Greg dropped Kal off at the pizza place while he headed to the supermarket. They figured if they split up, it would be a better use of their time.

Greg had left Pugsley in the waterproof dog bed in his bedroom with the door closed. He had no hopes that Pugsley would actually stay in the bedroom, but he hoped he would at least stay in the apartment.

Norah was really not going to be happy if she learned that Pugsley was there, so he'd sat him down and told him to wait and that they would be right back.

He'd felt like an idiot having the conversation. He had no idea if Pugsley understood anything he was saying, but he didn't know what else to do.

Greg parked and hustled into the supermarket. He grabbed a cart and quickly filled it with potato chips, diet soda for him, and regular for Kal, who didn't yet have to worry about calories. Then he swung through the ice cream aisle and grabbed two gallons of Rocky Road along with a container of mint chocolate chip. He was back outside in about twenty minutes and heading back to the pizza place.

He pulled up in front and texted Kal: *I'm outside.*

Kal's response came back quickly: *They're running a little behind. It'll be a few more minutes.*

*No problem.* Greg shifted to his email app and started going through the security procedures to get in. Five minutes later, he was finally able to flick through his inbox to see if there was anything immediate that needed his attention and hoping there wasn't. For the first time in a long time, he really didn't want to do work. He just wanted to relax and enjoy the time with Kal.

This was probably going to be the best weekend he'd had in a long time.

# CHAPTER 36

The scent of freshly baked pizza seemed to permeate every surface in the pizza place. Kal loved the smell of it. Although he had to admit he was a little worried about what upstate New York pizza was like. Not that Greenwich had a monopoly on phenomenal pizza or anything, but he'd heard that once you got outside of the New York metropolitan area, pizza standards went decidedly downhill.

His Uncle Greg had assured him though that this place was actually pretty good. And Kal had to admit that the pizzas he saw being pulled from the oven did look delicious. His stomach rumbled in response. Plus, the place was pretty busy, which he always took as a good sign.

"Number forty-seven."

Kal bounced up and headed to the counter. The bald guy behind it nodded at him and pushed four pies toward him. Kal had figured he should order an extra few, that way they'd have leftovers throughout the weekend. "Have a good one," the guy said.

The pies smelled so good. Kal grabbed them from the counter with a grin and headed for the door. "Yeah, you too."

He backed out of the door clutching the pizza boxes, the warmth heating his arms. He scanned the parking lot and saw his uncle had parked toward the back, away from all the other cars. The pizza boxes were really hot. He kept shifting his hold to avoid burning his fingertips as he waited for a slow-moving Chrysler to pass.

An older couple sat in the front seat. They were only going about ten miles an hour. The driver was leaning forward with thick glasses as he watched the road.

Not that he was the world's best driver, but Kal didn't think that guy should be driving anymore. But eventually, the car passed. He took a step off the curve as a van pulled into the end of the parking lot with a squeal of tires. Kal frowned, pausing to watch it.

It was a white van with no windows, and it was moving awfully fast. He and his friends had always joked that those were "child abduction vans." Probably not the most sensitive thing to say.

Kal's heart rate ticked up, expecting to see the car crash or flip. It was really moving way too fast for a parking lot.

A few other people had stopped what they were doing to watch the van as well.

The van made a left, barreling down the lane of the parking lot. Now everybody seemed to have stopped to watch where the van was headed.

Looking between the van and his uncle's car, a feeling of dread rolled over Kal. The van was aimed right for it.

He took another step forward as a car honked at him. An SUV he hadn't noticed drove toward him. Kal stepped back quickly to avoid getting hit. By the time the SUV had passed, the van was almost at Greg's car. It slammed to a stop. The side door slid open. Three men in dark clothing and masks jumped out, guns in their hands. Kal dropped the pizzas and started to run.

One of the men used the butt of his gun to break the driver's-side window.

A yell came from inside the car, and then his uncle was dragged out through the window.

Greg turned and slammed his fist into the guy's face, but then another one slammed the end of his pistol into the back of Greg's head, and he slumped forward. Two of the guys dragged him over to the van and threw him in. In a flash, they jumped in behind him. The van tore off in the same reckless way it had entered the parking lot.

The entire attack had taken just seconds.

Kal stumbled to a stop, just staring before his mind kicked into gear and he pulled out his phone and started to take video. The van was already at the far end of the lot, but hopefully someone would be able to get a license plate off it. And then it pulled out onto the street, made a right, and with another left, it was completely out of Kal's view.

# CHAPTER 37

**B**right-yellow police tape cordoned off Greg's car. Two cop cars stood with their lights shining across the parking lot. Another two cop cars were parked near the pizza place. A group of witnesses was lined up to provide their names and statements.

Norah pulled into the parking lot with Mitch behind the wheel. Mitch's face was stony, his knuckles taut as he gripped the steering wheel. She'd gotten the call about Greg ten minutes ago.

Kal had called the department to let them know what had happened. She was impressed he'd figured out how to call the department. He'd actually contacted the Pentagon and told them he had an emergency for the D.E.A.D. and used Greg's name. The call had immediately been transferred to her. Kal's voice had been frantic as he explained that Greg had been abducted from a parking lot.

On the way over, Norah had contacted the D.E.A.D. response team to get them assembled. She didn't know what was coming, but she knew she needed to have a team ready to go as soon as she had a location on Greg.

Her gut clenched. God, someone had *taken* Greg. She'd met Greg when she'd met Maeve, Alvie and the rest of the gang. At first, she had thought he was just an extremely geeky guy. And he was, but he was so much more than that. He was a genuinely good guy, and incredibly smart. And he might not get the job done in the way that some others would, but he did always get it done. And he was the last one who deserved something like this to happen to him.

Mitch pulled to a stop. Norah had the door open before he put the car in park. She strode across the parking lot, pulling her badge as one of the officers tried to wave her away. "Norah Tidwell, Department of Defense. We're taking over the scene."

The officer's mouth fell open as he looked from the badge to Norah's face. "DoD? What are you guys doing here?"

"I'm afraid that's classified. I need to have all of your reports, all your evidence, any video. I need everything and I need it now."

The evidence turned out to be very little. Kal had managed to record the van leaving the parking lot, but zooming in revealed that the license plate had mud caked over it. Norah knew from experience they wouldn't get anything from that.

None of the angles of the parking lot's cameras provided any additional information that would help. And all of the men had been fully covered, right down to gloves.

Mitch walked over from where he'd been on the phone after Norah finished speaking with the sergeant who was having his people canvass the area for any additional security cameras or cell phone that might have caught something. "Anything?"

Norah shook her head. "Nothing."

It had been over an hour since Greg had been taken. In an hour's time, those guys could be just about anywhere. They could practically be in Canada.

She had a bird up in the air searching the area, but that was a desperate attempt. They had no real direction to go in.

"How's Kal?"

Kal sat in Mitch and Norah's SUV. Mitch had grabbed him as soon as they arrived. He looked devastated. Mitch shook his head. "He's blaming himself. He saw the van come into the parking lot and thinks he should have been able to warn Greg."

It was a useless feeling, guilt over something like that, but all too common. Norah stood up to go talk to him when her earpiece came to life.

"Director Tidwell, it's *Pegasus Two*." Pegasus was the name of one of the chopper units.

Norah clicked on her mic. "Go for Tidwell."

"We've got a white van on fire. It's about two miles from your location."

Norah's eyes flew to Mitch's. His jaw tightened. He couldn't hear what was being reported to her, but he could definitely interpret her face. "Is fire on scene?"

"No. They're on their way, but the entire vehicle is consumed."

Norah nodded. They had probably dumped the van. "Okay. Send me the location."

She stood up and nodded toward Kal. "We need to get him back to Greg's apartment." She paused. "Strike that. Let's bring him back to base. We're going to have to go through Greg's apartment to see if there's anything there. They found the van. It looks like they torched it."

"I see."

And those two words were enough that Norah knew he did indeed see. The van was the only clue they had to Greg. And if the van turned out to be the one that had taken Greg, then they had absolutely nothing.

# CHAPTER 38

Leaving Kal in the care of the Clay Police Department until a unit arrived form the D.E.A.D., Norah and Mitch hightailed it to the scene of the van fire. By the time they got there, the fire had been extinguished. Smoke still wafted up from the remains of the vehicle, which was little more now than a metal skeleton.

"An accelerant had to have been used for it to burn that quickly," Mitch said as he steered them over the uneven ground.

Not replying, Norah took a deep breath, trying to prepare herself for whatever they were about to learn. But she knew in her gut their one link to Greg's abduction had quite literally gone up in smoke.

By the time Mitch pulled them to a stop, Norah had her emotions back in check. Without a word to Mitch, she climbed from the car. A fire official walked over to them, his hands up. "I'm sorry, folks. This is a closed scene."

Norah held up her badge again. "Norah Tidwell, DoD. We need to know what you've got."

The man flicked a glance at Norah's ID with a frown. "DoD? The Department of Defense?"

Slipping her badge back in her jacket pocket, Norah nodded. "Yup."

"Why on earth are you interested in a van fire?"

"I'm afraid that's classified. Can you tell me what you've got?"

"Uh, yeah, I'm, uh, Chief Willis. Um, sorry, you guys threw me a little bit. Wasn't expecting any feds out here. Okay, anyway, it's definitely arson. I can smell the chemicals they used as an accelerant. It'll take a few days to identify it through the lab."

"We'll need a sample," Norah said.

"Any chance we can get fingerprints or anything off the van itself?" Mitch asked as he joined them.

The man shook his head. "Doubtful. The thing was burned to the frame. It's possible you might be able to get an ID from the body in the back, but you'll need dental records for that."

Norah went still, her heart beginning to pound. "Body?"

The man nodded, not seeming to notice Norah's response. "Yeah. Can't even tell if it's a guy or a girl. Body's burnt beyond recognition."

A tingling began at the edges of Norah's fingers. She rolled her hands into fists, taking a deep breath. Then she took another one. *Greg.*

Next to her, Mitch sucked in a breath as well.

Norah licked her lips and then swallowed hard, trying to get the spots that appeared around the edges of her vision to go away. She felt like she was walking at the end of a very long tunnel. "We're, um … We're going to need, uh, to take everything from the scene, um, whatever you have."

The fire chief shrugged. "Fine with me. There's not much that—"

"Chief!" one of the firefighters called from over by the van.

The chief glanced over his shoulder and then looked back at Norah. "Excuse me for a minute." The man hurried away.

Now the tingling was in her knees as they began to shake. She locked her legs, trying to keep herself upright. There was a body in the van.

It couldn't be Greg. He'd been alive just an hour ago.

But she knew it could be him. What were the chances in this sleepy little town that a body showed up in a van just like the one that had grabbed Greg, and it wasn't him?

"We don't know anything yet," Mitch said quietly.

But Norah could hear the doubt in his voice. They were both hoping that they were wrong. In her mind, she ran through his medical file and knew that they had the dental records back at the base. If it was Greg, they would be able to get a quick identification.

*Oh God, then I have to tell Maeve.* Her stomach caved in at the thought. Greg and Maeve were so tight. Then she'd have to tell Iggy and Alvie, and the list went on.

As she watched the fire chief, the thoughts of everything she had to do rolled through her head.

The fire chief was talking quietly with two firefighters who held something in a small bag.

The chief nodded, then grabbed the bag and walked back toward Norah.

Norah's gaze stayed on the bag as he approached—it was a wallet. The chief turned the bag around. The wallet was open and the driver's license could be seen through the plastic. "This might help with your ID. It was found next to the van. The name on the license is Greg Schorn."

# CHAPTER 39

The lounge in the D.E.A.D. headquarters was situated on the third floor. It was a large room with a pale speckled-ivory tiled floor. Two couches faced each other along the left-hand wall with a commercial rug and a metal coffee table between them. Blue cabinets with a wooden counter sat along the back wall, flanked by a large stainless-steel fridge on one side and a stove and microwave unit on the other. Six round dark-gray tables with four matching chairs were arranged to the right of the door.

The counter contained a row of cereals in plastic containers. Chips were in bags in the counter. Kal's stomach rumbled as he paced by them, but at the same time, the thought of food made him sick to his stomach. He had been starving before he and Greg had gone to get the pizza, but now he wasn't hungry at all. In fact, his stomach felt like it had been hollowed out.

He couldn't get the images of Greg being yanked from the car out of his mind.

*I should call someone. Do something.* For the umpteenth time, the thoughts rolled through his mind. But he couldn't do either. The two agents who had brought him here stood outside the door. And they had confiscated his phone, so he couldn't even call his mom and tell her what had happened.

Even if he had his phone, would he be allowed to tell anyone? He had no doubt that what happened to his uncle was related to his work. And his work was most definitely classified. Would he have to lie to his family about it? Would he have to say that he was on some sort of work trip when he knew that was most definitely not the truth? How could he do that?

And what if they never found him? Was he supposed to perpetually say that Uncle Greg was on a business trip?

Head in his hands, he sank into a chair at one of the tables. He should have done something. He should've moved faster. He should have called out to his uncle and warned him. He should have sprinted across the parking lot and helped him. But all he'd done was watch.

His head jerked up as he thought about Pugsley. *Oh God, poor Pugsley.* Who was going to take care of him now? From what Greg said, Pugsley was really only attached to him.

A glance at his watch indicated that it had been over two hours since his uncle had been grabbed. How much longer were they going to hold him here? Had they found something? Would they even tell him if they did?

The lounge wasn't a horrible place, but nevertheless, he was sick of being here. And if he had to wait, he'd rather hang back at his uncle's apartment with Pugsley.

He walked over to the door and pulled it open. The agents had gotten chairs and glanced over at him. "Everything okay?" one of them asked.

"Look, I want to go back to my uncle's place. Can you call someone and see if that can happen?"

The agent at the door nodded. "I'll give the director a call. See what she says."

Kal nodded his thanks and then sat back at the table to wait. Because it looked like that was all he was going to be able to do.

# CHAPTER 40

As soon as the body could be extracted safely from the wreckage, Norah had it transferred over to the base. She hadn't watched it being pulled from the van. She knew it was cowardly, but she just couldn't do it.

Mitch drove quietly behind the van that held the remains back to the headquarters. Neither of them spoke. What was there to say?

Norah prayed that the body in the van wasn't Greg. But the chances were high that it was.

She didn't know what she was going to do if it was. Greg was the heart and soul of the D.E.A.D. He was what made sure it wasn't what it used to be. He brought a sort of humor to the place that had been sorely missing before. And he brought humanity to the cases. It wasn't just Pugsley that Greg had saved. There had been innumerable cases where Greg had stepped between the acquisition team and the target. Greg could read these creatures like no one else.

And he wasn't just some crazy Pollyanna type, always looking on the bright side. Greg knew better than anyone on those teams just how dangerous these creatures could be. He had more experience with them than all of them combined. And yet, it hadn't hardened him against the potential for good.

The D.E.A.D. needed people like that. Norah needed people like that. Greg had been her respite from all the responsibilities of being the director. He had been her sounding board. He had also had her back whenever the teams pushed back, wanting free reign to take down subjects however they wanted.

Norah knew how easy it was to get caught up in a mission and let doing the right thing fall by the wayside in exchange for efficiency. The former D.E.A.D. director had done exactly that. Martin had made sure that when they acquired a target, they went after it not to study or capture, but always to kill.

Greg had a completely different approach.

Of course, Greg hadn't been the first one to introduce her to that way of doing things. Iggy had done that. How different her life would have been if she had simply followed orders rather than her gut. A chill ran through her every time she thought about if she had simply followed orders and pulled the trigger when she'd first met Iggy. What a loss that would have been for everyone, but most especially for her.

"We're here," Mitch said quietly.

Norah's head jerked up. She hadn't realized that they'd made it back to base. Mitch even had the car in park. She shook her head. "Got a little lost there."

Mitch looked down at her, his dark eyes somber. "We don't know it's him."

Norah looked back at him, her hand on the door. "Don't we?"

Mitch's response team stood outside waiting. When the van stopped, they walked to the back and pulled out the stretcher. Norah noted the watery sheen to Max and Kaylee's eyes, along with a few others. Security guards held the door open as the team escorted the body through.

The office was quiet, as it was Friday afternoon. But everyone on duty lined the hall. Norah and Mitch walked behind the stretcher, and she couldn't help but think that this all felt like a funeral procession. There was a catch in Norah's throat at the sign of respect. Greg really had touched all of them.

They made their way to the right hall. Two gowned members of the medical team stood waiting. The response team handed the stretcher off to them and then stood outside the door. They would wait there until they got word.

Norah stared at the doors, which continued to swing. She waited until the doors stilled, and then turned and headed for her office.

Mitch fell in step next to her. "What do you need?"

"I need everything. I want all traffic cams. I want all information of border crossings. I want all cell phone videos. Find anything and everything that was recording this afternoon. We're going through all of it. Somebody has to have seen that van before it was torched. Somebody had to have seen where whoever was in it went."

"I'll go light a fire under some people." Mitch peeled off at the next cross hallway while Norah continued on to her office. She nodded at the agent she passed but didn't stop. She stepped past her reception desk. Tracy wasn't there. She left early today to go out of town for the weekend with her boyfriend.

Norah would have to call in a temp.

But she'd get to that in a minute. Stepping into her office, she closed the door behind her. The she leaned against the door and wrapped her arms around her waist. "Please, God, don't let it be Greg."

# CHAPTER 41

They wouldn't let Kal go back to his uncle's apartment, but they did tell him they'd ordered him some food. Which was good, because he was hungry again. But he felt guilty for even thinking about himself and eating while all this was going on.

An agent walked in with two pizza boxes and a six-pack of soda. He smiled at Kal. "Hey, Kal. Remember me? Mitch?"

His face was familiar, but it took him a moment to place him. Then it came to him. He was one of the agents he'd met back in Connecticut. Kal nodded. "You drove us back to my grandparents' house."

Mitch placed the boxes on the table. "That I did. I heard you weren't able to get some dinner, so I thought I'd bring some in."

Although Kal's stomach rumbled noticeably, he shook his head. "I don't want any."

Mitch eyed him and then sighed as he took a seat. "I know you think it's wrong to do anything for yourself right now. But the truth is, you need to keep up your strength. You don't know what's coming in the days ahead. And from experience,

205

I can tell you: You need to eat and you need to sleep when you can. So take a slice." He flipped open the box and grabbed one himself.

Kal was hungry. But he couldn't shake the guilty feeling about eating while Uncle Greg was missing. But Mitch had no doubt been through this kind of thing before. Kal hesitated.

Mitch nodded toward the box. "Eat, Kal. Starving yourself won't help anything."

Kal held fast for a moment but then pulled out a chair across from the agent. Mitch placed a slice on a plate and pushed it toward him along with a soda.

The two of them sat and just ate without talking but Kal studied Mitch. He was obviously a soldier. He had those arms that showed off muscle even without flexing. He was probably in his mid-thirties. His shirt was pulled tight across his shoulders, although Kal doubted it was because he was trying to show off. He bet he just had trouble finding shirts that fit.

After finishing off his first slice, Kal wiped the sides of his mouth with a napkin and grabbed a second slice. "So, are you, uh, in the military?"

Mitch inclined his head. "Used to be. Special Operations capabilities specialist with the Marine Corps. I joined up with the DoD after I retired three years ago. I've been with the D.E.A.D. for about a year now. I've worked with your uncle most of that time."

"You said my uncle's done a lot of great things. That he saved a lot of people."

Mitch wiped his hands with some napkins. "That he has. Can't tell you the stories, unfortunately. They're all classified. In fact, some of them I can't even get access to myself. But I like to do my research when I find out I'm going to be working with someone.

The soldier paused. "Your uncle, his appearance is deceiving. I mean, don't get me wrong, he's a strong guy. In fact, from the pictures I've seen, he's put on a lot of muscle in the last couple of years. But he's more of a thinker than a fighter. I thought that would be a liability for us when we went out in the field, but I don't know, there's something about Greg. He's good to have around in a difficult situation. In fact, he just saved my life not that long ago. Not only does he accomplish what he sets out to do, he does it in a way that ... well, that keeps your morals intact. I've been very lucky to work with him. He's a good man. And he's gotten out of some pretty bad scrapes. So if there's a chance that someone could get out of this, it's Greg."

Kal felt comforted by Mitch's words, but he also knew that that wasn't all there was to it. He leaned forward. "I heard they found a body."

Mitch's gaze darted to his, and he nodded, not looking away. "Yes. But here's the thing, Kal, that body was burned beyond recognition. And yet, your uncle's wallet lay perfectly untouched *next* to the van." Mitch fell silent, his gaze still on Kal.

"You think they want us to believe it was my uncle?"

The soldier shrugged. "I can't say that for sure. They're running tests right now. But it was kind of sloppy. I mean, why would Greg's wallet be outside the van? And if they were just going to kill him, why not do that in the parking lot? Wasn't he unconscious when you last saw him?"

Kal nodded.

The big man shrugged again. "Like I said, I could be wrong, and I don't want to get your hopes up, but something seems a little fishy. Until we know for sure, I, for one, am going to hold out hope."

Studying the soldier across from him, a kernel of hope took root. Then he reached for another slice of pizza, suddenly feeling famished.

# CHAPTER 42

## MANTENO, ILLINOIS

One of Greg's neighbors was playing a heavy drumbeat. It pounded into his skull, forcing him to open his eyes.

That was when he realized there was no neighbor playing some Metallica marathon next door. The thumping was coming from inside his own skull. He lay on an old soiled mattress on the floor of a room in desperate need of a paint job, a cleaning, and maybe a demolition. He sat up slowly, wincing as the movement sent more pain through his skull.

He reached up and gently probed the back of his head, then yanked his hand away at the pain that erupted as he touched the goose-sized egg now on the back of his skull. He stared around the room for a minute, trying to figure out where exactly he was. The walls were a strange institutional green and peeling. The roof was also peeling, but that was white, which was broken up by water stains that were varying shades of brown. The floor itself was covered in old tile with some unknown substances caked in the corners.

There was one window, which had old metal bars on it. He stood up, swaying for a moment as the world shifted out of focus.

When the world righted itself again, he walked over to the window and leaned his hand against the windowsill. There was nothing to see. Just an unkempt lawn and a forest slowly trying to overtake it. There were no cars, no people, no nothing. He leaned forward, looking down. It looked like he was at least four stories up. High enough that going out the window would get him at least a broken leg if not a broken neck.

Staring out the window, he tried to figure out what had happened. He remembered being yanked from his car. He'd been knocked out by a blow to the back of his head, but consciousness returned as they loaded him onto a plane.

Bound and gagged, there was nothing he could do but let them treat him like a piece of luggage as they placed him in the back of the plane. He'd tried to stay awake, with some vague idea that if he kept track of how long it took him to get somewhere, it would help. But the droning and vibrating of the plane was as good as a sleeping pill.

It wasn't until they landed that he'd fully woken up. Not that there had been much to see at that point either. It was still bright out when he'd been shoved in the back of an SUV, and no one spoke for the forty-minute drive. He'd been unable to look out the windows in the SUV. When they arrived, someone threw a bag over his head. He hadn't seen anything as they carried him up some stairs and tossed him in this room, thankfully without restraints. He'd yanked the hood off in time to see the door close. Then nothing.

No one interrogated him. No one checked on him. Nothing. He heard people walking by, so he knew he wasn't alone, but no one opened the door. Eventually, he fell asleep.

He slumped back against the wall, not wanting to sit back down on the mattress. He wasn't sure how old the thing was, but he was pretty sure he'd gotten at least three viruses just by lying on it.

The incident in the parking lot flashed back through his mind. He'd been checking emails while waiting for Kal to get out of the pizza place. He hadn't even noticed the guy until his window had shattered in a hail of glass.

Before he knew it, he was being dragged out of the window, and then someone slammed something into the back of his head.

He let out a sigh, slinking down to the floor. At least this jail cell was better than the one he'd woken up in at the Draco holding facility. That one had been as charming as a dungeon.

This place at least had "abandoned hospital" as a theme instead. Which you would think wouldn't be an improvement, but at least it was relatively dry. He had no doubt that was because it hadn't rained in a while and not because someone had gone ahead and fixed the roof.

But still, all things considered, it was a step up.

However, with the Draco abduction, he at least knew who had grabbed him. Right now, he had absolutely no idea. In fact, a leftover branch of the Draco seemed to be the most likely suspect, although the Draco were supposed to have all been killed when the asteroid hit their base.

Yet Greg seriously doubted that. The Draco had been spread throughout the societies of the world. They had their tentacles—no pun intended—in all of the government pies. He knew that there were at least a few who were wandering around, not including, of course, Adam and his adopted son, Sebastian. They were also Draco, except they were good ones.

Greg's stomach rumbled, reminding him again that he hadn't eaten in a while. A glance at his watch showed that it had been close to eight hours. Which, of course, brought him back to thinking about the pizza that he hadn't had a chance to taste. Which led him to wondering about Kal. He hoped that

Kal hadn't seen him get grabbed. That kid didn't need that in his memory bank.

Of course, if he didn't see him get grabbed, then it was going to take a lot longer for someone to figure out where he was. He and Maeve had joked one night that they should lo-jack him. He had laughed it off, but now he realized that if he ever got out of this, he was going to insist that he get lo-jacked. This was one too many abductions for him to be comfortable with it.

The door opened, and a jittery guy in his late twenties stepped in. Greg had never seen him before, and he was pretty sure he wasn't a Draco or working with one. They wouldn't put up with someone with such peculiarities. The Draco had a habit of weeding out anybody who had any weaknesses, like, for example, kindness.

The jittery guy stepped in with a brown paper bag in his hand. "Oh, he-hey, you're awake. That's good, that's good. Boss man will be happy to hear it."

He placed the bag on the mattress and then straightened. "Uh, I didn't know what you'd like, so I just kind of grabbed you some fast food. I hope that's okay."

Greg's stomach rumbled in response. He knew that if he were one of those tough guys in movies, he'd toss the bag across the room, grab the guy, push him up against the wall, and demand that he let him out, or maybe just throw him out the window.

But Greg had never been that guy. "Uh, what kind of fast food?"

"Uh, I got you a cheeseburger with all the works and a side of fries. Oh, and there's a bottle of water in there too."

"Uh, ketchup?"

The man's face fell. "Oh, no. Hold on, man, I'll be right back." He disappeared back out the door.

Greg followed and opened the door. A man the size of a wall stood there. He looked down at Greg.

Taking a short step back, Greg gave him a nervous smile. "Oh, hey, um, do you have the ketchup?"

The man shook his head and then grabbed the handle and shut the door firmly.

Greg's shoulders slumped. Apparently he wasn't going to be able to just walk out of here.

He walked over to the bed and grabbed the bag, opening it up. The burger smelled delicious. He knew he should be suspicious and worry about there being drugs or something in it, but honestly he was so hungry, he didn't care. Besides, if they wanted to drug him, they could either feed it to him or strap him down and throw a needle in his arm. He'd rather just eat the hamburger.

Mindlessly, he grabbed a couple of fries and chewed them while wondering what exactly all this was about. He'd finished the fries by the time the jittery guy was back. He walked over and handed Greg four ketchup packets. "Will that be enough?"

Greg had to admit for a captor, he was awfully friendly. "Uh, yeah, thanks."

"Hey, no problem, no problem."

"You got a name?" Greg asked.

"Uh, yeah, um, Neil."

"Well, Neil, thanks for the food. I appreciate it."

Neil nodded. "You know, you got to keep your strength up."

His appetite dimming, Greg looked up at him. "Keep my strength up? For what?" He asked slowly.

The smile Neil gave him in return was full of warmth. "Oh, for the fights. You're the opening act."

# CHAPTER 43

## CLAY, NEW YORK

The phone sat on the desk, silent, although it was still warm. Norah had been on the phone for the last hour, calling and speaking to everyone she thought could be of help. She had unhesitatingly made all of those calls, but no one had been able to offer her any hope of finding Greg.

Now there was one more call she needed to make, and yet she couldn't quite get her hand to reach for the receiver. She pushed herself back from the desk and stretched her back. She hadn't called yet because she figured she really had nothing to say. They didn't have confirmation yet that it was Greg, so she was waiting on that.

Her phone beeped. She grabbed it, reading the text. *Dental records do not match.*

A grin broke across her face. But the happiness quickly faded. It might not be Greg in that van, but he was still missing. And they still had no idea where he was. So far, none of her people had been able to offer any help. But she knew someone who probably could. She grabbed the phone and dialed quickly. Maeve answered almost as fast. "Hello?"

"Maeve, it's Norah."

"Oh, hey. How's it going? I was just going to call you. I was thinking maybe you could come over for a visit. Maybe you and Iggy. I think that Claude is getting a little lonely."

Claude was another Maldek that they had uncovered last year when they were trying to prevent the Council from destroying the world. He had been around for decades, ever since the Rendlesham Forest Incident. He'd been found by a man that lived near RAF Bentwaters. And he and Iggy, after a not-so-great introduction, had become really close. "I'll see what I can figure out. But there's something else I need your help with. Well, you and Alvie."

Maeve's voice became serious. "What's wrong?"

Norah took a deep breath. "Greg's missing."

"Missing? What do you mean missing?"

Norah quickly ran through the incident in the parking lot.

Maeve was quiet for a moment and then spoke quickly. "Give me five minutes." She hung up the phone.

Norah stared at it with a frown. *Okay, that was weird.* She dialed the lab and got confirmation that the dental records definitely weren't Greg's. The individual who had been burned appeared to have been much older, according to the coroner's report. They would try and see if they could figure out who it was, but they weren't hopeful that they'd be able to figure that out anytime soon.

Hanging up the phone, Norah frowned not sure that the identity of the individual in the van was going to help. She had a feeling the body was just being used to throw them off Greg's trail. The dropping of the wallet was way too obvious. But that still left them back at square one. She reached for the phone again when a boom sounded from outside, the windows in her office rattling.

Norah's head jerked up, and her mouth fell open. *She didn't.* Norah hustled out of her office as a second boom sounded.

Running down the hall, she noted the alarm on the faces of the guards, their hands reaching for their weapons. "Stand down!" Norah yelled as she ran past everybody. "Stand down!"

She sprinted for the door, and the guards held it open for her. She headed outside and made her way around the side of the building.

The building was all glass on the exterior, although it looked black from the outside.

A parking lot and long driveway were out front. Around back were the barracks for some of the security staff, as well as a motor pool. Beyond that, a few hundred yards away, was the runway and hangars that held the D.E.A.D.'s two jets and a chopper. The entire facility sat on two hundred acres, surrounded by an electrified fence.

Norah and Greg lived at one of the two apartment complexes on site. No one got on base without authorization. And drones, along with electronic security and human security, constantly patrolled. It was a secure location.

But that didn't stop Norah's heart from pounding as she rounded the building and caught sight of a woman with long brown hair pulled back into a ponytail striding across the field.

Another boom sounded. Norah's eyes jerked up to the sky. Sammy's skin was a deep maroon as he flew down next to Maeve his large leather wings extended. With a nod at Norah, he carefully placed Alvie on the ground before he darted back into the air and disappeared with another sonic boom.

Norah shook her head as she looked between Maeve and Alvie. "Seriously? You guys couldn't give me a bit of a heads-up so I could make sure there weren't too many prying eyes looking out the windows?"

Maeve continued toward her. "Alvie's already been here, and everybody within eyeball distance is sworn to secrecy. Also it seems like time is of the essence. So, what do you need us to do?"

As Norah looked between the two of them, she warred between annoyance and hope. She thought for a moment about reminding them about the security protocols they had all agreed to. But Maeve had made protecting Alvie her life's mission. She wouldn't unnecessarily risk him. And she was right. Time was of the essence.

Deciding, therefore, to focus on hope, Norah turned her gaze to Alvie. "Alvie, I need you to find Greg."

# CHAPTER 44

The pizza was good, and Mitch had been pretty good company, too. He seemed like a decent guy. Kal could see why his uncle liked him.

Then Mitch got a call and had to leave. The soldier managed to get Kal permission to go hang out in his uncle's office. Kal figured that would be a better place to wait than down in some nondescript lounge.

He walked Kal to the door. The two shadows keeping Kal company stayed with them at a safe distance.

Mitch smiled as he ended his call. "It wasn't Greg. Your uncle's still out there somewhere."

Kal stared at him. "Seriously?"

"Seriously." Mitch replied as he cast a glance back at the guards, but they were too far away to hear. Nevertheless, he lowered his voice. "Now we just need to find him."

That the body wasn't his uncle's was good, really good. But Kal wasn't exactly ready to celebrate. "Yeah, but isn't there something about needing to find someone within the first hour or else the chances go down dramatically?"

Raising his eyebrows, Mitch asked, "What did I tell you

about your uncle? He's been through a lot more than most soldiers. Don't count him out until you absolutely have to."

Kal knew that was just a line. It was just something that people said. Even so, it did actually make him feel better.

Opening the door to Greg's office, Mitch nodded toward the back. "That cabinet in the back. The tall one with the doors?"

Spying it in the back corner, Kal nodded. "Yeah?"

"That's where your uncle's junk food stash is. And I'm pretty sure there's at least a Nintendo DS in there. So that should help you pass the time a little easier."

Kal grinned. "Thanks."

Mitch extended his hand.

Surprise flashed through Kal. Not a lot of people shook his hand. That was more something for adults, and he was still well, not one, no matter that he was already eighteen. But he shook it and looked Mitch in the eye.

"I'll let you know when we find something," Mitch promised.

Kal stepped into the office, and Mitch closed the door behind him.

He paused for a second to take a look around. Greg's desk was over to the left, pushed up against the wall. It was a long gray desk with a large monitor on it. There were no files or paperwork, except for a single handwritten note pinned to the wall behind the desk.

He walked over and peered at it. *H.A.L.T. Help! Alien Life is Terrifying!* had been scribbled on a piece of paper with red Sharpie. There was even a little alien with sharp teeth and antennae drawn in the corner. Kal grinned.

He turned around and took in the couch on the right-hand side of the office with a pillow and a blanket on it. His uncle had mentioned that he sometimes slept here to keep Pugsley company.

*Pugsley!* He was still back at the apartment. Or at least Kal hoped he was still back at the apartment.

And what if his uncle didn't return? What was Pugsley going to do? Was there someone here who would take care of him? Kal doubted they would, at least not the way his uncle had.

Walking over to the couch, he sank down. He grabbed the blanket and lay his head on the pillow. Then he stared up at the ceiling. He needed to call his mom. But he couldn't tell his mom anything. He couldn't tell anybody anything.

So this was what life had been like for his uncle for the last few years. No wonder he barely came around family. It had only been a few hours, and already Kal was struggling not to reach for a phone. The temptation to talk to someone about all this was huge.

He replayed the scene again, his uncle getting dragged from the car unconscious. When his uncle had told him about the internship, Kal had jumped at the chance. Even the situation in Greenwich, he had taken in stride. After all, nothing bad had actually happened, at least to him.

But now Greg was missing. And Kal was worried.

Heck, he was more than worried. He was terrified. What if that was the last time he saw Greg? And what if Greg's job was what caused his death? Did Kal really want to join this world?

He was intrigued by it. That was true. And Pugsley, man, Pugsley was incredible. Just picturing that little guy made his heart pound and his mind whirl. He wanted to try to figure out what he was and what he was capable of. His uncle mentioned something about some sort of protective expansion, whatever that was. Kal was intrigued, but was learning about these things really worth the danger?

Obviously for his uncle, the answer was yes. And Mitch was right. His uncle had seen a lot more than even he had.

In fact, earlier, his uncle had let slip a comment about the moon, saying it was a pretty amazing place. For anyone else, that would have been just kind of a blow-off comment.

But there was something about the way his uncle said it. It was with the confidence of someone who'd gotten a really close look.

Kal shook his head and closed his eyes, suddenly feeling exhausted. He felt guilt for a moment at the idea of taking a nap. But then he remembered what Mitch said about taking the time when you could get it. So he closed his eyes. And even though he hadn't prayed since he was a little kid, he found himself making up his own informal prayer.

*Dear God, please help my uncle.*

# CHAPTER 45

The dream was strange. A man walked toward him. His boots made a strange squishing sound on the hallway floor. Kal stared at the man, unable to move away. The squishing got louder as he approached. The man stopped in front of him. "Do you want your pizza or not?"

Kal's eyes flew open, his breath coming out a little jagged. What the heck was that?

He rubbed his hands over his face and stared at the unfamiliar surroundings before it came back to him. He was in his uncle's office.

A small cooing sounded from the end of the couch. He leaned up slowly and caught sight of Pugsley curled up at his feet.

His mouth dropped open. *Where the heck did he come from?*

He looked back at the door, trying to figure out how Pugsley had gotten in. His uncle had said something about Pugsley being able get out of any container, but still, they had to be a pretty good distance from his uncle's apartment.

There was a shiny slime trail from the door to the couch.

Greg had mentioned that Pugsley left that trail wherever he went.

Placing his feet on the floor, Kal sat up quietly and tried not to disturb the little guy. But Pugsley must have felt the movement. His eyes blinked wide up at Kal.

Kal smiled. "Hey, buddy. Looking for my uncle?"

Pugsley gave one of his little chirps.

A heavy weight settled on Kal's chest at the thought of Greg. He replayed the abduction again in his mind. Tears pressed against his eyes. "He's not here. We don't know where he is."

The little alien let out another little sound.

There was a knock at the door. Kal's gaze flew to it and then back to Pugsley. "Just a minute."

Mind and heart racing, his gaze scanned the room. Oh God. Quickly he leaned down to Pugsley. "Do not move."

He threw the blanket over him and then the pillow for good measure before he hustled across the room. He glanced back at the couch and then yanked the door open.

Norah stood there. "Hey, Kal, how you doing?"

He self-consciously wiped at the sides of his mouth, not sure if he had drooled while sleeping. "Good, I mean okay. How are you? Any news on my uncle?

"Maybe. I wanted to let you know that we're heading out to check a possible location. I'm going to have Sparrow and Hinckley stay here with you, and they'll relate to you any information as we get it. Okay?"

Norah started to turn.

Kal darted forward. "Wait. Let me go with you."

Turning back to him, Norah shook her head, although there was understanding in her eyes. "No Kal. You're not trained for this. You are not ready in the slightest. Let us handle it. Okay? If your uncle is there, we'll get him back."

There was no doubt that they were better trained for this.

Kal had taken Tae Kwon Do for one week when he was thir-teen and had dropped out after nearly breaking his neck trying for a high kick. So he knew she was right, but he also knew in his gut that he needed to go.

"No, Norah. I mean, Director, he's my uncle. And I need to go. Don't you think Greg is going to be worried about me? He'll want to talk to me as soon as you find him."

Crossing her arms over her chest, she raised her eyebrows. "We'll make sure that he calls."

Kal's mind whirled. "Well, if I'm stuck here, I don't know what I'm going to do. I guess I'll just have to call my family."

Norah's eyes narrowed. "Is that a threat?"

Man, she was scary. He wanted to take a step back but managed to restrain the urge. "Not a threat. But I'm sure that Greg doesn't want the rest of the family to know about all of this. And I don't want the rest of the family to know about all of this, but if I'm stuck here on my own, with no one to talk to …"

The director's mouth became a firm line. She stared at Kal for a long moment. And Kal imagined that she was playing through a variety of different scenarios on how to keep him quiet. He hoped she did not take any of those options.

"Fine. But you will be attached to Mitch. You do not *leave* his side. Do you understand?"

Kal nodded. "Yup. Uh, yes, ma'am, yes. Great."

"We leave in five. Be ready, or you are getting left behind."

Norah turned and strode away. Kal closed the door and slumped against it. What on earth had he been thinking? He just basically blackmailed the head of a secret government agency. He was lucky she didn't shoot him.

He pushed off against the door. But she hadn't. And now he was going. The blankets on the couch stirred, and then Pugsley slid down onto the floor, his body flat before reforming into his usual shape. Kal watched, amazed. So he could change the shape of his body, kind of like slime he'd made as a kid. That was really cool.

Then his mouth fell open. What the heck was he going to do with Pugsley? What if Pugsley went to go look for his uncle? He was pretty sure Pugsley being in the middle of a mall was not going to be a good idea. And he couldn't let him get caught.

He hurried back to the cabinet in the back of the office and flung it open. He snatched a backpack and then emptied it out. Grabbing a couple of his uncle's snacks, he threw them in the front pocket.

He rolled up an already-opened bag of potato chips and stuffed it in the side pocket. Then he walked over and knelt down in front of Pugsley. "Okay, buddy, here's what we're going to do. But you're going to need to be really, really quiet."

# CHAPTER 46

Five minutes later, there was a knock on the door. Kal only had time to use the bathroom, throw water on his face, and stash Pugsley in the backpack. He carefully picked up the bag and secured it on his shoulders. "Now stay quiet, little buddy, or we are both in serious trouble," he whispered.

Pugsley didn't say anything in response, and Kal took that as a good sign. He hurried across the office and pulled open the door.

Mitch stood waiting for him. "So I hear you managed to wrangle an invitation to this little shindig."

Feeling his cheeks heat up, Kal nodded. "Yeah. I know I shouldn't, but I just think that my uncle would want me to be there."

Grunting, Mitch shook his head. "Pretty sure your uncle would *not* want you to be there. But I'm also pretty sure this is exactly what your uncle would have done." Not waiting for Kal, Mitch started walking down the hall.

Breaking into a jog to catch up, Kal had to seriously

lengthen his stride to keep up with him. The guy was really fast and tall.

"Okay. Rules," Mitch said. "You are my shadow. Where I go, you go. I go to the bathroom, you go to the bathroom. I sit up, you sit up. I lie down, you lie down. I step right, you step right. Whatever I do, you do. Whatever I tell you to do, you do."

Pausing, Mitch eyed him and the bag on his shoulder. "What's with the backpack?"

Kal tried to keep his voice even. "Nothing. I mean, I just, I brought some snacks. I'm kind of hungry, and I wasn't sure what there would be on the plane."

"Well, it's a military transport, so there won't be any snacks. And it will be incredibly loud and really uncomfortable." The agent flicked a glance at him.

Kal quickly nodded back. "Loud and uncomfortable. Got it."

Despite Mitch's description and his worry for Greg, there was a little thrill in the back of his mind. A military transport. He'd seen them in movies, and now he was actually going to be able to ride in one.

Movement down the hall caused him to turn. He frowned. He could have sworn he just saw a little gray bald kid. He shook his head. *Nah.*

"Come on. Let's get moving." Mitch hustled down the hall. Mitch was a good couple of inches taller than Kal, which was pretty amazing. Kal didn't meet many people taller than him. With Mitch walking at a fast pace, Kal practically had to jog to keep up with him.

They hustled through the main entrance, and there was a truck idling by the curb. Mitch climbed into the back. Kal quickly followed. There was a group of eight people, all dressed completely in black, just like Mitch was. The towering agent took a seat, and Kal quickly sat next to him. As soon as he did, one of his shadows shut the tailgate behind him and then banged on it twice.

The truck took off. Kal had to grip his seat to keep from getting thrown to the floor.

Mitch nodded at the others in the back of the truck. "Everybody, this is Kal. He's Greg's nephew. Let's not get him killed."

Kal swallowed. *Well, that wasn't intimidating.*

It was a short drive to the airfield. It took five minutes tops. And during that time, Kal studied each of the people that were sitting in the back of the truck. Mitch explained they were a strike force and that they regularly worked with his uncle. The guy and the woman that he'd seen in Greenwich gave him a nod of recognition. The others he'd never seen before, but everybody looked tough. And he noticed that they were all fully armed.

Normally, a group of eight fully armed people would make him incredibly nervous. But right now, he liked the look of it. Each of these people seemed hard and focused. And they were all going to look for his uncle. It made him feel better about the chances for his uncle to survive.

The truck pulled to a halt, and Mitch reached over the tailgate and opened it up. "Everybody out."

Kal grabbed onto the handle on the side of the truck and then jumped down, gaping at a large plane idling on the runway. The rest of the team walked over to a Humvee and started grabbing crates.

But Mitch headed straight for the plane and walked up the ramp. Kal hustled right behind him.

Norah stood with her arms crossed, waiting at the top. She nodded at Mitch, who stepped farther into the plane. "Kal, your nondisclosure agreement is still in effect. So if you say anything about anything you see or anything you experience, you and your family will be sued, if not imprisoned. Is that understood?"

Swallowing nervously, Kal nodded. "Yeah. Understood."

"Good." She gestured to a jump seat.

Kal slid his backpack off his shoulders as he sat down. Carefully, he placed the backpack on the ground, trapping it between his legs, before he pulled the straps on quickly and efficiently.

Norah leaned down and tightened the straps . "Listen, if anything happens to you, your uncle will be devastated. So you do everything you need to do to stay safe. You glue yourself to Mitch. Do you understand me?"

Her eyes were like lasers focused directly on him. His mouth didn't seem to be working, so he simply jerked his head down.

Norah wasn't done, though. She leaned forward a little more. "And I'm not kidding about that nondisclosure. You are Greg's nephew, and he loves you. That is the only reason you are here. But I will throw you into the deepest, darkest hole if I think that you're even contemplating revealing anything that you have seen. Do you understand me?"

The laser eyes remained, and he knew she was not kidding. She was dead serious. And he realized just how much trouble he could have gotten into with his earlier attempt at blackmail. He nodded quickly, managing to get a few words to stumble past his lips. "Yes. Yes, ma'am."

Norah straightened. "Good. Now that you understand the risks, you can meet the rest of the team." She let out a whistle.

Running feet sounded on the plane ramp as something barreled up it. It landed at the top of the ramp, did a flip, and then landed next to Norah.

Kal's mouth fell open as he stared at the little creature. He had large ears with just a little tuft of white hair in between them and bright green skin. It was like a little ninja Yoda, except it had lobster claw hands. Kal could swear it was also wearing red Mickey Mouse shorts, complete with straps.

Norah nodded down at the creature who rubbed against her leg. "This is Iggy. He'll be traveling with us."

"What is he?" Kal asked.

"He's a Maldek. They were native to Mars. He's pretty good in a fight. And he loves your uncle. So he should be helpful."

Iggy leaned forward, but he wasn't looking at Kal. He glanced down at the bag and then tilted his head.

Holding his breath, Kal prayed that Pugsley didn't say anything. And that Iggy didn't say anything. But what were the chances the Yoda-like guy could—

"Ig?"

Kal's jaw nearly hit his chest. "He speaks?"

Norah shrugged. "He only says 'Ig.' I'm beginning to understand what some of them mean, but not all. Iggy, this is Greg's nephew. Look out for him, okay?"

The little alien looked up into Kal's face and then nodded. "Ig."

Norah nodded toward the cockpit. "I need to go check on some things, but the rest of the crew will be up momentarily. Just don't freak out, okay?"

*Well, that wasn't ominous.* But Kal nodded nevertheless. "Yeah, sure. Thanks."

Norah headed up the plane as more people started to pour up the ramp. Iggy hurried after her, jumping along the seats.

A woman with dark-brown hair pulled back into a ponytail stepped onto the plane. Unlike the rest of the people who boarded, she didn't look like a soldier. For one thing, she wasn't dressed like one. She was wearing jeans, hiking boots, and a purple fleece.

She scanned the plane, her eyes locked on Kal. She walked straight toward him. "Kal?"

He nodded.

She smiled. "Hey, I'm Maeve. I'm a friend of your uncle's."

Maeve. His uncle had mentioned her a lot. They were good friends. Really good friends. "Hi. He's talked about you. I didn't realize you were still here. I thought he said you didn't work for the same agency anymore."

Maeve took a seat next to him. "I don't. But when I heard about Greg, I had to come back to help." She paused. "Norah explained to you about the unusual nature of some of the people on the team, correct?"

Nodding, Kal flicked a glance down at the backpack and then down the plane where Iggy had disappeared following Norah. "Yeah. I met Iggy."

"He's pretty great," Maeve said. "But he's not the only one on the team."

She nodded down the plane. And once again, Kal felt his reality shift. A Gray walked onto the plane.

Growing up, he'd read all about the Grays, aliens that often abducted humans for experiments. They had disproportionately large, wide heads. Immense black eyes with no white visible, a small mouth and just two holes for nostrils. This Gray was shorter than how he'd imagined them, standing at only about four feet. And he wore a pair of jeans, hiking boots, and a striped green-and-blue T-shirt with a navy blue fleece wrapped around his waist. He also had a maroon backpack on his back. The Gray walked toward Maeve and Kal.

"That's Alvie," Maeve said.

The name stirred a recognition in him. "Alvie. My uncle's mentioned him, although he didn't tell me everything, obviously. He said he's like some super computer genius, right?"

Maeve inclined her head. "Among other things."

The gray walked over and stopped right in front of Kal. His dark eyes looked into Kal's as he held his breath.

Maeve smiled. "Kal, I'd like you to meet Alvie. Alvie, this is Greg's nephew."

A strange feeling floated over him. It was like he was

seeing a long-lost friend for the first time. Friendship and warmth flowed toward him from this strange creature. He sucked in a breath. "What was that?"

"Alvie doesn't vocalize," Maeve explained. "He communicates telepathically. He's letting you know that he's a friend and that he'll do whatever he can to get Greg back."

Alvie moved to sit next to Maeve. And Kal couldn't help but stare at the obvious alien.

These were the people that his uncle worked with on a regular basis. Holy cow.

Now he understood it. He got the risks and why his uncle was willing to take them. Because here he was, sitting on a military plane, and within a short distance were three separate aliens.

Yeah, this job was definitely worth the risk.

# CHAPTER 47

During the plane ride, Norah spent her time reviewing the different places where Greg might have been taken. They didn't have a lot to go on. It had taken Alvie ninety minutes to track down a link that got them in the air. Financial records had gotten them nowhere, but cell phone records had.

With Penny's help from Norway, Alvie had found one cell number that had been used in three of the known sites for the fights. There was no name associated with the cell, but it had been tracked to a small town called Manteno in Illinois before it was shut off. It was a long shot that the people they were looking for were still there, but Norah literally had nothing else to go on.

But they were working on the idea that it had to be a relatively big operation to have grabbed Greg and gotten him out of the area so quickly. That wasn't just a mom-and-pop situation. This was someone with resources.

When they landed, it was going to be a manpower operation. Norah had two other teams coming in to help shortly and another six that should arrive in a few hours. Once they hit the ground, Norah would break them up into groups so that they could examine each of the sites.

Sadly, there weren't any satellite feeds that would help them out in that regard. The DoD had gotten a little squirrely about them utilizing satellites for their cases. So unless it was a world-ending problem, they were disinclined to allow the usage.

Norah knew that she could get around that with Alvie or even Penny's help, but she really didn't want to go down that road just yet. Doing so would set off a red flag somewhere. Her program was being watched incredibly closely. So if she utilized a satellite, it needed to be for more than just a fishing expedition. In all likelihood, they wouldn't find anything at any of these sites, although Norah was hoping one would eventually lead to Greg.

So she'd put boots on the ground and see what they could find. And if there was any inkling that Greg might be at one of the sites, then she'd see what resources she had to call up.

Currently, she had a list of ten different sites that she could send people to. She glanced at her watch. The landing gear should be lowering soon; they would be on the ground in less than thirty minutes. Greg had been missing for five hours.

Her gut clenched at the thought of what he might be going through. It wasn't the first time Greg had been grabbed. And if they got him out of this, it would probably not be the last. She just prayed that the good luck that had seen him through so far would continue.

Maeve unstrapped herself from her seat next to Kal and walked down the plane toward her. She took a seat next to Norah, who nodded back toward Kal. "What do you think?"

"I think he's a lot like Greg," Maeve said. "Smart, a little clumsy, somewhat neurotic. And I can tell he's really worried about his uncle."

Norah had a feeling that the teen was a lot like his uncle,

too, which was the only reason that she had allowed him to come on this trip. It had most definitely not been his half-baked attempt at blackmail. Greg had an annoying habit of stumbling in and figuring things out. She hoped that maybe Kal had a little bit of that genetic code in his programming as well.

"What does Alvie think?" Norah asked.

"He thinks that Kal can be trusted. He also thinks that Greg is still alive," Maeve said.

Norah turned her head quickly toward Maeve. "Did he find something?"

Maeve shook her head. "No, no, sorry. Not like that. He thinks that there's an eighty-two percent chance that this is related to the Johansen case. If the Johansen case is related to the online fight club, the chances go up to ninety-eight percent. And if that's what's going on, he thinks that they're going to use Greg in one of the shows."

Norah agreed with Alvie that his abduction was related to the Johansen case. Right now, that was one of Greg's only open cases. Most of his other cases were quick grabs from a sighting. The Johansen case was the only true mystery. Plus, whoever was running those fighting rings obviously had the resources to make something like this happen.

Alvie's idea that it was also related to the group that appeared in Vegas was surprising but shouldn't have been. Alvie was still trying to fine-tune the location. Her analysts had been trying, without success, to get an invite to the online fight. But they would keep trying.

Norah's stomach bottomed out at the idea of Greg being even near of one of those fights. "As bait?"

Maeve's face was drawn. "He thinks he's going to be one of the opponents. According to Alvie, these guys are efficient, and they utilize resources well. Greg will be a resource. And as a result, they'll use him as part of the show. He might be a warmup. He might be a practice round. But he's another ..." Maeve paused before she continued. "Another body to throw at the situation."

Norah's head dropped as she shook it. "Greg's not a fighter," she said softly.

"No," Maeve agreed just as softly. "He's not. But he is resourceful. So let's just hope he figures something out to keep himself safe until we can get there."

"Do you think that's likely? That he'll be able to keep himself alive until we manage to arrive?"

Her eyes troubled, Maeve shrugged. "I don't know. But I hope so."

# CHAPTER 48

itch had been right about the plane ride. It was really uncomfortable. How did they make soldiers fly in these things overseas? Kal had only been in the plane for a couple of hours, and his back was aching. Maybe he needed to work out more. Maybe it was all that extra muscle strength that soldiers had that kept them from feeling bruised every time the plane hit an air pocket.

Maeve was over talking with Norah, and every once in a while, they'd glance over at him. It was making Kal feel a little self-conscious. But he supposed there wasn't much he could do about that.

He felt movement next to him and looked over in surprise as Alvie took Maeve's seat.

Maeve had explained that Alvie was actually half human, half Gray. She didn't explain where he had come from, but Kal got the impression that the two of them had an extremely close relationship, almost like mother and son or brother and sister. But definitely some sort of familial relationship.

The little gray had spent almost the entire trip on his

laptop. It was pretty amazing to watch. His focus was incredible.

But now the laptop was closed and placed in his backpack. And Alvie was pulling the straps on in Maeve's seat as if he was planning on staying a while.

Nerves rolled through Kal as he stared at the little guy. He didn't think he was dangerous, but he didn't really know what the protocol here was. Was there some sort of special greeting he was supposed to do? Something like the Vulcan greeting? He balled his hands into fists, suddenly unsure what to do with them. What if he insulted him by flashing the wrong hand signal?

Well, here goes nothing. "Um, hi," Kal said.

*Hi.*

The word appeared in Kal's mind, and his eyes grew large as his mouth fell open yet again. If he kept this up, he might as well just keep his mouth open, it was falling open so often. Maeve had mentioned that Alvie could speak telepathically, but this was the first time that Kal had experienced it. He grinned. "That's so cool."

*Be careful. Greg wants you safe.* Alvie's dark eyes stared into him. He didn't blink as often as humans did. It was a little unnerving.

But he did get the sense of worry coming from him. He didn't take the warning as an insult or an affront, just a genuine concern. "I will. I'll stay with Mitch."

Mitch grunted from the seat on his other side. "Damn right you will."

Kal ignored him. Alvie nodded toward the backpack at his feet. *Keep him with you. He'll keep you safe.*

Stunned, Kal looked into Alvie's eyes and then quickly glanced around. He dropped his voice, hoping that the sound of the plane would keep Mitch from hearing him. "You know about him?"

*He will keep you safe. He will help find Greg. Keep him with you.* Alvie's lips didn't move, but Kal heard him perfectly, at least in his mind.

His mouth dropped open again, and he quickly shot a glance at Mitch, but he wasn't looking at them at all. Kal turned to stare at the hybrid. Only Kal heard that, he was sure of it. He wanted to say something more, but the plane went into a deeper descent, and the engines roared, making conversation pretty much impossible.

Alvie knew about Pugsley. He was pretty sure that Iggy had known about him as well. Wow. That was awesome.

It was possible Alvie had just kind of sensed he was there, but when no one was looking, Kal had made a point of slipping some snacks into the bag. He made it look as if he was just wiping off his hands, but in actuality, he was making sure that Pugsley had something to eat.

He was also a little worried about Pugsley going to the bathroom in his bag. He wasn't sure exactly how he did that, but so far, everything seemed to be all right.

The plane touched down a few minutes later. Kal held on to his straps, keeping the backpack carefully between his legs. He let out a breath when they finally stopped.

Mitch undid his straps as the ramp at the back of the plane began to lower. "All right, kid. We're going to meet in the hangar and go over the plans."

Kal shook out his legs. He'd tensed them for the descent, worried Pugsley would go rolling across the plane.

Mitch stood up and stretched. "I'm going to hit the head, you good?"

"Uh, yeah. Do I really have to go with you?"

Mitch grinned. "Nah. Debra here will shoot you for me if you try to go anywhere."

Debra winked from the seat across the way.

Kal smiled nervously, hoping that both of them were kidding. He undid his straps and stood up.

Alvie did the same and then reached up and took his hand. It was warm to the touch. *Stay safe. See you soon.* Then Alvie released his hand and walked toward the ramp.

Awe flitted through Kal as he watched Alvie walk away. He was a Gray, an actual Gray. And Kal had been speaking with him.

*And he's not the only alien. I've still got one stashed away in my bag.* He carefully reached down and picked up his backpack, securing it to his shoulder. One plane ride, and he'd met two new aliens while carrying a third. He wondered if there was any way the rest of this trip could possibly get any stranger.

But then his smile slid from his face as he remembered why he was here. And Alvie's worry. And he thought maybe they might need a few more aliens, preferably some bigger ones.

# CHAPTER 49

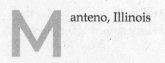anteno, Illinois

The team disembarked from the plane and met in the hangar next to the airfield. Norah had already had an advance team secure the entire private airfield. All other traffic was being held at bay to make sure no one spotted Alvie or Iggy.

Now Norah scanned the group in front of her. She'd brought in two response teams, for a total of sixteen people. She had another two on standby if she needed them, as well as another dozen agents to secure the site.

And then, of course, there was Maeve, Alvie, Iggy, and Kal.

The only wild card was Kal. But so far, he had responded pretty well. Meeting Iggy and Alvie were the tests on the plane. But just like back in Greenwich, he'd taken it in stride.

And Alvie had given his seal of approval. So it looked like, at least for right now, Kal was on the team, although Norah had no intention of sending him anywhere that was even slightly dangerous.

"Okay, I've got ten separate locations. We're going to break off into different groups and tackle all of them. I'm going to need you guys in civvies for that. Can't have you walking around and looking like you're invading the place." She nodded toward Alvie and Maeve. "Alvie and Maeve will be staying with the plane. They will be our eyes and ears and will be monitoring our communications. They'll let us know if anything critical pops up. If you find anything of interest, you contact them immediately. They'll be on channel sixteen."

All the groups quickly turned their radios to the correct channel.

"Okay, here're the assignments." She rattled off the first nine. "Remember, this is strictly recon. You go in, you see what you can find, you get out. You will be armed, but try not to do anything to raise any flags. If you spot anything, I want the full team going in. I don't want to take any chances with Greg."

There was mumbled agreement, and then Norah nodded. "Cars are out front."

She waited until everybody had dispersed and then walked over to Mitch and Kal, who stood in the back. Mitch's arms were crossed over his chest, making his biceps look even bigger. She hoped that the size of him would keep Kal in line.

"Okay, you two, I'm sending you to a warehouse. It's a long-term storage place, one of two around here. I just need you to find out if anybody's been moving heavy equipment."

"You think they're storing their equipment nearby?" Mitch asked.

"That's a theory. So just get in, get some information, and get out." Norah eyed Kal. "You stay with Mitch. You do whatever he says, okay?"

Kal nodded. "Yeah. I'm just going to go use the bathroom before we go."

Norah nudged her head to the back of the hangar. "Right back there."

Kal nodded and hurried away.

Mitch turned toward Norah. "Am I babysitting, or is this an actual site?"

Norah sighed. "It's not a site where we think they're holding Greg. But it's possible that they stored some equipment there. They would have had to move a lot equipment into the area in order to make the show happen. Which means they have to have stored it somewhere. This is one of a few possibilities. We just need to cross it off the list."

"Okay. Then we'll cross it off the list." He eyed Norah. "You okay?"

Norah liked Mitch. He was a good guy. And he was starting to become a friend. "Yeah. Just, it's Greg, you know?"

Mitch sighed, his shoulders dropping. "Yeah, I know. But like I was telling the kid, Greg's been through a lot more than most of us, and heck, we've been in the middle of wars. He'll find a way to get through this. He'll find a way to hold on until we get there."

"I hope you're right, Mitch. I really hope you're right."

# CHAPTER 50

The storage facility was located on the outskirts of Manteno. It was one of those old-time, long-term storage places. It looked like one of those places that would eventually be on one of those shows where they trade off the lots. Kal wouldn't be surprised to find that stuff had been left there for fifty years.

Mitch pulled in and cast a glance around with a sigh.

"Something wrong?" Kal asked.

"Nope. Just doesn't look like there's any security or cameras. So if our guys were here, we're not going to get any tape."

"There are places that don't have cameras?" Kal asked.

"Despite what you see on TV, not everybody can afford to have an expensive security setup. A lot of places still just rely on human surveillance." Mitch grabbed the door handle. "Okay. You stay with me. You say nothing. Got it?"

"Yep." Kal bent down, grasping the handle at the top of the backpack.

Mitch raised an eyebrow. "I think you can leave your bag."

Flicking a glance at the bag at his feet, Kal hesitated. "Uh, yeah, sure."

Waiting until Mitch stepped out of the car and closed the door, Kal quickly unzipped the bag. Pugsley's large eyes blinked up at him. "You okay?"

Pugsley chirped in response.

"You've been really good. Just keep it up. I'll be right back. Okay?" He quickly zipped the bag back up. He didn't like leaving Pugsley, but they should only be here for a short time. He was amazed that Pugsley had stayed so quiet this whole time. He thought for sure that once the plane stopped, Pugsley would give him away. But he'd stayed almost perfectly silent.

He could tell Mitch didn't think anything would come of this assignment. Still, Kal felt uneasy about leaving Pugsley behind. But he really couldn't think of a good excuse as to why he needed to bring the bag. Dropping a few potato chips in, he zipped the bag back up before closing the door.

Kal was beginning to wonder if maybe he actually understood what Kal was saying, or at least what he was trying to do. Greg had suggested that he thought Pugsley had some understanding, although he didn't seem to realize how far it extended. Which made sense, being that Pugsley only communicated through chirps. But taking him out in the world seemed to give Kal a chance to understand Pugsley in a whole new way.

The office for the storage facility was up toward the front of the lot. As Mitch pushed the door open, a bell over the door rang.

This place really was old school.

The scent of cigarette smoke hung over everything in the office. Kal tried not to cringe thinking of all the secondhand smoke that he was taking in just by being in the room. The man behind the desk had to be in his late forties, maybe early fifties, but he was extremely thin.

With confidence and a smoothness in his gait, Mitch walked up to the desk. Kal always admired people like that. They walked into a room just assuming that people were going to like them. Kal tended to trip into the room, figuring everybody was laughing at him. For the first time, he noticed the backpack slung over Mitch's shoulder. Why did he have that?

The man behind the counter wore a dark-blue jumpsuit with the name *Tom* embroidered on his left breast. Kal wondered if that was actually his name or if the jumpsuit had just been handed down from someone else, because it hung off the guy's frame. He also had a bit of a yellow tint to his skin, suggesting that maybe he had a liver problem. All in all, he was not a healthy-looking specimen.

Mitch pulled his badge from his back pocket. "Morning. DoD. I've got some questions for you."

The man's face rippled with shock. "DoD? You mean the Department of Defense?"

Sliding his ID back in his pocket, Mitch nodded. "That's right. We need to know if you've had anybody from out of town that has taken some of your slots for some rather large equipment. Maybe some metal bars, containment units, cages, things like that."

His lips pursing, Tom frowned. "Not real sure. I don't really see them entering the units. I tend to spend most of my time behind the desk here."

"Okay, well, any out-of-towners grabbing some bigger units? Maybe for the last few weeks or so?"

Tom shook his head and then stopped, his eyes lighting up. "Uh, yeah, uh, actually, there was some guy, he came in a couple weeks back, maybe two, three? He had this strong accent like New York or New Jersey or something. Anyways, he, uh, brought in a couple of trucks' worth of stuff, and then he kind of disappeared and just got back, actually. A couple of days ago."

Mitch leaned forward. "Has he emptied out his lots?"

"Don't really know," Tom said. "They paid for the full month, so they can come and go as they want."

"When's the last time you saw him?" Mitch asked.

Tom shook his head. "Uh, not since he first came in, but I've seen some big trucks going back there. We don't really go back and check things out unless there's a problem."

"Would you be able to give me those lot numbers?"

"Uh, yeah, sure thing." Tom rifled through the papers on his desk before pulling one out and jotting the numbers down on a little pad. Pulling the sheet off, he handed it over to Mitch.

Mitch took it with a nod. "Thank you very much, Tom. You've been very helpful."

Tom beamed. "Uh, great. Thank you."

Mitch headed for the door and turned Kal around, giving him a gentle push to get him moving.

As the door shut behind them, Kal looked to Mitch. "How come he just told you all that? How come he didn't want like a warrant or something?"

"Most people want to help. They're not looking to make trouble. Tends to be the younger generation that's more interested in warrants, them and the guilty people. I think Tom there was just kind of excited to have something a little different happening in his day. I'm sure he'll feed off this story for a while."

They had been walking down the long rows of the storage area. It looked like a bunch of garages strung together.

Mitch consulted the piece of paper that Tom had given him. "We're looking for lots seventy-two through seventy-seven."

The lot across from them read 44, and 45 was on the right-hand side. They had a ways to go. As they walked along the lot, Kal wondered about the people who left stuff here. How much stuff did they actually have that they needed an entire storage unit to put more? They couldn't all be traveling or selling homes. Some of them just had to have extra stuff.

He bet that they didn't even remember everything that was inside their storage units. His grandmother had been like that, on his dad's side, not his mom's. He was pretty sure his grandmother on his mom's side had a running inventory of everything in her attic. But his dad's mom, she had passed away two years ago. He still remembered going through the attic and the basement. Both of them had been filled to the brim. In fact, there wasn't even a way to walk through the spaces. They had to just start pulling stuff out from the door in order to make a path to get in.

Kal never understood having that much stuff. It seemed ridiculous. You didn't even know you had it. He just kind of wanted what he wanted. He liked how Uncle Greg had his apartment. He had clothes and a couple of plates and cups but not a lot of extra junk that he didn't need, although some comfier furniture wouldn't be a bad idea.

The thought of his uncle's apartment made his heart ache. He really hoped that Greg was all right. It all seemed kind of surreal that Greg had even been taken. Now, here they were, kind of just walking through a storage area a couple of states away from where he'd been abducted. No danger, and it was actually a nice day. Birds were chirping somewhere in the distance. There was a light breeze. It was easy to forget that his uncle was somewhere probably scared to death.

They turned at the end of the row and made their way down. The numbers 62 and 64 were on the nearest units on the left. Halfway down, they reached the units that they were looking for.

Mitch knelt down on the ground, slinging the bag off his shoulder and unzipping it. He pulled out a pair of bolt cutters and walked over to the lock on the first one.

Kal looked around nervously. "Um, pretty sure you need a warrant for that."

Mitch grinned. "I won't tell if you won't."

"Um ..." Kale hedged, not sure what he was supposed to say,

Mitch clipped the lock off and threw it to the ground. He placed the bolt cutters along the side of the garage door. "Look, we just need to make sure this isn't related to Greg. The reality is pretty much every single thing we do is in the nation's interest. I know you don't understand what's underlying all of this, but I can tell you that your uncle's abduction is part of a bigger issue. And that issue has some serious life and death consequences. So while some things I'm doing might look like they're against the law, the truth is there are different rules when it comes to the stakes that we're currently playing at."

Mitch grabbed the end of the garage door and flung it open.

The space inside was huge. Mitch reached along the wall and flicked on a light. There were crates lined up along the right side of the space and more along the back.

Mitch's eyes narrowed as he spied some dark crates in the back. He cursed softly. Kal couldn't see anything inside that warranted that reaction. "What's wrong?"

Not answering, Mitch pulled out his phone and dialed. "I've got some weapons crates here," he said into the phone as he moved toward them.

Kal's eyebrows rose as he looked at them, wondering how Mitch had been able to identify them from across the room and without opening them. But he figured he'd probably been doing this long enough to know.

Instead of heading toward the weapons crates, Kal made his way toward the other wooden crates. Some of them were pretty big, about eight feet by six. Others were much, much smaller, maybe two feet by three feet. He wandered down the line of them, wondering what was in them. He flicked a glance over at Mitch, but Mitch wasn't watching him, so he pushed against one. It moved easily. The thing was empty. Maybe they had emptied them out and just left the crates here. Strange.

Wandering along the crates, he pushed against a few more of them as he went by, but they all seemed to be empty. He stopped at the last one over by the garage door and looked around. Whatever had been in here looked like it was gone now.

Mitch slid his phone back into his back pocket and flicked open the crate in front of him.

Kal took a step toward him just as something pressed into the back of his neck.

"Don't move," a voice growled.

# CHAPTER 51

The ghosts of the hospital seemed to reach out for Trevor as he walked past. As he walked down the hall, he could picture the old patients lying in their beds, strapped down while being force-fed medications. Down the hall was the room where they gave lobotomies, and one floor up was the room where they did forced sterilizations.

The Manteno State Hospital, an hour south of Chicago, had been in business from 1930 to 1983. It peaked in the fifties before beginning its slow, steady decline. Over time, the hospital expanded to 1,200 acres. It had been started in the middle of the Great Depression and had massive staffing issues. At one point, only sixteen out of 120 'nurses' were actually accredited nurses.

But the staffing was the least of the hospital's issues. It had been the site of horrendous patient abuse, including secret medical testing without patients' consent. In 1941 alone, nearly 500 died from experimentation. Surgeries without consent, lobotomies, and shock treatment all went on underneath the roofs of the hospital. A nearby farmer eventually sold his property because he kept finding bodies in his field.

Most people would be scared away by such a history, but Trevor loved this type of place. And he thought even his performers could feel the past violence.

The darkness hidden within the walls didn't just energize them; it energized Trevor as well. He could feel the history as he walked through the building. It probably made him a bit of a ghoul, but he didn't care. He liked to soak in all the misery and despair.

After all, that was what life was, just a series of miserable, horrible experiences until you died. If you were lucky, you had a couple of good experiences mixed in as well.

Trevor didn't trust anybody who said they had a good life. He didn't see how that was even possible. His life had been one unending series of miseries piled on top of miseries up until around the age of twenty-five. But by that point, even when he had good experiences, he was waiting for the other shoe to drop.

Now, when it came to places like this, he felt at home. Comforted by the misery of others, he knew he wasn't alone walking through this world with torturous memories.

Of course, the people in this place, if the stories were true, had an even worse situation than he did. But, hey, that was what happened sometimes. That was the roll of the dice. His life had its own kind of misery.

Neil hurried down the hall toward him, a little skip in his step. He stopped next to Trevor with a smile. "Oh, hey, boss. Just got the prisoner guy some food."

Trevor nodded. He'd been a little worried about the scientist. His Pentagon connections had come through, and he'd gotten a little more background on the guy. Apparently, he was one of the scientists involved in the creation of these things.

He'd also been one of the only survivors of Area 51, which meant the guy had a little fight in him. He'd been happy to see the guy had a little bit of muscle on him too.

Prior to grabbing him, Trevor had vacillated between killing him and having him fight before finally settling on the latter. He would be a warmup for the last night. And why waste a warm body? They were going to have to get rid of them all anyway. Might as well make his death have some use and, of course, provide Trevor with a little extra dough. So he'd sent Neil to make sure that the guy ate and got some sleep before he was thrown in the ring.

"Did the guy say anything? Does he have any fighting experience?" Trevor asked.

Neil shook his head. "I don't know. He didn't really say much after I mentioned that he was going to be the opening act."

Trevor supposed that shouldn't be surprising. After all, the guy was smart. Master's at MIT, doctorate at John's Hopkins, and then straight to work for the U.S. government. He'd been involved in all sorts of top-secret programs that not even Trevor's sources couldn't access. So the guy was seriously up there in the brains department. He no doubt knew about their shows. Which meant he knew what was in store for him.

But he really didn't have to be much of a show. If it didn't go well, he just wouldn't broadcast it. Schorn's entire job was to get the bloodlust up for the other creatures. Hell, the doc could do that while tied to a chair.

In some cases, Trevor did have to tie someone to a chair to make that happen. But it was always more entertaining when someone fought. It was even entertaining when they were scared and just ran away. Because then the screams were awfully good.

"What about the creatures? Are they all in their cells?" Trevor asked.

Neil started to nod, then frowned and shook his head. "I'm not sure. Uh, Brad said he was, uh, finishing up last I saw him. You want me to go find out?"

Trevor shook his head. "No, I'm heading down there. I'll see for myself. You just go make sure that our numbers are looking good and get me a report for the latest viewership."

With a quick nod, Neil scurried down the hall.

Trevor walked to the end of the hall and then down the stairs. The creatures were being held in the basement. There was a large elevator down there that they could use to bring them down for showtime, but it was safer to just keep them locked up down below until then.

Helpfully, the hospital already had some cells, so it actually didn't take a lot of renovation to make it work for their purposes. Plus, there'd been a giant hole that went through two floors. Trevor had his guys expand it and set up the cages there. Now there was a containment room right next to the main room. It was perfect.

In the basement, Trevor stepped into a large open hallway. A few smaller crates were stacked up against the wall to his right. Inside were cats, dogs, goats, even a few sheep. They were used to feed the creatures. They had to make sure that they were in top condition for the show as well.

Beyond that were double doors with two guards with heavy electric-shock prods in their arms as well as machine gun backups.

The machine guns were a last resort. Used only if there was absolutely no chance of taking the creatures alive.

So far, they hadn't had any problems. Trevor had spared no expense to make sure that his shows were safe. And he made sure that he recouped those expenses with each production.

And then some.

He nodded at the two men by the door. "Hey, how's it going?"

"No problems, sir," the man on the right said.

"Good. Where's Brad?"

The other man nodded his head toward the doors. "Just

double-checking the creatures, making sure everybody's wrapped up tight."

Gesturing to the electric prod on the guard's belt, Trevor said, "Give me one of those, would you?"

The man handed it over. Trevor pushed through the door and into the large, cavernous space. Cells had been built into the walls. Some already had the metal bars, and it was just a matter of reinforcing some of them with glass used in shark tanks. There were eight creatures in all.

Brad was halfway down the wall on the right, looking from his iPad to the control panel on the wall.

Trevor walked over to him and glanced inside the cell he was standing in front of. It was the Blue Boy. The guy looked like a gorilla, but a blue bald one.

He'd read about the incident in Kansas where some woman had taken one on in her kitchen. That broad had some balls. Unlike some grown men, who he'd seen burst into tears at the sight of the thing. And yet she'd taken him on, in a kitchen of all places, and then tried to track one down on foot.

He wasn't sure what had killed the other one in the field, but something had ripped the thing apart. Whatever had ripped it apart—now *that* would be a showstopper.

"How we doing?" Trevor asked.

Shaking his head, Brad nudged his chin toward the holding cell. "This guy nearly got out earlier today. One of the new guards wasn't paying attention and didn't put the code in correctly. This guy slammed against the door, and it burst open. I mean, it wasn't a problem. We got him back in the cell, and the guy only lost an arm, but still. It was a stupid mistake. So I'm making sure that everybody's locked up tight. I don't want any problems like that before our last show."

Trevor sighed. It was a shame this would be the last one. Part of him had wondered if maybe they should have put some of these creatures away and just kept them on ice until he could get the show up and running again.

But the problem was that keeping these guys on ice was proving to be more and more difficult. Usually he had to kill them at the end of a show, especially if they were wounded. When they were wounded, they were even more dangerous than when they weren't. He'd tried fixing them up at first. It worked with a few, but it wasn't worth the cost in supplies and staff. Besides, most ripped out any stitches put in.

So he'd have to put all these guys down when the last show was done. There was no way to safely keep them under wraps.

He himself was going to go under wraps for a while until the furor around him died down.

He contemplated starting up again in Europe, or even Africa. But these creatures were homegrown. There'd been no sightings of them across either the Atlantic or the Pacific. They were strictly a North American phenomenon, so that wasn't an option unless he wanted to transport them. And even he knew that putting these things in the air was an absolute insane undertaking. He was pretty sure no one would survive that flight.

So it looked like this was going to be the end of the road.

Which really was a shame. He'd put millions away thanks to these creatures. And of course, thanks to the vapid nature of the elites' entertainment needs.

"Well, we got that scientist settled in. What do you think about him?" Trevor asked.

"Apparently he managed to get a punch off at Harvey when he grabbed him. Gave him a black eye. That's kind of impressive. I think the guy might have some chops."

Trevor raised an eyebrow. "Really?"

Brad shrugged. "It's possible. You might want to give him a weapon when he goes in. Maybe he could be a contender."

Trevor mulled it over. That would make the fight more exciting. Of course, he needed the professor to die, so he couldn't put him in with anybody easy.

He walked down the row of holding facilities and stopped at the one on the end. The creature sat in the back up on a pipe, its talons gripping it tightly. It didn't rush the cage like some of the other creatures did. No, this one was smart. This one liked to think and figure out what the best approach was. Trevor smiled. "We should put him in with this one. After all, they're both thinkers. What's it called again?"

Brad walked over to join him. "It's called a Kecksburg. It was found after the Kecksburg UFO incident back in Pennsylvania. But for some reason, the government types call it a Hank."

# CHAPTER 52

A bead of sweat rolled down Kal's back. The object pressed up against his neck felt like cold metal. And it didn't take a rocket scientist to figure out it was a gun. The man grabbed the back of Kal's shirt. "Who are you?" the man demanded.

"Mitch!" Kal croaked out.

Whirled around, Mitch pulled his gun from his holster at the same time. Two hands on the gun, he walked slowly toward the entrance, his gun aimed at Kal and the man who held him. "Let him go. Let him go right now," Mitch ordered.

The man responded by yanking Kal back toward the doorway. Then the man leaned to the side and pulled the trigger.

The noise of the blast sent pain through Kal's ear and he cried out as fear raced through. No, Mitch.

But the soldier darted behind some crates, looking unharmed. He also didn't return fire, for which Kal was grateful because the guy was being really careful about keeping Kal right in front of him.

Pulling on his shirt again, the man yanked Kal outside, gesturing to the entryway. "Pull down the door," he ordered.

But the words came out muffled thanks to the gun blast right next to his ear. "What?"

The man slammed the gun into the side of Kal's head. "The door, pull it down now."

Pain slashed through Kal's temple, but he reached up and grabbed the rope attached to the garage door and yanked it down.

"No!" Mitch yelled bursting from his hiding spot.

But with the gun once again pressed to the back of his neck, there was nothing Kal could do. The door slammed shut before Mitch was even halfway across the pace.

The guy yanked Kal to the side, and Kal nearly tripped over his own feet. The guy was shorter than he was, so it was kind of an awkward angle to be grabbed by.

Shoving Kal over to a large black pickup, the gunman brought Kal around to the passenger side. "Open it up."

Head aching, heart racing and hands fumbling, Kal finally managed to latch onto the handle and pull the door open.

The man shoved him forward. "Crawl over to the driver's seat."

His shins crashed into the door frame sending pain radiating through his legs now. Now he had matching aches at the top and bottom of his body. With a wince, he climbed across the passenger seat and awkwardly unfolded himself behind the steering wheel.

The guy reached into his pocket and threw a set of keys over to Kal as he climbed into the passenger seat. "Drive. Now."

With shaking hands, Kal found the right key and put it into the ignition. The engine roared to life. Putting the car into reverse, he pulled away from the storage unit. "Where am I going?" He asked.

"Head out the exit, then make a left."

Blinking hard, his head ached and his ears still rang from

the gun blast. He'd never heard a gun go off before. It was *loud*.

Shaking as if he'd been dunked in an ice-cold lake, Kal was amazed he didn't crash into the storage units as he turned down the main path toward the exit. His heart felt like it was going to jump out of his chest. Was this how his uncle had felt since he'd been grabbed? Kal didn't know how he could stand it. He felt like he was on the edge of a heart attack.

"Watch where you're going!" The man yelled.

Kal yanked the steering wheel back, avoiding the pole at the end of the storage units.

As they passed the office, Tom stepped outside, a phone to his ear. He'd obviously heard the gunshots and was now calling for help.

"Take a left," the man ordered.

Bumping over the curb, Kal yanked on the wheel.

Jogging after them, Tom stood at the edge of the lot, the phone still to his ear. For Mitch's sake, Kal was glad. At least Mitch wouldn't be stuck inside that unit. But Kal knew that the calvary wouldn't get here in time to do anything to help him.

# CHAPTER 53

There was a police car blocking the entrance to the storage unit. Norah didn't slow as she drove up. The officer standing by his car had to jump out of the way as he tried to wave her off.

In a cloud of dust, she pulled to a stop in front of the office building. Mitch looked up from where he was speaking with police, and quickly strode over to her.

Norah stepped out of the car, slamming the door. "What the hell happened?"

Guilt was splashed across the big man's face. "There was no one here when we went into the unit. The guy must have drove up while we were inside. He grabbed Kal and locked me in."

Norah ran her hand over her face. "First Greg, now Kal. God damn it. Do you have anything? Make, model, something about the guy's car?"

Mitch shook his head. "I didn't see it, but Tom, the yard attendant, he got a look. I gave it to the LEOs."

"What about the guy? Do we at least have a description of him?"

"He was just some white guy. Brown hair, wearing a base-ball cap. Honestly, I really didn't get a good look at him. He kept Kal in front of him the whole time. He was shorter than Kal and a little stockier, but that's about as much of a descrip-tion as I got."

*Oh, God, this is not good.* The rest of the group had been off at their different locations and hadn't come up with anything. Norah had sent Mitch and Kal to this one thinking that it would be a dead end. And of course, this was the one that actually proved fruitful.

"So we have nothing?"

Mitch gestured over his shoulder to an unhealthy-looking man in a blue jumpsuit. "Tom there said they headed east when they came out of the parking lot, but that's all we've got. He did get the make of the truck. It's a black F150, but he didn't get a license plate."

"Well, I guess that's a little better than nothing. Is there an APB out?"

He nodded. "Yes. But I made sure that they don't follow if they get a notification. They're going to let us know as soon as they spot it."

Norah didn't doubt that was what Mitch had told them, but she also knew that feds and locals didn't often get along. Which meant that in all likelihood, if the truck was spotted by the locals, they would undeniably go after the truck, looking to one-up the feds. But they were going to need all eyes on this one anyway.

"Was Kal hurt?" Norah asked.

Glancing toward the end of the parking lot, Mitch shook his head. "Nothing too serious. The guy hit him on the head with his gun, but he seemed okay. Tom said that Kal was the one behind the wheel when they took off."

"So, what have we got, then?"

"It looks like a lot of nothing," Mitch growled, his jaw clenched.

Her phone rang just as Norah was heading toward Tom. She wanted to get more information from him, see if maybe there was something he didn't realize he knew. She grabbed the phone, seeing that it was Maeve.

"Maeve, good. I need you to run all the cameras in the area around the storage unit. It's the tenth one on the list of possibles."

Maeve's voice was muffled as she called out directions to Alvie before she came back on the line. "You've got something?" Maeve asked.

Norah winced. "Not exactly. It looks like they were using this site. Mitch and Kal went to go check out one of the units, but a guy got the drop on them." She paused. "He grabbed Kal."

"What do you mean, *grabbed him*?"

"He took Kal with him. I'm sorry, Maeve."

Maeve was quiet for a moment, and then she relayed the information to Alvie. Norah could hear Maeve talking, although she couldn't understand what they were discussing. Then Maeve got back on the phone, her voice excited. "That's actually really good."

Norah frowned down at the phone. "Good? How is that good? Kal's a kid."

"Yeah, he's a kid, but he's a kid that Alvie put a tracker on."

# CHAPTER 54

The guy in the passenger seat kept drumming his hands on the dashboard and mumbling to himself. Sporadically, he would call out directions usually when Kal was about to miss a turn. It was making him even more stressed.

Nerves rattled through Kal's body as he gripped the steering wheel. Every once in a while, he would glance in the rearview mirror, but no cars seemed to be giving chase.

He knew that Mitch would be looking for him. But he didn't know what he could do to help with that process.

His cell phone wasn't even on him. He'd left it in the truck in the backpack with Pugsley.

Pugsley! He'd forgotten about Pugsley again. Oh man, he really hoped that the little guy didn't take off and go looking for him or Greg. If that happened, they'd never find him again.

"Make a right," the man ordered.

Nearly past the road the guy indicated, Kal pulled on the wheel hard and turned down the gravel path. Sweat soaked the back of his shirt. The guy next to him looked unbothered. In fact, he looked a little more relieved.

Which meant they were probably nearing the end of their ride. Kal swallowed hard, wondering what that meant for him.

The truck bucked on the uneven drive. An old sign was off to the left, partially covered by bushes. Only the last word was still visible: *Hospital*.

If the drive was any indication, whatever hospital they were heading to hadn't been in use for years. That was not good. In the back of Kal's mind, he had a vague plan of attracting attention somewhere that would get to the cops or back to one of the people with very big guns he'd flown in with. Now that was blown, and his panic increased. "Where are we going?"

"Shut up," the man barked.

Biting his lip, the trembling in Kal's hands increased. He gripped the steering wheel hard, his hands feeling a little numb. He thought and discarded the idea of wrecking the car. With his luck, he'd get hurt and the guy next to him would be fine. He thought about demanding an answer, but he was pretty sure that would not end well either. Basic survival suggested that you never argue with the guy holding a gun on you.

So he drove in silence.

The main hospital building came into view a few minutes later. It had three floors and a large clock tower in the center. But they drove by avenues of buildings after buildings, all looking abandoned.

"Take a left."

Following the command, Kal turned, making his way across the front of the hospital building before he was directed around toward the back. Half a dozen cars were parked there. It was the first sign of life, and Kal was relieved. The rest of the place looked like an excellent place to dump a body without anyone seeing.

"Over there." The man pointed to a spot close to a door where two men stood outside, one smoking a cigarette.

There were no designated parking spots, so he merely pulled up to the edge of the asphalt and put the car into park. The man reached over and pulled the keys from the ignition. "Now get out."

Kal stepped out of the car, looking around. The two men by the door straightened and then headed toward them. Both carried long batons. Wire was wrapped around half of the baton, suggesting it was electrified.

"What's going on?" one of the guys asked Kal's abductor.

The man slammed the door shut with a growl. "We've got a little problem. Take him down to holding while I go speak with the boss."

With one last burst of optimism, Kal shot a glance behind him, noting the open fields. He was fast, but not faster than a car. And the guys by the door each had guns attached to their belts. Plus, the nearest group of occupied buildings had to be miles away. If he was going to make a move, it should have been before now.

The men seemed to sense his indecision, and they moved forward quickly. "Take it easy, kid. Don't do anything stupid," one of the men said.

Knowing that "stupid" was the only option available to him, Kal raised his hands.

The two men grabbed him by the arms and pulled him to the door as his abductor disappeared inside. His abductor turned to the right, heading up the stairs, but Kal was pulled along the hallway to an old elevator. Kal looked at it dubiously.

The man next to him chuckled. "It works. It's ancient as hell, but it still works."

The doors to the elevator opened as if to accentuate the point. The man who'd laughed grabbed his arm and pulled him inside. The other man went to the control panel and pressed the button for the basement.

Trying to tamp down his rising fear, Kal looked around. The walls had faded green paint chipping in lots of places, the floors were cracked tile, and some spots had even worn away completely, showing the rotting wood beneath. "What kind of hospital was this?"

"It's an old mental hospital. They say the ghosts still haunt the basement." The man gave an evil laugh.

"Cut it out," his partner said.

The doors to the elevator opened after the car stopped with a jolt. The men headed down the hall, and Kal followed. The men stepped through double doors, one holding the door open.

Kal stepped inside, his gaze down. The men stopped, and Kal looked up.

His mouth fell open. Cages lined the space. But instead of humans or even animals, they were creatures that he had never seen before. One looked like a giant gorilla, except it was a pale blue. Another looked like an oozing starfish except that the thing was massive, easily ten feet across. Each cell held something more and more impossible.

The man who laughed opened up the cell nearest to the door. The other guard nudged him forward. "It's okay, kid. It's empty."

Swallowing, Kal stepped forward, glad to see the guy wasn't lying. But he still didn't want to step inside.

But that wasn't his choice to make. He was shoved into the cell, and the door clanged shut behind him. "Hold tight, kid. The boss will come down in a little bit and tell us what to do with you. You'll probably be a snack."

Picturing all the creatures in the other cells, Kal didn't need to ask who he was going to be a snack for.

# CHAPTER 55

**P**ocketing her phone, Norah nudged her head to Mitch, who hurried over.

"What's going on?" he asked.

"Apparently on the plane, Alvie placed a subcutaneous lojack on Kal."

A grin broke out across Mitch's face. "I'm going to give that little guy the biggest hug the next time I see him."

"Get in line." Her phone beeped, and she pulled it out. "Maeve's got a signal. Kal's on the move." She paused, reading the text accompanying it. "Did Kal bring a backpack with him?"

"Yeah, it's in the car."

"Alvie said we need to bring it with us."

Mitch frowned. "Why?"

"Doesn't say. Just grab it. I'll meet you at the car." Norah headed for the parking lot, typing out instructions to other team members to get them to head back. She wanted everyone ready to go when they got a lock on Kal's phone.

A few minutes later, the backpack secured in the backseat, they were heading toward the blinking light on Norah's phone that indicated where Kal was located. He was no longer moving. The signal pointed to a long-abandoned sprawling mental institution. It looked like a perfect location for a secret fight club.

Norah quickly brought up the online information on it. The thing was huge. And its history was decidedly disturbing. Apparently it hadn't been used in decades. She could just picture it with its old halls and ghosts creeping through them as they took affront to the behavior that had landed them there and led to their deaths.

Getting schematics for the place proved more than a little difficult. It had been abandoned for over three decades. The plans, therefore, hadn't been digitized.

But even if they were, she wasn't sure how much good they'd do. During its fifty years of operation, it had been expanded time and time again. Nevertheless, she sent two of her team to go to City Hall to get a hold of the blueprints, with permission to break in if they needed to. She and Mitch headed toward the site while she called in all the other teams to have them meet them there.

Mitch nodded to the road ahead of them. "Check it out."

Norah looked up and then narrowed her eyes, looking at the car in front of them. "Is that a Maybach?"

"Yeah, and there's a BMW Gran Coupe in front of this one."

Norah looked around with a frown. Both cars had a six figure sticker price. The town of Manteno was a nice little town, but it certainly didn't have residents who were of the high-end car crowd.

The cars turned onto the road to the hospital.

"Hold on. Pull over here," Norah ordered.

Mitch slowed and steered off the asphalt to the grassy strip. They sat there and watched as half a dozen cars, all of them expensive luxury brands, pulled into the hospital drive. A few of the cars Norah, who prided herself on her knowledge of automobiles, didn't even recognize.

"I guess it's Fight Night," Mitch said quietly.

Damn it. That meant there was going to be a bunch of extra people on site. It would make it more difficult to extract Greg and Kal.

Norah swallowed, hoping that Greg was still alive and hadn't already been used as some sort of practice round.

"What do you want to do?" Mitch asked.

Norah's phone beeped at the same time Mitch finished speaking. She pulled it up. "They found the blueprints. Hold on a sec."

She pulled them up and quickly got her bearings. The cars were going down the main drive, but there was a service entrance a little farther down the road. She directed Mitch toward it.

A few minutes later, they were located only about two hundred yards from the hospital itself but hidden behind a group of overgrown bushes. Mitch pulled the car to a stop. As Norah stepped out, Mitch grabbed Kal's backpack, placing it on the hood of the car. "I need to see what's up with this thing."

Norah glanced over at him, but her attention was more focused on Max and Kaylee, who pulled up next to them. Two other SUVs pulled in behind them.

"What the—" Mitch jumped back as the backpack toppled to the side. Some sort of liquid leaked out of the fabric and then rolled down the side of the car. On the ground, the liquid solidified.

Norah's mouth fell open as Pugsley let out a chirp. Then he scooted toward the hospital. "Grab him!"

Mitch sprinted toward the creature, but in the dim light, it was tough to even see him. The rest of the team gave chase as

Norah flicked on the flashlight on her phone, focusing the beam on Pugsley.

Max dove for the creature but ended up just missing him. Kaylee sprinted forward, but nearly knocked herself out on a low tree branch. The others joined in, and Norah couldn't help but think that her well-trained response team looked like they were at a county fair trying to grab an oiled pig.

Finally, Mitch dove, wrapping his arms around Pugsley. "Got him!"

But the celebration was short-lived. Pugsley oozed between Mitch's arms and reformed as he dove under a bush. Max and Kaylee sprinted to the other side but couldn't find him.

Norah squeezed the bridge of her nose. "Crap."

# CHAPTER 56

The sky had darkened dramatically. The sunset had actually been beautiful. Greg had taken the time to appreciate it. He had a feeling it would be his last.

In the parking lot below, a lot of activity had been happening for the last two hours. The lot had been cleared of the large weeds that had grown over it. Orange cones had been arranged to direct traffic, and they even had a red carpet by the entrance. Now that darkness had fallen, the lights blared into the sky, while individuals in black suits waved people on with those lights used to direct airplane traffic on a runway.

But even with the limited lighting, he could see the expensive mix of cars. Apparently, "the boss" was getting ready for his next and probably last show.

More and more people streamed into the old institution. All of them were dressed to the nines, laughing, talking happily, their jewels flashing, ready for a good night on the town.

The fact that they'd be watching humans get killed apparently was not something that would dampen their spirits. In fact, that was why they were coming here. That was what they wanted to see.

Greg finally stepped away from the window, disgusted by human nature. He supposed he had his role to play in all of this. After all, he had been Hank's first researcher. He hadn't created him, although he'd had a hand in it, at least theoretically. But he had been the one who had analyzed his behavioral tics and his biological characteristics. Without people like him, none of the research would have been possible.

Of course, not all of it was bad. Alvie and the triplets, Iggy, and even Pugsley were proof of that.

Greg worried what would happen to Pugsley when he didn't return. Because he had no doubt that he would be taking his last breath within these walls.

Pugsley was a pretty sweet little guy. But who knew what the impact Greg's abandonment would have on him? They still had no idea about his emotional state or how he responded to situations.

Of course, Pugsley had been taking care of a mom and her pups when they first found him, so he definitely had the empathy gene in tall order.

Empathy, however, was not a trait of most of the Setis. Yet despite that, Greg couldn't help but feel a little bad for the creatures. They were being forced to fight one another for their survival. First humans had created them, and then humans had set them free, followed by humans chasing them down, and now they were forcing them into cages again and demanding they fight.

But sure, the Setis were the monsters, not the humans.

Greg flung himself on the mattress. His aversion to the disgusting thing had disappeared as he accepted his fate. Any diseases or illnesses he contracted wouldn't have enough time to take hold before he died, so why bother? Besides, it wasn't like the floor was any cleaner.

He stared up at the water marks on the ceiling, wondering who had lain in this room before him. Had they been someone in the middle of a psychotic break or some poor slob who had simply been incarcerated because that was easier for the people of society?

*Man, I'm really a downer right now,* Greg thought.

Footsteps sounded in the hall. Greg sat up, staring at the door. He'd heard footsteps on and off all day, although in the last hour or so, he really hadn't heard any. He tensed, somehow knowing these footsteps were heading for his room.

The door swung open. Neil stepped in, jittery as always. "Uh, hey, man. It's, uh, time to go."

If it were just Neil, Greg actually would have a chance. But Greg's two shadows were still standing outside the door. So he stood and nodded. "Where are we going?"

"We, uh, just need to go pick up someone else."

Greg felt bad for whoever else was stuck in this misery.

He followed Neil without a word, and they headed down the hall. But instead of taking the stairs, this time they headed to an elevator. He stepped inside, glancing around, picturing patients strapped to beds being wheeled in and then dragged into some terrifying room for some hideous procedure.

Neil hit the button for the basement, and Greg rolled his eyes. Of course. Where else would they go but the basement? It would be nice if for a change if bad guys actually had their lair on, say, the third floor.

The elevator car jolted when it reached the bottom floor. Neil stepped out first, walking quickly, his whole body vibrating.

Greg watched him, wondering how the man had survived to this age. The fact that he was incredibly thin suggested that he either didn't eat much or burned an incredible amount of calories.

Although Neil reached the door far in advance of Greg, but

the guards with him didn't prod Greg to walk faster. Greg wasn't exactly sauntering. He was walking at a normal pace, and apparently, the guards saw no reason to keep up with Neil. Which made it very clear as to where the man stood on the pecking order.

Neil pushed through the doors when Greg reached them. But even before he reached them, the noise from inside reached his ears. His feet stumbled only slightly as the hair on the back of his neck rose. He knew what lay beyond those doors. He stepped inside, unsurprised to see the cages lined against the walls. The creatures were worked up, no doubt sensing the energy of the crowd in the building. And once one got worked up, much like at a zoo, the rest followed suit. Greg scanned them all with a jaundiced eye. He'd seen more than a few of them before.

But the room did hold one surprise. The guy who could only be the boss stepped forward with a big grin on his face. "Dr. Schorn. So glad you could join us. I'm Trevor Austin, master of ceremonies."

Greg crossed his arms over his chest. "What do you want?"

"Oh, don't be that way. We're going to be great friends, you and I, at least for a little while." He pointed to the cage closest to the door. "And look, I even brought you a familiar face for your big debut."

His breath catching, Greg didn't want to look. He didn't want to know even as he tried to picture who they meant. Turning slowly as dread pooled through him, his heart pounded. And then it plunged into his feet as he stared into Kal's terrified face.

# CHAPTER 57

After losing Pugsley, Norah decided that was a secondary problem. Alvie must have known he was in the bag. Kal had brought Pugsley onto the plane with him. She shoved that little piece of information to the back corner of her mind because the rage it brought up was not productive.

And right now, getting Kal and Greg back was the priority.

Especially after her analysts reached out to her—they'd finally gotten in. According to one of the dark web IDs they'd set up, the fight was scheduled to begin less than an hour from now.

Strapping the bulletproof vest more tightly around her waist, she walked toward the row of bushes where her team was set up. Cast in shadows, it was difficult to pick Mitch out as he stood along the edge. He glanced over his shoulder at her as she approached. The rest of the team was gathering their gear at the cars behind her.

Mitch shook his head. "Too many heat signatures. I can't get a read on exactly how many people are in there."

Max walked up with a small remote in his hand.

"Send up the drone," Norah said.

Without a word, Max started fiddling with the control. Norah turned to the camera feed that had been set up on the hood of her and Mitch's car.

The drone flew over the ground and quickly moved toward the hospital.

"Do a perimeter sweep."

The drone swept to the side, going around the front and then toward the back.

Norah sucked in a breath. There were dozens of cars. Which meant there had to be at least seventy people inside.

Mitch looked at the screen over her shoulder. "Well, things got a lot more complicated."

Norah nodded. "They certainly did."

# CHAPTER 58

Greg's heart jumped into his throat as Kal looked at him. Trevor snapped his fingers, and one of the guards that had been stationed in the room opened Kal's cage door. His nephew's shoulders sagged in relief as he stepped outside.

"You're alive." Kal stepped toward Greg, but one of the men behind him dragged him back.

Although Greg glared at the man, he didn't step forward. He turned his gaze to Kal. "Are you okay?"

Nodding, Greg scanned his uncle from head to toe, the same way Greg was doing to him.

"Ah, see this?" Trevor said. "Family. That's what's most important. Why don't we give these boys a minute alone?"

Trevor waved the goons off. Greg strode forward, quickly grabbing Kal and pulling him over to the side of the room. They stopped in front of a glass-walled cage. Inside was the same type of creature that had chased Greg at the gym that he had once worked at. Greg nodded at the creature. "Bob, nice to see you"

He turned back to his nephew, dropping his voice. "What

are you doing here? Did they take you at the same time they grabbed me?"

"No. I saw you get abducted. I contacted Norah. She, Mitch, and a bunch of people with weapons flew out here along with Maeve." Kal flicked a glance at the other men before he whispered. "And Iggy and Alvie are here, too."

Hope surged through Greg. "They're here? At the hospital?"

Kal's smile faded. "No, but they're in town. I got grabbed when Mitch and I went to go check out a storage place."

"Is Mitch okay?" Greg asked, as his fear spiked once again. There was no way Mitch would just let Kal be taken.

"Yes, he's fine, but they made me lock him in a unit. The guy had a gun on me. I didn't have a choice. But I mean, he should have raised the alarm by now, right?"

His mind spinning, Greg nodded as he looked away, Mitch and Norah being in town along with Maeve and Alvie, that was good, although if they hadn't shown up already, then chances were they hadn't been able to follow Kal. It was definitely good that they weren't too far away. But the question still remained as to how quickly they'd be able to find them. He needed to stall, giving them enough time to at least get here to rescue Kal. So that was the plan: he would just stretch things out.

Greg leaned toward his nephew. "Okay, listen to me. We have to stall. We have to make sure that we give the team enough time to find us."

Trevor clapped his hands from across the room. "Well, gentlemen, I hope you've had enough together time, because now it's showtime!"

# CHAPTER 59

**T**revor glanced at the two men. The kid couldn't be more than eighteen, but he looked like a younger, taller version of his uncle. The genes were strong in that family.

He nodded to Frank and Herbert. "Take the kid."

The men walked over to Kal and reached for him.

Out of nowhere, Greg swung wide, catching Herbert on the side of the face and then threw a stomping kick in the middle of Frank's chest. Frank went flying back against the glass wall.

Camden and Brad rushed over and pulled him back, wrenching his arms behind his back. "Get off me," the doc yelled.

Trevor laughed out loud. This guy had spunk. That was good. He raised his hands. "Whoa, whoa, whoa. Now that's the kind of excitement we like to see. But let's save it for the ring, shall we?"

"The ring?" Kal asked.

Ignoring the question, Trevor waved to Neil. "Show the good doctor his options."

Neil walked over to a large cabinet and pulled the doors wide open. Inside were the combatant's weapons of choice. No guns, of course, because that would make things too easy. But there were plenty of good options: some machetes, some tall swords, even a pair of nunchucks. Trevor indicated it again. "All right, Dr. Schorn, pick your weapon."

Greg glared at him, crossing his arms over his chest.

Trevor chuckled. "I wouldn't waste time, Doctor. You either pick a weapon or you go into the cage without one. And I assure you, having a weapon is the much better option."

The scientist's eyes narrowed further, but this time he turned his gaze toward the cages arrayed before him. "Are you going to tell me who exactly I'm fighting? Or rather, what?"

Trevor chuckled again. He really liked this guy. Most of the combatants just grabbed the sharpest weapon, but the doc here wanted to know who he'd be fighting, no doubt to try and figure out which weapon was best suited for him. He knew that it wasn't always about the sharpest weapon. Sometimes there was the perfect weapon that fit the situation.

But despite the fact that he liked him, he couldn't provide him with too many advantages. After all, people did not come to see the humans win. "You're the first one to ask me that. I'm afraid I can't tell you that, though, Doc. But I can assure you that it is one of these guys in the cages in this room."

The scientist didn't move toward the weapons immediately. Instead, he looked around the room, his eyes hardening as he took in all of the creatures surrounding him. He shook off his guards and walked up to the array of weapons, looking them over carefully before reaching in and pulling out a most unusual choice.

A spear.

Trevor grunted. "Really? A spear?"

Greg hefted it in his hand as his two guards took out their

electric prods, keeping them in their hands, at the ready. Greg shrugged. "Seems like a good choice."

Now Trevor had some serious doubts about whether his initial assessment of the doc was correct. But hey, maybe the doc had a plan. "Okay. It's your funeral."

# CHAPTER 60

A spear. Out of all the options available, his uncle had chosen a spear. What the heck was he thinking?

But Kal didn't want to say anything because the cabinet was now closed, and that was the only weapon Greg had.

"All right, Doc, let's get you to the starting line," Trevor said.

Two of the guards moved toward Greg. His uncle stepped back. "I'd like to say goodbye to my nephew first."

Trevor tilted his head and then shrugged, waving the two guards back. "Sure. Why not?"

Greg walked toward him. Kal felt light-headed. His uncle couldn't fight one of these things. He'd be killed. Panic roared through him, and he started to shake.

But his uncle didn't look worried. And he definitely wasn't trembling like Kal. He looked in Kal's eyes before he hugged him tight, whispering in his ear. "Stall. Whatever you do, stall. Give them time to get here."

Then he released Kal and stepped away. "Love ya."

"Ah, that's very touching. All right, Doc. We'll see you later." Trevor nodded to the two giant mountains that were his bodyguards.

Terror lanced through Kal. His gaze shot to Greg.

But Greg just nodded, giving him a smile. "It's okay. Go on. I'll be fine."

Kal knew he was lying. His uncle knew Kal knew he was lying. But what else was he going to say?

One of the guards nudged Kal's shoulder to get him moving. With one last look at his uncle, who nodded back at him, Kal turned and walked down the hall with his guards, following Trevor. When they reached the end of the hall, he glanced back, but Greg was nowhere to be seen.

Taking a shaky breath, Kal followed Trevor up a flight of stairs and down an empty hallway. He could hear the crowd milling around down another hallway they passed, but instead of turning down it, Trevor continued forward. He took another left, and then a woman in a short black dress opened the door at the end of the hall. "Everything's ready, Mr. Austin."

Trevor smiled. "Thanks, Clare. Why don't you go down and make sure everything's working well for our guests?"

She gave him a small nod and then headed down the hall. Trevor paused to watch her walk away, letting out a slow whistle. He looked up at Kal. "Good-looking girl, huh?"

Kal had absolutely no idea what to say to that. But apparently Trevor wasn't waiting for a response. He stepped inside the room.

One of the mountains pushed on the edge of Kal's shoulder, shoving him into the room as well. He turned and glared at the man, but the man didn't even look at him as he ducked in the door. The other mountain stayed outside the door.

The inside of the room was surprising. Sheetrock had been put up and freshly painted. A leather chair sat in the middle of the six-by-six space, looking like a throne. The deep-red carpet underneath only supported that impression. A small buffet had been set up on the left-hand side of the booth with chafing dishes, and a metal bin was filled with waters, sodas, and a bottle of champagne set in its own container.

Trevor walked over to the window. He waved Kal forward, not even looking back.

Kal didn't want to do what he said. He wanted to resist somehow. But he also wanted to see. Stepping forward, he joined Trevor at the glass.

Arrayed in front of them was a massive octagon. It looked like something out of a movie. A wired metal cage completely surrounded the space. Two alleys, also surrounded by wire, led to the octagon.

"The cage is electrified. Twenty thousand volts. Anything that tries to go through that is going to seriously regret it." Trevor grinned at him. "You've got the best seat in the house."

Outside the window, well-dressed people milled around in stadium seating. Waiters and waitresses in tuxedos walked through the crowd, holding trays of champagne.

Trying to accept that this was real and he wasn't actually in a movie, Kal shook his head. A rumble ran through the crowd, and everyone looked toward the stage.

Trevor reached over to a control on the left-hand side. "Oh, sorry, my bad."

All of a sudden, the sound from down below filled the box. "... and gentlemen. Welcome to this final night of the Creature Spectacular. You are in for an absolute treat, as we have something very special to begin with. You may have wondered how these creatures came to be. You've certainly never seen them anywhere else before. Well, tonight, for one time only, we have one of the scientists who helped start the projects leading to their creation. Ladies and gentlemen, put your hands together ... for the Brain!"

Jaw dropping, Kal leaned closer to the window, placing one hand against the glass as his uncle stepped into one of the alleys leading to the cage.

# CHAPTER 61

A roar filled Greg's ears as he stepped onto the white surface that led to the cage. He wasn't sure if it was his blood pounding or the crowd yelling.

Around the cage, people in the audience laughed and talked, mingling with one another, drinks in hand, having a great a time. No, it was definitely the blood in his head. The people in the stands were barely paying attention.

Greg glared at all of them, wanting to yell, wanting to scream. But he knew there was no point. They weren't going to run to his rescue. They had paid to see this.

He'd been led down the hall after Kal had left to the combatant waiting area. Three men had been in the room, warming up. None of them had guards. For some insane reason, they seemed to have volunteered for this suicide mission.

Greg wasn't even given a chance to speak with them before he was pushed out into the alley.

He walked forward slowly, stepping into the octagon while keeping an eye on the other gangplank. His opponent had yet to appear.

The announcer's voice cut through the room. "Now it's time to meet his opponent. The one, the only, the Ripper!"

The door at the end of the other alley slid open. He pictured the one creature he prayed with all his being did not step out of those doors. *Please, no, please, please, no,*

But apparently the gods were not in a listening mood.

The Hank stepped into view.

# CHAPTER 62

The breath was sucked from Kal's lungs as his uncle's opponent appeared. It looked like some sort of walking alligator. It had strong thick arms and legs. Even standing here, fifty feet away, in an elevated room, with that thing still in a cage, Kal was scared for his life.

He swallowed hard, his gaze shooting to his uncle, who now had his back to him. Greg merely tightened his grip on the spear, which might as well have been a toothpick for all the good it was going to do against that thing.

Why, out of all the weapons that had been in that room, had his uncle chosen a spear? And he realized, that's where Kal could have helped. He should have insisted that his uncle choose the big scary-looking machete.

But Kal hadn't, he hadn't done anything. His mind had gone blank when the doors to the cabinet had opened. But he should have forced himself to move, making his uncle at least choose something bigger and sharper.

"Why don't you get something to eat? The food's good," Trevor said from behind him.

Kal ignored him.

"Mr. Austin is talking to you." The mountain gripped Kal's shoulder. Kal flung the man's hand off of him.

A laugh escaped Trevor. "There's no need for that. I'm sure Kal here is happy to go along with the plan."

Kal glared at him.

Taking a bite of a chicken wing, Trevor raised an eyebrow. "Oh, a little spark. Perhaps you're a little more like your uncle than I thought."

*I wish*, Kal thought. No, he wasn't like his uncle. His uncle stood down there looking completely unafraid.

Not that his bravery was going to help him. Greg was going to be sacrificed to that thing, and there was nothing Kal could do to help him.

Yet Greg's last words to Kal had been about Kal stalling. At first, Kal though he meant stalling the fight.

But standing staring at that creature, he knew now that wasn't what his uncle meant. Greg didn't want him to stall the fight. He wanted him to stall whatever Trevor had planned for *Kal*. He wanted to make sure Kal had enough time for Norah and Mitch to ride to his rescue.

Because there wouldn't be any time to save Greg.

Kal placed a hand on the glass, his fingers splayed, wanting desperately to do something but knowing there was nothing he could do. He turned to Trevor. "What is that?"

Trevor grinned, moving to the window. "*That* is a champion."

Kal's breath started to quicken, and he felt light-headed. Greg was going to die. And Kal was going to have to stand here and watch it happen.

He closed his eyes and turned away from the window, not ready to see this. He couldn't watch Greg die.

But before his eyelids fully closed, he saw Trevor watching with glee.

# CHAPTER 63

The crowd let out a cheer. The Hank didn't even look at them. Its gaze was locked on Greg.

Greg's breathing turned shallow. His gaze shot to the gate at the end of the Hank's alley, the one keeping it from the octagon. It wouldn't stay shut for long.

The Hank strode forward slowly. Its nails gripped the runway as it made its way toward Greg.

At the same time that part of Greg's mind was screaming in terror, another part was categorizing the Hank that he had worked with and the Hanks that he had run from. Their hides were incredibly thick, like alligator skin. Bullets often had trouble making it through, even the armor-piercing kind.

Talons extended from their hands and feet, each generally about three inches long, although some could be shorter on the younger ones.

Full maturity in a Kecksburg didn't occur until they were about five years old, at which point their speed and strength were incredible. Before that, they tended to be a little more impetuous, without the more logical approaches of their elders.

Regardless of the age, though, they held no compassion, no emotion. Their entire goal was to destroy their prey. And they tended to think of everyone and everything as prey.

In fact, Greg didn't think he'd ever seen one turn away from a fight or even be intimidated by one. He wasn't sure if that was because of the bloodlust pumping, or if that was just who they were: incredible killing, fighting machines. He also wasn't sure that there was an answer to that particular question.

And he doubted he'd get the chance to do the research on it.

Gripping the spear in both hands, he looked into the creature's eyes. Its eyes were, in fact, one of its weaknesses. But Greg harbored no illusions that he would somehow be able to reach the creature's eyes with this weapon.

The thing was simply too fast.

At the same time, he knew that this was the only weapon that gave him a chance against a Hank. It was the reason he had chosen it. The Hank would just shake off an electric prod, or the shock might not even register with its thick hide. A knife or a machete wouldn't make it through its hide either. He knew that from personal experience. And it wasn't like bazookas were part of the weapon choices he was offered.

He swallowed hard, sweat rolling down his back. A bead of sweat also rolled from his forehead, down his nose, and onto the mat. He paused for a moment, thinking about wiping it away but quickly discounted it. If he stopped even long enough to do that and the gate opened, the Hank would be on him. And it would be over just that quickly.

Of course, even without a slight distraction, this fight was going to be over awfully quick. After all, he was basically standing in front of an incredible killing machine with the equivalent of a slingshot. In fact, a slingshot would be more useful at this point than the spear. And even then, he was no David. And this was most definitely a powerful Goliath.

A few people in the crowd looked over and laughed. A few women squealed at the sight of the Hank.

The gate between the hall and the octagon still lay closed as the Hank approached.

Greg had no doubt the gate remained closed because the Hank moved too quickly. He was betting in previous cases that the Hank would shoot out of the alley and the fight would be over in mere seconds.

Trevor would want to draw out the action. He would want to give people their money's worth.

And even though he knew he shouldn't, Greg flicked a glance up to Trevor's box. A glance that Trevor was apparently waiting for. He raised a glass in toast to Greg, or maybe it was in farewell. Kal stood next to him, which only angered Greg. His nephew shouldn't have to watch this.

The announcer's voice boomed out. "Welcome, ladies and gentlemen. Tonight, we have a true fight for you. A classic matchup of brain versus brawn."

Some people in the crowd were finally interested in Greg. They peered down at him, tilting their heads as if he were an exhibit in a zoo. Which Greg supposed he actually was. They scanned him as if looking to see the brains that the announcer spoke about. And then looked away, dismissing him from their thoughts.

The announcer laughed. "I know he doesn't look like much, but he's come through other difficult situations before. So let's see how he does, shall we? After all, the Ripper needs a little warmup before his real event. Or should I say, a snack?"

A few people in the audience laughed.

Greg ground his teeth. Bastards.

The gate at the end of the hall slowly began to pull back.

His hands now slick with sweat, Greg gripped his spear, his heart pounding.

The gap between the gate and the cage slowly widened. The Hank picked up its speed. Greg tensed, watching the space, waiting for it to be wide enough for the Hank to burst through.

The crowd receded into the back of Greg's hearing. He wasn't sure if they were standing on their feet cheering, sitting in their seats ignoring the action in the cage, or booing. They were not a concern at the moment. The only concern was the Kecksburg, which moved at a rapid clip toward him as the gate slowly opened.

From the stride of the Kecksburg, he knew that it was used to these running starts. It had the opening of the gate timed so that as soon as it reached it, it would slide through.

Then Greg would be done.

It would pick up enough speed through the alley that Greg wouldn't be able to dive out of the way in time. Then it would be game over. It just needed to get through the gate.

*Which means I can't let it.*

Greg sprinted across the octagon. Careful not to touch the wires of the cage, he slid the wooden staff of the spear through the wire, blocking the gate. With a jerk the gate's opening stayed fixed. The Hank, unable to slow crashed into the gate and fell back. Sparks flew from the gate where he hit.

But the spear stayed put, keeping the gate from opening further.

Grinning, Greg's gaze shot up to Trevor. Score one for the brains.

# CHAPTER 64

K al turned his back to the window. He knew it was cowardly. The least he could do was watch his uncle, offer him some sort of emotional support, but he couldn't watch him get gored by that thing. And there was no way his uncle was going to avoid that.

Trevor cursed.

Kal's eyes flew open as he whirled around.

Glaring at the cage, Trevor held out his hand. "Phone," he ordered.

The mountain handed Trevor a phone, and he quickly spoke into it. "Tell someone to push the spear out."

Through the glass, the sight was not what Kal expected. His uncle had stopped the gate from opening, using the spear like a bolt lock.

A grin broke across Kal's face. That was awesome.

But then one of the guards approached from outside the alley and pushed the spear away, and Greg hurried to the other side of the octagon.

The gate began to open again, and Kal knew that while that

trick had been good, his uncle couldn't possibly have any more up his sleeve.

# CHAPTER 65

The Hank let out a screech of disapproval and then slammed into the gate. But it wasn't wide enough for it to get through. No more sparks of electricity danced across the wires as it reached its talons through, swiping at the air. Apparently the gate was no longer electrified.

A guard hustled over to the edge of the octagon. He thrust an electric prod through the holes in the fence, moving Greg away from the spear.

Greg backed away, his hopes of a reprieve dashed as another guard hustled over to the gate wearing thick woolen gloves. The guard pushed down the end of the spear, sending it clattering into the octagon.

The gate restarted its opening, but this time at a much faster pace. Greg started back for the spear but then stopped as the gate reached a space wide enough for the Hank to burst through.

It barreled straight for Greg, lashing out with a talon. Greg dove for the ground and then rolled. The talons caught on the edge of his shirt. He felt a tug and knew that it had ripped but didn't slow as his fingers wrapped around the spear. He whirled around and swung the spear wide. The Hank reared back.

But that was just a momentary glitch. It surged forward, and Greg shoved the spear toward its face. The creature ducked out of the way and then slashed toward Greg. Greg darted to the left, barely avoiding getting ripped open. He backed up toward the other side of the octagon, sweat now pouring down his forehead, his shirt clinging to his body.

*Come on, Greg, think. Think.*

The edge of his spear touched the cage wires. Sparks flew but didn't travel down the wooden pole.

An idea flashed through his mind. It would take luck, daring, and skill—three qualities that had never really been in Greg's wheelhouse. But he didn't give himself a chance to doubt. He backed up closer to the cage and hunched his shoulders, making himself a smaller target.

The Hank charged. Greg waited until the absolute last second and then flung himself at the ground. The Hank reached out with its talon into the space Greg had just been. And its talon raked the cage wires.

Electricity rolled through its body as the Hank screamed and screeched. Greg crawled from underneath it as it started to vibrate, electricity crawling over its skin.

Breathing hard, Greg stumbled to his feet. Just one more thing to do, and this nightmare would be over. He gripped the spear and plunged it into the Hank's eye. Then he took a step back and looked up at Trevor in triumph.

Tilting his head and smiling, Trevor looked down at the octagon. The man pointed at the mat.

Oh no. In disbelief, Greg followed the direction of his finger to where the Hank was slowly getting back to its feet.

# CHAPTER 66

The cars coming into the parking lot had dwindled down to just one or two every few minutes.

Norah knew that meant that it was getting close to showtime. There had to be over three dozen cars here. Most had at least two people in each, although there were some limos that groups of people in evening wear had piled out of.

Which meant there had to be at least a hundred people inside.

She and her team would definitely be outnumbered, but she couldn't wait for the others. She doubted Greg had that kind of time. And besides, she didn't think the rich and entitled would be jumping in to fight them off.

She'd called local police to have them block the exits at the roads, so hopefully if anyone slipped through, the locals would nab them.

With Iggy, Kaylee, Max, and Mitch at her sides, she moved forward through the grass. Together, they stopped at the edge of the parking lot. The rest of the team moved in from the other end. Norah spoke into the mic at her throat. "Now."

All the parking lot lights immediately went dark.

Norah moved forward quickly as cries of dismay came from the entrance of the building.

Her team had shot out the lights. She didn't want to take down all the electricity because she wasn't sure what she would find inside. And if they were smart, they were using at least some electricity to keep the creatures contained. She didn't need this to be more of a disaster than it was already going to be.

Luckily there was a full moon, so they didn't need night vision goggles.

Her team quickly made their way through the parked luxury cars. The other team was coming in through the southern entrance. They would breach at the same time.

They approached the entrance. A couple in a tuxedo and a short cocktail dress stood looking around next to two men in black suits.

Raising her tranquilizer gun. Norah took down the two men in black. Mitch took out the couple.

Hustling forward, Max pulled out zip ties and pulling the tranquilizers from their necks. "Secure."

Once again, they moved forward.

Kaylee held the door open, and Norah and Mitch went through first.

There was no one in the main vestibule. A bright-red carpet had been brought in to cover the floor, and chandeliers had been hung from the ceiling, but the walls were still peeling plaster. "Secure the room," Norah ordered.

A tall skinny guy looking down at his phone came out a side door. Norah grabbed him by the front of the shirt and slammed him up against the wall. "You're going to show me where the stage entrance is."

The guy looked down at her, his eyes large as he nodded. "Uh, sure, sure."

Keeping a hand on his shoulder, Norah pushed him forward. "Which way?" She demanded.

The guy's eyes nearly bugged out if his head as Iggy bounded over to Norah. "Uh, this way." He turned to the right, headed down a hall. Max, Kaylee and Mitch followed behind her as she had Neil push open the door to a stairwell.

The whole time Norah held the man he shook so hard Norah thought she might lose her grip on him. At first Norah thought that it was nerves that was making the guy shake. But now, as he led them down the stairwell, she realized that it must be some sort of neurological condition.

"What's your name?" Norah asked as they headed down the stairs. The rest of the team would be following after securing the main entrance.

"Uh, Neil, Neil Tedeschi."

"And who do you work for?" She asked.

"Uh, Mr. Austin," he said with no hesitation.

"He runs this place?"

"Yeah."

"So, Neil Tedeschi do they keep the creatures in a storage room next to the stage?" Mitch asked.

Neil nodded quickly. "Yep, um, yep. Uh, Jerry, he does all of the technical stuff, and Brad, you know, he does the security. They're both good guys, you know? I mean, sometimes they're a little mean to me, but you know, overall, they're pretty good."

Norah couldn't help but feel a little bad for Neil. He didn't seem like he was a full-grown adult. And she had a feeling that he had been horribly taken advantage of—not just in this situation, but throughout his life. Part of her hoped that she could figure out a way to lessen the charges against him if he cooperated.

Of course, if Greg died, then all bets were off.

They approached an intersection, and Mitch held up a

hand. Norah nodded at Max, who grabbed Neil and pushed him up against the wall, covering his mouth with his gloved hand.

Mitch put up two fingers. Norah nodded, sliding down to the ground below him. Together, the two of them peered around the corner and took their shots. Norah's first one missed, but the second one got the guy in the leg.

Unfortunately, when he fell, he fell into the swinging doors next to him.

Vaulting to her feet, Norah sprinted down the hall, Mitch right next to her and Iggy on her other side.

Max hustled behind them with Neil. Kaylee was behind them.

Norah looked through the door. There were three men inside. One was frantically tapping away at his tablet.

Norah's stomach turned. That was never a good sign.

"Go, go!" She yelled.

They burst through the doors just as the lights above the cages around the room containing the Setis turned green.

# CHAPTER 67

S moke rose off of the Hank's body. The smell of burnt flesh drifted through the octagon. Yet the Hank still got to its feet with a snarl. It was moving slower than it had before. The spear still hung from its eye socket. It reached up and yanked it out.

The weapon hit the mat and rolled out of the way, and out of Greg's reach.

Greg backed up, knowing that had been his one-in-a-million shot. That had been his Hail Mary. His only chance.

Now he stood defenseless. And although Hanks didn't have a lot of emotions, one of the emotions they did have was anger. And this Hank was going to be really, really angry.

But the electricity seemed to have weakened the Hank a little bit. Not enough to give Greg a fighting chance, but enough that at least he seemed a little hurt. It wasn't a lot of solace, but it was something.

The Hank across from him shook his head, as if to clear his thoughts or maybe the ringing in his ears. Saliva dripped from the edge of its mouth.

Greg stared at it and looked around the cage, his mind fumbling for any sort of plan of something he could do.

But there was precious little that was coming to mind. And all the ideas he did have were basically suicide. Scaling the cage was suicide because even if the electricity didn't knock him out, the Hank was a much better climber than Greg would ever be.

Going for the spear was also suicide. It was only a foot or two to the right of the Hank. But the Hank would be on him, plunging its talons into Greg's back before Greg's fingers even brushed the staff.

And as for fighting the Hank, well, Greg struggled when fighting a human. Fighting a lethal killing machine with talons on both the ends of its feet and hands didn't seem like it was going to go any better.

But Greg had to try.

He got on the balls of his feet the way Mitch had taught him, bringing his hands up. After all, what else was there for him to do?

He circled to the left, looking to put as much distance between himself and the Hank as possible, and also with a small idea of maybe getting the Hank away from the spear so he could grab it again. Not that it had helped overly much the first time he had used it, of course. After all, the Hank was still standing, looking at him now with just one eye, blood staining the eye socket of the other one.

Of course, with a blind Hank, he might have a small chance of avoiding it. Although their sense of smell was pretty darn good too.

Hopelessness tried to crawl into the edges of his mind. Greg shoved it away. He wasn't going to give Trevor the satisfaction of seeing him lie down on the ground and just let this thing kill him.

He squared up with the creature as it raised its head. Its snarl ripped through the octagon.

The hairs on Greg's arm stood at attention, and he knew this was it. After everything he had been through, this was the last moment. He wasn't going to survive this one.

But he hoped that Kal did. He hoped that Norah managed to get here in time to at least save him.

And he hoped that Norah and Mitch didn't feel guilty for not getting here in time to save him. He knew the two of them were moving heaven and earth to find him. But he also knew that sometimes luck played a role in how these things turned out.

And luck was definitely not on his side tonight.

The hunched shoulders of the Hank indicated that it was still feeling the effects of the attack and the electricity. But Greg knew that wouldn't slow it by much.

Greg prepared, bouncing on his feet, knowing that if he was lucky, maybe he'd be able to dart out of the way again.

The Hank bolted. Greg was caught mid-bounce. He dropped down, but then his right ankle turned over itself as he moved to the side. He stumbled.

And inside his brain, he screamed, knowing that stumble meant it was over.

The Hank reached for him almost as if in slow motion. Greg watched it coming. The talons extended. Saliva slowly dripped toward the mat.

He scrunched up his shoulders, knowing he should close his eyes but unable to take his gaze away from the certain death heading straight toward him.

# CHAPTER 68

For a moment, Norah's heart seemed to go still as all of the gates unlocked at once. She had been in this situation before, and it was not a good place to be. Images of other creatures giving chase rolled through her mind.

But the paralysis only lasted a split second before her survival instinct kicked in. She quickly issued orders into the mic. "Containment breach. Switch to lethal ammunition. Remember, flame throwers and grenades when bullets won't work."

Then she tightened her grip on her weapon and pulled it firmly into her shoulder. "Iggy, find Greg."

He looked up at her, and she knew that he was torn. But she need him to do as she said. She glanced down at him. "Find him."

Without another moment of hesitation, Iggy bounded toward a set of doors on the opposite side of the room. On his way, he sliced his talons across a guard who aimed his weapon at Norah.

"Greg and Kal are the priority. Guests are secondary," Mitch ordered through the radio.

The first gate opened. Norah held her breath, hoping that whatever emerged, they had the fire power to stop them.

# CHAPTER 69

The fight was turning out to be surprisingly good. It definitely wasn't like the usual ones. Perhaps Trevor should get some of these brainy types in a little more often. After he got back up and running, of course. This could be a whole new avenue.

The kid next to him didn't seem to be enjoying the fight, though. He'd stepped to the back wall of the box, trying to disappear into it.

As the phone rang, Trevor stepped away from the cage and frowned when he saw Jerry's name on the screen. Jerry knew he didn't like to be disturbed during the fights. He quickly answered it. "What's wrong?"

"Federal agents in the building. You need to get out now."

"Damn it. Initiate the escape protocol," Trevor ordered.

"Already did. You need to move." Jerry disconnected the call.

The kid took a step toward the door, looking like he was going to bolt. Trevor hustled toward the emergency door, flicking a glance at the kid. "Bring him," he said.

Camden grabbed the kid, yanking him toward the door.

"What's going on? I'm not going with you." The kid pushed against Camden, but it was like fighting an oak: completely pointless.

Trevor flung open the door which led to a short hallway that would take them outside. "Oh yes, you are. You're my insurance. I'm not letting you out of my sight. Now let's go."

Setting off at a slow jog, he hustled down the hall. He'd had these escape routes created in each of his stadiums, but until today, he'd never had to use one.

He cursed himself for pushing too hard. He should have backed off on this last event. Then he could have made a clean getaway. He'd become like one of those gamblers he always made fun of. He had to go for one last score. And the last score was always what did the gambler in.

But he wasn't done yet. He still had the kid, and he would use him to get his own safety. Assuming, of course, that anybody cared about the kid's safety.

He frowned, thinking that the scientist had to be dead by now. Which meant that maybe they wouldn't. Doubts flooded his mind.

But he shooed them away. The decision had been made. And if the kid couldn't help him, then he'd just have to kill him.

# CHAPTER 70

The range of creatures in this little zoo of horrors was pretty damn diverse. Norah wiped at the sweat that dripped into her eyes, ignoring the blood from the Blue Boy that now covered her torso. It lay at her feet.

A blob-like creature oozed its way toward Max, who stood in the corner firing at it to no effect.

"Grenade!" Norah pulled the grenade from her waist, yanked the pin out with her mouth, and chucked it across the room. It landed in the center of the creature.

Max dove for the ground, covering his head with his hands as the creature erupted in flames with a screech of agony. Kaylee stepped forward, using a flamethrower to further toast the thing. Max crawled along the wall, scrambling to get out of the creature's way.

Norah felt a presence moving up behind her and dove for the ground, rolling out of the way as a second Blue Boy swiped in the air. It let out a roar of frustration, banging its fists on the ground.

There was no hesitation as Norah rolled onto her back and fired from the ground, catching the Blue Boy in the chest. It staggered back with another yell and then sprinted away at a lopsided run.

Rolling to her feet, she realized that there was one more person in the way of the Blue Boy.

Neil stood in front of the door, his mouth gaping open.

Max had secured his hands and left him outside in the corridor. But Norah had noticed him enter the room a few moments earlier. But being she and her team were busy fighting for their lives, she hadn't had time to deal with him. He was way down on the threat scale. In fact, he wasn't even on it.

But now he was in danger as well.

With a curse, Norah rolled to her feet, slammed in a new magazine, and took aim. "Neil, move!" she yelled as she pulled the trigger.

But Neil either didn't hear her or was too scared to respond.

Her bullets crashed into the Blue Boy, and then she shifted her aim for its skull as she launched herself forward. Her aim proved true. Three bullets went in through the back of the creature's skull and exited through the front. The creature kept moving forward for another step or two before it dropped, face-planting in the ground below.

Neil backed up, his eyes wide. His shaking increased.

Screams came from the door where some of the creatures had escaped. And where Iggy had gone to find Greg.

Norah ran over and grabbed Neil by the arm. "You need to show me where the controls are for the other room."

She started to drag him toward the door, but Neil shook his head, stepping in the opposite direction. "Not that way. This way."

He dashed across the room to a door that no one had approached. He nodded toward it, his hands still wrapped behind him. Norah yanked it open, swinging her gun inside, but all that was there was a ladder.

"It leads to the electronics booth," Neil said. "There's another door up there that leads into the crowd."

Norah looked him in the eye. "How many people are up there?"

"Just one guy."

"You wouldn't lie to me, would you?" Norah asked.

Neil shook his head, looking completely shocked by her question. "No. You saved me. I wouldn't lie to you."

And Norah might be a sucker, but she actually believed him.

"Max," she called over her shoulder, "get him out of here." Then she swung her M4 around her back and started to climb.

# CHAPTER 71

The hallway was short, only about twenty feet, as the mountain of a guard pulled Kal through it. He dug in his heels, but it had no effect.

Up ahead, Trevor burst through a set of doors and into the night. An SUV stood idling at the curb. Trevor nodded to the man who stepped out of the driver's seat. "You coming with us?"

The man shook his head. "No, I'm getting Brad. We've got another car. I left you one guy for extra security. We'll meet you at the rendezvous."

With just a nod at the man, Trevor didn't waste any more time. He hustled into the backseat of the SUV. The mountain threw Kal in after him before climbing into the driver's seat. Kal righted himself, ready to make for the door when Trevor pressed a gun into his side. "I wouldn't do that if I were you."

It was the first time Kal had seen Trevor with a gun, but he had no doubt that the man would use it. And even though Kal's heart was racing and his nerves were pounding, Trevor's hand seemed awfully steady.

The mountain tore away from the building and shot down

the drive. Kal fell back against the seat, the door next to him slamming shut along with any chance of escape.

There were no cars in front of them. Whatever escape route Trevor had mapped out, it was away from all the other guests.

Staring out the back window, he didn't see anyone giving chase. "What happened? Why did we leave like that?"

"Your uncle's friends arrived a little earlier than I thought. But no matter. It doesn't look like they realize where we've gone."

The confidence of Trevor's words cut out what little hope Kal had. His rescuers were back at the hospital, which meant Kal was someone who would not be getting rescued anytime soon.

# CHAPTER 72

Tensing, Greg knew the moment of his death had arrived. And then he paused. The fast-motion pace he thought that the Hank was charging at him with decreased to practically slow motion. He blinked once, then twice. The Hank wasn't moving. It was as if it was stopped in . . .

A chirp erupted from behind the Hank. Greg slowly straightened and peered around it. Pugsley blinked back at him, giving him another little chirp. Greg followed the slime trail and saw that Pugsley had slipped through the wires of the cage and had now encapsulated the Hank in a bubble of his gelatinous muck.

Greg broke out in a grin. "Pugsley, I could kiss you."

"Ig, ig."

His mouth dropping open, Greg's gaze flew to the side of the octagon where Iggy stood. Two guards lay flat on the ground.

"Greg, get out of there!" Norah yelled.

His head jolted up as he searched for Norah, finally spotting her in the control booth.

The alleyway to the octagon lay open. Greg wasted no time bolting through it. But first he glanced up at Trevor's box. There was no one there. The box was empty.

*Kal.*

Greg barreled down the alley. He needed to find a way outside. He had no doubt Trevor was escaping. He burst through the doors into the locker room for the human combatants. It was empty except for one guy who was unconscious.

Screams erupted from down the hall.

Greg didn't know what that was all about and wasn't sure he wanted to find out. But then his gaze flew to where one of the cages in the hall lay splayed open as if something had ripped through it.

*Idiots.* Why would they think letting those things go was a good idea? But then he shook his head. Of course they let something out. Why couldn't the bad guys just give up nicely one time?

He bolted out into the hall and saw Mitch running toward him. Mitch pulled to a stop, handing Greg an M4 and a tactical vest. "Good to see you. We've got Setis running loose."

Greg slipped the tactical vest on and was surprised at how much comfort he found in the feel of the M4 in his hands. He really was a different person than he had been a couple of years ago.

"They've got my nephew. Trevor, the main guy, he disappeared from his booth. He's, uh, well, he kind of looks like a gangster. Has anyone seen him?"

Mitch tapped the microphone at his neck. "Anybody got eyes on Kal?" After a moment, he shook his head at Greg.

Strapping the vest one, Greg said, "Oh, Pugsley is holding a Hank in some kind of security blob."

"Yeah, Max is already there. He nullified the threat. Pugsley scampered off with Iggy."

Greg grunted at the word choice and hoped Max had nullified the threat quickly and with as much pain as possible to the Hank.

"Okay." Greg started down the hall, then stopped and looked around. "You got this, right?"

Mitch grinned. "Hey, this is what we do. Go get your nephew."

That was all the encouragement Greg needed. He bolted down the hall. Trevor no doubt had a pre-planned escape. Now Greg just needed to figure out where he was escaping to.

Greg burst into a hallway and crashed into a man and a woman in evening wear. They looked at him in alarm, but Greg just barreled on through the rest of the formal-wear-clad crowd trying to escape.

Knocking into two men, he sent them rolling down the stairs. Normally Greg would feel bad about that. But since these guys had just been willing to watch him get gutted without so much as pausing their conversation, he didn't bother.

He jumped down to the next landing and then sprinted forward. Screams erupted behind him. Flicking a glance over his shoulder, he caught sight of a blob rolling over the back of the crowd.

Picking up his pace, he cringed. Gross. But he didn't even think about going back to help. They deserved what they got. He burst out of the door into a parking lot. A sea of expensive cars greeted him.

Straight in front of him was a guy with blue-hair who couldn't be more than twenty or twenty-one. He stepped toward a bright-orange Ferrari. He wore bright-yellow pants with a white leather jacket.

And Greg recognized him: Thad Chavez, a YouTube sensation who made his money pulling pranks on unsuspecting old people. Greg ran up to him. "Hey."

Thad turned around.

Greg slammed the edge of his M4 into his face, snapping his head back. Thad let out a yell as he hit the ground, blood bursting from his nose.

Okay, for that Greg felt a momentary twinge of guilt.

But he hadn't knocked the guy out. And he'd seen him do worse to others. Thad scrambled to his feet, his hand over his nose. "What the hell, man?"

Ignoring the outburst, Greg turned the muzzle of his gun toward him. "I'm taking your car."

Hands up, Thad started backing away. "Yeah, yeah, whatever, man."

Greg jumped into the driver's seat. That was when he realized that it was a stick shift and not an automatic.

He'd driven automatic most of his life. In fact, the only times he'd ever driven a stick shift was during a vacation once with his youth group. One of the camp counselors had a stick shift, and he'd felt bad for Greg, who was having trouble making friends with the other kids, so he'd shown him how to drive a stick shift in the parking lot.

He stared at the dash and stick for a moment. "How do you drive this thing again?" He murmured.

The passenger door opened. Iggy scrambled in, followed by Norah. Even Pugsley slid in behind Norah's chair. "It's a stick shift. You need to push in the clutch on the left, put it in first gear, then press down on the gas while releasing the clutch."

Gripping the steering wheel, Greg pulled up those long-ago memories. "I know."

He slammed his foot down on the shifter, shoving the stick into first gear. The car rattled forward. Greg worried that the car was going to stall. But it stayed steady, and they shot forward, the engine revving. "Do you have any eyes on Kal yet?"

"Yeah. There's another entrance around the back. Kal was

taken out that way. Apparently this Trevor guy had a separate entrance to make sure that he could escape should anything like this ever happen. I've got the chopper heading here right now."

Gravel and dirt spit up into the air as Greg yanked on the wheel at the end of the parking lot.

"Second gear!" Norah yelled over the roaring of the engine.

"Right, right." Greg fumbled with the stick, trying to find second and met resistance.

"Clutch!" Norah yelled.

Punching down on the clutch, Greg shoved the stick into second gear. The car burst forward again.

Eying him from the passenger seat, Norah said, "You've never driven stick before, have you?"

Wincing at the grinding of gears, he shifted into third gear. "Once, when I was thirteen. And now that I think about it, I think I only drove it about ten yards in first gear."

Norah shook her head. "I'd say pull over and let me drive, but I don't think we have time for that. Just remember push down on the clutch every time you want to shift gears and downshift every time you go around the corner."

Greg stared at her for a second. "Downshift?! What do you mean downshift?!"

# CHAPTER 73

As the SUV ate up the road, Kal's heart dropped, thinking about what was happening to Greg. That creature had been nearly on top of him when he'd last seen him. But maybe there was a chance that Norah and Mitch had gotten there in time. Maybe they could get Greg to a hospital, or maybe . . . His thoughts drifted off.

The reality was that if that thing reached him, his uncle wouldn't survive, not with those talons. That thing wasn't going to leave Greg alive. Those talons had been three inches thick. If they got into Greg, he was a dead man, no matter how fast he received medical care.

At the same time, Kal couldn't help but wish that they'd arrived just a little bit earlier. Even minutes could have made the difference between Greg's life and death. He also wished that they had noticed Trevor's SUV pulling away from the hospital.

But he supposed with the size of the place, it would be hard to cover all the exits.

For a brief moment, he considered flinging himself from the car. But the world whizzed by the windows. The car rocked as it took the uneven drive at unwise speeds. All he'd accomplish by jumping would be breaking his neck. Now wasn't the time to escape. But he'd have to look for a chance. Because no one was coming for him.

They drove on for a few minutes in silence. And then the mountain behind the wheel spoke. "Headlights."

Whipping his head around, Kal stared out the back window. In the distance, he could see two lights bouncing along the road, making their way steadily forward.

Trevor squinted, looking at them. "It could be one of the guests." But there was doubt in his voice.

And the lights behind them were gaining steadily.

Kal couldn't help but wish that the gaining car would go faster. He glanced at the driver, trying to figure out some way that he could do something to slow them down to give the other car time to reach them.

Trevor, who'd had the gun in his lap, raised it. "Don't get any ideas, kid."

Swallowing hard, Greg looked from the gun and the man's face. Then he glanced back behind him, praying the car behind them had some sort of plan because he certainly didn't.

# CHAPTER 74

**N**orah gripped the dashboard as she nodded up ahead. "There, see those taillights? I think that's our target."

Wasting no time, Greg crushed his foot down on the accelerator, amazed at how fast the sports car responded as he pushed them into fourth gear. He understood now why people liked these cars. They really did have a lot of pep.

Of course, why that kid got it in this god-awful orange color was beyond him. Now black, black was the color that you got a Lamborghini in, or maybe bright fire-engine red. But orange? How ridiculous was that?

Up ahead, the taillights disappeared over a dip in the road. He pushed down on the accelerator even more, shifting into fifth gear.

Next to him, despite the roaring of the engine, he heard a sharp intake of breath. Greg flicked a glance at the speedometer and realized they were going a hundred miles per hour. One serious pothole and they'd be launched. Swallowing, he quickly diverted his eyes from the dashboard. He didn't need to know how fast they were going. That would only distract him.

They tore down the road, dirt spinning up behind them. They tore over the rise so fast that the road disappeared underneath them, and they went airborne for a minute. Greg sucked in a breath. Norah gripped the door handle, and Greg was pretty sure he heard her whisper a little prayer or maybe she was cursing him.

Iggy had been standing between the two seats, and his feet went flying up in the air. "Ig!"

Pugsley let out a little chirp.

They landed with a hard slam, and Greg nearly lost control of the wheel. Norah lunged over and gripped it, helping right it back onto the road.

"Thanks," he said with a nervous smile.

Norah just gave him a tight-lipped nod, her face a little paler than when she'd first gotten into the car.

The car in front of them was moving at a fast clip, but Greg was catching up to them quickly.

But he had no idea how he was going to stop that thing. How did people in car chases do it? Didn't they normally bump the other car? But that car was an SUV, and his was a Ferrari that would probably crumble as soon as he touched the thing, especially at these speeds.

"Um, any idea how we can, uh, I don't know, stop that thing?" Greg asked.

"Hold on a second." Norah pulled out her phone, sending off a quick message.

"Are you *texting*?" Greg asked, his voice nearly a shriek.

Norah rolled her eyes. "Yes, Greg. I thought I'd touch base with a girlfriend and see if she had plans for Wednesday night. I'm calling in reinforcements, you idiot. Car's a little loud, I wasn't sure if they'd be able to hear me over it."

"Oh," Greg said, feeling a little sheepish.

She placed the phone down. "Okay, he's on his way."

"Who's on his way?" He demanded.

Norah grinned. "You'll see."

From the tone of her voice, Greg knew Norah was planning something unusual. He tensed, looking around, trying to figure out what exactly Norah had up her sleeve. They were in the middle of farmland. There was absolutely nothing around them. No headlights in the distance, no taillights in the distance either. So Greg had no idea what she had in mind.

# CHAPTER 75

The car behind them was definitely gaining, but Kal wasn't sure how exactly they were going to stop the SUV. As it grew closer, he could tell it was a smaller car. In fact, it looked like a sports car, a bright-orange one.

A heavy thud sounded on the hood of the car. Everybody in the SUV jumped, even the mountain. It almost sounded as if someone had landed on the car.

Kal's heart threatened to gallop out of his chest as he stared out the windshield. Then h blinked, wondering if his eyes were deceiving him. He could have sworn someone just darted across the road.

Someone with *wings*.

Then they were gone, bursting back into the air.

A second thud landed on the roof again, and the guy in the passenger seat leaned out and fired. With a scream, he yanked his hand back in, without the gun. His wrist flopped over, obviously broken. Kal cringed.

Another thud hit at the back of the car and sent the vehicle spinning into the grass on the side of the road.

Looking toward the window, Trevor screamed.

Kal launched himself toward Trevor. He grabbed for the gun with his left hand and threw an elbow into Trevor's face.

The gun dropped from Trevor's hand, falling to the floor.

The car slammed to a stop in a ditch. The driver's door was yanked open. And then the mountain disappeared.

Trevor's mouth fell open, and he fumbled for the door, stepping out and running into the night.

# CHAPTER 76

A boom rang out through the sky. Mouth dropping open, Greg flicked a glance at Norah. "You didn't."

She just grinned in response.

Staring up into the sky looking around, Greg didn't spot Sammy until he slammed down onto the roof of the SUV.

He couldn't help it, he cringed in response. The SUV swerved over the road. And then someone leaned out the window with a gun.

This time, Sammy dropped onto the roof, crouching low, and grabbed the arm of the person who had reached out the window and slammed their arm into the side of the doorframe.

That got a wince from Greg. The guy's arm was definitely broken.

Then Sammy vaulted up into the air and charged back down, hitting the back of the SUV. It spun, turning around and around, and finally swerved off the side of the road, stopping in a ditch. Sammy dropped down, tore off the driver's-side door, and yanked the driver out.

A man bolted from the backseat, tearing off into the field.

Greg turned the Ferrari off the road and bumped and bounced after him. As they got closer, he slowed. Norah rolled down her window. "Iggy, take him down."

Iggy climbed out of the window and onto the top of the car. Greg came up alongside Trevor. Iggy leapt over toward the man, slamming his feet into the man's shoulders. Greg slammed on the brakes.

The back fishtailed, and he fumbled with the steering wheel before bringing the car to a bone-jarring stop. Shaking, he grabbed his M4, and threw himself from the car. He ran for Trevor. Trevor fell to his hands and knees and looked up, starting to rise, but Greg slammed the M4 into the back of his head. Trevor went face first into the cornfield.

Norah waved him on as he looked back at her. "I've got him. Go."

His heart in his throat, Greg sprinted back for the SUV. He hoped and prayed that Kal was okay. *Please, please, please, let him be okay.*

He stumbled over a divot but managed to keep himself upright. Sammy stood next to the SUV, his arms crossed over his powerful chest, his wings expanded out. He truly looked like a demon.

Greg groaned. *God, Kal must be terrified.*

But then Greg realized that Sammy wasn't alone. Kal stood in front of him. Greg sprinted forward and then stumbled to a halt.

Whirling around, Kal's eyes widened. "Greg?"

In the dim light, Greg couldn't see any injuries, but he still scanned him, looking for anything off. "Are you okay? Are you hurt?" Greg demanded.

There was a tremble in Kal's voice. "I'm fine. I'm not hurt. But ... have you met this guy?"

Greg's shoulders sagged in relief. He was okay. It wasn't fear that was making Kal's voice tremble but excitement.

# CHAPTER 77

**N**orah had brought in extra forces to help contain all of the audience members. Ambulances were strewn across the parking lot. Local police and FBI were on the perimeter, keeping the area contained, and she'd pulled in D.E.A.D. agents from six states to help with the crowd.

The back doors of the ambulance were open wide, and Greg sat on the lip with Kal next to him. Pugsley was safely contained in a backpack between them. Iggy was in one of the SUVs, hidden from view.

When they had driven back to the hospital, the place had been lit up by spotlights that the locals brought in. Mitch had managed to contain the site and catch or kill all the remaining creatures.

It was an impressive feat. Corralling all them, or even killing all of them, wasn't an easy undertaking. Mitch was truly an invaluable member of the team. And Greg was glad that he was with them.

Norah stood about thirty yards away, speaking on her cell phone, her arms waving as she emphasized her point.

Greg did not envy her position. She had dozens of incredibly wealthy individuals in her custody. They were not getting access to lawyers due to national security concerns.

Typically, in these situations, they pressed upon the individual the need for secrecy and then threw in a bunch of threats of what would happen to them and the things they held dear if they revealed anything. But Greg didn't think that was going to work with the wealthy class. He had a feeling more restrictive steps might be needed.

He'd already heard Norah mention incarceration. He had a feeling some of these people, if they put up too much of a fight, were going to be guests of the United States government for a while.

Part of him hated the idea. No one should be unfairly held. He believed in the Constitution and the individual rights provided within it.

However, these individuals had been ready to happily sit by, sipping drinks and eating canapes while a Hank killed him for their entertainment. And they had probably sat by and watched others get killed already.

He knew that the rules should still apply to them, but from his experience, the uber wealthy didn't think the rules applied to them at all. And society seemed to agree. The wealthy seemed to pick and choose which laws they wanted to follow. So another part of him was looking forward to them getting a bit of a comeuppance.

Kal stretched next to him. He had a small cut on his forehead from where he'd hit the side of the car when the SUV spun out. But other than that, Kaylee said he was fine.

But Greg was still worried. "Are you sure you're all right? I mean, it's not a problem if you want to go to the hospital and get checked out."

Kal shook his head. "I'm good. No dizziness, no headache. It's just a scratch, Uncle Greg."

But Greg knew it could have been so much more than a

scratch. He could have lost Kal tonight. The idea of that ate him up inside.

Greg took a deep breath. "Kal, I'm so sorry about all this. But this is exactly why I've been keeping everyone so far away from what I do. I think it's best if we just go back to the way it was. And you pretend not to know what it is I do. As far as the family's concerned, I just work for the government doing some sort of biology stuff. The internship—"

Kal cut him off. "Whoa, whoa. What are you talking about? I'm not giving up the internship."

Greg stared at him. "You nearly died tonight. You get that, right?"

His nephew shrugged. "Yeah, I do. But I also met three really cool aliens. Wait, no, four."

"Setis," Greg mumbled.

A grin lit up Kal's face. "See? They even have a cool code name. And I like to think that I partly helped bring down this, well, whatever this was."

Greg had to admit that was true. If Kal hadn't gotten grabbed, Norah wouldn't have been able to track him down. So technically Kal getting grabbed had saved Greg's life. Greg conceded the point. "Okay, that's true, but—"

"But nothing. That is the point. I was able to help. And I mean, it's not like this all the time, right?" Kal asked.

Opening his mouth to answer, Greg found himself without words. He wasn't quite sure how to answer that. He supposed most of the time things were pretty quiet, when he wasn't going off on missions. And he was going to make sure that Kal was under lockdown every time he went on a mission if he was nearby. It would be nice to have Kal there, to have a little piece of family in his everyday life.

Pugsley oozed over the edge of the bag and onto the floor of the ambulance. Greg quickly grabbed a blanket and wrapped it around him. Then he pulled Pugsley into his lap.

Pugsley looked up at him, blinked, and then gave a contented sigh.

"Thanks, Pugsley," Greg whispered as he smiled down at him. The little guy was really something.

Looking between Pugsley and Kal, he realized that these two actually made him feel a little more connected, a little more like he had his own family.

Maeve was back at the plane, and she was family, but she lived in Norway now. And Norah, they were close, but they weren't quite at the family stage. Mitch, he had his own family.

Maybe having a little family around wouldn't be such a bad thing. "Okay. We can try it. But only on a trial basis."

Kal's grin nearly split his face. "Thanks, Uncle Greg. You won't regret it."

Greg shook his head. "I hope not."

# CHAPTER 78

## CLAY, NEW YORK

H ours later, Greg and most of the response team flew back to upstate New York. Maeve and Alvie decided to come along for the ride. Norah had to stay in Illinois for a little while, so she asked Greg to take Iggy back with him.

Now they were all set up in Greg's kitchen. Mitch had run out and picked them up breakfast before he headed home. Now Kal sat between Iggy and Alvie, his eyes wide, a giant grin on his face. Pugsley sat in the middle of the table, eating his saltines. Maeve and Greg were over at the kitchen bar, watching the little group.

A small smile was on Maeve's face.

"What do you think?" Greg asked quietly.

"It's a risk. That's true. But the fact is, you didn't invite him into this life. And he already knows about it. You could keep him away from it, but you and I both know that if it were you —and he seems an awful lot like you—he'd find a way to insert himself into it."

"Yeah, but shouldn't I be the adult? Shouldn't I be the one keeping him from being part of this?"

Maeve hesitated for a moment before she spoke. And when she did, she reached out and squeezed his hand. "Greg, I like the idea of Kal spending more time with you. I worry about you being here on your own. And Kal is family. I don't know, I think it could be a really good thing."

The same thoughts had been running through Greg's mind, although he thought maybe he was just being selfish by thinking so.

"Are you sure? I mean, it could be dangerous."

She nodded. "It could be. But if someone's going to try and get to any of us, they're going to do it through the people we care about. Kal is already family. That already places him on the list. At least if he's around you, there's a chance that he'll be protected."

He knew that was true. But he also knew that was the answer he wanted to hear.

Maeve stretched out her back. "I was thinking maybe Alvie and I would stay for the weekend and hang out. Maybe we could all have a movie marathon."

"Really?" Greg perked up. "That would be great."

She nodded toward the table. "I know you think that this would be good for Kal and you, but I think it could be good for Alvie as well. Look at them."

Kal was looking down at Alvie, nodding intensely, and Greg knew that meant that Alvie was communicating with him.

"Alvie doesn't get a chance to talk to a lot of humans, especially ones Kal's age. It would be kind of nice if he had a friend."

There would definitely be a benefit to Kal and Alvie getting to know one another. Alvie had been so isolated through his upbringing. And even with his relatively expressionless face,

Greg liked to think that right now, he could see a little bit more of a glow in him.

"Staying the weekend would be great. And yeah, I do think a friendship between those two would be pretty cool."

A yawn caught Greg by surprise. It must have been contagious, because Maeve let out one almost immediately as well. There hadn't really been any good ways to nap on the plane. And dawn was already creeping across the horizon.

Greg nodded down the hall. "Why don't you and Alvie take my room? I'll bunk in with Kal."

Maeve stood. "Are you sure? We can take the guest room."

Greg shook his head. "No, it's fine. All my clothes are in the washroom anyway, so there's nothing I need out of my room. And Kal's bag is already in the guest room."

"Okay."

She looked like she was a few steps away from falling asleep on her feet.

"Go on. You look like you desperately need a bed."

"That I do," she said with a smile.

She started for the kitchen door and then stopped, turning to look back at him. "Hey, do you realize this is the first time in a long time we went on some sort of mission that didn't involve world-ending or country-destroying possibilities? It was just basically a good old-fashioned underground fight ring."

He grinned. "Yeah, I have a feeling that the D.E.A.D. cases from now on are going to be like that. One and done, with no overarching, world-ending mystery."

"It's kind of nice, isn't it?" She asked.

Greg let out another yawn, all the stress of the last couple of weeks falling off him now that the case was closed. "Yeah, it really is."

# EPILOGUE

The bike lay sprawled half on the path and half on the grass. Mitch walked over and picked it up, climbing the stairs with it in his arms, and then placed it against the railing of the front porch. He'd have to talk to Marissa about being more careful with her things.

He pulled out his key and unlocked the door, opening it quietly.

Her dark hair pulled up, pajamas still on, his wife, Maya, walked in from the kitchen just as he stepped into the living room. Baby Otis lay on her shoulder. And without makeup and probably without even brushing her hair, she looked absolutely beautiful.

Mitch grinned at the sight of them. "Hey. He's awake."

Maya leaned forward and kissed him on the cheek. "And he would love to spend some time with his daddy." She handed Otis over.

Mitch took Otis carefully, cradling him in his arms. When they'd had Marissa, four years ago, he had been amazed that such a little tiny thing could possibly survive in this world. He was always half convinced her head was going to roll off her shoulders at any moment, her neck seemed so wobbly.

Now with Otis, he thought he'd be a little bit more confident. Yet here he was again, still nervous about dropping his child.

"If it's okay with you, I think I'm going to go take a shower."

Mitch eyed his wife. He and Maya had been together for ten years. He'd met her when he was on leave one weekend. She had been waiting tables as she put herself through law school.

She had been a powerhouse, even back then. Now that she was a mom, he truly knew what a strong woman she was. But right now, his powerhouse wife looked like she needed a nap. "Why don't you go lay down for a little bit? I'll keep the kids quiet, and you can just maybe take a nap and then grab a shower afterwards?"

Maya leaned into him, and he could tell she was barely keeping herself from falling asleep standing up. "Have I told you how you are the greatest husband ever?"

"You may have mentioned it."

Maya walked toward their bedroom, her eyes at half-mast. "Marissa's finishing up her breakfast."

Mitch walked into the kitchen. Bright-white subway tiles sat underneath the white cabinets. The walls were a bright, cheery blue. In the corner of the room was a round wooden table with four chairs. Marissa sat in one, four braids in her hair, as she leaned over her bowl of Froot Loops.

Spunky, the puppy he'd brought home from Detroit, sat next to the chair, waiting for the any cereal pieces that slipped off the spoon.

"Hey, sweetheart."

Marissa's head shot up, a grin splashing across it. "Daddy!"

She hurried over to him and wrapped her arms around him. Mitch stood there, one arm around his daughter, the other carefully holding his son, and realized this was the best he'd felt in days.

He'd been so worried about Greg and Kal. They were good people. They didn't deserve what had happened to them. But this world rarely gave people what they deserved. And the D.E.A.D. was lucky to have Greg on their staff. He hugged Marissa a little tighter and then ushered her back to her chair. "Come on, why don't you finish up."

Spunky rose up on his hind legs, scrambling up Mitch's leg for his attention. Mitch squatted down to pet him as the pup tried to crawl into his lap. He only succeeded in getting his top two paws on Mitch's thigh. But Mitch stayed there for a moment while Spunky licked Otis's feet, his little tail wagging furiously.

This was what life was about: spending time with family. It was these small moments that he always looked forward to.

Two hours later, he had both kids bathed and Otis back down for a nap. Marissa sat on the couch, curled up with a bowl of chips that she occasionally shared with Spunky, when Maya wandered out from the bedroom.

Mitch looked up in surprise. "Hey. I thought you might sleep through till evening."

She grabbed her breast pump from the side table. "Yeah, if that were an option, I would have. You guys good?"

"Otis is down, and Little Miss here will be going down as soon as her show is finished."

Maya nodded. "Well, I can take over here if you want to go grab a shower."

The mention of it made him yearn for one. But he glanced at his wife. "You sure? I don't mind waiting a little while longer."

Grabbing a few chips from Marissa's bowl, Maya shooed

him down the hall. "No, it's fine. Go on. Besides, your mom stopped by yesterday and dropped off something in your office. I don't know what it is, but she said you should take a look at it when you got home. I was so tired, I completely forgot."

Mitch frowned. His mother hadn't said anything about leaving something for him. He stood up immediately. "Okay. Well, I'll just go check on it, grab a shower, and then I'll come back and put Marissa to bed."

Maya was already moving toward the dining room after picking up her tablet. She'd sit there for the next few minutes, watching a show while she readied a bottle so he could feed their son.

Once again, Mitch was completely in awe by the female of the species and the way they juggled so many things. He kissed Marissa on the cheek. "Don't bug Mama. If anything comes up, come find Daddy, okay?"

With her mouth hanging open and without removing her gaze from the puppies fighting a tiny fire on the screen, Marissa nodded.

Mitch rolled his eyes. Marissa got very zombielike when the TV went on. He knew that they'd have to cut down her TV hours soon, but right now, he and Maya were just kind of trying to get through.

His office was halfway down the hallway off the living room. It wasn't fancy. In fact, it was barely an office. It also served as a guest room. But it had a desk and some book-shelves on the left-hand side and a queen bed pushed against the wall on the right. Sitting on the desktop was a black case. Mitch's eyes grew wide at the sight of it.

Quickly closing the door behind him, he locked it. He walked over to the window and pulled down the blinds. He turned and stared at the black box. It was two feet by two feet. What was his mother thinking, bringing it here?

Slowly, he walked toward it. He could feel the energy being emitted from the box, even from across the room. He was surprised that Maya couldn't feel it, although he knew that she probably was completely unaware of it.

It took a special type of individual to feel this type of energy. It was possible that Otis or Marissa might one day be able to sense it, but they were still too young.

Still, it was a risk even having it in the house with them. He'd have to talk to his mother about it.

There was no lock on it, nor any noticeable handle. In fact, the box was essentially indestructible and unopenable to almost everyone. Mitch placed his large callused hand on the box's top. Warmth spread across his palm before the top of the box popped open. He removed his hand and carefully slid the lid aside. Sitting inside was a perfectly round metal sphere. Normally, the sphere vibrated at a low intensity.

With dread, Mitch noted how much faster it seemed to be moving. Picturing his family, and then Greg, Norah, Alvie, and Iggy, he grabbed the sheet of paper tucked into the lid of the box as dread rolled through him.

They've been activated. Things are moving quickly. You need to prepare.

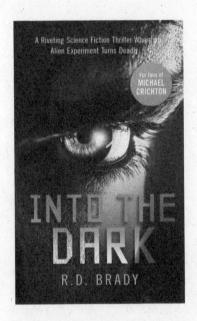

# INTO THE DARK - PREVIEW

## PROLOGUE

**Clearwater, Florida**
**June 20, 1997**

The laughter of Shelly Crumb's children drifted through the kitchen door as she placed the frying pan back in the lower cabinet. Straightening, she leaned against the countertop as she finished drying the last mug.

With a happy sigh that the chore was done, she placed the now-dry mug on the countertop and filled it with coffee. More laughter slipped in through the kitchen doorway. Her heart lifting, she smiled. She'd worried they were growing apart, but these last twenty-four hours had changed all of that.

Her coffee mug warm in her hand, she headed to the living room. As she stopped in the doorway, she leaned against the doorframe. Sipping her coffee with a smile, she watched the miracle unfold: Her eight-year-old son, Luke, and her twelve-year-old daughter, Sandy, played happily together on the living room rug. There was no arguing. No one yelled at the other to go away, though in fairness that was usually Sandy's request, not Luke's. Luke still adored his big sister. Sandy, however, was fast approaching the dreaded teenage years.

But today, she still looked like Shelly's little girl as she rolled the strange silver ball toward her brother. Luke stopped it with a grin before rolling it back to his sister. They'd found the sphere in the woods just yesterday and had come running back to the house all excited. Shelly had trekked into the woods with them to look at it. It was perfectly round, like a bowling ball, and about the same size.

A tree had uprooted, revealing the sphere, which meant it had been there for a while. Shelly thought it might actually be a cannonball from Renaissance-era Spanish colonizers. She had taken pictures of the object and dropped them off at the university's history department to see if anyone had any answers. She hadn't heard anything yet, so she supposed it was possible it was nothing. Even so, she knew this was definitely not a normal cannonball.

Sandy, who had her father's brown hair while Luke shared Shelly's pale blonde, stood up. "Let's see if it follows us again."

Luke jumped to his feet and hurried to Sandy's side. The two of them walked toward the front door.

The silver ball, which had been rolling in the opposite direction, slowed and then switched directions on its own, following them.

The kids burst into laughter. "It worked. It worked!" Luke cried, clapping his hands.

It was an odd trick of the ball, and probably the reason the history department hadn't called her back. Shelly wasn't sure exactly why it did the things it did, but it must be some sort of new technology or kids' toy or something. If this was going to be on the shelves at Christmastime, they were lucky to have gotten one early.

But how it ended up in the woods near her house, she had no idea. Maybe it was dropped by someone engaged in corporate espionage. She nearly laughed out loud at the idea, her imagination spinning away from her.

A knock sounded at the door. Shelly looked up. Sandy was closest to the door and hurried over to it. Peaking through the glass panel next to it, she said, "Mom, it's a guy in a uniform."

Placing her mug on the dining table, Shelly frowned as she hurried across the room. "A uniform?"

"There's a cable truck out there too," Sandy said.

Had she gotten a notice about a visit? She couldn't remember seeing one. Maybe her husband arranged it and forgot to mention it? That would be just like him. She shooed the kids back as she stepped to the door.

Sandy grinned as she squatted down and, with a grunt, picked up the silver ball to cart it back to the other side of the room.

Shelly opened the door as the kids sat back down.

A tall African American young man in a dark-blue cable uniform stood there.

"Can I help you?" Shelly asked.

"Mrs. Crumb?" he asked.

"Yes?"

"Morning, ma'am. I'm Carl from the cable company. We've had a number of outages in the neighborhood, and they sent us out to make sure that your system is all right."

Shelly glanced over her shoulder at the kids, who had once again resumed their game with the ball. "I think we're okay."

"Have you tried your TV recently?"

She shook her head. "No, actually, we haven't."

"Well, do you mind if I just check it out and make sure? It'll save me having to come back later if there's a problem."

"Sure, yeah, come on in." Shelly stepped back.

Across the room, the kids barely looked up from their rolling game.

Carl chuckled. "I wish I could get my kids to be that focused on a game and not on the TV. Is that a bowling ball?"

"We're really not sure what it is. We found it in the woods yesterday. It's … I don't know, maybe some kind of new toy or something."

The man knelt down in front of the TV and turned it on. "Toy?" He asked.

"Mommy, let me show him what it does," Sandy said.

Shelly nodded with a smile. "They're very excited about it."

The man turned around to watch as the ball followed the two kids around the room.

His eyebrows rose. "How does it do that?"

Shelly shrugged. "We have no idea. But it seems to just kind of switch direction if people try to leave it behind. We actually had to lock it in the bathroom when we went to the store this morning."

"Well, don't that beat all," he said. He flipped through a bunch of the channels on the TV. "And you just found it in the woods?"

Shelly shook her head. "Yeah. It was just sitting out there. The kids found it. At first, I thought it might be a cannonball left over from Spanish colonizers. I even brought some photos over to the university, but now, honestly, I'm not sure what it is."

"Does it do anything else?" Carl asked as he stood.

"It hums a little bit sometimes," Shelly said with a shrug, "and other times it kind of vibrates. It's actually kind of cool. And the kids really like it, as you can tell."

"I can see why. I'll have to see if I can find one for my kids." He reached down and turned off the set. "Well, it looks like this is all fine. Whatever is happening with your neighbors doesn't seem to be affecting you."

"Well, that's good to hear," Shelly said. "Can I get you some lemonade?"

"I would love that. Thank you very much," he replied.

Shelly disappeared into the kitchen and returned with a glass of lemonade. The man now sat with the kids, rolling the ball back and forth. He grinned up at her. "I can see why you guys like this so much. It's pretty cool."

She handed over the lemonade as the man stood. "Yeah, it really is. I mean, we all saw *Star Wars*. It kind of reminds the kids of R2-D2."

The man took a long drink. "I can see that. I really can."

\* \* \*

The small two-story home sat on the edge of the Everglades. From the van, Matilda Watson watched as her young agent was welcomed inside.

She didn't doubt that Jasper Jenkins would get the information that they needed. Even though he'd only been with R.I.S.E. for a short time, he seemed to have a way about him. He was very good at charming people. He quickly got them to believe that he was harmless while he sucked them dry of all the information he needed. He was going to be an excellent addition to their ranks.

The sun was hot up ahead. Tilda had cracked the windows, although she wasn't sure if that helped or hurt as the humid Florida air rolled over her.

Time was ticking away. She glanced again at her watch. He'd been inside for a good fifteen minutes now. With any other agent, she might become worried, but Jasper was probably just having a good yarn, as her grandmother used to say. The man could get people to talk like no one she'd ever seen.

Within minutes, he could have someone spilling their guts as if Jasper were their long-lost best friend.

The front door opened, and he finally appeared. The homeowner had followed him to the door and stood smiling and chatting with him. Jasper took his leave, giving her a friendly wave. Mrs. Crumb waved in return, a smile still on her face.

He really did have a way with people. He walked down the sidewalk and then crossed the street, sliding into the passenger seat of the van.

"Well?" Matilda asked.

Jasper blew out a breath. "It's the strangest thing. It's about the size of a bowling ball, and it's silver. It follows them around, like a little, I don't know, ball dog. They said that when they had to go out, they actually had to lock it in a room so that it wouldn't try to follow them. They kept trying to close the door, but it kept attempting to slide through."

"What do they think it is?" She asked.

"At first, they thought it was an artifact left over by Spanish colonizers."

Tilda grunted. Not a bad guess, given where they were. In fact, it was because of that guess that they had found out about it. Tilda had a contact at the university. She had a contact at most universities, and they'd reached out to her. That and the meteor shower the other night in the area had piqued her interest.

"And now?" Tilda asked.

Jasper stretched out his legs. "Now they think it's some sort of high-tech kids' toy."

"They think that a high-tech kids' toy was just lost in the Everglades?" She asked with raised eyebrows.

He shrugged. "It's a nice family. I don't think they really think too much about conspiracies or UFOs."

*That must be nice,* Tilda thought. Conspiracies and UFOs were pretty much all she thought about.

348

In fact, it was UFOs that had brought them to this little slice of Florida. There had been a meteor shower the night before. That wasn't unusual. The earth was actually bombarded by meteors every day, but the atmosphere kept them from getting through.

It would be impossible to check each time a meteor hit even just the United States. They'd spend all their time doing nothing else.

But this meteor shower had been different than the others. In a typical meteor shower, small pieces of rock managed to get through the atmosphere and land on the earth. This time, though, something bigger got through, something the size of a bowling ball.

Even that wasn't enough to attract the attention of R.I.S.E. They had more than enough things to keep them busy. But this particular piece of meteor was giving off a radio frequency, and it had slowed down shortly before it made impact.

Meteors didn't do that.

So, they needed to find out why this one did. And the Crumbs had very helpfully sent those photos to the university, making it easy to track the object down.

"So what do you suggest?" Tilda asked, wanting to see what the new recruit was made of.

Leaning back in his seat, he studied the house. "They let slip that they were going to a friend's for dinner tonight. Shelly joked about getting a babysitter for the orb. I suggest we break in, take it, and replace it with the lookalike. They'll assume that the batteries that were in it stopped working."

She had been thinking the same thing. "Will the sphere we brought work?"

Shelly Crumb had kindly included the dimensions of the sphere in her email to the university, along with a guess as to its weight. Prior to making the trip down, they'd recreated a sphere from steel in case it turned out to be something. And it looked like they would be needing it.

"The size is right, but the weight's a little off, and the finish. But if we shine it up, it should work," Jasper said.

Tilda nodded, looking at the home. "Okay, we'll go pick up some spray paint and then we'll get back here and stake out the Crumbs. When they leave, we'll replace it."

Although he nodded, Jasper asked, ""But what exactly is that thing? I mean, it's certainly not some high-tech toy."

Tilda started the car. "It *might* be a high-tech toy. It's just not one humans created."

## CHAPTER 1

*Present Day*
*Clay, New York*

The gymnasium/training area was located in the basement of the Department of Extraterrestrial and Alien Defense (D.E.A.D.) headquarters in upstate New York. It was set up like an extraterrestrial version of Hogan's Alley that police academies used to train officers. But instead of criminals with guns jumping out at people, it was aliens that jumped out at you—and criminals with guns.

As the simulations began, the lights were dimmed to represent early evening or midnight. Right now, the lights were still bright as Dr. Greg Schorn stood at the beginning of the obstacle course in his combat suit, ready to begin. Next to him stood his partner/pet, Pugsley.

Standing at two feet tall, Pugsley was a pale blue, slightly transparent creature that resembled a gumdrop with eyes. He had little arms that could extend out of his body but generally stayed within his Jell-O-like form.

Pugsley was one of the projects from A.L.I.V.E. (Alien Life

In Vitro Experiments) although Greg had been unable to find his files on Martin Drummond's database. Of course, the former head of the D.E.A.D had tried to erase all of the files from that same database, so that wasn't really a shock. Gigabytes of data had been lost.

When it came to Pugsley, they'd had to learn as they went. Greg had been on the mission that had first located him in Detroit. Pugsley had been staying in an abandoned home, looking after an injured pit bull and her pups. Greg had protected Pugsley from getting shot, and Pugsley had bonded to Greg in that moment.

Or at least, that's what everyone was assuming. Pugsley wasn't exactly talking. In fact, he made no vocal noises at all, save a little chirp and hum. But from the moment they captured him, he had made it clear that Greg was his chosen person. Wherever Greg went in the D.E.A.D. facility, Pugsley would appear. They still hadn't figured out a containment unit that would hold him.

That bond was so strong that he'd even unofficially gone on a D.E.A.D. mission to find Greg when he'd been kidnapped. To avoid that in the future, or at least to make sure Pugsley didn't get himself or anyone else hurt, Norah Tidwell, the director of the D.E.A.D., approved the training of Pugsley for missions.

And left it to Greg to do the training.

Now Pugsley looked up at Greg and blinked. Greg smiled down at him. When he'd first met Pugsley, he had not been enamored. The little guy had been cute—sort of—but at that point, he hadn't been Alvie or Iggy cute. He'd been really translucent, and it was hard to get a good look at him.

The slime that Pugsley left everywhere didn't exactly help. Nor did the early wart stage of his development that coincided with the slime stage. Pugsley, though, hadn't been put off by Greg's resistance to his presence at all.

Luckily, the slime had all but disappeared, and the warts were completely gone. Greg and the other scientists believe the slime might have been part of some form of alien puberty. And the warts? Alien acne.

One attribute that had remained, however, was Pugsley's ability to expand outward and encapsulate someone or something in a protective gel. Basically, his body just inflated until it wrapped entirely around either the person or the subject, completely immobilizing the target.

And it could happen fast. That ability had saved Greg's life not that long ago.

"Okay, little buddy. Now, remember, you need to focus on grabbing the bad guys but leaving the good guys alone, okay?"

Pugsley didn't answer, but his whole body vibrated.

Greg was making a little headway in understanding the small alien. He'd begun to notice a slight difference in the tone of the vibrations. The one he'd just emitted was a little higher pitched. Those vibrations seemed to indicate agreement.

And while they were all kind of guessing as to what Pugsley was saying, he seemed to understand them just fine . . . suggesting that Pugsley might be the smarter of the species.

Grabbing his M4, Greg pulled it up to his shoulder. There were no live rounds in it, but he wanted Pugsley to get used to the weapons being around. The hope was that maybe they could take Pugsley out into the field. So far, the trainings hadn't exactly gone great.

But Greg had made it his mission to make sure that Pugsley at least got a shot. He tapped the mic at his throat. "You got us, Kal?"

Kal was Kal El Haddid, Greg's nephew through his oldest sister Martha. Greg had never intended to introduce Kal to his work but life happened. His nephew sat up in the observation booth that overlooked the training field. Through the massive glass window above the starting point of the simulation, he gave Greg a big thumbs-up.

Kal had just finished his first year at MIT. He was doing really well, and his mother had actually agreed to allow Kal to stay with Greg for the summer for his internship with the D.E.A.D.

Of course, his mother didn't know the internship was with a sub-agency of the Department of Defense. She thought Greg worked for the Department of Agriculture. But this was the second summer Kal would be spending with Greg, and Greg had found himself really looking forward to his nephew's arrival.

"I got you, Greg," Kal said over the earpiece.

"Then let's begin."

The lights dimmed. Next to him, Pugsley took on a faint turquoise glow. That was another trait that had developed lately. Apparently, his little buddy came with a glow-in-the-dark setting.

"Turn down the glow," Greg whispered.

Next to him, Pugsley's light dimmed.

The two of them started forward. The cardboard cutout of a woman holding a small chihuahua burst out from the alley to the left.

Turning his weapon, Greg aimed at the woman, but he didn't pull the trigger. Next to him, Pugsley expanded but didn't unleash himself at the woman or Greg.

Greg nodded. "Good."

They made it through the next four surprise individuals without any problems. And Pugsley even managed to expand himself around a mean-looking Kecksburg that startled him from the right.

Greg grinned. *This is actually going pretty well. Maybe I can—*

The door to the back of the gym opened just as a cardboard cutout burst out from Greg's left.

Pugsley's light exploded as he expanded out.

"No, Pugs—" Greg slammed his mouth shut as Pugsley's goo wrapped around him and the offending cardboard cutout of a grinning Labrador retriever. Unable to move, Greg simply closed his eyes. *So close.*

Footsteps approached as Greg looked up.

Mitch Haldron smiled as he stepped into the alley. "So I take it training's not going well."

*You think?* Greg thought as he glared at Mitch. But he didn't even attempt to speak. He couldn't. Pugsley's goo worked as a paralytic. It had an immediate effect but thankfully wore off just as quickly.

"You can release him now, Pugsley," Mitch said.

The goo slid away from Greg's body but left a cold trail over his skin. Shuddering, Greg shook out his hands and sent goo flying across the space. The smiling Labrador tilted over on its side and crashed to the ground.

Greg sighed while Mitch chuckled.

"We were doing so well. But then you opened the door, the dog popped out and ..." Greg shook his head with another sigh.

Pugsley scooted forward and leaned against Greg's leg, looking up at him with big eyes.

Even as slime slipped down Greg's forehead and off his nose, he leaned down and patted Pugsley. "It's okay, buddy. I know you were just trying to keep me safe. We'll try again later. Why don't you go see if Kal has some cookies?"

At the mention of cookies, Pugsley's glow brightened before he scooted across the floor and disappeared up the stairs.

Mitch chucked a towel at Greg. Snatching it from the air, Greg started to wipe some of the goo off his face, knowing he needed a shower before this stuff dried. The goo was like beach sand: It got in everywhere. "He's actually getting better.

We made it through four separate obstacles before he slimed me. That's a record," Greg said.

Watching Pugsley disappear, Mitch said, "You know you could just take him along as your own personal protection bubble. He won't let anything happen to you."

Greg grimaced. "Yeah, but I'm afraid that I might be in the middle of something completely innocuous, and he'll slime me anyway. So I'm hoping we can get him trained a little bit better before we do that."

"Well, I'm afraid training is over for today."

"Why? What's up?" Greg asked as he ran the towel over his hair. A large piece of goo slipped down the back of his head and under the collar of his jacket. He squirmed as it slid down his back.

"The boss wants to see us," Mitch explained.

Wiping the back of his neck, Greg flung some of the goo that slipped onto his hand away. "Do I have time for a shower?"

With a curled lip, Mitch took a step back, eyeing him. "Normally, I would say no. But for all our sakes, yes, definitely yes."

## CHAPTER 2

Five minutes. That was all Greg needed for showers these days. With the amount of times he'd been slimed by Pugsley, he'd gotten it down to an art form. Wasting no time, he zipped into the locker room next to the training area. He was back out the door in fresh clothes in four and a half minutes, a new personal record.

He'd left his mic and earpiece in the locker, so he pulled out his phone to call up to the observation booth. "Hey, Kal, I need to go see Norah. Can you keep an eye on Pugsley for me?"

"Sure thing. I'll take him down to the cafeteria. I'm meeting Alvie there in a few minutes for lunch."

"Okay, sounds good." Greg disconnected the call, then smiled, imagining the lunch scene. Kal now stood six feet, four inches tall with a slim muscular build and dark wire-rimmed glasses. He looked like a younger, better-looking version of Greg.

And his two best friends at the D.E.A.D. were both aliens: Alvie and Iggy. Well, aliens and Greg.

Alvie was in town this week working on some top-secret project for Tilda. But after the workday was done, he and Kal spent most of their nights playing video games. Iggy would often just hang out with them, not playing but just kind of enjoying the company. Pugsley would sometimes wander down too, especially when there were snacks.

Greg shook his head as he hurried out of the training area and down the hall. What a strange world he lived in. The D.E.A.D. facility was a completely secure building. Everyone here had top-secret clearance, which meant that Alvie, Iggy, and Pugsley could walk around freely without having to worry about being seen.

Greg wouldn't trade it for anything in the world. This was where he was meant to be. He loved what he did and the people that it had brought into his life.

And in a weird sort of way, it had actually brought him closer to his family. Before he had joined the D.E.A.D., he hadn't spoken with his family in years, in part because, well, he, along with Maeve and the others, had been hiding from the world.

Even before that, though, his relationship with them, would have been best described as strained. For some reason, getting a doctorate from MIT and working on top-secret projects for the government was not viewed nearly as prestigiously as working for an accounting firm, the family business.

Reconnecting with Kal and bringing him into the D.E.A.D. had actually resulted in Greg seeing his family more often than he used to before he joined the D.E.A.D.

Not that that was always great. His sisters were still super judgmental of him, and now their latest thing seemed to be focusing on when Greg was going to get married. His mother had also joined in talking about her needing grandchildren from him every chance she got. The fact that she already had a bunch from his sisters hadn't swayed her from her argument.

His father, at least, wasn't giving him any grief about getting married or providing him grandkids. In fact, like normal, his father was barely talking to him at all, and Greg was fine with that. He'd accepted long ago that that was how his father and his relationship was going to go.

But the best thing about all of it was getting to spend time with Kal. He saw a lot of himself in his nephew, a young smart kid who didn't quite fit in with his peers. But Kal, too, had found a place where he belonged amongst the eccentric halls of the D.E.A.D.

Not everyone adjusted so easily. Every once in a while, a new individual was added to the staff, and their eyes nearly bugged out of their head when they saw Iggy taking a hopping jump into the cafeteria or Alvie scrolling through a tablet as he walked down a hall.

Speaking of which, a young woman in a white lab coat, her dark hair pulled back in her usual French braid, walked down the hall toward him at a fast pace. Her head was down, her glasses reflecting the glow from the tablet in her hands.

Greg had to sidestep quickly to avoid getting run over. "Hey, Hannah."

Dr. Hannah Eldridge's head jolted up, her eyes widening behind her glasses. "Oh, Dr. Schorn, I'm so sorry. I didn't see you."

"It's okay, and I told you to call me Greg."

Her cheeks flushed bright red. "Yes, sorry, Greg. And I'm sorry I'm running late. We had a situation in the lab."

"What happened?"

"One of the new techs didn't have his filtration suit connected properly, and he inhaled some noxious fumes from a sample. We had to rush him down to the med bay."

"Is he okay?"

"He's fine, or at least he will be."

"Was Dr. Kerwin on duty?" Greg asked

"Um, yeah. She took care of him."

Dr. Cheryl Kerwin had been brought in nearly a year ago, and Greg had been working up the courage to ask her out. His track record with women wasn't exactly great. In fact, it wasn't much of a record at all. It was really more of a Post-it note. But Cheryl, she'd been really friendly and open with him when she first arrived. He just couldn't tell if that was who she was or because she was actually interested in him.

Buoyed by her friendliness, about two months ago, he'd finally decided he was going to try. But before he could, he felt this shift in her interactions with him. She was less friendly, more professional. It wasn't a radical change, but it was enough that it got him second-guessing himself.

But hope sprung eternal, and he found himself looking for little nuggets of information on her. He also found himself in the cafeteria when she usually took lunch. Not that he was a stalker. And with all the MeToo stuff out there, he definitely didn't intend to cross any lines. But good old-fashioned pining was still all right, wasn't it?

"How did Pugsley do this morning?" Hannah asked. "Are you guys finished already?"

Greg pulled himself back from his thoughts and focused on Hannah. It wasn't just idle curiosity on her part. She was leading the team overseeing Pugsley's development. She normally attended the training sessions, a small quiet specter up in the observation room.

"He did well until Mitch opened the door during a run."

Hannah winced. "You got slimed again?"

"Yup."

Her hands flew over the tablet. "What was the subject this time?"

"A Labrador retriever."

Her gaze met his. "The smiling yellow one?"

"That's the one."

With a shake of her head, Hannah turned her attention back to the tablet, her lips a tight line as she jotted down some notes.

"What are you thinking?" Greg asked.

Hannah looked up, her gaze unfocused before it cleared. Greg tried not to smile. He knew that look. That was the *getting lost in your thoughts and being surprised that there was a world outside of those thoughts* look. "Oh, well, I'm wondering if maybe Pugsley has difficulty telling the difference between animal silhouettes in Hogan's Alley."

Greg was floored. She was right. Almost all of Pugsley's mistakes involved animals. "Why do you think that is?"

"I'm beginning to think scent plays a large role in how he distinguishes between people."

"You think he has bad vision?" Greg immediately pictured Pugsley wearing glasses.

"Not necessarily. I'm wondering if he simply doesn't process stimuli that way. We humans process with all of our senses, but vision is probably the top sense. But there's no reason to believe that that's the case for all creatures. So perhaps wherever Pugsley is from, vision is less critical or less able to discern differences."

It was an intriguing thought. If Pugsley came from a dark world, vision would be difficult to rely upon to make distinctions. It would still play a role, but other senses would take the forefront.

"I think I'm going to see if we can add scents to Hogan's Alley. I'll have to figure out how to do it so they don't release until just when we want Pugsley to sense them. But it would be a way to see if he is relying more on scent to make distinctions between good and bad. Of course, getting the scents right won't be easy."

He knew what she meant. It wasn't just the scent of a Labrador that they could put in. All animals gave off different pheromones when they were angry, stressed, sad. They'd need to find the right combinations to make it work.

"You're going to need some help."

"Yes, I could definitely use some help." She looked up at Greg.

Greg nodded, agreeing. "It's a big project. I'll speak with Norah about getting you more people and diverting some resources."

Hannah's smile fell before she nodded. "Uh, great. That would be great."

Greg smiled. "I'm going to see Norah now, in fact. I'll mention it to her. And the training session was recorded. Kal should have sent it to you along with the data."

"Good. I'll check it out," she said.

"Catch you later," Greg said, hurrying past her and ducking into the stairwell.

He jogged up the two flights to Norah's office and smiled at the fact that he wasn't even slightly out of breath. Years ago, he would have been hanging on to the railing by the time he crested the second floor.

But once you'd been chased down by multiple aliens on multiple occasions, it really inspired you to get in shape. So, Greg had become a bit of a fitness fanatic, and he'd even turned Kal into one. Now they started their days with a three-

or five-mile run, depending on how much time they had before they had to get to the office, plus weights three or four times a week. And then on the weekends, when they could, they took some seriously long bike rides.

Yeah, the guy Greg was now was nothing like the guy he'd been years ago. Part of him kind of missed that old guy, but at the same time, he liked the more confident guy that had stepped into his shoes.

Up ahead, he nodded at Norah's assistant, Brie. Brie was petite, age thirty-two, and looked completely wholesome and unassuming. But she was a highly trained operative that Norah had brought over from the DoD. She was the last line of defense if someone was trying to get the head of the D.E.A.D. And being that Greg had seen her in action down in the training rooms, he was always very respectful.

She smiled as he approached. "Hey, Greg, go on in. She's waiting for you."

"Thanks, Brie," he said as he slipped past her and opened the door, letting himself in.

Norah Tidwell, the director of the D.E.A.D. and one of Greg's closest friends, looked up from behind the desk. A former Marine, Norah sometimes joined Greg and Kal for their morning runs, although Greg knew she was holding herself back for their sake. Her brown hair was pulled back into a ponytail, making her look young, and she was already young for running such an important government agency. But she had earned the position.

After leaving the military, she had joined up with the D.E.A.D. under Martin Drummond. She had gone on dozens of retrieval cases that always turned into destroy cases. She'd thought she was keeping Americans safe. But after meeting Iggy, she knew she couldn't go along with the planned objective of the D.E.A.D., which was to kill all of the creatures that escaped from Area 51. And she began to question whether all of her previous kills had been necessary.

Greg knew Norah was still wracked with guilt over some of those cases. It wasn't that the creatures that escaped Area 51 weren't dangerous. Most of them were. But some, like Iggy and Pugsley and the triplets, were peaceful and deserved a chance to live. After all, they hadn't chosen to join this world. The US government had forced them to.

So when faced with Iggy, a Maldek who actually could be quite lethal when the situation called for it, she had hesitated, and then she went on the run with him against the agency she now ran. She had linked up with Maeve and the others, and now she'd been made head of the D.E.A.D. She was a good boss—smart, efficient, and completely thorough.

And right now, she looked stressed.

"What's going on?" Greg asked. He nodded at Mitch, who sat in one of the chairs in front of Norah's desk as he slipped into the other one.

Norah ran a hand over her hair. "We are starting to get some pressure from the White House."

Greg raised his eyebrows. He didn't think the White House played much of a role in their activities. He always figured they knew they were around but tried to pretend they weren't. "What kind of pressure?"

"The President's got a good friend," Norah said as she sat back.

Mitch coughed. "Donor."

She rolled her eyes before nodding. "Yes, actually, that's probably more accurate: a big donor who contacted the White House. Apparently, the son of the donor was abducted by aliens."

Greg went still, looking between the two of them. "He's missing?"

Norah shook her head. "No. It happened years ago."

Well, that was a relief. He wasn't sure exactly who they would complain to about an abducted human. The first stop would probably be the Council. And Greg really didn't want to talk to them. In fact, he tried to avoid even thinking about them. The Council had made it clear that humans were on a short leash. A very short leash that had nearly been snapped recently. It was only through the actions of Greg, Maeve, and the others that they had, not that long ago, avoided a world-ending catastrophe started by Martin Drummond's actions.

Just thinking about it caused Greg's pulse begin to race. He took some slow breaths. Nope, he was not going to think about that. He shoved those fears aside in his mind and instead focused on what he knew about the Council and alien abductions.

According to Agaren, the Gray who acted as a sort of spokesperson for the Council, abductions were no longer allowed. Decades ago, it had been normal for aliens to basically do a flyby of Earth and grab humans as specimens, do some tests, and then send them back. But it was not supposed to be happening anymore.

"So, if it happened years ago, why is it an issue now?" Mitch asked.

Leaning forward on her desk, Norah clasped her hands in front of her. "Apparently, he's lost time again."

Losing time was a hallmark of an alien abduction. People would find themselves driving on a road only to realize that four hours were gone without any memory of what had happened. It was theorized that the aliens did something to their subjects to make them forget, although sometimes memories bled through.

Norah continued. "They don't know where he's been, and neither does he. The donor's worried, and he made his fears known to the White House. Years ago, the President would have thought the donor was crazy, but you know what it's like in the media these days."

Unfortunately, Greg did. As much as they tried to tamp the lid down on the escape of creatures from Area 51, the information had made it into the news. Usually, it was just the tabloid rags that people weren't paying too much attention to. However more recently there were more and more suggestions in the mainstream media that something was going on and that the government was covering it up.

"On top of that, more former abductees have reported losing time. The President has assured his donor that he'll have his top people look into it." Norah looked across the desk at Mitch and Greg.

As Greg straightened up in his chair, he grinned. "And we're your top people?"

Norah nodded. "That you are. So, I'm going to need you to go run out and see what's going on with this guy. To be honest, he's probably got a drug problem, or maybe he's having an affair, I don't know. But you need to just run out there, talk to him, write up a report, and that'll make the President happy."

"Do you think there's anything behind this?" Greg asked.

Norah shook her head. "No. I think this is the President just trying to appease a guy with deep pockets. So go out there, make the President happy, and let's close the book on this."

"When do we leave?" Greg asked.

Norah smiled at him. "Five minutes ago. The plane is idling on the runway. Apparently, you needed a shower."

Greg grimaced. "Pugsley's getting better. I swear."

"I'm sure he is. I'll make sure he and Kal get home if you don't get back in time," Norah said.

"Where are we going?" Mitch asked.

"You're heading down to DC." Norah paused. "Is that a problem?"

Greg shook his head, wiping away his frown. "No, I was just supposed to have a video meeting with Maeve. But I'll call her to reschedule." He pulled out his phone.

"That won't be necessary. Tilda reached out to say she has Maeve working on something right now that will be fully occupying her attention for the day."

Greg stood, stretching his back. "Probably burying her in paperwork. Maeve is definitely leading the quiet life these days."

www.vinci-books.com/into-dark

# FACT OR FICTION

Thank you for reading *Into the Cage*. I hope you enjoyed it. If you get a chance, I would appreciate it if you left a review.

As with most of my books, Into the Cage was based in part on real events or facts. So read on to see where some of the story line developed.

### The Existence of UFOs.

Governments around the world have increasingly shown signs of admitting that UFOs are real. The US government has acknowledged the presence of objects in the sky that they cannot explain. The Pentagon has even recently confirmed that the UFO program is still in existence.

The most recent government official to come out in support of UFOs is an Israeli security space chief. He maintains that not only do aliens exist, but there is also a galactic federation that has been in contact with humanity. They are waiting until humans are more evolved to allow their presence to be known.

### The Milky Way.

The milky way where our solar system is located, contains many, many other solar systems (planets surrounding a star).

According to NASA, there are 200 billion suns in our Milky Way.

Of those suns, it is estimated that approximately half have habitable planets.

**Intelligent Species within the galaxy.**

We've already addressed how many suns there are in our galaxy. Now the question is, how many intelligent species are there? On Earth, there are anywhere between 8.7 million species, not all of those however are intelligent species.

In the galaxy therefore, we would expect there to be some species that are not intelligent. For example, life was just found on Venus but it is highly unlikely to be intelligent life.

Astrophysicists have estimated that there are 36 intelligent, communicating species within our galaxy. A large part of the calculations rely on the habitable zone, i.e. A location not too hot or not too cold.

Now thirty-six doesn't sound like much. However, our galaxy is one of potentially trillions. The idea that we are the only species in all of the vast cosmos has been disproven. Now, the idea that we are the only intelligent species becomes less and less plausible.

**The Stability of Galaxies.**

In *Into the Cage*, I mention an argument than galaxies need to be stable in order to support the growth of intelligent civilizations. Early on, galaxies were too chaotic to support that kind of growth. But there is one glazy we know of that seems to go against this argument.

**The Size of the Universe.**

First off, it's impossible to say exactly how big the universe is. The universe is 13.8 billion years old. Right now with our technological restraints, we can only see 28 billion light years,

14 billion in each direction at the time of the big bang. But due to inflation, it's actually 91 billion light years in diameter. Or at least that is what is observable. Other estimates of what we can't see suggests its actually closer to 250 trillion years in diameter. In other words, the universe is much larger than what we can currently see.

## Mixing animal and human DNA.

In the Belial Series and the A.L.I.V.E. series, we have previously discussed the science behind the mixing of human and animal DNA. We have created a sheep from a test-tube, a human ear on the back of a mouse, and cows that provide human milk. They've even mixed human DNA with pig DNA and then promptly destroyed the embryos of the new species. Science and science fiction are beginning to get indistinguishable.

## The Intelligence of Dolphins.

Are dolphins intelligent? Short answer: yes. But generally, in examinations of dolphin brains, the structures of the brain show complexity in areas associated with problem-solving, self-awareness, and a number of other traits associated with human intelligence.

Thank you once again for reading *Into the Cage*. The story continues in *Into the Dark*.

Happy reading!
RD

# ABOUT THE AUTHOR

**Author, Criminologist, Terrorism Expert, Jeet Kune Do Black Sash, Runner, Dog Lover.**

Amazon best-selling author R.D. Brady writes supernatural and science fiction thrillers. Her thrillers include ancient mysteries, unusual facts, non-stop action, and fierce women with heart.

Prior to beginning her writing career, RD Brady was a criminologist who specialized in life-course criminology and international terrorism. She's lectured and written numerous academic articles on the genetic influence on criminal behavior, factors that influence terrorist ideology, and delinquent behavior formation.

After visiting counter-terrorism units in Israel, RD returned home with a sabbatical in front of her and decided to write that book she'd been thinking about. Four years later she left academia with the publication of her first book, *The Belial Stone*, and hasn't looked back.

To learn about her upcoming publications, sign up for her newsletter here or on her website (rdbradybooks.com).